Wade Tabor lives with his wife, daughter, and a collection of pets in Charleston, South Carolina, where he teaches English and Creative Writing at Fort Dorchester High School. He is currently at work on his next novel.

the **long-range** plan

wade tabor

HAZARD PRESS
publishers

For Reese
The substance of things hoped for…
the anticipation of things unseen.
Everything.

And for Scott Alalof and Gary Dunlap,
who know why.

Thank you.

First published 2004
© 2004 Wade Tabor

ISBN 1-877270-56-3

Published by Hazard Press Ltd.
P.O. Box 2151, Christchurch, New Zealand
www.hazardpress.com

Printed in the United States of America

The educator recognizes the magnitude of the responsibility inherent in the teaching process. The desire for the respect and confidence of one's colleagues, of students, of parents, and of the members of the community provides the incentive to attain and maintain the highest possible degree of ethical conduct.

– Code of Ethics of the Education Profession

The effective teacher does more than teach; the effective teacher touches lives.

– Harry Wong

Never underestimate the power of cash.

– Wall Street Maxim

AUTHOR'S NOTE

There is no Winter's Cove School District in South Carolina. Neither is there a Coosaw Creek High School in either Charleston or North Charleston, and there is not to my knowledge a town of Winter's Cove anywhere in the South Carolina lowcountry.

This book is a work of fiction. The miscreants within, as well as the mischief, are selections from my personal stock. So too the angels.

It is all, from "I" to "enough" and everything between, entirely the product of the author's imagination.

Make of that what you will.

ACKNOWLEDGMENTS

As is the case with each book, I could never have completed it without the help of others and, in this particular instance, a touch of Blanche Dubois's kindness of strangers.

As ever, Shannon, who gave me Reese, and with her a reason behind each breath I draw.

To the memory of my Uncle Bill, who taught me the stuff they don't put in textbooks. I think he would have liked this story.

My friend and agent, Dan Myers, of the Robert Dean Agency, who took a shot on a no-name teacher with a story to tell, and whose perseverance, cynical optimism, and unabridged professionalism has made this all possible. Fifteen percent isn't enough – though it's all you're getting this go around.

Antoinette Wilson, project manager at Hazard, for seeing this book into the world with professionalism and care. Sam Gil for catching my mistakes. Mike Bradstock, who cleaned Cole, Savannah, and the rest of them up a bit. And Quentin Wilson, for giving me this chance.

Weezy, Poo's favorite Aunt, and the first to buy each of my books.

Scott Alalof, who understands that it's not a world of men. For the past sixteen years of friendship, support, and therapy, for helping me keep the Benz locked, and for being there when it's counted – every last time.

Pat Villegas, senior partner at Bendini, Lambert, and Locke – my wing-man in the Red Zone, the original dipman, the guy behind the guy behind the guy – who doesn't know how to read but is always willing to listen, for the years upon years of support and encouragement.

Shaylyn Casciotta, for the fantastic job on the frontispiece.

Jack Radcliffe, for sharing his unique philosophy of teaching, and for reading all my stuff in draft.

My parents, for their support over the years.

Pop and Grannie Peagler, who continue to brighten our world.

Dr. Sandy Parker and Mrs. Cindy Ritoch, who made their library available to me numerous times after hours, and Dan Wright, who assisted me with all things technical.

Nancy Cogburn, who showed me – on paper – how to steal zillions.

Vicki Sweatman, whose too-early retirement is a loss to every child – but particularly my own – who'll never have the chance to call her teacher. It is also a testament to all that which is wrong with this most honorable of professions.

Keith Guess, the hardest working teacher I know, for being a true friend and mentor these past years, and for understanding that fair weather is fine for sailing and would-be sailors, but no way to navigate a friendship.

Tim Payne, for tolerating my tenure on the learning curve.

The Admiral, Chuck Welty, for sharing the wisdom of the Old Guard, one nugget at a time.

Stephanie Morris, in whose class I first began to feel the possibility…

Ben Greer, who took the time countless times to cast pearls before swine.

Venus Morris, who won't have a clue as to why her name is mentioned here. On an October morning in 1993, she told me a story that altered the course of my life forever, and in virtually every way imaginable. Very rarely does one encounter such a cardinal moment so completely out of the blue – I think it important to acknowledge the source of mine.

Carson the Courageous One and Mark the Mohrmann, each of whom had particular insights crucial to this book's completion.

Bill Lavin, for being such a rock, and for making me laugh during those years when little else could.

Chad Dvorak, my left-coast connection, for perspective, and for hanging in there all these years.

Mike Lorick and Ernie Varner, who each, oftentimes unwittingly, contributed to this book.

As he does with every story, my little man Roma endured countless all-nighters out in the study, softly purring with the whispers of the keys. And, of course, The J-Man stood guard at the door.

ONE

Introductions, admonitions, and other sundry incidentals; intermezzo

I got a hand-job in a bookstore once. I was standing in the literary criticism aisle at the Barnes and Noble Booksellers near the campus, fanning through a faux-leatherbound version of *Dickey's Deliverance*, when my then-girlfriend got the urge and set about doing her thing. It was late, almost closing time, but the lights were still up and there were still a few browsers lingering around, all of which served, she later told me, to intensify her mood.

Throughout the whole deal she was examining with passing interest the puppies and kittens calendar that she held in her other hand. She just stood there, right arm tugging away furiously – all the motion concentrated in her wrist, her elbow and shoulder as still as monks at prayer – left arm holding that calendar, enjoying all the effort I was putting into not making noise. My frustration fueled her. If I'd bitten my lip clean through she probably would have come.

So there it is. Stay away from bookstores. Not because you might find yourself getting a hand-job in the Southern Writers section – in my infinite hours spent in bookstores, that only happened once, and was much more the product of the woman I was dating than the places I was going – but because bookstores are at their most base level inherently bad. Trust me on this. I spent a lot of time in bookstores. I used to love them – their smell, the warm, comfortable ambiance within, the soft lighting raining down and inviting you to sit, sip, and read yourself into another world – but it's a changed love now. It's an unhealthy love, the love the battered wife has for her husband, or the druggie for the little silver spoon. I kept going to them though; like the lush who sips his vodka from a Sprite can on lunch break, I returned again and again to bookstores. With their hundreds of thousands of alternate worlds and realities, their millions of strange and new characters, their truly infinite number of ideas and possibilities, today's bookstores are the intellectual's den of iniquity. They are enablers of addiction, and like all addictions, their effects linger.

I gave up on posterity when I decided to take this route. It wasn't an easy call. The decision to leave anywhere – not to mention your country – in such a fashion as to ensure your never being able to return isn't come to lightly. Expatriation is a big step. Furtive expatriation under cover of night in order to avoid criminal prosecution is an enormous, irrevocable step with implications I've no doubt yet to experience. God knows I agonized over it my fair share.

I did a lot of things I'm not proud of during my year as a teacher. I worked myself into such a mess that the only way out was the way I took, and if I hadn't taken it when I did I'd be in jail now, end of story. But during that year, at every turn, I did what I thought was right. If there's a line of continuity running through those nine months, it is that. The particulars of my sudden absence caused pain – they caused and most likely will for some time continue to cause problems for people at all levels. The Governor, the Superintendent of Education, the rubber-stampers at the Winter's Cove District Office, the school board, the principals, teachers, parents, and – perhaps more than any of the rest of them – the students. I'm aware of that, and the knowledge makes me sad. But I had to go. And I had to go the way I went. Prison wasn't an option.

According to the playwright Arthur Miller (one of the multitude of men who got to see Marilyn Monroe naked before she got mixed up with the tarnished Knights of Camelot) the loved ones of persecuted pilgrim John Proctor pleaded with his wife to intercede, to convince her husband to confess to something he believed was wrong so that his life might be spared. She steadfastly refused, stating that, in standing for principle, "he hath his goodness now."

When I think of Savannah, I know that I do, too. Therein lies my redemption.

Now, next to the window of my little motel room here below the Texas border, less than a stone's throw from the breathtakingly beautiful azure-blue coast of the Gulf, I have to force myself not to think of her, not to remember the smell of her hair, the smoothness of her skin, the taste of her saliva. It takes all I have to keep from wondering where she is this moment, this very second, wondering what she's doing, if she's happy, if she ever thinks of me or our time together. If I thought she did, there's a strong part of me that is afraid I'd change course and try to find her, try once again to convince her to accompany me, to journey through with me the days and nights ahead with nothing familiar save the feel of each other. That's a great deal of why I let it end the way it did. In order to run, I had to be sure that there was nothing I was leaving behind.

Most days I am.

I finished college at The University of South Carolina Magna Cum Laude, Phi Beta Kappa, the whole bit, and spent the summer after graduation working as a mail clerk for an insurance company. My boss was a forty-one-year-old woman who'd kept her smile and figure rather well, given her age. She'd rounded a bit around the middle; the years had left her with a few permanent creases at the edges of her mouth and fanning outward from her eyes, and gravity had done what it does best to women's breasts, but her eyes had a burning in them and her skin still gave off that healthy, pampered glow. According to her, her attorney-husband didn't appreciate these things to the degree she felt he ought.

I was twenty-two that summer. I worked from 9:00 to 4:00, sorting out-going mail and stuffing fire-extinguishers into cartons to be shipped to new homeowner-policy buyers. I worked literally in the basement, a dingy, factory-like room with no windows and too many overhead fluorescent lights. I was one of three mail clerks, and the only one who spoke English.

We never saw her much. She came down every two weeks to hand out paychecks. Her hair was an expensive-looking beach-sand blonde, and her clothes and skin smelled of moisturizing cream and perfume. We had mailboxes in the employees' lounge she could have stuck the checks in, but I think she got a kick out of handing them out. I always got those kinds of vibes from her, like being in charge meant something to her, and being in charge of men meant even more.

On my second to last day there was a note in my box in the employees' lounge. COLE, SEE ME WHEN YOU RETURN FROM LUNCH. – J

I'd seen her memos before, and it was always the same ending. No name, just the J. She probably thought it was friendly and cute.

It came off as arrogant to me.

But she was my boss and it'd been a good job, and I knew I'd need one the next summer too, so I returned from my Blimpie's Best lunch ten minutes early and rode the elevator up to her office on the seventh floor. She was sitting behind her desk reading something, the door wide open, and I sort of half-leaned in and knocked gently with a single knuckle.

'You wanted to see me?'

'Yes, Cole. Please, have a seat.' She rose, motioning to one of the chairs, and circled around behind me to shut the door. I thought that was a little odd. I heard her turn the lock inside the handle and check to make sure it was indeed locked. I thought that was a lot odd.

'My husband's been having an affair for over three years now,' she said, circling back around to her chair. She said it in the same business-is-business tone in which she might have said 'We need to revisit our double-indemnity policy.'

She sat back down, her eyes never leaving mine. She was wearing a pale yellow suit that made me think of the caramel candies I used to find in my Christmas stocking as a kid.

'He's been fucking his twenty-something paralegal at his office. She stayed with us – in my home – during her divorce last year, which means he's probably fucked her in our bed.' Pause. 'In the bed I sleep in, Cole.'

'I'm sorry to hear that.'

'Does it surprise you that I'm telling you this?' Still all business. All single-initial signature.

'Not really,' I shrugged.

'Why not?'

'Women talk about their troubles more than men. It's probably what makes them healthier.'

She didn't say anything. She just sat there looking like an older model modeling a thousand dollar outfit and hundred dollar hair, as reserved and collected as if she was explaining to me the difference between term and whole-life.

'When I confronted him about it he didn't even have the decency to lie. He said younger women's cunts are less experienced. Less used-up, was the way he put it.'

I nodded dumbly, as if this were something I'd researched extensively in my own life, and had come to the same conclusion as her husband.

'My husband can be obtuse at times.'

Then, as abruptly as a scream, she stood and began unbuttoning her blouse.

'This has nothing to do with you, Cole,' she said, removing her clothes and folding them on her desk. 'You've been a good employee. You come on time, you've never forgotten to clock out, and your stacks are always sorted correctly.'

I was still processing her words as she stepped backwards out of her shoes. I looked at her standing there in her black Victoria's Secret bra and matching panties and wondered what her house looked like. I bet it was a big one, the kind couples earning half a million a year lived in, with marble floors and a spiral staircase and cold, limbless statues on pedestals in various corners. I didn't know if she had kids or not, but if she did I bet she made them take off their shoes in the foyer.

Her skin looked warm and pampered in the early-afternoon sunlight washing through the window. Pools of shadow shimmered like a reflection across a pond in the spot between her legs. I wondered what she tasted like down there. I'd never been with anyone who had their own office.

'I put him through law school so that he could fuck the help and brazenly justify it in terms of elasticity. Have you had head before, Cole?'

I didn't move.

'I hope so. You'll need a point of reference.'

She came around the desk. I thought she'd remove the bra and panties but she didn't. She stepped between me and her desk and dropped to her knees.

'My husband's penis is the size of a cocktail frank,' she said, unzipping my fly.

'I'm sorry,' I said again.

'Don't be. Seventeen years of marriage can make anything seem normal.'

I was so hard I thought I would puke.

With a cold confidence I associated with world leaders, hired killers, and IRS auditors she said, 'Tell me if my mouth feels used up, Cole.'

For some reason I was picturing what I thought her house looked like again. 'Does your family use cloth napkins?' The words and my dick came out at the same time. She ignored the former in favor of the latter.

I watched the clock on the wall behind her desk through the entire thing. It lasted exactly three minutes and a second. It never occurred to me to tell her I was about to come, probably because it'd never occurred to her to tell me that I needed to.

When I was through she rose and held her expressionless face less than six inches from me. Her neck and cheeks were red.

'When you get married one day, Cole, make it a point not to run around on your wife.'

Her lips were flush and raw looking. There was a single milky-white drop in the center of her lower lip. It balanced there like a tear trying not to fall.

If she'd tried to kiss me I would have let her, out of gratitude and awe as much as anything else. But she was finished. I'd been a tool for retaliation, and I'd served my purpose.

She stood, rubbed her lips together as if she'd just applied lipstick, and began putting on her clothes. I just sat there, my shriveled dick shiny and sticky and retreating back into its den. I tried to think of something to say, but nothing came. It was too much effort just to regulate my breathing.

That fall I began law school, intent on becoming a filthy rich and successful commercial lawyer, working down in Charleston on Lawyer's Row, wearing Matlock suits and lunching (that's when you know you've really arrived, when other people's nouns become your verbs) at Charleston Chops, Mint Juleps, and The Harbour Club. I threw myself into the world of Torts and Civil Procedure and Con Law. I spent endless hours with The Rule of Perpetuities, The Battle of the Forms, The Statute of Fraud and The Commerce Clause. I learned that if you live in New Jersey and throw a party, you're responsible if one of your guests has too much to drink then drives his car into a gathering of pedestrians. I also learned that if you live in California and knock your neighbor's fourteen-year-old daughter up, you can with near impunity take her for a hoovering the day before her water breaks, but if your check bounces at the supermarket you can do six months in the can. If you find a piece of land you like in South Carolina, you can sit on it for seven years, and if the owner doesn't say anything, you can claim it as your own. I learned the abbreviation for 'contract' is the letter 'k'. Legal writing professors hate adjectives, adverbs, or any other descriptive language. All law libraries smell vaguely of morning-breath, and the highlighter of choice in library casebooks is jet black. I learned I could study seven hours straight, night after night after night, and learn very little. I learned that female law students fuck exponentially more than female undergrads, and they do it with an abandon that suggests academic frustration. But most of all, I learned I had no love for the law, which is why I quit three months into it.

Also, somewhere in there the girl I'd been dating for four years and was engaged to marry, a perfectly exquisite brunette named Autumn with big brown eyes and a honey-sweet Southern accent that made my insides warm, found out I was making it with this large-breasted airhead on the side, and so that relationship, like the dreams of an office on Charleston's Lawyer's Row, ended pretty much the same time and in the same mind-bendingly bad way.

I loved Autumn. Had her safety or well-being required my death, I would have paid the reckoning without a thought. But I was getting married five months later, and for reasons whose answers seemed significant at the time I allowed myself to be lured into a remarkably pleasurable, emotionally vacuous, and ultimately wrong fling with a bottled blonde possessed of double-D guns and a GED. She was a checkout girl at the local grocery, impressed with the law school gig. I was an aspiring law school dropout, enticed by the boobs and the possibility of one final, meaningless romp with someone I wouldn't have to respect during or call afterwards. But one final romp turned into one more final romp, then just one more after that, and so on and so forth. Given the opportunity to rewind that one, I'd simply choose another line at the supermarket to push my cart through. Not so much because of the morality of it all – though I know what I did was reprehensible – but because of the pain it caused Autumn. Large, firm, late-adolescent breasts come and go, but hearts as pure and unadulterated as Autumn's are as rare and delicate as rainbows. Even now, knowing that in sullying myself I'd also scathed her has exacted from me a penance of Biblical proportions.

I pulled some strings over in the Humanities Department, where they knew me from my undergrad days, and was able to roll over into the MFA program – Master of Fine Arts; I'd decided to try my hand at writing – but I spent most of the next five months drunk and stoned, studying very little, writing even less. I moved home to Augusta, Georgia, to live with my mother in a bid for some form of nonsexual feminine attention, the kind I used to find in Autumn before I'd driven her away. I commuted to Columbia five days a week and tried not to think about her. I spent a lot of time crying in the shower, wondering how I could have thrown away everything good about my life in such an efficient fell-swoop, and I leaned on anyone I could. I had long, tender conversations with my mother, who sat across the kitchen table and cried and commiserated with me. I called every friend I had at all hours of the night just to talk about her. I alternated between an intense desire for space and privacy, and an almost pathological need for company. I spent nearly every night of the week in one of Augusta's two main sports bars with a buddy named Bill, a heavy-set fellow with hard Irish eyes and a face as tough and grizzled as a bull's elbow. We'd drink Foster's oil cans, five or six to a sitting, then we'd go out back and smoke whatever he'd been able to pick up that day on the job.

Bill was a meat-cutter at the local butcher-shop, and his blue-collar hardness and honesty sustained me through those days the way the pain reminds the tortured they're still alive.

'You ran around on her like she was a weekend piece,' he'd say to me, holding the joint in a fist at the end of a forearm the size of my thigh, 'so what's the difference now she's gone? If you'da loved her, you never woulda fucked around. Suck it up and deal with it.'

Bill was hard, but he was a rock, and there're times when a rock in your corner is what you need.

I was going to be a writer, it was clear, so when the semester came to a close I packed my things, thanked my mother for her cooking and her kind shoulder, and drove my old Honda Accord down to Charleston, South Carolina, the jewel of the old South. I rented an apartment in the West Ashley area and waited tables at a steakhouse to pay the bills. I'd wake around noon, write until four or so, then serve steak and seasoned potato-wedges to Charleston's twenty-something crowd, which is to say my own. I slowed the drinking down. Some. Rather, I slowed the drinking alone down. I still spent my off-evenings in bars and clubs, alternating between imported darks in frosted mugs and lemon-garnished shots, popping ephedrine and Valium at the same time. I got sick my fair share, vomited in most of the bathrooms and moonlit alleyways up and down Market and East Bay, but I succeeded fairly well in prying loose the hold Autumn's memory had on me. Her face and voice and touch haunted my dreams less and less. I quit looking for her in crowds. I stopped pretending she was going to call. A good friend of mine once said the only way to get over a woman is to get over – and under, behind, and between – lots and lots of other women.

I fell in love with Charleston that summer, with her history and heritage, with the secrets and scandals that seemed to seep like mist from the century-old oaks lining the cobblestoned streets downtown. And like any good love, I became codependent upon her, deciding definitively that I was never leaving again, and taking great comfort in knowing that she could never leave me. I'd found my home, and here I'd raise my flag.

As I pushed my little beige Honda up I-26 in the early morning hours of June 2, nine months and one school year later, I glanced into the rearview and realized with the finality of the moment that I was leaving Charleston forever. The closest I'd come to her for the rest of my days would be postcards. I would have had to struggle to keep from crying, but I was thinking of Savannah's face, which meant the tears came without any real resistance from me. By that point I knew better than to fight it.

Had I waited any longer to leave – just twelve more hours – I'd be in prison now. It took them no time at all to figure out what happened to the money; the trail leading to me was an easy one to follow, complete with videotape and eyewitnesses. Of course, all that was intentional. I just didn't know it at the time.

By the time I reached the Mexican border it was federal, and the FBI and Treasury Department were looking for me.

But this story actually starts a year earlier, so it's there that we need to return for now.

TWO

The first day of school

I figured roll was the place to start, so I flopped open my class roster, found my chair, and began calling off the names.

'Tyson Adams,' I said, trying to sound as if I'd done this sort of thing before, an old hand and all that, not at all nervous, which of course I was. Intensely. I felt like I had a quart of diarrhea sloshing around in my colon. One wrong move and I'd blow it out of my ass like ink from a squid, which I suppose would have ended my teaching career at Coosaw Creek High. No one wants to be known as Mr. Shits or the Shit-man at his place of employment, and teenagers aren't exactly known for their sensitivity or discretion.

'Here,' the second kid in the second row called out. 'And it's Flash.'

'What's Flash?'

'My name. I don't like Tyson. I like Flash. I tell all my teachers to call me Flash.'

'Okay. Flash it is. Is Adams all right or have you changed the last name too?'

He just looked at me, like he didn't understand what I was saying, which I didn't have any trouble believing.

'Abigail Alders,' I said.

Abigail raised her hand.

'A.A., huh?' I said, trying to be cute. 'You know, like the support-gr…uh, never mind. Cynthia Banes?'

Another hand went up.

'Wendy Bannister?'

A hand, this one attached to a girl whose face was a bright red bed of zits. I instantly felt a wave of pity for the poor child; she was perfectly painful to look at. The acne ran wide and deep, like some rushing tide of fire-ants across a snow-covered prairie. It ran from chin to eyebrow, and from where I was sitting it appeared there were even one or two on the verge of sliding down her forehead onto her eyelids. I looked away as quickly as I could so she wouldn't feel my stare, assuming her adolescence had been traumatic enough. She didn't need her teachers puking at the sight of her.

'Pizza-face,' one of the kids – a mouthy little squirt of piss named Roy, I'd later learn – said under his breath. Wendy Bannister withdrew – visibly shrank in size – and tried to keep from crying.

Welcome back to school, Wendy.

'You,' I said, indicating the mouth in the back. He was a skinny, mousy-looking kid, one of the ones whose hormones had kicked in enough to allow that pencil-thin pubescent mustache fifteen-year old boys are so fond of, but not enough for actual muscle yet. 'What's your name?'

He looked at me wide-eyed, a who-me-I-haven't-done-anything mask of surprise plastered across his face.

'Yeah, you. You know who I'm talking to.'

'What did I do?'

'So far you've been rude and stupid, and the school year's not ten minutes old. Now what's your name?'

'Roy,' he said, looking fairly shocked that I'd actually called him stupid. I guess he hadn't heard much of that at home.

'Roy what?'

'Watherstein.'

'Well Roy Watherstein, didn't your mother ever tell you it's not polite to pick on other people, particularly about their appearances?'

He shrugged, looked down at his desk and began fidgeting with his pencil.

'Look at me, Roy Watherstein.'

He looked up, barely.

'I asked you a question. Did anyone in your home ever tell you it is impolite to criticize the way others look?'

Another shrug. 'I guess.'

'But you decided to do it anyway, is that right?'

And still another shrug.

'Roy,' I said, standing, slowly making my way towards him. 'that shrug-and-look-away routine may work at home, but not here. Here you're in *my* world, do you understand me? You're on Planet

19

Archer. And on Planet Archer, Mr. Archer calls the shots.'

I had the full attention of the rest of the class at this point, as they rotated in their orange plastic seats like little screws being turned, each of them transfixed by what was occurring here, in school, where kids picked on kids and made them cry as a matter of course, where a blank stare and a shrug was supposed to be enough to get the teacher off your back, and where little shits with pubic hair like Roy Whateverstein weren't used to being challenged and embarrassed.

'You're in Mr. Archer's classroom now, Roy, and if you intend to stay in here, you'd better learn the rules.'

'What rules?' he asked, as if the concept eluded him.

'You Jewish, Roy?' I asked, even as I knew I should probably not venture down this particular path. Nothing in my Methods classes included singling out a child's religion as a means of classroom management.

'Yeah. So?'

'Well, tell me Roy, how would it make you feel if someone called you, say, a dirty little Jew? Would you like that?'

I wish you could have seen his face when I tossed him that one. I knew I'd gone too far, that I was still in the first hour of my career and perhaps stomping it straight out of the womb, but there wasn't much I could do about it at that point. It couldn't be unsaid now. About all I could do was push ahead, drive my point home, make sure Roy got the drift.

'Or how about a money-grubber? Or a sheeny? A kike? Hook-nose? Any of these make you feel good about yourself, Roy Watherstein? They don't, do they? Know why no one in this class has called you that this morning? Is it because you're not Jewish? Of course not. You are. You just told me so. So that can't be the reason, can it, Roy? Could it be manners? Politeness? Parents that have taught their children the difference between right and wrong? Any chance that's it, Roy?'

He looked at me square on, his teen-age chin beginning to tremble. 'I'm telling my father you called me a hook-no –'

'Shut your mouth, Roy. In Mr. Archer's room Mr. Archer talks, and the students listen.' The first thing they taught you in the Methods courses was to Be A Bastard the first few days. It showed the kids the boundaries, let them know you weren't one to be trifled with. Once they saw the line and knew to toe it, you could ease off a bit. But in the beginning, you had to Be A Bastard. I thought I was doing a fairly decent job so far.

'Now Roy, you're going to apologize to Miss Bannister, and if you don't, you and I are going to march down to the office, call her father, wait until he gets here, and let you explain to him why you're calling his daughter names on the first day of school.'

I was directly in front of him now, so I could see the tears not only fall but form. They grew up out of the inner corners, clung a bit to the lower lid like morning dew on grass, then fell heavily down his cheeks. I didn't feel bad a bit. The pecker deserved it. I surmised I'd have no more trouble out of Roy that year.

'I'm sorry,' he said, turning to Wendy, who was understandably mortified at the whole scene. 'I'm sorry I called you a pizza-face. I was just cracking around. I won't do it again.'

'Very good, Roy,' I said, my tone suddenly one of praise, 'thank you for being so adult about it.'

And then we finished the roll.

'See here's the thing,' Mr. Collins was saying to me from behind his big, deeply polished desk. He looked more like a Fortune 500 executive than a high-school principal, even a white-bread high-school like Coosaw Creek High. His gray pin-stripe was cut with a razor and tailor-fit. He wore a gold Rolex on his right wrist, a gold bracelet around the other.

'You can't really do the sort of thing you did in there today. Parents ...' he ran his tongue under his lip, as though the word he was looking for might be lodged up there somewhere with the remnants of his breakfast, 'parents don't care for it. They damn well hate it, actually.'

Ricke Collins – it's pronounced 'Rick'; no clue about the deal with the 'e' – Ricke Collins was a short, slightly pudgy man in his mid-fifties with square shoulders and thick forearms. He was an ex-marine from the Tennessee mountains who'd come to teaching late in life, discovered he hated kids but liked boffing attractive teachers, and as such had made his way in spurts and jerks up the ladder into that abyss of ineptitude called ADMINISTRATION.

Sitting there, it occurred to me that he looked a lot like what a beagle would look like if it were a man. His ears were fairly well floppy, his eyes beady and tight, and he was constantly sniffing. From snot or snow, I'm not sure, but the man loved a good sniff.

'Now I know you're new and all, this your first year, no experience, nervous' – sniff – 'but let me tell you – let me give you a
tip on how things work. Parents,' – sniff – 'they're the wild cards
of education. They're the things you have to look out for, you get
what I'm saying here? They're where the rubber hits the road. If
the parents aren't happy, they bitch to the Board, and if they bitch to
the Board enough,' – sniff – 'the Board comes down here and crawls
up my ass with their questions. And I hate their questions, Archer.
Hell, some days' – sniff, sniff – 'some days I hate the Board. And
I've got the Board and the DO I've got to answer to. So go easy on
the Jew stuff. Colored, too. Proper term now is African-American,
and' – sniff – 'God forbid we mess that one up. The Indians, too. We
don't have too many of those. One, maybe two, but you know it's
Native-American now, don't you?' Sniff.

'Uh, yes sir. Yes, sir I do. I was attempting to make a broader
point, and I just let it get away from me. I don't want you to get the
idea I'm some racist or anti-Semite. My best friend's Jewish –'

'Oh I know, I know.' He dismissed my words with a wave and a
sniff. 'I wouldn't have hired you if I hadn't thought you'd turn out.
We all have to learn. Down there in the trenches.' Sniff. 'That's
where the learning takes place. For you and them. Both. You see
Mrs. Harris about your benefits yet?'

His shift in topic threw me. 'I'm sorry?'

'Benefits. Health. Life. Eye. The 403. That sort of thing. You
married, Archer?'

'Uh, no sir.'

'On the verge?'

'Not that I'm aware of, sir. Week's still young yet, though,' I said,
trying to lighten the moment a bit.

'Well, you'll still' – sniff – 'still need benefits. Things are
happening all the time. Car wrecks. Accidents. Never know, one
of those trench-coat types might walk in here and decide to take a
crack at you with a sawed-off. You have any idea how much it costs
to get a leg amputated these days? And a prosthesis? Not cheap.
You don't want to be a self-pay in this cold world. It's the HMOs,
of course, doing this to everyone. The tight-fisted sons of bitches…
Gotta have health insurance.' Sniff. 'I tell all my teachers that. Get
the Health. Pass on the Dental if you need to cut corners, but get
the Health.'

'Yes, sir. I'll speak to her after school. And about the Watherstein incident, if you'd like me to call his father and apologize –'

'We'll see what happens with it. I think I calmed him fine. Don't worry about it for now. Just be careful. And get the Health. Not Life so much, since you're single and whatnot, but get that damned Health.'

I promised, figuring I'd take my exit before he launched into the ups and downs of each available HMO. 'Thank you for your time.'

'Any time at all,' he said, and threw me a sniff in case I missed the first forty.

The night of my first day, the Roy Watherstein night, I found myself alone at a downtown Charleston bar called Capone's. It's a small little place, a locals-only type establishment nestled in on King Street without a sign. I was rifling tequila shots and sucking lime wedges every fifteen minutes or so, pumping money into the video-poker machine – South Carolina, buckle of the Bible belt, had at that time more sites at which to gamble than Vegas – and getting very little out of it. I was talking with one of the bar-girls that worked there, a former flame of mine named Marla Grossman I'd dated on and off a bit back at USC. She'd been a German major and had moved down to Charleston after graduation to teach in neighboring Berkfield County, but had been caught in a compromising position with one of the much older and much more married Social Studies teachers. Probably wouldn't have been that big a deal had it not been in a faculty bathroom, in the middle of the school day. Rumor was a student somehow opened the door and caught them in the act, so a year later Marla was serving me Jose Cuervo and enjoying my stories from my first day on the frontlines.

'Different than what you expected, isn't it?' she asked, leaning against the machine, holding a wet tray layered in empty shot glasses and beer bottles. Her eyes were big and brown, almond-shaped in that exotic way that suggests a hint of foreign ancestry. And the bar gig was suited for her, too, or suited for her body, in any case. She wasn't particularly thin, and this always bothered her a bit, but what she was carrying she carried well. She had those hips you could make out two city blocks away, all tightly-coiled and curvaceous in the Rita Hayworth sense of the word. There was an almost maternal, child-bearing quality to them which was wonderfully arousing in the right circumstances. She'd been a swimmer in her teen years, so she carried more muscle in her upper arms and shoulders than your average girl. She'd be fat one day, I was fairly certain, or would at the very least spend her life counting calories and measuring portions, but for now all that full fleshiness which would no doubt vex her in later years was terrifically placed and proportioned. Her breasts were round; nearly mirror images of one another. Her ankles were a little thicker than you'd have thought – sounds petty, I know, but I'm sort of into ankles and feet. Her winning feature was her face, though. As I said before, it wasn't so much pretty as it was unique. You could see people noticing her when they walked in the place, their eyes drawn to her the way a toy-store draws a child. There was something visually fascinating about her. Those deeply set, wet-brown eyes with the almost Egyptian flare at the corners. The overly-large mouth which wasn't afraid to try new things, but which had, rest assured, difficulty finding things that were new. Those lush, naturally-arched eyebrows that held a hint of mystery there. They were right. Marla Grossman was a walking enigma, an elixir of juxtaposed contradictions.

We'd dated pretty steadily for a year or so, breaking up a few weeks after I'd caught her in the sack with her German roommate, who was this hefty exchange student named – dig this – Helga. I'd tried to handle it; in truth, I was more than a little excited at the prospect of dating a full-fledged bisexual, but alas, Marla put the skids on those notions in a hurry.

'My sex life isn't for your entertainment,' she'd said, once Helga had gathered her clothes and exited, rather embarrassed at least, stage left.

'That's exactly what your sex life *is* for,' I'd countered. 'You're my girlfriend. When you have sex, I'm supposed to be there. And I'm supposed to be entertained through it. Why else would we do it? We're not making children.'

'You usually are.'

'Making children? Like hell. What do you think all those damned condoms are about?'

'There,' she said. 'Usually, when I have sex, you're there. And I dare say you're well entertained through it all.'

It would've been funny if it hadn't been my life at the time.

'Usually? Marla, you're not hearing me here. You were fucking – this,' I said, pointing at the bed, the sheets all twisted and damp, 'this...this is fucking! I don't care if it was another woman – you can't do that without me.'

'Why the hell not?' She asked, and the amazing thing was, she really wanted to know. Why couldn't she? Of course, there was a litany of answers, and of course I could think of none of them then.

'Because,' I offered as convincingly as I could manage, 'because you just can't. It's cheating, for God's sake. How long has this been going on?'

'Me and Helga, or me and other girls?'

'Yes. Both. Either, shit, I don't know.'

Her responses were as cold and clinical as if she might be describing how to de-flea a dog, or bake a potato.

'Helga and I were nearly finished when you barged in – completely abusing the key to my apartment I gave you, by the way – and I stopped limiting myself to just guys somewhere around my sophomore year in high school.'

'You have got to be shitting me,' I said. 'You've been…I don't even know what to say to that.'

'No, you knew exactly what to say to it. You said the same thing every brainless jock would say. 'Can I join in?' I thought more of you, Cole.'

'Me? How in the hell has this become about me? You're the one that's cheating and –'

'Oh, honestly. Grow up. It's not cheating when it's with another girl. Another guy I could see, but –'

'You mean to tell me if I was ass-tagging some other guy that'd be just kosher with you?'

'That's different,' she said. 'That's intercourse. Helga and I were hardly having inter –'

'It doesn't matter. You were naked together. Doing – doing shit that you're not supposed to be doing unless I'm there doing it, too.'

'So if you'd been there with Helga and me it wouldn't have been cheating? Cole, are you honestly listening to yourself? How can you be so obtuse?'

'This isn't about me, dammit. This is about – never mind. Have you slept with other guys?'

'What kind of question is that? Ever?'

'No. Since you and I have been dating.'

'Well,' she said. 'That depends. Exactly when did you and I start dating?'

That was a good question. We'd never had a formal conversation about it, never your basic Define The Relationship tête-à-tête. But her need for clarification left me weak.

'Pizza at the park,' I said. 'We got the Papa John's and took it to Finlay. Climbed the rocks. I almost fell in.'

She thought for a moment. 'Was that the same night we ended up at Bar None?'

I shook my head. 'This was after that.'

'Pizza at the park was after Bar None?'

'Way after,' I said. 'Like a couple weeks.'

'Oh. Then no, I haven't been with anyone since then. Other than you, that is.'

'And other girls?' I added, my stomach sick with betrayal, excitement, forbidden desire of the taboo, all of it.

'Yes, but I don't count that,' she said, smiling that smile she flashed on the Tammany Hall dance-floor the night we met.

That conversation went on a bit longer, but you get the gist of it by now. My girlfriend was a switcher, and I could neither get her to admit it was wrong nor allow me to join in. I was stuck in some lunatic purgatory. I hadn't even managed to extract some semblance of a promise that she'd discontinue the practice while we were involved. I'd tried, but she wouldn't budge, and that's where the whole yin-yang contradiction thing comes in. It wasn't wrong for her to do it, she reasoned, because I knew about it and implied my acceptance, if not my consent, by remaining involved with her. And she wouldn't tell me she'd stop, not even to make me feel better, because she had no plans of stopping, and lying after all wasn't a moral thing to do.

It was enough to make your head spin if you looked at it too hard.

I shrugged, pulling myself back into the moment, out of her Columbia apartment bedroom with the pink curtains and the piles of stuffed animals and the heavy smells of a dickless rendezvous, and back into Capone's in Charleston.

'I don't know what I expected, to tell you the truth.' I shot another tequila, my third of the night, and chewed thoughtfully on the lime. 'I didn't expect so much paperwork. Or so many dumb students. Or such dumb administrators, for that matter.'

Marla nodded agreement. 'Oh, Cole, the stories I could tell you.'

I leaned back on my stool and stretched, taking Marla in as I did.

She saw me do this.

'So Cole,' she said, 'any of the little teeny-bops making the eyes for you yet?'

'Me?' I said. 'No, no. Hell no. I teach eleventh graders. We're talking fifteen, sixteen years old here. I doubt many of them have had their first kiss yet.'

'Sweetie, tell me you're joking. First kiss? That really is rich.'

'What do you mean?'

'Honestly, Cole. I can't think of a single friend I had in high school who was a virgin in the eleventh grade.'

I wanted to say something along the lines of that's because all your friends were just like you: dirty little come-catchers who spent their high-school years nibbling cock like it was cheese at a wine-tasting soiree. Of course, I didn't say that, probably because the pragmatic part of me understood that it wouldn't have had any real effect at all. You couldn't shame Marla Grossman. You could only push her away, and occasionally, when I've had a few drinks, I could think of things to do with her more fun than pushing her away. I don't allow myself thoughts like that often; in fact, I don't allow them at all. They come unbidden every once and again, like gas, usually when I'm drinking, also like gas.

So I settled for a surprised, 'You're kidding. Eleventh grade?'

She smiled, almost laughed, and I had a sudden and unpleasant flash of déjà vu as I recognized the look in her eyes. She was mocking me. Mocking my naiveté. It seemed she'd spent most of our relationship mocking me in one fashion or another. Even the lesbian thing was an indictment of my abilities, or so I thought at the time.

I realized then why I'd been so relieved about our break-up – apart from the bisexual thing, of course which, had she shared a time or two, probably would have kept me around a touch longer, truth be told. But it was her personality. Marla Grossman was an overwhelmingly arrogant individual. Everything she did was arrogant. She even fucked arrogantly, as if she were in a vacuum; she'd writhe and roll and moan and claw in a selfish, single-minded manner that, despite its surface-level compensations, left me feeling empty and cold many a night. Some of the loneliest moments I'd spent with her were during her orgasms, which were always loud and violent and wildly animated, and which would without fail give me the strange sensation of being a voyeur, of watching someone pleasure themselves alone and without care for anyone else in the world.

But it was like that out of bed, too. Her ego was enormous, which, I suppose, is how she could stand there and shoot the shit with me, looking me in the eye all the way, knowing I knew what kind of unfaithful, morally flexible, virtually virtue-less woman she was.

'How old were you the first time?' she asked.

Seventeen, I thought, and shrugged. 'I don't remember.' I wasn't dating her anymore. She wasn't entitled to any of my past, present, or future.

'I'm sure,' she said. 'Well, I was fifteen, and before you say what you're dying to say about that, let me give you a piece of advice. Eleventh-grade girls have sex on the mind as much as eleventh-grade boys. And they think about it in much the same way, but with one notable exception.' There was a gleam to her eye just then, a glow to her cheeks that suggested she was now traveling through familiar territory.

'Unlike eleventh-grade boys,' she continued, 'who channel most of their sexual tension into late-night sessions jerking off in their beds and bathrooms, eleventh-grade girls know they can have it the minute they want it.'

'Sure,' I said, 'but I'm their teacher.'

'And that's what makes you so desirable, Cole. Trust me on this. I know, believe me. You're older, more mature, attractive, a quasi-father figure in a position of authority. Half the girls in your class haven't seen their father in the last ten years.' She winked, stood, and gathered her tray. 'And all of us deep down feel the need to be submissive now and again.'

She left me with that, the arrogant bitch, and went about her business of serving drinks, collecting money, and wiping down tables.

THREE

Chesterfields, beer, and Cole takes a sick day

I left Capone's that night – morning, actually; I'd watched the hands of my watch strike twelve right after doing three shots of tequila in as many seconds with a fairly attractive blonde co-ed from the College, me thinking I might have company for the night, she apparently thinking she'd be drinking for free, both of us wrong – at a quarter after two, three hours and forty-five minutes before my alarm would rip through my tiny two-room apartment to herald the dawn of my second day on The Job. The mere thought of it left me nauseated. I'd have to look Roy Watherstein in the eye, knowing that he would know that Mr. Collins had apologized on my behalf, doubtlessly sharing this bit of news freely with his classmates. Day two in the career of Cole Archer the Teacher, and already my authority was diluted.

I was driving up King Street towards Calhoun, which cut through the city and would eventually lead me to the bridge crossing the Ashley River. I'd be home in another twenty minutes, provided I didn't get pulled for swerving or driving too slowly or any of the number of things intoxicated drivers do to call attention to their intoxication.

I was doing the math in my head – 180 days of students per year multiplied by 30 years of teaching equaled out to 5349 more days like today – when I couldn't bear it any longer and pulled over at the BP for a six-pack of beer and a pack of Chesterfields. I'm not a chronic smoker but Chesterfields always soothe me and beer made the world go numb, and I figured I was entitled after a day like the one I'd had today.

I bought Beck's, the cigarettes, and a pack of Mousers for Brasco, then climbed back into my car and debated my options. It was 2:30;

plenty of places were still open in downtown Charleston. I could hit Henry's, which was a pretty decent second-time-around spot, packed wall-to-wall with divorcees out giving it another try. One thing about divorced women you can always count on, and it's a quality they share with a good number of unhappily-married women, and that's that all they need is a caring ear and an understanding nod in the right places and their guard begins to melt like snow in the rain.

But listening took energy and pretending to be listening took even more, and I was pretty well spent. There was Acme, which was more of the college scene, but it had its drawbacks, as well. It was a dance club that stayed open till four on weeknights, six on Fridays, and there were plenty of interesting people to meet, but the thought of all the lights and smoke and bone-deep bass made my head hurt. And I was worn out. From the drinking, sure – drinking, if done correctly, can be extraordinarily tiring – but from my conversation with Marla as well. I didn't want to admit it, but she still had an effect on me, still stirred my imagination with the suggestion of possibility as she had since the night I'd met her, as she did throughout our ill-fated relationship. There were large parts of her that repulsed me, but I was still on a visceral level drawn almost magnetically to her raw wantonness. Like good, high-quality coke, the ride with Marla Grossman could be so damned good for the moments they lasted that you allowed yourself to forget that waiting for you at the end of it all was a drop that left you empty and depressed and filled with self-disgust. But being there tonight with her had sent a current through my bloodstream that I was having trouble shaking.

So there I was, driving up Highway 61, a half-residential, half-industrial stretch of four-lane that you could ride all the way to Myrtle Beach if you chose. I had half a Chesterfield wedged into the corner of my mouth, my head was spinning pleasantly about a foot above my body, and all I could think of was how depressing my little one-room West Ashley apartment was going to be. Brasco would be there waiting for me, curled up into a tight little ball of fur on the couch, and he and I would sit there together while he ate his Mousers and I drank my beer and smoked my cigarettes and tried not to think about either work or Marla.

I spent a few minutes rolling around with Brasco when I got in. He'd heard my steps approaching the door, and had been waiting for me when I entered into the dark, too-hot living room. One thing about pets: So long as you treat them right, they'll make you feel like you're the whole universe and everything in it, which I guess I was, so far as he was concerned. He'd been a house cat ever since I picked him up at the shelter some four years earlier, and except for the few times he'd sneaked out through my legs, he'd never been outside. These days, he didn't show much interest in what was out there. He knew I was coming back eventually, and so long as I brought the food and litter and the occasional pouch of Mousers he was fine.

I finished the Chesterfield and knocked back one of the beers in about half a minute. The Beck's was thick and full, and the simple taste of it seemed to lighten my mood a bit. Beck's is good for that. There's something about the dark beers that'll settle you in ways the Ambers and Blondes won't.

I surfed the tube and drank the beer and an hour later I'd cleaned them all out, so I killed the TV with the remote, sending the apartment pitch black. I stumbled across the room and found the halogen lamp (Wal-Mart, sixteen bucks) and stood there, considering my options. I thought this probably said something about me, about my attitude towards my career of choice. It was almost four in the morning, I had to be up in another two hours, and I hadn't slept a wink yet. I'd spent most of the night at a bar, talking to an old flame I never really liked much but still fantasized about for some reason. The rest of the night I'd sat home alone drinking with the cat, too tired to even jerk off, until now here I was, four A.M., alone and pathetic and trying to figure out what to do with the rest of my life.

They give you twelve leave days a year when you work for The Winter's Cove School District. Regular saints, that bunch at the DO. Get hit by a bus and need thirteen, they dock your pay a full day.

You get nine sick, three personal. The personal were for whatever the hell you wanted them for, and had to be scheduled at least two days in advance. The sick days were for when you were sick, as I was then. Sick of doing something for a living I didn't believe in. Sick of hoping like hell whoever I meet for the first time won't ask me what I do, forcing me to either lie or say 'teaching,' both of which are equally emasculating. I was sick of missing Autumn and fantasizing about Marla. Sick of this apartment – this stinking little one-roomer with no overhead lighting and no washer and dryer – that was running me five yards a month. When I moved in there was a grease-spot on the wall from where the previous tenant had rubbed his head while he slept. The refrigerator had, and still has, for all I know, the brownish-yellow crust and film lining the edges that was there when I moved in. Every time I took a shit I wondered who else had sat right there, their cheeks where mine were, their turds plopping beneath them just like mine. It was all I could do to make myself sit down. How do I know the person before me wasn't a fat, nasty, redheaded woman with bad teeth and freckles all over her face and ass? I wouldn't have thought it would matter, but it apparently did, because I thought about it every time I had to pinch one off. About a week after I moved in I found a red pubic hair in the shower, which is probably why I said redheaded. The fat part I'm assuming. I could have said Angie Everhart, or some other redheaded bombshell instead of a fat one with bad teeth and reckless freckles, and maybe that says something about my state of mind lately, as well, like the glass being half-empty or half-full. The previous shitter on your toilet was either an obese skank or a beautiful model. Pay your money, place your bets. Hope the hell it turns your way.

I needed to get out of here, that much was obvious. I picked up the phone and called the automated sub-caller, punched in my employee-code and then a '1' for 'sick,' and hung up. Then I lit a cigarette and went to bed.

Brasco was waiting for me, as he always was. He draped himself over my calves like a tarp, and his purring lulled me to sleep.

FOUR

First sick day; intermezzo; orange-juice and rainbows on King Street; Grey on the beach

I awoke on my first sick day at nine that morning; I'd let the alarm sound its soulless 6:00 A.M. wake-up just to have the pleasure of turning it off before rolling back over for another few hours. There are times in life when you have to take your kicks where you can get them.

When I finally did force myself out of bed – Brasco fighting me all the way, his tastes having never bent towards anything that involved much effort – I skipped the shaving/showering routine and climbed into a pair of old Gamecock sweats from my college days. I did brush my teeth and wash the crust out of my eyes, but that was about it. I probably wouldn't have even bothered with that, but the Chesterfield had been fermenting in there for a good five hours, and my breath was enough to make my eyes water. That's always a compelling sign.

I drove the fifteen minutes downtown and ate breakfast at a little sidewalk café on King Street. I took a table near the street and watched the tourists pitter-patter this way and that like little marching ants. The sun had that early-morning warmth to it, that cleansing, basking feel that is like some sort of soothing balm. It poured over my head and back and sent a million tiny stars of color through my half-filled – already I was feeling more positive – glass of orange-juice. I tilted my head back and let it wash over my face, felt my skin tighten and saw the world go pink and black behind my closed eyelids.

For those few moments I was able to forget about Coosaw Creek High School and Roy Watherstein and Mr. Collins and his annoying sniffs and fixation on health plans. All that nonsense was worlds away, and I was here, in the center of the most amazing city in the world, the sun raining down on me and everything suddenly feeling all right.

I decided then and there, at that café on King, to drive to neighboring Isle of Palms and spend the rest of the morning on the beach, watch the gulls dive into the gray Atlantic and listen to the waves crashing on the sand.

We drove. When you're out of options and out of time that's about all you can do.

Just drive.

I'd driven my little Honda all the way across the belly of the Deep South, running a zigzag line through the heart of Lee's original Confederacy, until I reached the Louisiana/Texas border. We'd begun burning oil badly somewhere in Alabama, so I'd pulled into the first all-night Wal-Mart I came across and bought twenty quarts of 10W-40. I had to stop every hundred miles or so and pour another half a quart in, and there were still stretches where the muffler belched white smoke out the tail-pipe and the engine knocked and whinnied beneath the hood so loudly I could turn the stereo up to 'ten' and still barely make out the song. But we got there, bless her heart. That car – that '83 Honda my mother and I pitched in together to buy for me when I was a junior in high school myself – got me all the way to the edge of Texas, nearly a thousand miles away from Charleston. I'd driven seventeen hours straight, stopping only for gas, oil refills, bathroom breaks (for myself and Brasco) and food – all of which I'd taken care of at a series of off-road gas stations and all-night truck-stops. It'd been 5:00 a.m., Eastern Time, when I'd left my Charleston life behind forever. It was ten minutes shy of straight-up midnight Texas time when I reached her border. Mexico was still another couple hundred miles. I'd gone through thirteen quarts of oil, fifty-odd gallons of gas, four packs of Chesterfields, half a bottle of ephedrine, and a floorboard full of Pepsi and Frito Lay products. While I was driving, the authorities – first the local police, then shortly after the Feds – had gone through my apartment, slicing open my mattress, tearing up my carpet, checking the bottoms of my drawers, gathering prints from the countertops and hair samples from the bathroom and taking pictures from every possible angle. They were looking for anything they could find; evidence of Savannah's presence, evidence of the missing money, evidence of anything at all. All I was looking for was a horizon over water.

The next morning I traded the Honda plus a thousand dollars cash – a sizable chunk of my traveling stash – for an old utility van that still had the outline of the words 'Stanley Steamer Carpet Cleaner' running along its sides and front. It was hard to leave the Honda behind, harder than I'd thought it'd be. I'd spent the two or three hours prior to reaching Texas talking to it, explaining why I had to abandon it, trying to frame it in terms of retirement rather than abandonment. Mexico's a harsh country, I whispered to the dash, and I'm going to have to run harder than you're going to want to run at this stage of your life. You've been a loyal and faithful friend, seen me through a lot of shit and a lot of good, and retiring you to an old folks' home for loyal and faithful cars is the best gift I can give you right now.

It sounds infantile and even a little insane, I know, but aside from the cat I was leaving everything I knew behind, and doing so permanently, and that car came to symbolize for me during those last few hours the sum total of all I'd ever known or done in my old life up to that moment; on one level or another it was involved with every relationship or attachment the Cole Archer of old had ever established. Wherever I might have traveled the previous thirteen years – whoever I'd been dating, hanging out with, or carpooling to or from high school, college, or graduate school with – that car had taken me. The feel of its wheel at the base of my fingers, where the first knuckle and the palm come together, was as familiar to me as the sound of my own voice. I'd left everything in the world behind in exchange for what waited for me beyond the Mexican border, and that car was simply the last little bit of 'then' that I had to get rid of if I wanted to ensure for myself a new 'now.' You'll forgive me if I cried a bit.

When I reached Brownsville it was noon Texas time, 11:00 back home. No. That wasn't quite right: 11:00 back in Charleston. Home wasn't Charleston anymore. Home was somewhere I hadn't seen yet.

I found a small used-car lot, one of those side-road types where all the cars are parked on dirt and the office is a sawed-off little single-wide without windows. I gave the guy the van and five hundred dollars in exchange for a '86 Ford F150 with over 300,000 miles on it. I insisted on signing nothing, and the salesman/manager/owner nodded understandingly.

'Been here some twenty years now,' he said through teeth of

varying degrees of yellow and brown. 'Not many folks ever sign anything. Not many drive north, neither,' he said, chuckling as he fingered my bills – twenty-five twenties, fresh from the teachers' credit union in Charleston – in his oil-stained hands. That five hundred plus the thousand for the van put me down to three hundred dollars. Three hundred dollars and one hell of a lot of hope.

I checked the tires, the oil, and the brake/taillights. I was less than ten miles from the Mexican border by that point, and I couldn't risk getting pulled by some local deputy who noticed my left-blinker wasn't operating properly. Not this close.

I tossed the duffel bag into the truck, got Brasco situated, and drove two miles to the nearest motel. I was near exhaustion. I'd been able to get less than two hours sleep the previous night, my first as a fugitive, tossing and turning in a cheap motel bed on the Texas line that smelled of old urine and older come. Now it felt as if someone were lighting matches, then putting them out against my eyes. My stomach was roiling with the nausea of non-sleep; the ephedrine had worn off and I was coming down hard.

Five minutes later I was on my back atop the worn purple bedspread, the drapes pulled closed, the lights off. I had the air-conditioner on high, and the television tuned to CNN for the sake of familiarity more than anything else.

A line from one of my favorite movies occurred to me just then. These two characters, roughly my age, were talking about skipping out on their miserable lives and looking for brighter tomorrows somewhere else. I've always wanted to see what TV looked like in other countries, one of them says. The other one nods her head: me too, and the two of them hit the road.

Brasco had found his way to my chest, and was nervously kneading my skin beneath his paws. He'd never cared for travel, and twenty-plus hours of it was simply beyond the feline pale. It was like six weeks of cat-time. He'd had to piss four times and shit once on the way here, each time on the side of the road while I held his shoulders tight enough so he couldn't get away. I was reasonably sure he'd never fully forgive me for that particular indignity.

I scratched his ears a bit, trying to pull a purr out of him.

'What do you think, boy? You ever wonder what TV in foreign countries looks like?'

But I was asleep before he could answer.

I went back to the apartment and changed into shorts and a tee shirt, then took the Mark Clark to Mt. Pleasant, and the connector to Isle of Palms. I was reclined in a beach chair out on the sand, a Gamecock hat perched backwards on my head and my dark prescription shades on as I scanned the classifieds of *The Post and Courier* looking for condos for sale.

I found a few I was interested in, creasing the page to mark them. Had money not been an object I would have liked to buy in Mt. Pleasant, which is a small, pristine little peninsula that juts off the city and caters to the young professional crowd, but I was a teacher and money was an object. The average three-bedroom, one-and-a-half bath condo in Mt. Pleasant was going for about a buck thirty, which was more than I could spend. I didn't have much saved yet, having only worked at a real job for two days (and only actually working in the literal sense for one of those two days), so my only hope was an FHA loan, which are federally-backed. Their interest rates are a bit higher but they don't require nearly as much cash up front.

That's just about as far as I'd gotten with the process when Grey happened along, and changed everything about my life forever.

I hadn't seen her approaching; she came shuffling up behind me, dragging her beach chair in one hand and a novel in the other, unfolding the chair about ten feet off to my left. The book, I noticed as she walked by, was one of those big hardbacks you got from the library, with the clear plastic wrapped around it for protection. I caught the author, Judith Michael, and knew it was a romance. I could have guessed that, though. She was a woman on the beach alone. You don't see many of them toting *Windows for Dummies* around.

She was wearing one of those big touristy-type hats with the wide rim that blocks the sun from your face, and had on sunglasses as well. I looked her over quickly, out of habit more than anything else, then returned to my newspaper. That's something males learn at a young age, from our fathers and big brothers: The art of looking at a member of the opposite sex, of sizing her up and mentally cataloguing the results without appearing to be doing so, is probably on the Y chromosome.

I'd seen enough to know that she was an older woman, in her late thirties probably, with short dark hair that leaned to red beneath the early afternoon sun. She was wearing a skimpy white bikini, which ordinarily would have looked misinformed or even desperate on someone else, but she was in surprisingly good shape for her age: her legs thin and toned, and her stomach flat, if a little overcooked by the sun. She was brown all over, and had, judging by the leathery look of her skin, been tanning for years.

All of this was catalogued automatically by the part of my brain that handles that sort of thing; the rest of me was busy looking in the classifieds for a place free of red pubic hair.

'Moving?' I heard her ask, and wasn't sure whether she was speaking to me or no. I was the only other person nearby, however; except for a few old folks strolling along at the water's edge, and the usual crop of runners huffing their way down the beach with their walkmen and wristbands.

'I'm sorry?' I said, setting the paper down in my lap and looking over at her. She was squirting something – baby oil, I saw – into her hand and rubbing it into her calves and thighs. As she pointed her leg out you could see the muscle flex. I assumed she was probably an aerobics instructor or something.

'I saw your paper there,' she said, offering me a cordial smile as she rubbed the oil into her skin with practiced vigor. 'I only said anything because I've recently moved myself.'

'Oh yeah?' I said, 'from where to where?'

'James Island to downtown,' she said. 'And it's the best thing I've ever done in my life, next to each of my divorces. Except maybe the first one. But then again, had I not divorced him I would have never married the next, and would have never had the pleasure of walking out on him.'

She was rubbing the baby oil into her stomach now. I had the feeling she was talking to herself as much as to me, as though she might enjoy the sound of her voice in the clear, salty air.

I tried not to watch her rub herself down with the oil, glancing away, then back at her stomach, then to her face to see if she'd caught me, then away again before she could. If she noticed any of this she didn't show it.

'James Island that bad?' I asked. 'I always thought it was kind of nice.'

'Oh, there's nothing wrong with the island itself. I think most all islands are inherently charming places, except perhaps Australia, which doesn't really have that island feel, despite its being surrounded by water. Of course, I'm terrified by marsupials, so naturally I'd think that. But James Island is free of marsupials and perfectly lovely; it's merely with whom I shared it that turned me off.'

'Ah,' I said, not sure what 'ah' meant, but it sounded like the sort of thing one says in situations like that.

'I'm going through my latest divorce,' she continued. 'Finally. It takes a year, you know. Are you married?'

'No,' I shook my head. 'Not even close.'

'The not-even-close of the recently divorced, the not-even-close of the happily single, or the not-even-close of the confirmed bachelor?'

'Uh, well, I've never been married, so not recently divorced.'

'And since confirmed bachelor means hopelessly gay, we'll assume for serendipity's sake that you've never been married?'

'No. Yes. Never have been, no.' I made a mental note to look up 'serendipity' when I got home. And me the big English teacher.

'Well, keep it in mind, should you ever choose to make the leap.'

'What's that?'

'It takes a year.'

'To get divorced?'

'Yes,' done with the stomach, rubbing into the tops of her breasts now, peeling back an inch of white bikini top and rubbing it in, the skin there just as brown as everywhere else.

I felt myself go hard in my shorts and held my breath to kill it, a trick I taught myself in middle school. It works sometimes.

'First you have to legally separate, then you have to actually remain separated – sexually, that is – for an entire year. One little slip up and it throws you back to the starting point. But I don't mean to sour you on the subject. Marriage is wonderful, and I absolutely think you should do it. Positively. I've done it several times. Four to date, to be exact.'

I whistled. 'That's a lot of I do's.'

She nodded. 'It's a wonderful way to get to know someone. Of course, the problem comes when you actually *do* get to know them, know them too well sometimes, and by that point you're stuck with them. Would you mind getting my back for me?'

'Sorry?'

'Oh, don't be so shy. Surely you've had your hands on a woman's body before.' She extended her arm, every inch of her shiny with the oil, the bottle in her outstretched hand.

'Well come on,' she said, smiling. 'I won't tell anyone, I promise.'

I figured what the hell and stood, folding the newspaper on my chair and walking over to her. I took the oil from her and she turned her back to me, bending her head forward.

'Make sure you get everywhere,' she said. 'I'm quite averse to splotches.'

'Yes, ma'am,' I said. Like the quick surveying of her when she walked up, the 'ma'am' was a habit.

'Oh no,' she said, as I squirted the oil into my hand. 'That won't do at all.'

'What's that?'

'You ma'am'd me. I'm not that much older than you.'

I rubbed my hands over her back and shoulders, covering her in the lotion.

'If you say so,' I said, rubbing, Mr. Bojangles cooperating not at all.

'I definitely do. How old are you?'

'Twenty-six. Almost twenty-seven. Next week, actually.'

'There, you see. In just another eighteen years, you'll be the age I am now. Eighteen years is no time at all. You'll see it really does fly right by.'

'You're forty-five?'

'For another two months.'

I couldn't believe that. 'So you'll be forty-six in two months?'

She nodded. 'That's the way it works out, yes.'

'Well,' I said, wiping my hands over her lower back, which was far too firm for a woman her age, 'I hope you don't mind my saying so, but you are in absolutely fantastic shape.'

'Thank you. It's amazing what they're doing with silicone and saline now. I made certain I bought my breasts before filing for divorce. Be sure to get beneath the string.'

I did, then stopped rubbing and she turned around to face me. I tried not to let my eyes wander down to her breasts. Her nearly-forty-six-year-old breasts, bought not too long ago.

'I'm Grey,' she said, extending her hand. I shook it.

'Cole,' I said. 'Cole Archer.'

'Oh,' she said with a dismissive wave of the hand, 'let's not bother with last names. Last names are too formal, don't you think?

I'm much more fond of first names. Besides, you've already coated me in oil, so we're far past any pretense of formality.'

I laughed at this. I was surprised at how much I was enjoying talking with her.

'I guess you're right,' I said. Then, 'I notice you're still wearing your wedding band.' Ordinarily I don't notice that type of thing, but her diamond was enormous, and insofar as refracting the sun went, it put my orange juice glass from the café to shame.

'Yes,' she said. 'I'm waiting for the right day.'

'The right day?'

'To take it off. My last husband proposed to me here, at the end of that pier out there actually, exactly eight years ago tomorrow. So tomorrow I'll come out here and toss the diamond over the edge, which is what I should have done in the first place. Saved us both a great deal of headache, but of course then I wouldn't have gotten the boobs.'

'Why don't you just sell it if you don't want it?'

'Oh, no,' she said. 'All they'll give me for it is money, and all the money in the world couldn't buy the satisfaction I'll get from throwing it over the edge and watching it sink. There's a certain bit of symbolism there that is wonderfully refreshing. Don't you agree, Cole?'

I guess I did. 'Sure.' What I knew was we were sitting on the same chair, less than a foot apart. I could smell her breath when she spoke. Spearmint. I was strangely uncomfortable, then, the mechanics of this situation something with which I was completely unfamiliar. In a bar or at a club or in a class or any of the rest of it, I knew the drill. But I was out here on the beach with a woman every bit my mother's age, and so far both the parameters and the tone of the situation were being controlled by her. The role of beta-male wasn't one to which I was accustomed.

'So tell me, to where are you moving?'

'Looks like it's going to have to be Winter's Cove. I can't really afford anywhere else.'

'I love Winter's Cove,' she said. 'Particularly the quaint little downtown area. I could live there except that it's too far from the beach. And I'm deeply in love with the beach, as you probably assumed by now.'

I was getting ready to say something – I'm not entirely certain as to what, now – when she took off her sunglasses and stared up at me from beneath that absurdly large hat.

'I tell you what, Cole,' she said, her eyes a bright, metallic green, 'let's not say any more to one another. I've very much enjoyed talking to you today, and would like to do it again sometime, if you wouldn't object, of course. But we've only just met, and I find that when people have only just met and they enjoy speaking to one another, they tend to search for things to talk about, simply because they enjoy talking to the other person so. And that really can have a watering-down effect on what might otherwise be a quality introduction and conversation. So let's do this instead: give me your phone number – just say it aloud once and I'll remember it – and I'll call you one evening. We can have coffee. Do you drink coffee, Cole?'

I felt like I'd been caught in a tornado. 'Yeah,' I said. 'All the time.'

'Really good coffee should only be had at night, after dinner. Around eight or so. But see, this is something we should talk about over coffee – around eight or so, of course. So give me your phone number, and then one of us must go.'

'You mean leave the beach?'

'At least this part of it. Otherwise we'll be tempted to talk, and risk spoiling it for later. Or we might just ignore each other, and that would be awkward, in light of how well we've gotten along here this afternoon.'

In an odd, off-center way, she was making sense. And while the idea of going out on a date – and that's what it would be, if the two of us met for coffee sometime – with a woman who was closer to fifty than forty was pretty strange for me, that part of it didn't bother me much. She was an interesting woman, someone with whom I thought I could enjoy sitting around and just shooting the breeze. Any woman who marries to get to know people and makes appointments to throw massive diamond rings off of piers had to have some good dinner conversation. And again, from a purely physical standpoint, she looked at least ten years younger.

So I gave her my number and grabbed my paper and walked off. Twenty yards away I turned back, but she didn't see me. She was lying on her stomach, soaking up the sun, and as I turned to walk away, I could have sworn that I heard her singing.

FIVE

Meeting Capers; day three;
places without couches or porches

Day three. I arrive at work – school, everyone else calls it, as in 'I'll be staying after school today so a few of my students can make up a test,' but I can't bring myself to say that; I need the dignity associated with 'work' – at a quarter after seven, before most of the other teachers. I'm a rookie, and as such am held, at least unofficially, to a different set of standards. Aside from the Induction Year Class, required of all first-year teachers by the Great and Powerful Professional Educators at Winter's Cove, there is an entire sub-level of expectations associated with being a first-year, and I was learning this as I went.

For starters, there's the attitude thing. I'm supposed to be happy to be there, even downright jazzed, while my more seasoned (read: grizzled and jaded) colleagues bitch from sign-in to sign-out about everything from the kids to the temperature in their classrooms to the district tie policy. But I'm fortunate, you see, to be working there, to be working anywhere apparently, and need to be ready to genuflect at a moment's notice to All Who Have Come Before Me.

There were a few gems on the faculty, however; men and women I considered myself fortunate to have met. Bert Rogers, the History and Econ teacher; and Zack Capers, who taught English better than any professor I ever had and took me under his wing those first few months. Jim Heathcliff, who 'taught' driver's ed. and coached every sport known to man; Kevin Geist, the poly-linguist who taught German, French, and Spanish, and somehow found the time to chair the Winter's Cove Democratic Party, for which we shall forgive him.

In any case, there I was on day three of the 180-school-day year, sitting in my classroom, my feet propped on my desk, the *USA*

Today folded and unread in my lap. I was watching the clock above my door tick off the seconds, trying to figure in my head how many seconds there were in a 30-year career. I was fairly sure there were more than I could handle without a great deal of drugs. I was thinking this when Zack Capers, the English teacher down the hall, poked his head in the door.

'Someone's on dawn patrol,' he said through his closed-mouth smile. He was a big guy, with receding dark hair going gray around the ears. His face had that deep, metallic red that came from countless hours spent in the sun and wind.

'Yeah,' I said, smiling over my feet, removing them from my desk, figuring it wasn't a good impression from a guy not quite into his third day On The Job. 'They said I needed to be here at a quarter after.'

'Who said,' Capers asked, coming into my room, glancing around casually. 'Don't tell me the folks at the DO?'

I nodded. 'Dr. Louis herself. During my clearance interview, as a matter of fact.'

He rolled his eyes. 'Well,' he said, 'that's about par for the course for that bunch over there. Your contract doesn't require you to be here until five till. I'm always here early 'cause I need the peace before I face the kids, but it's not required. Guarantee you the lights are off at the DO right now.' He extended his hand. 'Zack Capers,' he said. 'You're Cole Archer, right? I'd heard we'd hired another male. Good thing, too.'

'Oh yeah,' I said, shaking his hand. 'Why's that?'

'Because this profession is short on men, plain and simple. Our department picked up four new teachers this year, and you're the only male. Two new teachers last year, no guys. Two the year before that, same story. Last male teacher we hired quit his second year, and they replaced him with a woman.'

'And this is bad?' I asked, fairly certain I'd be stepping on his professional sensibilities – I'd already pigeonholed Capers as Mr. Teacher himself, a professional educator honestly committed to the cause on some deeply visceral level; I had a touch of envy of him then, as I recall. It must be nice to be able to believe in something other than yourself and the moment.

'Well, they're good teachers, by and large. One or two of them outstanding, actually. But it's bad for the profession, for the kids, particularly in today's day and age, with the current shortage of fathers in the homes.' He sighed. 'Rearing children on one's own seems to be in vogue these days.'

I didn't have much to say to that, but there he was, still standing there like there was something that needed to be said and my not saying it would be testament enough to my incompetence. As I think I've already said, my morale wasn't much those first few days. I was given to self-doubt a bit.

He smiled again. 'It'll do these kids good to have a male up in front of them reading poetry. Add a masculine tint to things.' He glanced at his watch. 'You up for a bite?'

'Sure,' I said. 'Here?'

He nodded. 'Cafeteria crew serves breakfast for the teachers from twenty after to ten till. The eggs aren't much, but the coffee's free, the bacon's salty, and the biscuits and gravy are the eighth great sin.'

'Yeah, you bet. Coffee and sin, all before eight. Who can beat it?'

He laughed, and we walked down the long, quiet hallway towards the cafeteria, our footsteps echoing in the empty silence of the early morning. Coosaw Creek High was a new high school, built with new state money that trickled down to Winter's Cove two legislative sessions ago thanks to a goofy-looking Governor who rode Education into the mansion. Coosaw Creek High was one of the forty or so like it being built across the state, complete with all the amenities politicians and bureaucrats had decided shortly after the last election that schools needed to be successful. Brand new shiny lockers lining either side of the extra-wide halls, brightly painted walls, noise-absorbent ceilings, the works. The library was state of the art, with over 50,000 volumes and some sixty computers hooked up to the Almighty Internet. Every classroom had a minimum of three computers, a wall-mounted television, and a multi-media projector I still didn't know how to work. The District was, it seemed, suddenly flush with cash, and our end came in the form of free coffee. As many cups as you like.

'You met any of the others in our department yet?' Capers asked as we entered the cafeteria and headed for the breakfast station in the corner.

'No, I haven't really had the chance yet. I didn't have the greatest first day, and I was sick yesterday, and –'

'Yeah, I heard about that. The Jewish thing. Not something you want to do on a daily basis. Take my word for it: you don't want to make headaches for Ricke.'

'Ricke? Oh, Mr. Collins.'

'You'll drop the 'Mr.' business once you've worked for him a while.' He pointed to the eggs, bacon, and biscuits and gravy. An old black woman with discomforting green eyes offered him a 'Morning Mr. Capers,' and scooped his plate full. 'Extra gravy, as you like it,' she smiled.

'You know me too well, Virginia,' he said. 'You let me know when you're single.'

And she laughed and laughed at that. 'Help you, young man?' she finally asked me.

'Yes, ma'am. Just three strips of bacon and some biscuits and gravy. Thanks.'

She fixed my plate – no extra gravy, I hadn't earned that yet – and I followed Zack into the teachers' dining area and joined him at the table. He was already eating. We were alone this early in the morning.

'So tell me Cole,' he said, working on the eggs first, leaving the rest alone for now. My mother always said that told you something about a person, if they ate all of one thing before moving on, or just ate off the plate in whatever order struck them at the time. She said the ones who ate one thing first – first the meat, then the potato, then the steamed carrots – were control freaks, alpha-types who were accustomed to leading the way. I figured Zack Caper fit right in there.

'Where you from? Where's your family?'

'My mother lives in Augusta, Georgia, where I grew up, and my father's wherever. Haven't seen him in twenty-something years. Far as I'm concerned he's just a faulty condom in the back of some Buick twenty-seven years ago.'

He nodded, full of empathy and understanding, a standard tool for any teacher. 'Any brothers and sisters?'

'One of each. My brother's a twin, believe it or not. He's doing three to five for insurance fraud in Atlanta. My sister's an entertainer in New York.'

'Well there's an interesting contrast.'

I took a sip of my orange juice. No beautiful downtown sun refracting through it. This one was Styrofoam, and I was in a high-school cafeteria, waiting for The Kids to arrive. I wondered what the lawyers were doing just then, down on Broad. I wondered what Stephen King was doing up in Bangor, or Thomas Harris, over in Italy. I wondered how in the hell I was going to get out of this gig, now that I was so hopelessly in it.

'Not really,' I said. 'She's a call-girl. It's not exactly Broadway.' If I sounded callous, it's only because I'd worked through all the dysfunctional Conroyesque family stuff long ago.

He finished the eggs and went for the bacon, apparently saving the biscuits and gravy for dessert. His manna more precious than Mammon.

'My sister went the wrong way for a while, too,' he said. 'Damned hard thing to handle at the time.'

I nodded; sipped the coffee. I don't even like coffee, but he'd seemed so pleased with himself when he'd told me it was free, I hated to hurt the guy's feelings.

'She'd been married and divorced twice by the time she was twenty-one, the first at sixteen, mind you. And my father the ex-marine at the time? Forget it. We're talking postal, right? Anyway, she runs off, gets herself pregnant, a judge had to step in…it was a mess. Lasted maybe six months. Maybe. He beat her up right before she had the baby, and my father went over there and beat him up, put him in the hospital for almost a week.'

The night we graduated from college, my buddy Jules and I went to a bare-all strip club on the outskirts of Columbia, where we drank and inhaled our way into a vaporous haze. Sometime between midnight and closing an equally inebriated black man jostling for position at the bar threw a little too much elbow into old Juliet's side. Jules is a reporter now, here in Charleston, being groomed for CNN or Fox and a million-dollar contract with all sorts of perks. That night, some five years back, he was a drunk Mexican who'd been disrespected by a black man with an unfortunate lack of forethought on one of the bigger nights of his life. In that smoky dark strip club I saw Jules do things to that hyphenated-American fellow you can't put in R-rated movies.

So I wasn't too impressed with whatever Zack's old man had done to his sister's first husband or whatever. But I raised my eyebrows anyway, let him know he'd struck some macho-male chord covered over by my Oxford button-down and Structure tie.

'I'll put it to you this way,' he was going on, nibbling the crunchy bacon reflectively, 'did you see The Godfather? The scene where Sonny finds out his sister's husband is abusing her? That was something like what my father did to Steve. Now I'm twelve at this point. My sister is sixteen. Four years later she's almost twenty-one and it's love all over again. Same guy again, only the name has changed. Seemed they were all the same guy. They stay together long enough to have two kids. Then he robs a shoe store and leaves.'

'A shoe store, huh?'

He nodded. 'Tells you something about the guy's brains, doesn't it? They catch him a couple days later, in a swamp-cabin in West Georgia, and far as I know he's still in jail somewhere.'

'Your sister recover from all that?'

He shrugged. 'Depends on what you consider recovered. She joined a monastery shortly afterwards, then moved out to Colorado. Tried her hand – or feet, as it were – at ballet for a while. Now she makes donuts for the stars at a Krispy Kreme in Aspen, and lives with her black lesbian lover in a three-room mountain bungalow.'

'Wow,' was all I could find to say. 'That's a … I don't know. Damn.'

He shrugged. 'Damn indeed. So don't give up on your sister.'

I didn't mention to him that I hadn't spoken to her in over four years, and had no plans of doing so down the road.

'No,' I said. 'I won't.'

We were into the biscuits and gravy before it turned to shop-talk.

'Stay away from the lounges,' he said. 'Go there to use the copier, the phone, the Coke machine and the microwave, but don't hang out in there. Don't lounge there, as it were. You'll notice the English department lounge is the only one in the building without a couch in it. That's because I had it taken out a couple years ago when I was Chair. Social Studies took it, so now they have two. Any idea why I took it out?'

No, and I don't much give a shit either, Zack m'boy.

I shrugged. 'No.'

'For the same reason Social Studies was so hot to have it. Couches invite people to sit on them. And once that happens, it isn't long before the people start talking. Talking about the weekend, the spouse, the weather or the game, all that's fine. But it all eventually comes back to work, and then people begin to air their grievances publicly. So and so had a bad parent-conference.

This person's parking place is closer than this one. Her classroom is bigger than mine. He's got more desks and fewer students. Blah blah blah. And these grievances, they take on additional weight in the presence of others similar to them, Cole, and before long you've got a group of people bent out of shape because of lunch duty, or the DO's charging for athletic passes, or conferences are always scheduled at 3:30 when everyone wants to be going home. And as you can imagine, nothing ever gets done this way. Pretty soon the petty complaints about the job overshadow the importance of the job, and we begin to lose what vestiges of professionalism we as a profession still have. All because of a lousy couch.'

Like I said. Mr. Teacher. All he needed was the cape.

'Sounds like you're talking about collective complaining,' I said. 'Isn't that how the labor unions cleaned things up for the truckers a few decades ago? I mean, labor organization is the essential root of –'

'There's your first mistake. There is no collective bargaining in South Carolina. Check that notion at the door. This is a right-to-work state. No unions. Anywhere, save for some of the Federal jobs. If you want a union, you need to be a letter-carrier, or drive a UPS truck. The state sets everything down here, and they do it without a union, without concern for supply and demand, without much regard whatsoever for Adams's Invisible Hand. The lounge is filled with the poison of malcontents, and it bubbles and breeds and grows in intensity with each passing year. It can cause someone like you on the front end of a thirty-year career a hell of a hard time, convince you that something good is really not so good after all.'

He stopped talking long enough to chew some more. I struggled to keep my interested face on, but I could've given two shits about this stuff.

'For example, we got a four percent raise last year, which is pretty good, by any standard. My wife works for Bosch and hers was two point five. Now, the day after we get word from Columbia that the four percent was coming, there're five, six veteran teachers sitting around on the Math lounge couch, bitching about how up in Pennsylvania or Ohio or some other union state the teachers got a six point five percent raise.

'So we did away with the English lounge's couch. Like Bradbury's porches, it had to go.'

Now, the Couch-Is-The-Root-Of-All-Evil Speech was one

thing, but Bradbury's porches was pure bush-league stuff. In Bradbury's classic, *Fahrenheit 451*, the characters live in a world where porches are illegal, thereby preventing the populace from sitting around talking, questioning the wisdom of a society fucked up enough to employ fire departments to burn down the houses containing books. I figured he was testing me – Mr. Teacher feeling me out on my content knowledge, the gatekeeper of the integrity of his department – so I mentally ran through my knowledge of similar works of literature. I drew a blank at first, but Huxley came through for me.

'So it's a *Brave New World*,' I said, 'filled with lounges sans couches.'

He smiled a knowing smile of understanding. He'd caught the heavy-handed reference and apparently stamped me 'Approved.'

'Just ours,' he said. 'The others have them, which is why I avoid the others.'

We finished the breakfast in much the same manner. He was right: the biscuits and gravy were out of this world, the off-white gravy thick and loaded with chunks of sausage, and the biscuits the kind your mother used to make if your mother ever made biscuits. Mine did, along with sweet iced-tea and tomato sandwiches and homemade peach preserves, and sitting there eating it made me miss her some. I resolved to call her tonight, once I got back to the apartment.

Zack Capers gave me over the course of that breakfast what I suppose he saw as a crash-course in RealPolitik 101: The High School.

'Read every memo they put in your box,' he said. 'You're responsible for knowing or learning or complying with whatever is on it. The paperwork – grading – is incredible, so go ahead and set aside three hours a night, five nights a week to stay ahead of it. Most of my energy goes into grading, and believe me when I tell you it's intense. Try to stagger the writing assignments you give your kids; the first time you get back ninety 200-word essays to grade, you'll wish you'd done it differently.'

'What about Scan-Tron tests,' I asked. 'They told us at The Citadel –'

'Scan-Trons don't teach anything. They're great for you, easy to grade, but they're a cop out. You're an English teacher, and English teachers deal with words, not little black spaces neatly bubbled in.

You need to roll up your sleeves and get them accustomed to words. Reading them, writing them, spelling them, using them, defining them. This is what you do. The stories and novels and other works you'll assign are all vehicles for introducing them to words. They'll remember very little of what you teach them – particularly at the eleventh grade level – but if you instruct them on how to handle words, you will have done them a service from which they'll benefit until they're dead.'

I was still stuck on the three-hours-per-night thing. My stomach, filled with biscuits and gravy and bacon and free coffee, began to flutter. But Capers was on a roll at this point.

'Don't miss faculty meetings. The door prizes they give away aren't just gifts because they like you. They're a de facto form of roll-call. Definitely don't miss department meetings. You haven't met our chair yet, but when you do you'll understand.'

'Bad?' I asked.

'They call her the Ice Queen,' he said. 'And it's a generous title. Just don't cross her and you'll be fine.'

'I'll make a note of it.'

He laughed, stabbed the last triangle of biscuit onto the tip of his fork, smeared it around in the gravy in a repeated figure-eight, and tucked it into the corner of his mouth.

He didn't chew it right away, preferring apparently to suck the flavor from it. Savor it as long as possible.

'Be particularly nice to the secretaries. They run this place. Mr. Parker, Madeleine in Guidance, Glenda in Attendance, and Susan in Finance. When you want something done, they're the ones that actually live and work where the rubber hits the road.

'And Virginia, here in the cafeteria. She's a sharp one. I don't know if you caught the Shakespeare thing...' his voice trailed off to let me fill in the blank, provided I could.

'As You Like It,' I said. 'The comedy. She did that on purpose?'

He nodded. 'She's worked in the district for forty-four years, longer than anyone else alive. Her husband's retired from the railroad, and she swears she'll retire the day after she dies. Day after the Good Lawd takes me, she says.' He smiled at that, shook his head. 'Lots of knowledge and secrets stored up in that old head of hers. Her eyes have seen a lot.'

We ate on in silence then, and I caught myself, only for a moment, thinking of Grey, wondering whether or not she'd actually call, and if I even wanted her to. Looking back, our meeting and conversation seemed oddly surreal, as if I'd watched it all from some objective, detached point of view, like a story in a book.

I tried to picture her, but couldn't. All I could remember was the big hat and the leathery skin. And that her store-bought tits looked thirty years younger.

'Oh, yeah,' Capers piped up, pulling me back, 'probably you would have caught on to this one too, but I'm only telling you this next thing because I doubt any of the others will. You're teaching sixteen- and seventeen-year-olds, and you're young and attractive, and it's going to be interesting to see how they react to you, particularly the girls. My first group was tenth-graders, and there isn't much different between them. They're liable to touch you quite a bit. A hand on your forearm when they come to your desk to ask you a question, a brushing of your lower back as they pass you in the crowded hallway, a closer-than-comfortable lean into your frame when they're talking to you one-on-one. Don't take any of it the wrong way, and don't make too much of it. It's what I call safe-sex. They have all these swirling feelings and stirrings inside, and are unconsciously looking for a way to act upon them. So they touch you, flirt with you, whatever. They know you're safe, unlike the boys they migrate the halls with all day. Problem comes in when you're no longer safe.'

I knew what he was talking about, and I had no desire even to begin discussing it.

'Hey,' I said, a little irritated, only halfway trying to hide it. 'Listen, if I had a thing for little girls I wouldn't be in this business. I'm –'

He held up a callused hand, which irritated me even more. I was learning rather rapidly that Zack Capers didn't mind driving his words right over yours if he felt his were more important.

'Of course you would never think of such a thing,' he said, sensing, I think, my chagrin. 'But I just wanted to let you know that that is the Big No. It'll kill your career quicker than anything else. Happened a couple years back. Young, good-looking, single Social Studies teacher, coached girls' track, had an apartment a couple neighborhoods over. Back over there behind the McDonald's? No? Well anyway, he started having a few of them over after practice, just to watch videotapes of their meets at first, then for other reasons. Rumors swirled for two years, but the man's uncle was on The Board, and The Board in this town wields a lot of power. But one of the girl's boyfriends found out about it, told his parents, they told her parents. The girl denied it at first, but they pushed until she broke down, told them she was pregnant. Tests proved it was his, and Mr. Slaughter, who was Assistant Principal at the time, walked into the man's classroom in the middle of class and escorted him off campus.'

'The girl a minor?'

Capers shook his head. 'Eighteen by a month. When they found out. But she'd been a minor when she got pregnant. Had he gone quietly all he would have had to do was leave the district. They probably would have even recommended him to Berkfield or Charleston. But he fought it, and his uncle fought it, and the papers had their way with it, and before the year was over he was being charged with statutory rape by the state, sued by the girl's parents for a bevy of things, and once Columbia got wind of it his certificate was revoked. His uncle lost his seat the next election cycle, too.'

'So it does happen, then? Teachers and students. You hear things, but never much official. Except for that lady out in Washington that had the thing with the eighth-grader, there isn't much made of it.'

'It doesn't happen often, and when it does the school tries to keep it under wraps as best it can. But kids talk, and nothing stays secret in these halls for long.'

And with that we rose from the table and walked into the mailroom, where we gathered our day's mail and headed back down the hall towards our classrooms. I thanked him for breakfast, for the tips, shook his hand as he wished me luck, and went inside my room to wait for The Kids.

Looking back on things, it's ironic how that last statement of his pretty well sums up the lot of what happened to and around and with me that first year.

Nothing stays secret in these halls for long.

I started class that morning the same way I had the first day of school, the same way I would every morning thereafter. I sat at my desk and flipped through the myriad memos – Annual Blood Drive, faculty and staff encouraged to participate; Reminder from the Principal: District Policy states that males will wear ties Monday through Thursday, ladies slacks or dresses, Fridays are Spirit Days;

faculty meeting Friday, at 3:30; Departmental meeting Thursday, at 3:30; All Teachers must pick up their parking passes before the end of the week or risk having their vehicles towed, and so forth – as the students filed in. They came and took their seats and drummed their pencils on their desks and tapped their toes to an unheard rhythm, waiting for the bell to begin class, waiting for the bell to end class, waiting for Friday, waiting for Christmas vacation.

It was day three for the Coosaw Creek High Penguins, and they'd apparently not overcome the shock of summer's end enough to begin chattering with one another yet. This suited me fine.

Roy came in just before the late-bell, ignoring me as he took his seat. I felt my heartbeat kick it up a notch, felt my face grow warm, its standard reaction to anger or nervousness, both of which Roy elicited from me without really trying. I was fairly confident he'd have an attitude with me this morning, this being my first time back after the unfortunate Jew comment. I assumed that Mr. Collins no doubt kowtowed to his father on my behalf, all of this, of course, shared with great enthusiasm with his classmates while the sub looked guilelessly on. Everyone remembers how it was. Subs don't give a shit about anything. In Winter's Cove they make sixty bucks a day, whether the kids learn, behave, whatever. They could break off into pairs and rim each other and the majority of subs wouldn't care enough to take names.

As it was, however, Roy didn't appear any different. He just slumped in his chair and tapped his fingers on his desk, staring out into the space before him as if the wonders of the world were being played out there. Maybe Mr. Collins didn't give in too much to the father. They say he'd killed people in Vietnam. Maybe he got on the phone with Mr. Watherstein and stood his ground on behalf of his teacher, saying something like, 'Look, Mr. Watherstein, if one of my teachers offended your son, I'm sure if was for a good reason. My teachers are the best in the district; hell, they're the best in the business. I'm sure your boy misinterpreted whatever was said in there. Have a nice day.' Maybe Roy's a royal pain in the ass for everyone, and Watherstein senior knows it. Maybe I've got a bonus check in my teacher's box in the mailroom, and Natalie Portman is waiting at the apartment with Brasco, naked and missing me. Just maybe.

I managed to get through the roll this time without any career-ending blunders – one for two on that front, and not even MacGwire hits .500 – and went into the lesson.

'All right class, I'm sorry I had to be absent yesterday. I had that flu that's going around.'

A pudgy hand from the back went up. I acknowledged it with a nod.

'I didn't know there was a flu going around.'

Jonah something was the kid's name. Jonah the lawyer. Jonah-I'll-analyze-every-word-teacher-says, because I'm fat and have no friends other than the cupcakes hidden beneath my bed at home.

'Sure is, Jonah. So be careful. That goes for all of you. Get your vitamin C.'

This seemed to satisfy Jonah.

'So,' I continued, 'let's get out our DOL notebooks, and copy down today's sentences.'

DOL stands for Daily Oral Language. You flash a badly constructed sentence on the overhead, give the kids a couple of minutes to copy it down in its wrong form, then another couple to correct all the grammatical errors in it.

I killed the lights and turned on the overhead. Today's sentence read:

After the pep rally begins marlene take these here banners to the booster club at the school located West of hear.

A couple minutes later a girl in the back – Melody, last name still a blank at this point – raised her hand.

'Yes, Melody.'

'Marlene needs to be capitalized. Proper noun.'

I corrected it on the overhead. 'Very good, Melody.'

Another hand went up, Melody having broken the ice.

'Yes…uh, Johnny.'

'Jimmy,' he corrected.

'Sorry. Jimmy.'

'Yeah, it's the wrong "here".'

'This second one here?' I asked, placing my pen next to it on the overhead.

'Yeah.'

'That's right. What's wrong with this "hear"?'

'It's like when you hear something. With your ears. It needs to be h-e-r-e.'

55

'Very good, Jimmy. Anybody see anything else?'

No one raised their hand.

'What about that first little bit there, in the first line,' I said. 'Anything missing there?'

Still no takers.

'I'll give you a hint. We're missing a comma somewhere in the first line. Does that help some of you?'

'After Marlene?' a voice, male, said from the back.

'No,' I said. 'Not quite. Close, though.'

'After take,' Tyson – excuse me, Flash – said.

'No, that's too far to the right. Come back a bit, Flash.'

'Back where?'

To wherever it is that you started getting so dumb. The womb, maybe.

'Back a few words closer to the beginning,' I said.

Melody raised her hand again. 'After begins?'

'Very good. That's exactly right, Melody. Why do we put a comma there, right after begins?'

She shrugged.

'Okay,' I said. 'That's okay. We haven't covered this yet. This is what you call an introductory phrase. You see how you can take it out of the sentence,' – covering the 'After the pep rally' with my pen – 'and you haven't really changed the meaning? Whenever you can do that to a group of words, and the group of words comes at the beginning of the sentence, that's an introductory phrase. And we put a comma after introductory phrases.'

Another boy, this one named Greg and sporting a Coosaw Creek football jersey, with the bright purple-and-gold colors, said, 'Why don't we just take out that part of the sentence then, and not worry about where the comma goes?'

A perfectly good question, for which I hadn't a perfectly good answer, or any other for that matter.

'Well, one of the reasons we do this DOL is to learn exactly how to write – how to integrate our words together to form tight, concise, compelling narratives. That's one of the reasons we're going to be doing so much writing in this class.' As I spoke, I turned the overhead off – there were several more errors in it, but I'd lost most of the class at this point; pushing on would have been an act of futility – and flipped the lights back on.

'In fact, we're going to write a bit today. But first, if you'll take out your literature books and turn to page 165, to the section entitled 'A Growing Nation'. We'll be beginning the year with some of our earliest American writers – men like William Cullen Bryant, Washington Irving, and James Fenimore Cooper. You may not know it just yet, but many of the movies you've seen are either directly from or based upon works by these writers and others like them. Now, what we're getting ready to read together was written by a man named Alexis de Tocqueville, who we'll be studying a good deal in the coming weeks. So let's all follow along as I read the first paragraph. I'll call on you randomly to read aloud as well, so pay attention and follow along.'

I surveyed their faces; I'd just given them the preliminary bit to the beginning of what I truly consider to be the greatest period in American literature, hands down. As far as their expressions – and lack thereof – suggested, I might have just recited the first page of a vacuum-cleaner manual.

I sighed, and began reading de Tocqueville: 'America is a land of wonders, in which everything is in constant motion and every change seems an improvement …No natural boundary seems to be set to the efforts of man; and in his eyes what is not yet done is only what he has not yet attempted to do…'

SIX

Fortuitous phone call; Jules growing horns; beer at George's; intermezzo

I was on my back on my couch in my miserable little apartment – Brasco on my chest, purring and drooling – when the
telephone's shrill ringing pulled me out of a shallow sleep.

I opened my eyes slowly. It had turned dark while I slept; the
only light on was the television, and it caused the room to glow
blue, sending wavy blue shadows across the wall and ceiling as if
the entire room were underwater.

I lay there for a few seconds, listening to it ring. I watched
Brasco's eyes slowly open, his tiny pupils dilating as they focused
on my face. His face always has the same expression upon first
waking; it's a combined look of recognition and approbation that
says, 'You may be a total fuck-up, Cole, but we're still pals. I love
you, man.'

I wasn't in any hurry to answer it. I paid four bucks a month
for voice-mail specifically so I wouldn't have to rush to the phone
when I was home. I ran a hand over Brasco's head, remembering
how I'd read somewhere that rabbits that were stroked regularly
had fewer plaque deposits in their arteries.

'There you go, little buddy,' I said, scratching his ears, under his
chin, the back of his neck. 'Didn't know this was good for you, did
you?' He purred loud as an engine.

Finally the phone stopped, and I reached over to the wicker
coffee table and killed the television with the remote. The room
went black, which I didn't like, so I turned the TV back on.

'Well boy, what are we going to do about dinner?'

Well, I'll probably eat the same shit I always eat, that greyish-
brown stuff you throw in my bowl over there, and you'll either boil
noodles, go get Arby's, or do without.

I was looking at him, pulling at his whiskers and tickling the little hairs inside his ears, when the phone started ringing again.

'Dammit,' I said, rising, Brasco jumping down and following me into the kitchenette, sitting at my feet as I answered the phone.

'Hello,' I said.

'There's the bitch,' the voice on the other end said. 'Mr. Don't-Stand-So-Close-To-Me-himself. The teacher-man.'

'Well look at this. My favorite Spick. What's up, bro?'

'The price of pussy, son. How's life in ye old halls of learning? You giving those little peckerheads the what's what?'

'Hey, you know how it is. I'm just trying to make it to the weekend.'

'You didn't know I knew that, did you? That Sting was a teacher before The Police?'

'Anyone with MTV knows that. Just because you're a Mexican doesn't make you completely stupid.'

'Some days I wonder,' he said. 'It's getting crazier and crazier on this end. You heard about Jani?'

Jani was Jules' girlfriend of the last seven years. She was a lithe little brunette who'd graduated from Clemson with a 4.0 in Accounting, had been heavily recruited by all the Big Six firms, and had chosen Price Waterhouse because, in addition to the $50,000 salary and company-leased car, it required approximately a hundred days of travel each year. The travel would afford Jani, who'd grown up in a tiny little Pee Dee town called Aynor, the chance to see places beyond the borders of South Carolina, something she'd never been able to do and had always felt lesser for. As far as Jules – a third-generation American, but a first-generation South Carolinian, and a fervent one at that – was concerned, the sun rose in Charleston and set in Spartanburg, and everything in between was God's Own Garden. Most everything beyond that, and certainly every inch of earth north or west of the Mason-Dixon line, could be consumed in fire and he wouldn't be interested enough to read it in the paper.

Some believe that men cheat more than women, or that it is in a woman's nature to be true and loyal, and inherently part of a man to wonder and wander. Certainly Jules had had a peccadillo or two, and more than likely he found some form of morning-after solace in this notion of duplicity belonging solely to men. And perhaps Jani relied upon her boyfriend's steadfast subscription to the Infallible Woman in Love Doctrine to sweeten her trips out of God's Garden. Probably we'll never know, though Jules had begun to wonder.

'I hadn't heard anything definite,' I said. 'I talked to Max a couple days ago – Sunday night, I think – but he wasn't positive about anything.'

I tried to tread carefully. Jules was tougher than leather to his very core, but growing horns is a painful process. Becoming a cuckold can wound even the strongest man for some time. Based on what he'd been telling me for the past few months, I'd pretty much decided that yes, Jani probably was seeing someone else, and yes, it was probably the same guy. So perhaps they're right, those who believe it's in a woman's nature to be true and loyal. Perhaps it's just that they can switch loyalties as easily as men might switch socks.

'I'm pretty sure it's true, Cole,' he said. 'I finally swallowed my pride last night, confronted her with it … my suspicions, all of it. The way she's been acting lately, like I can't do anything right, all of a sudden I'm this south-of-the-Rio migrant worker without a stitch of education because I drink beer and chew tobacco and watch football all weekend. You know, it's like there's this other standard she's been exposed to now, and it's all out there somewhere, these fucking business trips she's always taking, and she comes back home to everything she grew up around and all she sees is my flaws.' He paused.

'She even called me a redneck a couple days ago. Said I was the tannest redneck ever to walk a step, but a redneck just the same. Said it disgusted her when I dipped. Now Cole, tell me something, how in the hell is this just coming to the surface seven years into something. I've been dipping since … hell, since middle school.'

'I remember.'

'I dipped on our first date. I dip in bed with her. I dip on air. I'm dipping now. I always dip.'

'You're right, dude. You're right. You're always dipping. I don't think I've ever seen you not dipping. Come to think of it, I don't know if I've ever seen you pack a dip. You just always seem to have one in there. It's like chipmunks drinking.'

This caused him pause. 'What's like chipmunks drinking?'

'I saw a show once, nature guy said in all his years doing that sort of thing, tracking animals and all, he'd never seen a chipmunk drink.'

'What, alcohol? How the hell's a chipmunk going to get alcohol?'

'Not, not just alcohol. Anything. Water, whatever.'

'They have to drink, Cole.'

'It's what I heard on the show.'

'Everything drinks. Chipmunk's a fucking mammal, for God's sakes. Mammals drink. It's part of what makes them mammals. If it were a Volvox or something, maybe that I'd understand. But a chipmunk's like a fucking hamster or something. He's a forest hamster. They have to drink.'

'Well, I'm sure you have to not dip sometime, but damned if I remember seeing it.'

'That's my point. Neither does Jani, but she comes back from one of her trips and all of a sudden I'm Juan fucking Valdez.'

'I don't know what to say, man,' I said, and it was true. He hadn't asked my opinion, probably because he knew what it was. And I could tell him all I wanted to and it wouldn't do any good anyway. It's not always enough to watch someone else get hurt; for many of us, it takes the sight of our own blood before we realize what's going on.

'I wish there was something I could do ...' realizing how hollow that sounded, wanting badly to say something meaningful, something with weight, 'but if you're not happy...even if she isn't, you know, seeing someone else...if you're not happy, maybe you should just end it. I know seven years is a long time, but if you don't trust her, if you can't trust her, then you sure as hell don't need to end up marrying her. And those are your only options, pretty much. Break up or get married.'

'Or keep this purgatory shit up.'

'Pretty much,' I said.

'Yeah,' he said. There was an extended pause, during which Brasco, having never understood the concept of the phone, decided I was talking to him and began rolling over on my feet to show his approval.

'You know,' Jules said, 'I found a bruise on her ankle the other day ... about the size of a thumb. I know it's the ankle and all, but ... shit Cole, she bought lingerie in Chicago a few weeks back. I found the receipt when I rifled through her purse. I didn't say anything, and she's never worn the lingerie around me.'

'Maybe it was a gift,' I offered. 'Maybe she bought it for a cousin or friend or something and it was a gift.'

'Maybe it was,' he said. 'But I shouldn't be wondering, should I?'

'No. It's a bad sign.'

'Well,' he said, his tone changed, 'you know she's in town tonight.'

'What – here in Charleston?'

'Yeah. They've got a big conference down here, through Friday. The Marriot.'

I knew where he was going with this. I would've loved to say no, but he'd do it for me, no questions asked.

'You want me to keep an eye on her?'

'I can't ask you to do that, man.'

'I offered, Jules.'

'I was thinking we'd get together, drink a few beers.'

'Tonight?'

'Yeah, tonight. I'll get a case of something imported, we'll drink, maybe find ten miles of dirt road to ride down. Smoke a little lettuce.'

'Maybe end up at the Marriot, see what the out-of-town account-ants are up to tonight?'

'Hey, who knows,' he said. 'Couple of old pals like you and me get together, fucking world's our oyster, right?'

After hanging up with Jules ('I'm walking out the door now, bitch. Be there in ten, so don't leave me hanging') I called Winter's Cove's automated sub-caller for the second time in four days, the second time in the first four days of the school year. Still batting .500, I told myself, and punched in the requisite codes. Cole Archer, induction teacher, and chronic absentee.

It's a fifteen-minute drive from my place to George's, over on the Savannah Highway, most of it down 61. Sixty-one is some of the prettiest backcountry the Lowcountry has to offer, winding its way through marshlands and cypress swamps, twisting and turning along like an artery through muscle. The air is pregnant with the moisture and the smells of the Atlantic, captured and fermented in the heat of the forests, smelling vaguely of spoiled milk and semen. On either side stand massive, crooked, sweeping oaks hanging low with Spanish moss, their limbs stretching over the road into a canopy through which the moon slips in thin, silky sheets, pooling a milky gold on the asphalt before you.

It was a harvest moon that night; it was a harvest moon the

morning I left for good, too. I'll always remember that, because I thought it was so apropos.

I checked my watch. It was a little before nine. We'd be drinking within half an hour, drunk in another two, and probably trying to find Jani sometime shortly thereafter. We'd skulk around town like high-schoolers – like those little lollipops I teach when I bother to go. Try to spot Jani. Hope she was without the wrong kind of company. Maybe end up downtown, if the night was right. See what there was to see. Do whatever it took.

I slept without dreaming for nearly sixteen hours; the bright red numerals on the bolted-down alarm clock read a quarter after eight in the A.M. when I my eyes clicked open. The Day After, I thought, sitting up, rubbing at them, glancing around the room in search of Brasco. Everything I'd ever done had been yesterday and before; everything I'd ever do for the rest of my life would be a direct result of what I did today.

Today was the first full day of my life on the lam, that tiny sliver of malleable time wedged in between two wholly and entirely different lives. This was the day I had told myself was coming, had prepared for mentally, physically, and logistically for the past month. I'd set it aside like some sort of temporal savings account, just waiting for me safely should I ever need it, should shit start to crumble, should I feel myself beginning to lose control.

But I had made it this far, so now I was here, in this room, in the middle of that little sliver of time that belonged to me and me alone, before the people behind me knew where I was and the people ahead of me knew I was there. Today was the first day in a long line of days, all of which would begin and end after Charleston.

I took a moment to collect myself, let that last thought settle in. I'd burned a scorched-earth trail from Charleston, South Carolina, to Brownsville, Texas, and soon they'd be after me. By now my apartment and everything I'd left in it would belong to them. The computer in my classroom would be on its way to a lab somewhere. They'd be compiling a list of my colleagues they'd be interrogating. They'd call it a debriefing, or maybe even an interview, but it'd be an interrogation nonetheless. It was a quarter after seven back in Charleston; the entire community was gathering together for graduation today at the Charleston Coliseum.

Inside of a few hours someone would tell someone else that Mr. Archer was wanted by the police, that it had something to do with that Savannah Bellington girl, you know, the real quiet one in Trig with the long, curly hair. Someone else might mention the murder downtown two nights ago, or maybe something about the money, and that that's why Mr. Archer's not here for commencement. The news would spread like mono through the halls and cafeteria, going from mouth to mouth like spit at the after-prom party. By dinnertime tonight, parents throughout Winter's Cove would be hearing various versions of the story, and calls to the Board would begin in earnest about this time tomorrow.

Yeah, that's the way it's likely to fall, which is why I'm here now, in this motel room, halfway between this world and the next. My running hasn't caused any of this. My running is the reaction to the chain of events that began with Savannah. She's the first domino.

Brasco meowed to me then, from the foot of the bed. I smiled, tapped my hand on the bedspread next to me. He was there in two leaps, stroking his face against my elbow, purring loud enough to wake the people in the next room.

'Hungry, buddy?' Scratching his ears, his cheeks, under his chin.

I'd picked up a couple packs of semi-moist cat food at the last 24-7 Mart I'd stopped at for gas and oil. They hadn't had any Mousers. They didn't carry Chesterfields, either, so I had to go with the Winstons. We were both sacrificing a bit.

I rose from bed, fed him on the floor, and retrieved from my duffel bag an old, worn shoebox. I set the shoebox on the counter next to the sink and climbed into the shower.

Ten minutes later I was out of the shower, and I spent the next four hours in front of the mirror, getting ready for the world that was waiting beyond my motel room door.

SEVEN

Batman returns; Jani's ring shines too bright; bad night for a number-cruncher

There's an emotion in life we've all had but haven't put a name to yet. It's that moment prior to the onset of a familiar déjà vu, such as when you slide into a winter's coat you haven't worn for three years, the smell of chopped firewood or burning leaves still lingering in the material, just beginning to remind you of the comfort of home. Or when you come across someone you haven't seen in a while, and their smile or smell pulls from you that feeling you hadn't had since the last time you saw them. I was feeling that – this sense of an impending *déjà vu* – now with Jules.

We were at a sports bar in West Ashley called George's, which for my money had the best wings in all the Charleston area, regardless of what the good folks at Wild Wing downtown try to tell you. We'd been there for a couple hours; it was approaching midnight. He'd guzzled Bud Lights from the can on his way there, and we'd each had another two out in the parking lot before coming in. We were working our way through a plate of fifty hot wings, sitting across from one another, when it struck me.

I'd tilted my mug of beer back and saw him through the bottom of it, the taste of Tabasco and chicken in my throat, my nose running, my head fuzzy. His image across the table from me: thick dark hair, the hard, solid lines of his face and jaw, the imposing, angular squareness of his shoulders, a beer in one hand, mouth moving around words I couldn't quite make out over the cacophony of televisions and drunken laughter, the entire scene distorted by the bottom of the foamy beer glass. It was a scene made familiar to me through four years of college and a semester of law school, one which I discovered that evening was as integral a part of my unconscious well-being as nicotine or chocolate might be for you.

It had become so routine and commonplace that I hadn't noticed its importance until, inured to its absence, I again felt its presence. But this – this sitting and drinking and disclosing and confiding – this subtle but definite descent into intoxication together was where most of my adult memories that mattered had been made. It was where virtually all of the healing I'd done since Autumn had occurred. Somewhere along the way you learn to leave little pieces of the pain behind, perhaps in each glass that's emptied and taken away before being replaced by another. And as you slide down the hill together you begin to forget most of what it was that drove you to the top of it, that made you want to take the ride down at all, and through the haze and the dizziness you look across that table and see the one going there with you, your wingman riding shotgun, just going there because it's where you're going and you don't want to go there alone, and this profound and ultimately unspeakable rush of gratitude overwhelms you and you know in that single, crystalline moment that there isn't much beneath the stars you wouldn't do for him. If he needed blood, you'd bleed.

'You remember Batgirl?' he asked around a wing. His lips, like mine, were raw and inflamed from the hot sauce. 'The times we had with that one?'

It's a truism that when men are wounded by the fairer sex they often treat the wound with memories of previous conquests, the rehashed stories a soothing balm that, while unable to heal, can temporarily ease the sting.

I rolled my eyes and tried not to remember, knowing the memory would come unbridled, knowing I had no say in it now; it'd been summoned much the way it'd been born – in a smoky haze made fuzzy with alcohol.

'Yeah,' I said. 'I'm gonna forget?' I half-sighed, half-laughed. 'We walked the edge with that one.'

Jules finished off his beer, motioned the waitress with a nod of his head, and ordered us another bucket of Beck's.

'Never see anything like that again,' he said, shaking his head, his eyes glassy from the memory and the beer.

'For some things once is enough,' I said. 'For a lot of things, actually. For Batgirl, definitely.'

'What do you think she's doing now,' he asked. 'You ever run into her?'

I shook my head. 'No. Imagine she's still working on her doctorate.

What'd she say it was … conceptual physics, or some such? Last time I saw her was with you, right before we went to the emergency room. I'll have that scar the rest of my life, you know.'

'You? Bitch, I almost died that night. That goddam crown of hers nearly impaled me. And when I fell off the bed' – shaking his head, remembering, looking as though he might be holding back a shudder – 'she didn't stop, either. Just kept going, like she was being graded on it. Like me tied up naked on the cheap carpet, gagged and damned near gorged on her fucking crown, was her number one fantasy.'

'It was,' I said. 'She told me on the way home that night.' I took another long swallow of the Beck's, felt it fill my throat and expand on the way down. 'I thought she was exaggerating.'

'That's because you're stupid,' he said. 'Any girl says she wants to come home with you to party a little, says she wants to play with you and the roomie, that's just jim-dandy, but she brings her own tarp, for the love of God…and you in your cape! Your dad should have raised you better.'

I'm a visual man, and it's both a blessing and a burden. If I see something, actually see it and tag it and catalogue it in my mind, it's there forever. It's a skill that's served me well my entire life, something I have no memory of cultivating or sharpening, something that has simply always been there, like the ability to exhale. I got through college and part of a master's degree that way. I also nearly killed myself drinking in an attempt to scrape Autumn's image from my memory, which I've never fully done. (It's why I had to leave Columbia once we broke up: when you spend nearly every day with someone for four years you create an enormous amount of history. You leave your litter all across the landscape. Every restaurant houses a special moment you shared, every inter-section a conversation. For the man who remembers in pictures, each street, road, and avenue previously traveled becomes a series of painful visual cues.)

Sitting here in this motel room off the beautiful Mexican coast, the sun beginning its slow westward arc, tinting the endless sky a glowing pink and blue, I can still bring back every detail associated with that night. It isn't something I generally care to do, the details of some memories better off left alone to decompose and, one hopes, disappear altogether.

But I can still recall all of it. The silvery glimmer of the tiara she wore as the light from my little closet reflected off it. The feel of the hard box springs – and then the shag carpet – beneath my knees, the friction rubbing the epidermis away. The noises in the room, akin to what I imagined injured animals moving en masse might sound like. The smells hanging in the air, heavy smells of perfumes and lotions and alcohol; heavier ones of effort and want and excitement beneath that. And the specifics – the slight pinkish scar above her clavicle that darkened with arousal; the syncopated noise of hips meeting; the bone-white impression of Jules' college ring in the ivory white of her right ass-cheek, the way it rushed to rosy and whelped in a matter of seconds; the kink of dark hair that hung down over her forehead absurdly like a comma; the darkness of the blood that dripped from Jules' nose from her punch; the salty-sweet taste of her sweat mingled with Hershey's syrup; the burn of it in my eyes. If I close my eyes right now, I can be there again, see it all, do it all, again.

Sometimes – when the memories of my more tender moments with Autumn would come rushing over me like a tsunami – I would pull the night with Batgirl out from the shadows of my mind, and live them over and over again in an effort to drown the image of Autumn. Occasionally it would work, but it had its price. Like using uppers to counter downers, there was freight to be paid.

Batgirl was what we called her, and the reason is singular in its simplicity: She wanted to be fucked by Batman. Yes, Batman. The guy with the mask and the nifty gadgets and the cave outside Gotham City. I learned this sitting at a bar with her in Five Points, downtown Columbia, one Thursday night. I'd gone there with Jules and, upon arriving, had made my way to the bar to start drinking while he busied himself with a few games of pool. I don't remember her approaching. One moment I was drinking my beer, aware of the general mass of milling people behind and around me, and the next she was just there beside me at the bar, ordering five shots of Tequila.

'Now there's a round,' I said, taking her in, not overly impressed with anything I was seeing, but not overly picky that night, either. Tall, thin, plain around the mouth and eyes. Glasses too big for her face. Lots of kinky brown hair. She had the bohemian look of a self-absorbed intellectual.

She smiled at me pleasantly enough, then shot three of the five in as many seconds.

'Bad day?' I said, but my words were lost in the music.

She leaned over and yelled something into my ear that I pretended to understand. I nodded, smiled again, signaled the bartender. Time to play ball.

I ordered four shots of tequila, and two more beers. She ordered a strawberry wine cooler, which I took to mean she didn't drink beer.

We had six shots in front of us, my four and her two, and we each did three. Somewhere in there she mentioned her name was Chris, but later that evening she changed it to Paula. It doesn't matter, though. She'll forever be Batgirl in the annals of my memory.

'You a student here?' I managed to get out during one of the brief gaps in the music.

She nodded. 'Conceptual and Theoretical Physics. Ph.D. I'm defending my dissertation next month.'

I nodded. Impressed, but not overly so. I'd figured she was an intellectual.

I'll spare the barroom banter, and most of the bedroom stuff as well. Suffice it to say that we did in fact end up at my apartment, in bed, Brasco watching disinterestedly from atop my ink-jet printer which rested on a card table in the corner. We were almost naked when she dropped the bomb.

'At the Wal-Mart up the road their Halloween stuff is out. Go up there and buy a Batman costume and put it on, then come back here and rape me.'

I said I'd spare most of the bedroom stuff but a few crumbs are needed to appreciate the unique contours of the night.

'I'm sorry?' I said, absolutely positive I hadn't heard her correctly. 'Come again?'

'Buy Batman, then come back and rape me.' She bit my lower lip, whether to inflict pain or pleasure, I couldn't tell. The result was a bit of both, as many things are.

'And rape me right,' she said.

I looked at her. 'You're kidding, right?'

She shook her head, stood, finished undressing, and found my closet. I had four ties in there, hanging over nails hammered into the plaster wall with the heel of a shoe. I bought them for important occasions, of which I'd had none thus far. Batgirl had just found one.

Fully naked, she took all four ties and returned to the bed. She began working them into slip knots.

'When you get back,' she said, not looking at me, concentrating on her work, seemingly speaking to the ties, 'I'll be tied up to the headboard, splayed open like a crippled bird. Have the Batman suit on. You're not trying to rescue me, remember. You're trying to rape me, hurt me with your cock. You're Batman gone bad. My keys are on the floor there. You can take my car. In the glove box there's a crown from a watermelon pageant I once won, and on the floor of the back seat there's a big blue tarp. Bring both of these in. Make me wear the crown before you fuck me. The tarp we'll use later. When I resist, slap my face. Hard, if you have to. Be careful; I'll bite at you. Claw you if I can, and I'll do it without empathy or remorse. But you'll be Batman, and Batman isn't easily deterred.'

She lay back on the bed, naked as a newborn, the diminished light from my closet illuminating patches of her legs, waist, and face. The light looked almost blue against her skin, creating a surreal, almost underwater scene as she worked the first tie around her left wrist and a peg of the old thrift-store headboard. She pulled it tight with her other hand.

The scene bothered me inexplicably, so I nudged the closet door open and allowed more light to flood the room. If she noticed, she gave no sign. She was busy with the ties. I stood there watching her, barely cognizant of the fact that she was nude, her tuft of brown pubic hair less the draw than the mysteries she wove with her hands. I was entirely transfixed by what she was doing, by what she was proposing.

'Like any victim of rape,' she said, working the second tie around her other wrist with her teeth, deftly maneuvering her hand through the hole, pulling it again with her mouth until the blue-green veins in her wrist bulged like little worms swallowing, 'I'll be hysterical. I'll be singularly determined to prevent you from penetrating. I'll do all I can to land a heel in your groin. Anything you put in my mouth I'm liable to bite off, unless I'm properly subdued.' She smiled at this, not to me, but to herself.

'You'll have to be convincing,' she said.

She was fastened to my headboard now, a stripe of white skin punctuated with brown hair on either end. Her breasts, small to medium, lolled over towards her sides. She struggled against the ties; the ties held.

I had no clue as to what had just occurred before me; this ghastly scene had evolved of its own accord. I'd merely watched.

'You've done this sort of thing before,' I said. 'The tie-knots and all.' I sat on the edge of the bed, my bed, feeling in control because it was my room and I was not entirely naked and I was not tied down. That's a note of humorous irony to me now, the notion of my being in control that night.

'Tell me something,' I said, reaching out, touching her leg above the knee. 'What the hell do you want a crown and tarp for?'

She pulled her knee forward – I caught the fleeting glimpse of her vagina slit opening, meaty brown yielding to pink, an eye in a reverse wink – then kicked my hand away. Her countenance was that of determined defiance.

'Get the suit,' she said. 'And then get in here and act like something other than a pathetic little priss.'

I looked at her a moment, briefly and only briefly wanting to climb atop and grudge-fuck her until it hurt, but of course that's what she wanted. Her game was clear; she was merely suiting up now, getting ready for the main event.

I glanced at her breasts, then down to her thatch of pubic hair, her legs together now, the little pink triangle waiting benignly. I considered everything I could think of, but as I sat there and took her bound and naked figure in I began to respond physically, and there seemed to be less and less to consider.

'Be back in a sec,' I said, gathering my wallet and her keys off the floor where they'd landed. She wanted to be fucked by Batman, fine. I'd put on a Batman suit, fuck her till I came cartilage. What the hell did I care about the fantasy? They were all Ashley Judd when the lights were off, anyway.

I was almost out the door when she called out to me.

'Oh – and Cole,' she said. 'You're right. I have been here before. More than once.' She let her legs slide open then, brought her knees partly to her chest, her ass cheeks rounding and tightening with the stretch. When she spoke, her voice was long and smooth, like a bolt of satin. 'There's a Batman down in Panama City whose cock has a permanent rightward bend because he took me lightly. Another needs medicine to function properly now. These days he's Batboy, at best.' She smiled a pleasant, comfortable, perfectly content smile. I gathered the memory of Batboy pleased her.

'I can be quite emphatic in my protestations. You may find you have to turn me over, use alternate routes. Don't be shy about it.'

As I drove the short distance to Wal-Mart, I decided two things simultaneously. One, I would not at all be shy about it. She was going to know Cole Archer the fucking Dark Knight of Gotham City had been there. And two, I wasn't going in there alone. If the plight of Panama City's Batboy told me anything, it told me that this woman was not your garden-variety one-night thrill-fuck.

I gathered my purchases inside and took them to the counter, watched the check-out girl tally them up. One Batman costume, complete with mask, cape, bat-belt and bat-buckle, and two bat-boots. One bottle of aspirin, a pack of Chesterfields, and a ten-pack of Nonoxynol-9 condoms.

I also picked up the Robin costume, to complement the Batman. Because as I said, I was not going in there alone.

I'd like to be able to say we sat there for another four or five hours, eating wings and drinking ourselves sober enough so we could actually see the cab Sera – our waitress – had to call for us at three that morning. I'd like to say that we went from George's back to my place, where Jules passed out on the couch and I made it almost entirely to Brasco and my spinning bed before falling. I'd like to say that the worst thing that happened that evening was my vomiting on the off-white bathroom tiles and Jules pissing his pants on my flea-market couch.

I suppose it doesn't matter tremendously now – amazing what sudden wealth and relocation can do for one's perspective – but it wouldn't bring me any pleasure whatsoever to have to say that Jules and I left George's after finishing that last bucket of Beck's, and that I – being the less intoxicated of the two – drove us across town to North Charleston, where the Marriot and all her out-of-town accountants were located.

If I said that, I'd have to carry it a bit further, say that I sat in that parking lot praying I was wrong about Jani while Jules used his cell phone to call the front desk and have them patch him through to her room, his brown face growing red and his knuckles white as the desk clerk broke in after a thousand rings to tell him no one seemed to be answering, and he'd be happy to take a message.

Had we gone straight home from the bar Jules wouldn't have said, 'Yeah, tell her Julian called, and to call me back at my place whenever she gets in, whatever the time.'

Had we gone home, we wouldn't have been waiting in the

parking lot for the better part of an hour in pure, black silence, Jules going through all the emotions a man goes through during a time like that, and me sitting there wishing there was something I could say and, lacking that, somewhere else I could be.

Then I wouldn't have been there to see Jules see Jani drive up in front of the Marriot at a quarter after four in the humid Charleston morning, climb out of the passenger side of a pearl-black BMW IS dressed in ways accountants don't dress for business. I wouldn't have seen him see her walk around the front of the car to the man who got out – a man neither of us recognized. I wouldn't have seen her smile, or them kiss, or his hand ride down with familiar ease through her hair to the small of her back, then over her butt and to her bare leg. I wouldn't have seen his hand move up under the skirt a bit, then a bit more. I wouldn't have seen Jani pull him closer, or lift her leg up over his hip in a fluid motion that was anything but new to them.

'Oh my God,' isn't something I would have said. And I wouldn't have turned to look at Jules, and see instead a rock crumbling, see whatever parts inside him willing to doubt and deny falling away like doves killed in mid-flight.

I wouldn't have seen his single tear, burning silver on his eyelid, as if struggling not to fall, and I wouldn't have ached for him at that moment, ached more completely, more wholly, than I had ever ached for myself. My pain, at least, had been mitigated by guilt. But not Jules's. Sitting there, I struggled vainly against a single thought which assailed me like a blade: this – this moment, this pure, unadulterated pain – this is what I did to Autumn. This is the hurt I heaped upon the woman I'd asked to share forever with me.

Had I not been there I wouldn't have seen the unmistakable look of recognition turned fear in her eyes as she ignored her partner's efforts and focused instead on my car, associating the car with me, and me with Jules. When her eyes narrowed and sharpened on my friend slowly appearing from my car – moving through the space between them with the steadiness and purpose of one who has weighed his options and found himself with none – I wouldn't have seen it. When those same eyes widened as she realized with horrifying finality what she was seeing – the image of her boyfriend standing twenty yards to her left, which was, incidentally, twenty yards to the right of the man fucking her – I wouldn't have seen it.

Of course that part, and most of the parts that came next, I kind of enjoyed seeing.

I'd like to be able to say that when we left George's that night, we went directly back to my place and let the hangovers settle in; but we didn't, and there it is.

EIGHT

A succession of bells;
why we write; Savannah

There's a tenet of quantum physics that postulates that time is but another form of space, that the Western world's orderly sequencing of yesterdays leading into tomorrows is only orderly because we are limited in our view of time as linear. There's also an African people known as the Hopi who say that time's a wheel and what comes around goes around. I'm still not sure which hook I hang my hat on.

The weeks following my night out with Jules moved quickly, much quicker in retrospect than I would have ever hoped for. I became lost in a blur of short-story discussions and essay-grading, of vocabulary quizzes and grammar group-work. I had four periods a day, the first of which was planning and therefore free of students. The next three were all juniors, succeeding one another in rapid-fire succession until 3:15 when that magic bell rang and they all disappeared as quickly as they'd come.

Before I realized it Guidance was sending out notes informing us that first quarter grades were due in three days – I had to check my calendar to be sure we were really into October. The weather had turned colder and the days shorter and I'd noticed it on a daily level, but it seemed that time for me was speeding up as it progressed, the way an object rolling down a hill will do.

I'd wanted to be out of the apartment and into a condo by Christmas, but it didn't look feasible now. I was literally swamped with work. Capers, I quickly learned, had been low-balling me that morning over the biscuits and gravy. Where initially I had scoffed at the notion of taking home any work in the afternoons (three hours per night my balls, I remember thinking when Capers had suggested it: they want me to work like a six-figure executive, they can pay me the six figures. Till then, their thirty-one K buys them punctuality and a necktie).

But it doesn't work that way, and this I was learning fast. Follow me:

It's Monday morning and you've got thirty kids pouring into your room, none of them any happier about being there than you, and one or two of them exceedingly less pleased with your presence than you are with theirs. They're going to be there for ninety minutes – your kids, turning to you for instructions and directions – and you've got to find something to fill that time for them. You can't stand up and just talk to them about literature, the way your professors talked to you about literature, because these kids don't know how to listen. They hear, but they don't absorb. These kids aren't college kids, and the bulk of them never will be. They're adolescents in the point-and-click generation of the Internet and Playstation. They were raised on microwave meals and instant messaging and real-time chatrooms. They've got no attention-spans, no lasting tolerance for any sort of input that isn't digital, or done through AOL, DVDs, or MP3s.

Fortunately, you're an English teacher and you've got a secret weapon, something the teachers of Math and Science don't have. You've got The Novel, and her gorgeous cousin, Sustained Silent Reading. Together these twin swords serve as both filler and fall-back; filler when you need to chew up thirty minutes here, twenty-five minutes there, and fall-back when all that alcohol from the night before has your skull pulsating beneath your scalp so badly you can't stand the sound of your own voice, much less theirs.

But, you learn, today's high school juniors are a funny lot; you say 'silent reading time' and they hear 'naptime,' and one by one their heads drop to the desk as if the lights had gone down and they'd just had a big meal. Or, as is the case with some of the more blatantly apathetic pillars of tomorrow's society, they simply sleep with their heads upright and immobile, their necks seemingly concrete. These students you don't mind so much – what initially you view as an affront you begin to be thankful for, as you realize how much less desirable some of the alternatives are. Such as the zombie burn-out types who enter your classroom in a cloud of black clothes and gray smoke, the unmistakable jingling of myriad chains announcing their every step, their faces pierced in strange, medieval fashion. They lock their empty eyes on yours the moment they sit down, refusing to blink, their heads rotating throughout the room in unison with you as you oscillate from one side to the other. Every now and again one of their lip-rings catches a glimmer of the institutional fluorescent light from overhead and calls your attention, and you notice then that they're still staring at you, still not blinking, their stone-and-metal faces not moving, nothing to suggest they might be hearing anything you say. It occurs to you then that they're plotting your death. Yours, their classmates', possibly those of All Who Dare To Stare. Then the bell rings and their auto-pilot switches on, and they rise in synchronized motion like Druids at fucking Stonehenge to take the willies to their next teacher.

But those that are awake need to be occupied and, ideally, taught something, so you run through the streams they gave you in your education courses. For the English teachers they run like this: you've got the grammar stream (which you'll use often, as the kids haven't the first damn clue about it, and it burns time like nothing else), the vocabulary stream (group-work, or cooperative learning, in educational jargon) Sustained Silent Reading, the Literature stream (a seemingly obvious one, but it requires a textbook, and kids bring their pagers more reliably than their textbooks), and, of course, writing. That's right, the composition. It's something the kids have never gotten enough exposure to, and that's largely the fault of the teachers. I don't presume to speak for all the nation's English teachers, but I know firsthand that nearly half the thirty-odd English teachers at Coosaw Creek High won't teach writing, claiming they don't know how to assess it. I might have bought that, had I not been stricken with the irony of a cadre of English teachers bitching about the reading and writing skills of their students while refusing to teach them how to write, and therefore how to read.

In any case, I gave writing assignments, one a week, every week. Gave the kids forty minutes to get it done: two hundred properly spelled, well-organized words, and gradually they began to learn a thing or two. Topic sentences. Developed ideas. Transitional sentences. I watched with satisfaction after handing out their first writing assignment (discuss a defining moment in your life, and explain its significance) as their little heads bent over the desks and their pencils started working. There is, I must admit, something nearly intoxicating about knowing you're helping kids, touching them in some positive fashion during one of the more delicate, formative times of their lives. That I was touched by this is an enormous self-revelation for me.

And then they were finished, and they passed the work up, and it hit me then that I had thirty writing assignments to grade. Thirty 200-word handwritten assignments, for a total of 6000 words. And there were still two periods left in the day.

That evening, I got a taste of Zack Capers' world. I carried home over ninety writing assignments in my manila folder, sat down next to Brasco on my garage-sale couch, and began grading. It was seven when I started. It was nine-thirty when I quit. I'd gotten through twenty-eight of them.

I'd be lying if I said I wasn't tempted to simply stop teaching writing. I was. Deeply. It would have been so easy to simply dump vocabulary dittos and grammar workbooks on them, watching the clock like some of the others. After all, I wasn't being paid the six figures, and a hot seam of resentment twisted through me when I thought how blithely the Powers That Be expected me to just donate my time, my life, my entire being, to this job. But the fact of the matter was that these kids couldn't write – they were terrible writers; I cannot overstate how bad they were. Forget subject-verb and pronoun-antecedent agreement. Never mind dangling modifiers or improper participle usage. We're talking sentences nine words long with six commas, or entire 200-word papers comprised of two – honest to God, two – sentences. Periods placed in the middle of sentences. Periods eschewed all together. Half-formed ideas that wandered into others and melded into complete mutants before dying messily and badly. Others aborted at the fetal stage; still others carried well past senility. And – and no one could ever be more surprised than I – I felt a modicum of responsibility for it all. Not for their current ineptitude; my colleagues – the clock-watchers whose chief concern was whether the legislature was going to reduce the retirement quota from thirty years to twenty-eight – who refused to undertake the hours of requisite grading were to be blamed for that. But for their future, for that day they'll have to fill out a job application, or write a college essay, or even compose a love-letter, I felt responsible.

I don't want to sound pious. My desire to help these kids did not come close to piety. But it did resemble duty, and for that I have a nugget of pride. Whatever else might be said of me, whatever diatribe is written by that bunch at *The Post* and *Courier, The State,* or those leftist rags like *Newsweek* and *Time,* know that I really did come to care about the kids. In fact, it was probably my concern for these kids – and one in particular – that got me into this whole mess.

That, and Grey.

When you have ninety kids a day, what you really have is ninety different personalities, ninety different sets of problems and secrets and pressures. Ninety different smiles and ninety different attitudes. Ninety different little entities moving in and out of your life at the sound of bells, each requiring something different from you, each drawing their own apportionment of your day's energy. If you do your job right in the classroom you're exhausted when you get home. If you do your job right at home, you're exhausted when you wake up the next morning. If you teach, it isn't long before you realize that Christmas vacation was created for the teacher.

As the days progress as they did for me those weeks after my night with Jules, you come to know your students, their individual personalities, their little quirks and habits. By the time a couple weeks passed I knew who I'd have to tell to stop talking before they started, who would laugh at what joke, which students did homework and which ones would not. I learned which ones smoked, who was dating whom, which ones worked after-school jobs and which ones drove, who was in the band and who played sports. None of this came to me through any direct attempt on my part to glean information about my kids; you simply learn things when you deal with people day in and day out. I dealt with ninety of them every day, and as a consequence, I learned about what it was that made them who they were when they weren't in my classroom.

And of course I had my favorites. You can't help but have favorites. Some you look forward to speaking with, some you'd just as soon avoid. Some you care enough about to inquire into their world beyond the high school, and are in turn willing to share yours, and others you could never see again and not notice enough to care.

The purists who insist that it's different for the rest of the world are right: teachers owe all the kids in their classes – irrespective of their individual personalities – the same level of instruction, interest, and direction. I agree, and I did my best to provide that. But beyond that, I was to some degree hostage to my own tastes. You can't help but be a little fond of the student who pops in between classes for no reason other than to say 'Hi, Mr. Archer.' Or the kid who brings you her report card to show you her B+ in Geometry, her face beaming with pride and accomplishment, or the student who invites you to his basketball game, and is clearly, visibly happy when he sees you in the stands. As I said, part of being a teacher is caring about that sort of thing, and that part of the job I warmed to quickly.

But it has its perils, this connecting with students. A casual, innocent gesture or word on your part can be confused for something more significant. In a high school, perception is everything, and sixteen-year-olds' perceptions aren't always accurate. But I established my boundaries at the outset, remained professional and well behind all the right lines, and vowed to never cross them.

It's a vow I strove mightily to keep, even when it became clear to me that I was going to fail.

I didn't have a teacher's pet, in that I didn't strive to single out or favor one student over the other. I didn't have the same kid take roll for me each day, or hand back all the papers, or erase the greaseboard at the end of class. For these tasks I simply went down my grade book and chose the students alphabetically.

I did, however, have my favorites, and that isn't something I could have helped. I already told you that I understood the rules (The Big No, as Capers succinctly put it that day over Virginia's biscuits and gravy), and agreed wholeheartedly with them.

But the folks in Guidance put Savannah Bellington in my class, and in so doing altered the course of my life forever. Grey played her part as well, but her role was secondary.

Of course, Savannah never knew a thing about Grey. She never wanted anything but to get good grades and ride a scholarship to somewhere other than where she'd spent all of her life thus far. And had I had the good sense to leave things as I'd found them, to limit my influence to grammar and literature and things of that nature … but there's no real point in what-ifs. There just is. Wherever you are, you are, and here I am, and there it is.

Savannah Bellington was sixteen when I met her, living with her mother and four baby brothers – two of them half-black – in a single-wide trailer less than a mile from the school. That alone was enough to tug at my heart.

She walked to school, cutting through a thatch of woods on the eastern side of the campus that separated her family's trailer park from the school. Occasionally I'd pass her on my way in to campus. I never honked or waved or any of that. There were lines that weren't to be crossed, and I was always mindful of them.

And then the weather turned cold and her clothes remained the same. She never wore a coat, and I don't think it was because it didn't match her shoes or her bookbag.

Coosaw Creek was a whitebread school, the majority of whose students came from affluent, upper-middle-class neighborhoods speckled throughout the Winter's Cove community. But travel through any old Southern town like Winter's Cove and you'll see the same thing; money and privilege and opportunity, and scattered in between like afterthoughts and reminders are the trailer parks. The Winter's Cove School District took great pains, I eventually discovered, to keep the majority of these trailer-park kids out of their schools. The district lines are a testament to the creative art of gerrymandering, running as thin as a two-lane road for one stretch in order to keep a splattering of shacks – and about thirty thoroughly uncultured blacks – out of the student population. But somehow Savannah's park slipped in, so she became a Penguin, a Coosaw Creek High student, and one of mine.

Ever, Fate has her way.

She was a hard worker, Savannah was, and never gave me any trouble. On the third day of class she thanked me on her way out the door. It caught me by surprise.

'Thank you?' I said. 'What for?'

'For teaching me. Us. I don't know if everyone else is as thankful as I am, but I know teaching isn't easy and teachers don't get paid a lot, and I just wanted you to know that I'm glad you're here.'

I'd be lying if I said it didn't touch me, but I'm not afraid to lie, if the occasion demands it.

'Well you're very welcome, Savannah,' I said.

And she smiled and left my room, merging with the formidable flow of traffic crawling through the halls.

What about another summons our attention? Is it physical? Intellectual? Something emotional, perhaps – a hole in our own internal fabric which promises to be filled. Maybe it's pity, or paternal – either way, a desire to care for and protect. These are difficult questions, and there may not be a single answer.

A couple of weeks later I noticed her in the courtyard during lunch, sitting by herself among the various groups and cliques. She was sitting cross-legged at one of the bright yellow plastic picnic tables, eating a piece of plain white bread and reading a textbook she had opened on her lap. I stood in the hallway outside my classroom and watched her for a moment through the wall of glass, watched her nibble on that piece of bread in bites that suggested scarcity, watched the way the other kids neither noticed nor ignored her. I stood there, my hands in my pockets, rocking gently on my heels, aware that the occasional teacher or student was passing behind me and might notice my preoccupation with the goings-on in the courtyard. But that was all right. There were over two hundred kids out there, and any number of groups or pairs or individuals I might be watching. If someone asked, I'd merely say I thought I'd seen an impending fight.

It can be said that I knew my interest in Savannah went beyond the purely academic, and that I had a chance to nip it early. But that's part of the job. Teachers are what are known as mandated reporters; if we see bruises or scabs or other suspicious signs of abuse or neglect, we're required by the state to report it to the appropriate administrators. Savannah never looked like she'd been abused, but not all bruises and scars are worn on the outside.

Every now and then she'd set her piece of bread down and copy a passage from the textbook into her notebook, then return to the piece of bread. She did this for a full twenty minutes, and I stood there and watched her for every one of those minutes. She never lifted her head from the book. And she never ate anything other than that piece of bread.

The next day I held her after class.

She approached me at my desk as her classmates filed out the door and into the hall. Savannah was in my second-period class, and had Honors Trigonometry third, which was just around the corner. I knew this because I'd checked her schedule on the computer during my planning period this morning.

'Did I do something, Mr. Archer?' she asked, her books held in both arms up against her chest.

'No, no, not at all Savannah.' I was sitting behind my desk, keeping a solid three-foot zone between us. There were lines that weren't to be crossed, and I was always mindful of them.

'I just wanted to make sure everything was going all right with you,' I said. 'You know. At home, in particular.'

Her facial expression, which had begun as one of concern, shifted slowly to understanding, and right then I saw her life. The home filled with want and the vague smell of something better on the horizon. The wandering mother and the nonexistent father; the subtle but sharp comments from kids her age who'd never know what it was like to try to sleep cold or hungry, to shower without warm water, or cut their own hair. I saw the teachers who'd seen and pried and offered bitter pity before, and I saw in that second Savannah's endless pursuit of redemption through books.

'No,' she said, her copper-colored hair falling curly down the sides of her face. 'I'm fine. Just lots of late nights studying lately, with quarter exams being just around the corner and all.'

'Do you work?' I asked her, and I wouldn't catch the hesitation until months later, in hindsight. Dear God, to have been clairvoyant for only that moment.

'No,' she said. 'I mean, I baby-sit for the neighbors in the trailer behind ours, but it's not really work. They don't pay me regularly or anything. I just do it for the quiet, usually. They only have two kids, and one of them is a newborn who sleeps all the time, so I can get pretty good studying done there.'

'It's noisy at your house, then?' I asked, knowing I probably shouldn't.

She shrugged. 'Most of the time. My mother's usually either out with her boyfriend or at work, when she's working. They don't call her in much now, since she's had my little brother. He's two months and has colic and she had to take too much time off to carry him back and forth to the doctor's. I guess they just got tired of it.'

She smiled at me then, an innocent, hopeful, unbroken smile, and if there was ever a chance of my not finding a special place in my heart for Savannah Bellington, it left with that smile. Everything that happened from that moment forward is merely degrees of the inevitable. Any alternatives I might have had are simply various paths to the same place, each beginning at that smile.

'I've got four brothers,' she said. 'Two of them half-brothers, actually, but I consider them my brothers. I think that'll be the worst part of moving away to college. Missing them. I'll probably want to come home every weekend, just to see them.'

'Do you know where you want to go to college?' I asked, relieved to be able to ask a question that had some business being asked.

'Anywhere but College of Charleston or Charleston Southern. My mother wants me to go to Tech for the first two years because she says it's all we can afford. Either that or beautician school, but I'm not going to do it. I don't tell her that because it makes her mad, but' – a conspiratorial little giggle here, the pleasures of sharing a guarded secret with one who'd understand – 'I'm definitely moving away from here. I've been here my whole life, ever since I was born, and I'm going to get a scholarship and work nights waiting tables if I have to in order to pay for my rent and books. I'm number fourteen in the class so far, and as long as I can get through Latin I should crack the top ten by the end of the semester. Ms. Fernando said that anyone graduating in the top ten from here shouldn't have any problem getting a scholarship.'

She smiled again, not at me this time but at her dream, a dream she'd doubtlessly fed and nurtured and protected from the world for as long as she'd realized she was living a life without. She wanted a life with, and was willing to work for it. I had all the respect in the world for that. Still do.

'Ms. Fernando's right,' I said. 'Top ten out of a school like this one shouldn't have any trouble getting in anywhere.' I leaned back in my chair, folded one leg over the other in an effort to seem more casual, to suggest to her that it was all right to lower her guard with me.

'I went to USC in Columbia and I know of at least three or four of my classmates up there whose grades weren't as high as yours and who received at least partial scholarships.'

She nodded. 'Partial won't be enough, I'm afraid. My mother thinks college is a waste of money. Says with six mouths to feed in one house, there isn't anything left over for big-bucks schools. That's what she calls them: big-bucks schools. I tried to explain to her about scholarships, about how they've got the Life Scholarship for anyone with high grades and good SAT scores – which I've already begun studying for by reading the dictionary every night before bed – but she just gets mad. So mostly I don't talk about it much.' She stopped, seemed to realize that she'd just peeled away the veneer and exposed her dream. 'But I am going to college,' she offered, in a tone that made it clear there was no alternative.

'I believe you,' I nodded, telling the truth. 'And what's more, Savannah, colleges were made for students like you. You probably know this, but for the student that's willing to study and apply himself, as you clearly are, a college education is without question the gateway to a much better life. Do you know what you want to study?'

She nodded. 'Medicine,' she said. 'I'm going to be a doctor. An obstetrician.' She turned and checked the clock on the wall then, and to prevent her from having to tell me, I said, 'You better hurry to your next class. Don't want you to be late.'

She smiled at me again, turned and headed for the hallway. My third period class was filing in, finding their seats, ignoring me as though I was the greaseboard or overhead projector.

Savannah was almost out the door when I called out to her. She turned around, her pale blue eyes seeming more so beneath the copper of her hair.

'I think you've got a wonderful plan, Savannah, and if anyone can do it I'm sure it's you.'

I don't know why I said that, or why I was willing to throw it all the way across my half-filled classroom like that, but I think it was probably meant to be some form of encouragement or support. Judging by her expression – which was something along the lines of a curious smile, if that makes any sense – Savannah took it to be politeness, and maybe even a little weird. I supposed this was because she didn't get much encouragement at home, or anywhere else, for that matter, and as such had never needed it for fuel.

Or maybe she'd never had a teacher be interested in her – not her circumstances or her history, but her – and wasn't sure how to respond.

Whatever the case, it wasn't meant to be anything inappropriate. After all, there were lines that weren't to be crossed, and I was always mindful of them.

NINE

Kevin Geist drops the dime; Grey

I didn't think of Savannah Bellington anymore once she left my classroom that morning. I passed her once in the hallway and simply looked away before we could make eye-contact. I didn't want to summarily ignore her after taking such pains to gain her trust and confidence a couple hours earlier, but I didn't want to compound any mistake I might have already made by singling her out in a hallway filled with students to say hello; if she thought my parting words to her were weird, then that would do plenty to confirm her suspicions that Mr. Archer was behaving inappropriately towards her. I could just see myself sitting across from Mr. Collins, my toes curling with each sniff, listening to a lecture on how important it is for a teacher – particularly a male teacher – to watch the boundaries between himself and his kids, particularly his female kids, and especially his cute female kids.

That afternoon at a quarter till four, I was walking across the faculty parking lot to my old but faithful Honda, thinking how nice it would be to be able to buy a new car – an SUV, perhaps – and diddling with the budget numbers in my head, when I heard a man calling my name from behind.

I turned and saw Mr. Geist, the foreign language teacher – the foreign language department, actually. He spoke and taught German, French, and Spanish. He also spoke but did not teach Portuguese and Italian and, I'd heard, bits of Latin as well. I'd had the opportunity to speak to him a few times before, and had quite rapidly come to the conclusion that the man was an absolute genius. He was an avowed liberal Democrat in a state with at least three or four, but he wasn't aggressive about it. He was a high-minded, refined intellectual, and belonged on some college campus somewhere lecturing and writing books that are never read but receive wonderful reviews.

He was wearing a bow-tie – his traditional attire – and a blazer, half-trotting to catch up to me, carrying a large cardboard box under one arm, the pleasant smell of a tobacco pipe emanating from his attire. I stopped and waited for him.

'Mr. Archer,' he said upon reaching me, 'I was wondering if I might trouble you for a ride home. My wife's car is having transmission troubles so she took mine today. I'd intended to catch a ride home with Gene in Science, but I'd forgotten that he's always out with a cold while coincidentally deep-sea fishing off the Florida coast this week every year.'

'Sure,' I said. 'Not a problem. You need help with that box there?'

I kept my own stuff in a leather briefcase Autumn's parents had given me upon my acceptance to law school. I had my gradebook, three manila folders filled with as-yet-ungraded compositions, and the literature book for lesson planning. When I got home, I had four hours of grading and lesson-planning waiting for me. That and Brasco and whatever I could heat in the microwave.

'No, no,' he said, settling into my stride. 'These are projects I'm having my French class do. They've got to go through their family histories and diagram their family tree, in French and with pictures. It helps them learn the terms for family members, and beats standing in front of them listening to them repeat after me all day. What about you? How are your classes coming?'

'Fine, I suppose. I don't really have anything to compare it to, since this is my first year. I'm only a couple weeks behind on my grading, and might get my first quarter numbers in to Guidance on time if they'll cut me a couple days' slack.'

He shook his head. 'You're doing better than I did my first year. I thought I was going to go insane. Had five preps, one of them Spanish, and I barely spoke the language back then.'

I looked at him quizzically.

'Charleston County School District,' he said, which explained a lot. Most of the teachers I know have said they'd rather clean septic tanks without gloves or masks than teach in Charleston County.

Kevin Geist was a twenty-three-year veteran of the teaching wars, having paid his dues before Governor Dick Riley and the EIA. The EIA is the Education Improvement Act of South Carolina, which essentially kicked up the pay scales to get teachers off food-stamps.

Geist, being a firm believer in the core Democratic Party principle that every worker should be in a union shop, was Coosaw Creek's SCEA liaison. The SCEA is the state's branch of the National Education Association, which is the largest teacher's union in the country. He was a terrific teacher, from everything I'd heard, and the kids simply adored him, as did his colleagues. If there was ever a fact or piece of trivia you needed to know, you'd be better off consulting him before the Internet, as the Internet is limited next to the information Kevin Geist has filed away in that mind of his.

After I dropped Kevin off I went home, which was only a few miles from his house. I spent the first few minutes as I always do, rolling around the floor with Brasco, kissing and chewing on his cheeks (a ritual we developed when he was a kitten, and which he genuinely adores now), letting him lick my ear until it tickled so badly I couldn't stand it.

I tossed him a few Mousers and listened to him purr with satisfaction while he gulped them down. He's at the point now he'll purr when he sees the bright purple (though I'm not sure cats have cones in their retinas, and as such probably can't see colors) Mousers package, or even when he hears the word 'Mousers.'

I was boiling water for my Ramen noodles (chicken flavor tonight, perhaps beef tomorrow, and shrimp the night after) and dumping two cans of Vienna sausages into a bowl full of vinegar when the phone rang.

I instantly thought of Savannah, and was laughing out loud at myself at the absurdity of that when I answered the phone.

I didn't recognize the voice at first, but it was female, knew my name, and used it with a comfortable familiarity, which meant, of course, that it was Grey.

Tennessee Williams once said that solitude is a gem, for it is only trapped within it that we can actually appreciate the singular beauty of the random interruption. I'd been in the midst of the gem of solitude that was my life of late – an evening alone with a micro meal, Brasco, and a million high-school essays – when Grey, aged 46, picked up the telephone somewhere else in the world and dialed my number, rang my phone, and asked me out.

'A kaffeeklatsch,' she said when I asked her, entirely sarcastically, if she was asking me out on a date. 'There's a darling little coffee-shop downtown on the corner of King and Calhoun. Port City Java – have you heard of it?'

'Sure,' I said. 'Been there a few times. Kind of a local college-type hangout, right?'

'Yes, but we won't let that bother us. It's a mere jump from the battery if things go well and we decide we need seclusion. We can take a carriage ride. The air is breathtaking tonight.'

Grey, I was learning, wasn't one to camouflage her thoughts. I suppose you gather that sort of aplomb over the years. She was, after all, nearly old enough to be a member of the AARP.

'Er – sure, I'd love to. Would you like to meet there, or –'

'You hesitated. Have I caught you at a bad time?'

'No, no,' I said. 'I was just settling down for some riveting student-essay grading. I could use the distraction.'

I realized how bad that sounded once I said it; Grey did too, and, true to what I was discovering was her nature, called me on it.

'Really, darling' – and when she said it I could picture her again as she'd been on the beach that morning, her Mediterranean-brown skin and her silly oversized hat and, perhaps most vividly, those surgically modified breasts – 'if we're only out to distract ourselves, we might as well do that sort of thing alone. The idea behind a union – any sort of union, mind you, from a meeting to a marriage – is that each brings some variety of pleasure to the other that otherwise would not have been there at all.' She paused, to allow me to absorb this last bit, no doubt.

'You do enjoy pleasure, don't you Cole?'

'Pleasure? Oh, yeah. Of course. I mean, who doesn't? That's why it's called pleasure, right? Because it's so pleasurable.'

'Well good, then. Now, rein in your composure and all those silly thoughts you're struggling to keep from having right now, and meet me at Port City Java at nine this evening. How's that for you?'

'Nine's fine,' I said.

'Wonderful,' she said. 'See you then, then.' And she hung up.

So did I, an indeterminate length of time later. I stood there stunned for a moment or two, I know, because it was that shrill, horribly loud buzzing that echoes through your house when you leave the phone off the hook that pulled me back into the present.

Brasco was on the counter beside me, rubbing up against my stomach.

'Man,' I said aloud, finally hanging up the phone and scratching him behind the ears. 'What in the hell has Daddy gotten himself into, little buddy?'

I tried to look at the facts objectively. You've got an attractive, mid-forty-year-old sun-worshipper who looks not a day over thirty-five and apparently thinks and acts closer to twenty, with four ex-husbands and God knows how many lovers in her wake. She's rich, or close enough to be able to toss multi-carat diamond rings off piers at the beach the way most people would throw crackers to the seagulls. Probably she's unemployed, which means she's essentially unencumbered in any way of a firm, grounded connection to reality. People with money and skin to burn rarely suffer the burdens of such connections.

And she's calling me on the phone, nine weeks after we'd bumped into each other on the beach, nine weeks after I'd rubbed oil all over her back. (Be sure to get beneath the string, she'd blithely said.)

Then you had the whole pleasure reference. You do enjoy pleasure, don't you Cole? Wow.

But I knew what part of me that line of thinking was coming from; it was the same part that got me interested in Chasey Lain, Janine, and all the rest of the Vivid Girls, the same part that still occasionally missed Marla. Somehow, though, I thought that in dealing with a woman like Grey I should employ more of my faculties than merely those that were domiciled in the strike zone.

It might have been her age; something about the fact that she was only four years my mother's junior, and probably a mother – and possibly grandmother – herself. It's difficult for me to see her in that light now, however, looking back. The lanoe-soft hands and enveloping compassion she would eventually come to show me have, in the glaring, unforgiving light of hindsight, been tarnished in my memory. There were elements to my relationship with Grey that I know I'll carry with me forever, that I've already hidden away in that secret room we all keep and in which we store our scars and wounds and fleeting fantasies. Whatever I learned from her, however, came at a terrible price. Now that I know her angle, now that I understand the impetus behind her lilting words and warm, deceptive actions, it's hard for me to step back and objectively view her at all. She was a central player in everything that unfolded in my life that year, everything that convinced me that my presence in America (or any country with an extradition treaty) was no longer in my best interest.

But back in October, standing there in my kitchenette while Brasco did his best to rub every inch of himself against my torso, it was the Oedipal thing that had me hung up. I wasn't too keen on experiencing the kind of physical reactions I was having to Grey with someone my mother's age, even though Grey and my mother had nothing more than gender in common. There was just something weird and unnatural about it.

But as I said before, when she'd called I'd been trapped in Williams' gem of solitude, where even time can seem frozen in amber, and was grateful for her random distraction.

Of course, I know now the randomness was anything but.

It was a little after five when she'd called. By five-thirty I was in the shower, scrubbing and scalding myself as though it were my wedding night. I debated what to wear only momentarily – I've never been one to worry too much about that sort of thing – and decided upon khaki slacks and a light blue button-down. It was mid-October and the weather was still relatively mild at night, but just in case she'd been serious about that carriage ride I put on a white turtle-neck beneath the button-down. There's not much less attractive in someone you've just met than a constant chattering of teeth, and the wind could get pretty cold whipping in off the water downtown.

Once I had my clothes on I brushed my hair, dolloping gel through it to get rid of any cowlicks that might have formed over the course of the day, and spent about a half-hour brushing it just so. I rubbed Cool Water skin-lotion over my face, neck, and fore-arms, and spritzed Cool Water cologne across my clothed torso. It was nearly seven by the time all this was finished, and I realized I still hadn't eaten. So I finished making the Ramen noodles and ate the Vienna sausages in vinegar while the soup boiled, alternating between CNN and VH-1 on the tube. I gave Brasco a few Mousers. When the soup was ready, I ate it in the living room, sitting on my musty garage-sale sofa, hunched over a ratty wicker coffee-table I couldn't remember acquiring, so as not to spill soup on myself. I had half a case of Beck's in the fridge, and drank three with the soup while I watched the national news, punctuated by videos every few minutes. The Beck's went a long way towards relaxing me, nibbling away at the anxiety that stemmed from the unknown portion of the night ahead of me, as well as the guilt that stemmed from those parts – like her age – that were known all too well.

The next time I noticed the clock it was twenty after eight, and I gathered my keys and wallet and left for the Port City Java on the corner of King and Calhoun.

TEN

*A brief history of Grey;
Cole's dream*

The weeks after my night with Grey moved surprisingly
slowly, as if everything transpiring around me was doing so
underwater. I rose each morning after my two clicks on the snooze
button and went to school and did my thing, drove home, graded
papers and watched TV over three or four beers, then went to bed,
all of it trapped in Williams' gem, none of it interrupted by random
distraction.

I found myself thinking of her a great deal – I couldn't call,
because I'd not asked for her number, still unsure at the end of our
evening that I could in good conscience see her again – though at
the time I remember thinking that it was probably loneliness as
much as anything else that precipitated this. Certainly it was loneliness as much as it was attraction. That's another thing I wanted to
believe (there's so much I wanted to believe, so very much during
those days in which I tried to find faith), for there were lines, and I
needed to be mindful of them.

The plain truth of the matter is, however, that whatever lines
existed between Grey and me were blurry at best. Whatever significance they might have was drawn more from abstract morality
than from the very real and lasting damage that could be done to
one of my students – Savannah Bellington, for example – were I to
cross them.

No. Grey, whatever else might be awry concerning the dynamic
of such a relationship, was not a teen-aged student of mine. She
was to me during those weeks after our evening at Port City Java
an enigma, one who walked nearly fully removed from the norms
and conventions which lined the perimeters of most people's lives.
Over the course of our 'kaffeeklatsch' she revealed, in terms whose

frankness made me blush more than once, that all four of her marriages had been mutually 'open', and thereby not constrained by sexual fidelity or emotional loyalty. She had not, she explained, worked since she was twenty-two, when she married her first husband, a fifty-year-old man who'd built his fortune in the North Carolina tobacco fields.

'Each Sunday he'd write me a check for a thousand dollars, and instruct me to make it last until the next Sunday. I was out of his hair this way, and out of his accounts. Of course, living on his family's estate I had everything I could ever dream of wanting or needing, so I busied myself reading, learning musical instruments, traveling, and having glorious and tragic affairs with beautiful men from all walks of life.'

He died on her thirtieth birthday – 'He'd bought me a pair of stallions, and was thrown off while showing me how to dismount them. He broke his neck and died instantly' – and she'd married her second husband three months later, who also happened to be her first husband's son by a former marriage.

'His name was Simon and we were much more similarly matched in age and interests. It took me three years to discover that his tastes in men far surpassed my own.'

So she left him – 'I wasn't all that upset, really; bored, more than anything else' – and took with her 'enough money to permanently dismiss the notion of ever selling chunks of my life for a weekly salary.'

Grey had spent most of the next decade in Europe, taking cooking classes, dance lessons, wandering through France and Germany and Italy. 'I lived with one perfectly divine man from Naples named Franco. who owned a resort in Rimini, on the Adriatic Sea. We stayed there for three years – his wife taught me Italian in exchange for my keeping her husband occupied. We were wonderful friends, she and I. It was hard to leave.'

But leave she did, as she apparently always had. She met her third husband in a bar in New Orleans and married him the following weekend. The Justice of the Peace performed the ceremony in the actual bar, a block off Bourbon, and the bride and groom consummated the marriage in the ladies' room. 'Cleaner than the men's room,' she explained.

They lived in abject squalor together for two years in an apartment above a record store in the French Quarter while her husband,

Todd, tried to get his jazz band off the ground. She'd never told him about her money.

'He was a terrible lover but a wonderful musician, and one shouldn't marry for sex, anyway,' she'd told me that evening in Port City Java, her words spoken across a small corner table through the rising steam of coffee and hot chocolate.

'If you marry for sex you'll divorce because of it. My mother told me that, and she was right as she could be. Much better to marry for love or infatuation or friendship, and divorce for something else entirely.'

Her fourth and final husband she'd met in Charleston, where she'd ended up 'two days after my fortieth birthday. He was a doctor. Nothing particularly mentionable about him save his outright worship of me, which can be as intoxicating as wine at times, as you probably know, Cole.'

I did. I'd been adored once – pure and unrestrained adoration had been my daily fare with Autumn – but you already know how that turned out.

'But it does get tiresome after a while,' she said. 'It can grow stifling, which is never a good thing in a marriage.'

I merely took it all in, listening to her over my hot chocolate, all the while developing an increasingly evolving picture of Grey as a woman who had, due to some early good fortune, been able to remove from her life's equation the variables with which the rest of us are consumed daily. Bedtimes and alarm clocks were not part of her life; she often walked the streets of downtown Charleston during the late-night-early-morning hours, having breakfast at one of the little sidewalk cafes before going home to read poetry or work crossword puzzles in her bed, then crawling naked with her cats beneath her goose-down duvet as the sun reached its apex outside her window. (I know this about her routine only because she told me; our night together started and stopped in the Port City Java.) Or she'd throw darts at the map and travel to wherever it landed, staying until she grew bored with the local customs and peoples, leaving the moment the fancy struck her. She was governed not by requirements and necessities nor even by time, as are you and I, but by moods and whims and impetuous desires. Monday and Wednesday and Saturday were all the same to her; she measured her life in seasons, not days. May began the beach season, in which she spent most of the day with a romance novel beneath the sun, turning her skin to leather and bleaching her brown hair reddish. September meant it was time for parks and lakes and long walks South of Broad, alone or with another, depending on her mood. In December when the leaves fell she'd usually go flying with the birds down Florida's panhandle, landing in Miami or Key West; she kept furnished homes in both places. Around March or April she'd return, in time for May and the beach at Isle of Palms where I, of course, met her.

She'd lived in over ten countries, 'had two or three times that many lovers,' studied five languages ('mastering none completely'), learned the piano and the harp, begun writing two different novels, had one child ('a beautiful girl named Dallas after the city in which she was conceived – thank goodness I didn't meet her father in Casper, Wyoming; she's studying Historical Preservation at the University of Chicago now'), and nearly died of a drug overdose in Munich twenty years ago.

Some things she'd never done, 'not that you're particularly intrigued by any of this,' were: intentionally harm any animal, including killing bugs or spiders ('I throw them out the front door'), told a lie ('aside from little white ones to spare people's feelings, of course'), gone to church, owned a dog ('I'm a cat person, and cat people don't mix well with dogs'), been to Australia ('I'm terrified of marsupials, as I may have already mentioned'), voted, remained faithful in a marriage, ridden a horse ('not since I saw what happened to hubby number one'), fired a gun ('but I do keep one by the bed'), gotten a tattoo ('it's on my list'), or eaten anything other than fruit, vegetables, or grains before noon ('not since my early twenties, anyway').

Despite her comment to the contrary, however, I was intrigued. Wonderfully, magically, incredibly intrigued. I soaked up her words and imagined myself living the same way. Imagine, the freedom to do whatever you wanted to do, whenever you wanted to do it. No artificial constraints, no boundaries other than those you place upon yourself. It was an inebriating concept, one I couldn't allow myself to dwell upon too long. Your world can grow immeasurably ugly if you stare out of it enough.

And through it all as the evening progressed and finally drew to a close, both of us stationary at the little table in the corner of the café for the better part of two hours, Grey became something more than an older woman with a colorful past; again, I think it was the loneliness as much as anything else that did it. I don't believe I would have had a place for her at all had Autumn's sudden absence not ripped such wide, gaping holes in my life. But regardless, Grey began, in the days and weeks after my evening with her (it's still hard for me to call it a date), to symbolize something else, something larger and epic. Freedom, inhibition, wealth, hedonism; I'm not entirely sure. I was a teacher, and a miserably unhappy one at that. Autumn was gone forever, and this fact was gradually working its way through my consciousness like a cancer. And here was this woman who had tasted the world and everything in it, and was sitting here telling me what I already knew but had heretofore been able to pretend I didn't: there is an entire universe of sensations and experiences out there, and absolutely none of it is going on in Room 111 of Coosaw Creek High School.

Weeks later – November 1st, I still remember – I awoke at 4:14 in the morning, in the midst of the first wet dream I'd had in years. My thighs and lower abdomen were cold and damp, the semen already drying stickily in the hairs there. I sat up, my head fuzzy, realizing what it was that had just happened.

The pieces were already beginning to fragment into that misty fog that separates dreams from consciousness, but I glimpsed enough of them to know what I'd been dreaming. It'd been Autumn, of course, as all my dreams were. We'd been making love on the beach, something we'd never done in reality, Columbia being in the dead center of the state and having nothing in the way of coastlines. We'd talked about it, though. We were going to drive down I-26 one day and wrap ourselves in a sleeping bag between the dunes, listen to the ocean roaring against the surf and make love through the night. It'd been something we promised ourselves for years, and like the rest of our promises it existed only in my dreams now.

But this one was different. Near the end, as the intensity grew and reached its climax, Autumn had turned into Savannah, and she'd been looking up at me, that same hopeful, unbroken smile that she'd shown in my classroom that day she thanked me, and she'd been saying – I distinctly remember her words – 'Will this help me get into college, Mr. Archer? Will this help me get a scholarship?'

I'd awakened then, thank God, and sat there and cleared my head. I'd gone into the bathroom and washed my face with cold water, tried to shake the image, and the words, of Savannah out of my head. But I left the light off. I couldn't bear to see myself in the mirror.

ELEVEN

Ernestine introduces herself; Marla sips the night; Savannah calls

I knew there was no way I was getting back to sleep, so after I finished in the bathroom (I was wracked with nausea for several horrible moments, and actually bent over the toilet in preparation, but it gradually passed) I made my way into the living room and sat on the couch in the center of the cool darkness.

Brasco followed me; I couldn't see him but I heard him chirp as he found me on the couch and took his place beside me. I reached out and stroked his coat for several minutes, tried to shake the images of the dream away.

I sat there in the darkness for close to half an hour on the VCR clock. The guilt washed over me in waves, guilt intermingled with self-disgust. What the fuck was the matter with me? I'd just had a nocturnal emission about one of my kids, a little girl for God's sake. A sweet, trusting, disadvantaged little girl. She'd made a point of thanking me for teaching her. For actually being a teacher. I was quite possibly one of the few stable males in her life thus far, and here I was, her teacher, having the sort of dream about her after which I had to wipe my come off my belly.

'I'm fucked up,' I said aloud to the darkness. 'Dear God in Heaven... I am seriously out there.'

My voice was hoarse and sounded foreign to me. Brasco responded with a meow. Yes, Cole, you are fucked up. A little more behind the ears there if you could.

I sat there and tried to get next to that dream, to the fact that it had actually come from somewhere inside my mind. I sat there naked and motionless until the little green numerals on the VCR said it was 5:00, at which point I stood, walked into the kitchenette, grabbed two Beck's from the fridge, and sat there and drank them in the darkness until it was time to get ready for work.

'Ok, class, you'll remember yesterday we were talking about complements, and how to determine which of the four we're looking for. Who would like to tell me the first step when working with complements?'

The usual array of hands went up, roughly one for every head that was down on the desk. It was an interesting mix, this bunch of eleventh-graders. I thought many times over the course of that year that you could walk in on any of my three classes and watch them for a half hour or so, and know with a fair degree of certainty which ones would grow up to be professionals, which ones would have a name-patch, which ones wouldn't grow up at all.

Savannah was absent that day, her first time all year. It was an irony for which I was thankful beyond measure, and for which I remained thankful until I learned the reason behind her absence.

'Okay, Tom, tell us the first step.'

'Isolate and identify the verb.'

'Very good,' I said. 'That's exactly right. How about step number two? Anybody?'

'See if it's action or linking,' a girl in the back, Dianne, called out.

'Let's raise our hands,' I said.

Dianne raised her hand. I purposely waited until someone else did to call on them.

'Okay, Walter, what do you think?'

'See if it's action or linking,' Walter said, then turned and smiled a shit-eating grin for Dianne. Oh, for the world to be so simple as it was to those kids.

'That's right. We see if it's action or linking. Good. Now, I'm going to write this sentence on the board for you' – I retrieved a red grease-marker from my desk and walked to the board, began writing out the sentence, reading it aloud for them – 'An anonymous donor gave an Olympic-sized pool to the school athletic department.' There. Now, you need to copy this down in your notes, then identify the verb, circle it on your paper, and write an 'A' above it if it's action, and an 'L' if it's linking. Go ahead and get that done.'

As they did, I walked casually around the room, fighting off what remained of the dream from that morning. I wasn't assaulted with images anymore, those having slipped away as subtly as smoke over the course of the morning. Now it was merely the knowledge of what I'd done. I hadn't meant to do it, of course. In truth, I hadn't actually done anything – how accountable can you hold the dreamer for the dream? – but I was responsible, nonetheless. The fact that I hadn't caused any tangible damage wasn't doing much for my conscience; I was slowly suffocating beneath the weight of the realization that from somewhere inside of me festered the potential to imagine one of my kids and myself naked, copulating. Even now, walking up and down the rows of desks in my classroom, my olive green khakis pleated and cuffed, my long-sleeved button-down professionally starched, my tie in a tight Windsor knot, I felt like a child molester, harboring his dirty secret behind expensive clothes and impressive carriage. I felt the way President Clinton might have felt, if indeed he had the capacity to feel anything at all.

The kids were done with the sentence, waiting for me to walk them through the next step. It was all I could do to make myself look at them, the irrational fear that they could see my sins on my face an almost palpable presence.

'Okay,' I said, my back to them, my attention to the board, red marker in hand poised to write. 'Now someone tell me step three.'

Of course I had to turn around in order to see them raise their hands, so I did, and felt my stomach lurch.

'Yes, Mary.'

'Well,' she said in her clear, high voice that rang of pigtails and dimples, 'if it's an action verb you have to look for the direct object. If it's a linking verb, you look for the subject complement.'

'That's exactly right, Mary. Good job. So what's our verb in this sentence here?'

'Gave. It's action, so you look for the direct object.'

'And how do we find the direct object?'

Mary wasn't too certain about that one, so she retreated into the mass. The girl next to her, Wendy Bannister, raised her hand. Wendy Bannister with the pimple problem, which hadn't gotten much better, for the record.

'Yes, Wendy.'

'It asks the question who or what received the action of the verb. That's why there aren't any direct objects in sentences with linking verbs, because you have to have action.'

'You got it,' I said, and if I was overly-animated it was simply because the girl was so profoundly cursed in complexion and I wanted to throw her a bone where I could. That's another one of the teacher's professional responsibilities, and it's another part of the job I warmed to. There were parts of teaching, indeed, that I loved, and that I'll miss. But there it is.

'And in that sentence there it's "pool". The pool is the thing that was given. "Olympic-sized" is an adjective modifying the object "pool".'

'That's right, it is. Good point,' I said. 'Very good point.' She was smart, and it would do the trick for her. In the end, brains would likely pull her through, even if her skin didn't clear up, which it would in time.

That's one of the first things I learned when I first reached the Caribbean. With enough time, everything clears up. These islands are loaded down with the sins and secrets of some of the world's worst, and the islands don't care. Time and sunshine are prevalent here, and both eventually change everything, whether you want them to or not.

The bell rang, the kids filed out, and I went and sat at my desk, savoring the eight minutes between this class and the next the way one might savor an exotic chocolate, wondering – but only periph- erally – where Savannah was. It wasn't like her to miss class.

Five minutes after the final bell I had my first real run-in with our department head, Mrs. Whitaker, and it was a beauty. It was the second week of October; I'd made it fairly far, according to Mr. Capers. (Zack Capers, consummate teacher, took it upon himself to serve as a kind of unofficial mentor to all the first-year teachers, and I found myself exceedingly grateful for his guidance and advice on more than one occasion.) Most of the twenty-seven teachers in our department had had run-ins with her more than once this year alone. It didn't matter whether you were a first-year rookie or a twenty-nine-year veteran, male or female, white or black.

So you can imagine me – disenchanted with the education profession, frustrated with what I honestly believed to be my unrealized writing potential, confused and disgusted over my sudden and apparently unhealthy affinity for one of my students – getting broadsided by this peach on the back end of yet another day in Paradise.

I don't know why she was the way she was, and I don't much care, either. I only know that she was, and it was my turn that day.

'Mr. Archer,' I heard her call from down the hall. I didn't look immediately – one of the first things you learn as a teacher is to hear selectively, particularly when it's your name rattling down a crowded hallway after you – choosing instead simply to continue locking my classroom door and venture in the opposite direction toward the parking lot.

'Mr. Archer,' she called again. 'A word, please, Mr. Archer.'

She was closer this time; Ernestine Whitaker had one of those roomy frames that doesn't so much move as displace space. When she passed you in the hall it was always fast and noisily, her moving mass pulling wind past you like a train.

It was obvious I heard her now, so I paused, glanced over my shoulder as if I'd only just heard her, and smiled. If she noticed, it was wasted on her. I doubt Mrs. Whitaker had ever smiled in her life.

'Mr. Archer,' she said, 'are you aware that I am the head of the department?'

I nodded, trying very hard not to ask her for her autograph. My mouth gets away from me like that sometimes.

'And then are you aware that as part of my duties as Head of the English department I have catalogued and referenced each English-related film in the media center by grade-level and curriculum?'

I wasn't, but I didn't think it prudent to say as much just then. Fortunately they were rhetorical questions, the kind people of little importance often ask to lend weight to their impending point. She wasn't expecting an answer.

'There are over one hundred and thirty films in the English holdings section of the media center, and I took the time to go through and segregate each one into its specific curriculum designation. What does this mean to you, Mr. Archer?'

This time she paused and pursed her lips, as if nothing I said could adequately answer her question.

I looked at her closely then – really looked at her. She was thirty-something, tall and square-shouldered and dense through the trunk and neck. She looked a lot like what a linebacker might look like if he traded in all the pads and gear for a wig and women's clothing. I would have thought that this was at least in part responsible for her miserable attitude, but some of the veteran teachers who'd known her for a while had said that once upon a time she'd been quite attractive and athletic-looking, and was just as much a patronizing bitch then as she was now. She wasn't particularly ugly; her face and hair were plain enough, but she was arrogant and condescending, and this was her chief feature to all I'd ever heard speak about her.

'I take it I did something wrong with one of the films,' I said, more in an effort to inject some levity into the situation, hoping the woman would lighten up. It was a no-go, though. Whatever I'd done had her panties in a real crimp.

'You certainly did, Mr. Archer,' her teeth clenched now, her face growing redder by the second. 'In my lesson plans which were made weeks ago I set today and tomorrow aside for *Death of a Salesman.*'

It clicked for me then, where I'd goofed. I showed *Death of a Salesman* to my classes late last week and had forgotten to return the film. It was still in the VCR in my classroom. We hadn't studied the play, but grades were due and I needed a free day, so I popped it in and pushed play. Had my grades in by 3:30, too. A full half-hour ahead of schedule.

'I checked the signature log in the library and I saw that you were the last one to check it out. Is this correct?'

I nodded. 'I just forgot to return it. It's right inside my room; if you want to wait a sec I'll get it for you.'

'What are you doing with it? *Death of a Salesman* is part of the twelfth-grade curriculum. You teach juniors. You have no business showing films out of curriculum.'

Her voice was rising now, which I suppose was meant to embarrass me in the hallway there, but it didn't. What it did do was piss me off. Still, I was an induction teacher and she was the department head, and whether I liked it or not she could do a lot to make my life at work more difficult.

'I made a mistake,' I said, my voice even and conciliatory. 'It won't happen again.'

'That's not good enough,' she snapped, punctuating each of her words with little jabs at the air with her fingers. This is another habit rude and unimportant people develop, this use of hand gestures when they speak. As if the rest of us just can't quite grasp it without visual aides and manual cues.

'I spent over two hours organizing those films. I posted a list of films by curriculum in the English workroom, and sent one out with an attached memo to every English teacher's box. Part of your job is to read those memos. It doesn't do me any good to spend all that time typing and copying them if people don't read them. Because of your negligence and dereliction of duty I've got a third of my classes next year who will have already seen *Death of a Salesman* when I go to show it!'

I held my breath and refrained from replying just yet. She'd begun shaking a little; nothing outright or overly noticeable, just that subtle little quiver people do just before they really lose control.

'It's not that big a deal,' I said. 'It isn't going to kill them to see a movie twice.'

'That isn't the point! I specifically stated in the memo that —'

'I know what the point is, Ernestine.' Using her first name took her by surprise. She looked as if she'd been stung. 'The point is that I failed to abide by a memo you spent a great deal of time typing, copying, and distributing, and in so doing have caused you a bit of inconvenience this year and potentially a great deal more next year. I've already apologized for that, and assured you that it won't happen again. If you aren't going to accept my apology and allow us to move on, then there isn't anything I can do about that.'

'You should watch your tone with me, Mr. Archer. I'm not one to be trifled with.'

'I'm not trifling with you, Ernestine. I'm just not trembling for you, either. I made a mistake. It isn't my first, and unfortunately it won't be my last. I'd appreciate it if you would be gracious enough to accept my apology and let this be over with.'

'The memos are there for a rea —'

'You know, I'd heard this about you.' This really got her attention. I knew I should stop, but I couldn't. Just then, at that moment in time, I didn't give an ounce of owl-shit for my job.

'That you were unforgiving, demanding, arrogant. And I have to admit, Ernestine, you're living up to your billing. Who do you think you are, coming down here to my room like this, asking me your patronizing questions and trying to bait me? I showed the wrong film. That's it. The wrong film. I didn't kill anyone, or treat a student or parent inappropriately, or forget to wear the all-holy tie. I showed the wrong film.'

'You are way out of line, Mr. —'

'And what's with the "Mr" stuff? You can call me Cole in department meetings and around the school, but all of a sudden you're a little upset and it's Mr. Archer? I'm not your child, Ernestine. And I'm not one of your students who has to sit there and tolerate this crap. I make one little oversight and all that comes out of your mouth is bile. Do you even know what you sound like sometimes?'

She stared at me, exhaling loudly through her nose, seemingly pushing it out for effect. I thought little boogers might come streaming out.

'Now if we're quite finished with our word,' I said, retrieving my keys from my pocket and jingling them in my hand for effect, 'I've got to get home and feed my cat.'

And I turned and left her there, her stare burning a hole in my back.

I knew it'd been a mistake to speak to her that way – she was, after all, our department head, no matter how she might have come by the position, or how arrogant she was in wielding its administrative duties – but it'd been one of those situations where I couldn't have won either way. Had I simply stood there and swallowed her shit, I would have spent the next few days irritated with myself, rehearsing in animated fashion all the things I should have said to her. I didn't need another reason to have trouble looking at my reflection in the mirror, so I opened my mouth and said what I said, and there it is.

In the end, though, it wouldn't matter a great deal. Had my teaching career been a conventional one, something of the magnitude of eternally pissing off your petty but vindictive department head would have likely had fairly far-reaching implications. But I was on the verge of so many enormous and irrevocable mistakes that engaging in a pissing contest with Ernestine Whitaker would simply get lost amidst the numbers.

They say that wild animals can sense the weakness in their prey; the wolf can lift his nose to the air and smell the suffering of caribou a dozen miles away. The shark can detect a single drop of blood spilled into a million gallons of water. And Marla Grossman can sip the night and taste my pain at will; those who doubt it are fortunate. They've been spared the emptiness of a relationship with one of her fold.

I'd been eating dinner – corn flakes and skim milk, two peanut-butter-and-jelly sandwiches – talking on the phone with Jules about a weekend fishing trip he and a couple of his buddies were planning. The idea of ditching Charleston and losing myself in the Lowcountry waterways for a couple of days had done wonders for my spirits. As if she'd known, Marla beeped in.

'Hello, Cole,' she said. Her voice filled me with mixed emotions, none I care to try to discern even now.

'Marla.' I said. A statement, nothing more. 'How are you?'

'Well, that depends on you, Cole.'

'And how might that be so?' I said. I never loved her, never even liked her a great deal. The phenomenal sex and the long-distance component of our relationship was the only way we'd survived as long as we had. If ever there were two people not meant for one another, it was Marla Grossman and Cole Archer. Her only allure was the random night here and again.

'I've made a pie,' she said, 'for a date I had tonight. He had to cancel at the last minute, leaving me with this pie.' She paused. 'It's key lime,' she added. 'Your favorite.'

'I'm kind of busy, Marla. I'm about a hundred and six years behind on my grading and I had a bit of a shitty day besides.'

'You remember what we did with the key lime pie that night in Boone?' she said, as if she hadn't heard a word of my protestation. 'That was our first night playing with food, wasn't it?'

'It sounds appealing, Marla, but –'

'I was standing here in my kitchen making it for my evening with Don when I started thinking about that, about the ski trip to North Carolina for my birthday, and how you bought that key lime pie from the gas station and we smeared it all over each other, and then it occurred to me, right about the time Don called to tell me his wife's plans had fallen through and that he wouldn't be coming over after all, that that night with you and me in the mountains was our first night for a number of things.'

Like I said, she was wild. Her date with the married man fell through and she doesn't want the pie to waste, so she calls me up to tempt me for a whirl. But I wasn't in the mood, and even if I was, I resented her thinking she could get over here so easily.

'That was a long time ago, Marla.'

'Do you remember what I asked you to do to me that night once we'd finished the pie? I was thinking about that while I made it. I got so involved in the memory that I began wishing it were you and not Don coming over for dinner. I wasn't even all that upset when he called to back out.'

I was about to say something when the phone beeped; it'd be Jules, tired of waiting and calling me back.

'Hang on, Marla. I've got someone on the other line.'

I clicked over.

'Sorry about that, Jules. It's Marla. She's got herself all hot and lonely over there and decided to call me up.'

'Mr. Archer?' Female voice. Young. Nervous.

Uh-oh.

It was Savannah.

'Oh, shit. Er – I mean, shoot. Wow. Uh, Savannah?'

'Yes, sir. I'm sorry I called you at home ... did I get you at a bad time?'

'Uh, no. I mean, actually yes, things are kind of crazy around here. I thought you were somebody else.'

'I heard. Marla?'

'No, a friend of mine. But I do have Marla on the other line. Can you hold on just a second?'

I didn't wait for her to say anything before I clicked over.

'Marla?'

'I'm still here, lover.'

'Marla, listen. We aren't lovers anymore. We tried that for a while. It didn't work out, remember?'

'The sex always worked out, as I remember. We had great sex.'

'Yeah, we had some good times. But we – we really didn't get along all that well. All we ever did was argue.'

'Arguing is the last thing I want tonight, Cole. No one is looking to rekindle any doomed relationship; I'm merely terribly in the mood right now and find myself in the frustrating position of having a freshly made key lime pie with no one to share it.'

'Another time,' I said. 'Sometime next week, maybe. I'll come over to your place, we can rent a couple flicks, see what happens. Maybe romp a while through Memory Lane. We don't need the pie for that.'

I found myself wanting off the phone with Marla very quickly, and felt a pang of guilt stab through me, for I understood the reason for my haste.

'Suit yourself,' she said. 'Come down to Capone's sometime. I'm working late all weekend.'

'I'll try,' I said, and depressed the receiver, thoroughly pleased with myself. When it came to dealing with arrogant women, I was two for two today.

I clicked over to the other line.

'Savannah?'

Nothing.

'Savannah? Hello? Savannah?'

Still nothing. Dead space coming through the line.

'Savannah?' I clicked the receiver a couple of times, got a dial tone.

'Savannah?'

I hung up the phone. 'Shit.' I picked up the phone once more just to check. Still no Savannah.

Okay, I thought. No biggie. She'll call back if it was important enough.

But that wasn't the problem. Ordinarily I wouldn't have particularly wanted to be reached at home by either my students or their parents. It didn't happen often – maybe once every two or three weeks – and when it did the calls were benign enough. They'd call to make sure they had the right novel for class the next day, or to let you know they'd be absent tomorrow and would bring a note when they came back. Sometimes a concerned parent would ring you up to make sure their kid wasn't mouthing off to you too much in class, or to tell you little Susie's parrot died the day before so Susie would be out of sorts for a while. Like I said, nothing major, but it still isn't the sort of thing you really look forward to. The last thing you want to do after dealing with ninety-odd teenagers a day is have one of them call you up in the middle of your Burger King dinner and Seinfeld rerun to talk about something you could really give a shit about now that you were home.

But it wasn't that way with Savannah, and therein was the rub. They say that self-realization is achieved by degrees, and I believe this is true. Drinkers, smokers, sluts, and gamblers all accept their problem gradually, its reality unfolding a single layer at a time until the weight and sheer ugliness of that reality becomes more than they can bear alone. That's where all the self-help books and support groups and twelve-step programs come in.

She was never really far from my thoughts. Never far from my dreams, as last night had borne out. I don't know why – I didn't then, and I don't now. She wasn't the prettiest student at Coosaw Creek High. She wasn't the sexiest or the shapeliest; she didn't have the best legs or the biggest breasts. And she didn't give me any real reason – no opening or opportunity, as it were – to imagine something between us. Perhaps it is because I felt she needed me, and, in such dire need of salvation myself, being someone's savior was an elixir for me. But it goes back to that earlier question, doesn't it? What pushes us in the direction of those we choose? What about another summons our attention? It's a difficult question, and there may not be a single answer.

Besides, putting words to it would do little good, for any attempt at nomenclature is little more than vanity or defense.

She was never far from my thoughts. In class I was a model of objectivity, oscillating before them during the lectures like a fan, glancing programmatically into the faces of each of them an equal amount of time. I'd been worried at first that I might linger too long on her or betray myself with the wrong look, but we rarely made eye contact. Her head was always bent over her paper as she busily took notes. During silent reading or essay-writing time I'd move about the room freely, never pausing more than a second or two near any one particular student. Part of being the teacher meant I had complete autonomy over my whereabouts; I could govern class from any point in the room, so I simply placed myself, quite deliberately, in spots where it would have been inconvenient for me to look at her.

But it was different during lunch. During lunch I would find reasons to leave my classroom and walk the halls until I found her; I'd grab a stack of papers and tread purposefully from one lounge to the other, or through the cafeteria in the direction of the office. Usually she'd be in the inner court eating a sandwich over an opened book. Other times I'd find just her and a book – having already eaten, if indeed eating had been an option that afternoon. When the weather turned too cold to eat outside she'd find a corner in the library and do her work there. As the days blurred into weeks that first quarter of the school year, I grew more and more religious in this lunchtime pursuit of her. I made certain that she never saw me, or that if she did, she didn't notice that I'd seen her.

I studied her during those lunch breaks. I'd stand at the faculty copier in the library and run off hundreds of unneeded copies of something official-looking, counting the curly, coppery-brown ringlets falling through her hair over her shoulders. They'd vibrate as gently as a whisper over water as she breathed, and when she lifted or turned her head they'd dance like smoke across the skin of her neck.

I memorized the curves of that neck as she bent over her books, turning pages and taking notes. I watched the way she blinked, the way the light filtered through her hair at certain angles, the way she always breathed through her mouth, her lips slightly parted. She had a habit of bouncing one of her calves as she read, always the right one, the left leg either folded over it or pulled up beneath her on the seat. She had exactly three pairs of jeans and one pair of tan pants, which she rotated through with half a dozen shirts and sweatshirts.

As time passed I even began making it a point to say something to her as I passed. It was a perfectly normal thing to do – I was her teacher, she was my student. Her education, regardless of what she might be studying at that particular moment, would naturally be of interest to me.

By the time first quarter came to a close she was staying after class a couple times each week to tell me about the good grade she got on her Chemistry project, or that her little brother had begun crawling, or that she was thinking about taking a job in secret after school to save money for college. I'd nod and smile and give her advice and encouragement, but she didn't respond to it the way most kids do. You could tell it wasn't something she needed. Approbation and encouragement wasn't her motivation; walking in footsteps different from her mother's was her impetus, and it was a powerful one indeed.

If I erred during those first few weeks – before everything went so crazy and I got swept up in the hurricane-like ferocity of the events assimilating around me – if I crossed the line with her, it was only in making myself available to her. She was a rare gem amongst the very rough driftwood that public schools take in and pump out year after year. She had the potential to do whatever she liked – be a doctor, an astronaut, an engineer, a housewife. She brought to school with her each day a singular determination to learn and perform and succeed that sets a fire within the teacher, the kind that makes us want to do whatever we have to do to help. You couple that with an almost nonexistent support network at home – no father to tell her she's pretty and worthy of respect, no mother to hug her after school or talk to her before bed – and you realize you're dealing with something fragile, something akin to a newborn child, innocent and vulnerable and full of possibility. If you come across something like that, someone like that, you owe them. I believe everyone they come in contact with owes them, but teachers most of all. It's a large part of what we do. Without that, you might as well put computers in front of the classroom and let all the kids simply log on.

'You never say anything about yourself,' she said one day after class, approximately two weeks before she entered my dreams with such force. The comment made me nervous and I instinctively glanced around the room, glad to see the rest of her classmates filing out into the hall. 'During your lectures you always talk about your friends and people you knew in college, but never anything about you.'

'Uh... well Savannah, I guess my life's pretty plain,' I said. 'I'm a teacher, you know, in case you hadn't heard.' I smiled as teacherly as I knew how. 'Didn't you know that all teachers are basically very boring people?'

'Most, maybe,' she said, and she gave me that look again, the one that said I wasn't fooling anyone, that she'd seen more of the dark side of the world than I could ever know, and that my little aphorisms were coming across as silly.

'I have a feeling you're not very boring at all, Mr. Archer.'

'Well, that's nice of you to say, Savannah. But you'd be surprised. You know what I do when I get home,' I said, aware that this was the first glimpse of my personal life, no matter how harmless, that I'd afforded any of my students. 'I usually pet my cat for a while –'

'– Brasco,' she said.

'Yep,' I nodded. 'You remembered. I've mentioned him before, huh?'

'Only a million times. Plus you keep that picture of him on your desk. You're about the only teacher I know who keeps a picture of a cat on his desk. Mrs. Smythers keeps a picture of her dog, but that's only because she doesn't have anyone else, and she probably had a spare frame.'

I laughed. 'That's terrible, Savannah. There's probably a Mr. Smythers somewhere out there that finds her beautiful.'

'There is a Mr. Smythers,' she said. 'But I doubt he thinks she's beautiful. He's gay.'

'How do you know that?'

She shrugged. 'How does anyone know anything? I just do.'

'Wow,' was all I could say. I didn't know Mrs. Smythers too well, and if Savannah was right I didn't foresee myself getting to know her husband any damn time soon, either.

'It isn't the same for you, though, is it?' she asked.

'What isn't the same?'

'You know … your having a picture of Brasco on your desk because there isn't anyone else.'

I didn't know what to say to that, so I smiled politely and sort of shrugged.

I was on the verge of saying something probably very dumb, but Savannah mercifully cut in.

'Well,' she said, glancing around, noticing that my next period class was beginning to make their way in, 'I gotta go. Stop and say hi if you're in the library tomorrow at lunch.'

'I'll do that,' I said.

And I did. We sat and talked most of that lunch away, and did it again the following two days as well. She told me more about her mother and her baby brothers, about her mother's abusive boyfriends, about colleges she'd been researching in Oregon and Washington and Hawaii and other states a million miles away from Winter's Cove and its trailer parks.

She pressed me for information, too, and I gave her a little. I told her a few sanitized college stories, mentioned that I'd been engaged once, that it hadn't worked out – 'we grew apart' was how I put it, that sounding much better than 'I got caught popping a set of big tits and she threw the ring at me and left' – that I harbored dreams of writing novels one day.

I kept it appropriate, every word. There were lines that weren't to be crossed, and I was always mindful of them. But there isn't anything wrong with connecting with your students verbally. It allows for an easier flow of instruction, benefits the students' self-esteem, instills them with greater confidence, and engenders in them a sense of respect for the teacher, which in turn assists with classroom management. All this can be found on page one of the induction manual Winter's Cove shits out each year.

I stood there by the phone and watched the second hand make its way around my watch. One minute. Two. It'd been three or four since we'd gotten disconnected, which meant a total of five by now.

Obviously she wasn't calling back.

I considered calling her back. I had her number – along with the home phone numbers and parents' work numbers of all my students – on a sheet of legal paper stapled into the back of my gradebook. It was lying right in front of me, on the kitchen table next to my corn flakes.

But what would I say if someone else answered? Hello, is Savannah there? This is Mr. Archer, her English teacher. And if she answered herself, what reason would I give for calling her? That I was concerned, thought something might be wrong or that she was in some sort of danger? That wouldn't raise too many eyebrows should word get out, but if I was truly that concerned, why would I wait a good six or seven minutes before returning the call?

So I stood there in my run-down little kitchenette and stared at the bowl of now-soggy corn flakes and tried to step outside myself, to see this situation as an objective observer might see it. A student had called me and we'd been cut off. Okay, no problem. I the teacher would simply call my student back. Still no problem.

But push a little further and it got, if not incriminatory, at least more interesting.

The student in question happened to be a girl, and a moderately attractive girl at that. And while no one could ever make the case that I favored Savannah Bellington in class, I could be placed – for the past six weeks or so – either with her or near her during lunch every day. I'd been seen – again, no smoking gun, but certainly bearing mention under the right circumstances – sitting next to her in her little corner of the library, engaged in conversation. I'd never touched her, or allowed my leg to brush by hers, or looked at her too long or in the wrong way – but still.

I checked my watch. It was a quarter after eight. I looked at the phone, watched it, wondering if it would ring. I was reminded of all the hours I'd spent watching that same phone after Autumn had left me. I'd lie in bed and ache and stare at it like it was the television, praying to a God I knew I'd angered that she'd just call once more. The worst part of all that wasn't that she never called again; the worst part was knowing that she'd never call again, and waiting for her nonetheless. There is a terrible emasculating effect involved with being left by a woman. It is a pain that lingers forever like memory in your blood.

I had a grand total of ninety-four students. Only one had called me that night. For reasons I could not at that time fully understand, I wanted her to call back. It wasn't happening, so I'd call her. In order to render that call as inconspicuous as possible, I decided, I'd have to bury it within ninety-three others. I'd call ten students a night, starting with second period, starting with the A's and working my way down. There were three A's and a B before Bellington. When they and the others answered, I'd inform the parents of the field trip downtown to the Dock Street Theater I was trying to put together, tell them I wanted to touch base with them before sending permission slips home, mention that I was looking for chaperones as well. It meant I'd have to plan a field trip downtown now, something I hadn't had any previous intention of doing. But it also meant I could call Savannah's home and not worry about how it might look to the objective observer.

So I grabbed my gradebook and started making calls. Fifteen minutes later I dialed Savannah's number, and found myself trying to picture her little single-wide trailer as the phone within it rang.

'Hello.' It was the gruff, don't-fuck-with-me voice of a man who'd been in the midst of something decidedly more important than you when you called.

'Yes, this is Cole Archer, Savannah's English teacher at Coosaw Creek. I'm sorry to bother you at home but I'm putting together a field trip to see Wilder's *Our Town* at the Dock Street theater downtown, and I wanted to touch base with –'

'Savannah's mother isn't here,' he interrupted. His voice sounded like it was being forced around a mouthful of Red Man and through a decade's worth of unchecked beard growth.

'Oh,' I said. 'Well is Savannah there? I could just give her the dates and she could –'

'Savannah's not here either,' he said. 'She's working.'

'Oh,' I said. 'I didn't know she'd found a job so soon.'

'So soon? Buddy, she's been working down there for damn near six months now. Long as I've been around, anyway.'

I thought about asking where 'down there' was, but I didn't want to appear hyper-interested.

'Okay, well I appreciate your time and sorry again for calling you at home. If you could just tell Mrs. Bellington I called, I'll try to reach her sometime later this week.'

'Yeah,' he grunted, and hung up the phone.

I sat there a moment, wondering what might have motivated

Savannah to call, then decided that I was over-thinking something which I had no business thinking about at all. Had I not felt so bad about last night's wet dream I doubt I would have given her call much thought, and certainly not as much attention as I had thus far. But that's a quality of dreams; they can make you feel – if only ephemerally – some connection to their subject. Though all Savannah and I had ever shared were mild, teacher-student words, my feelings for her had clearly crept beyond that. Paternal concern, pure agape, or, worst of all, erotic curiosity, I was still uncertain. Last night's dream had for the hours since cast her in my mind as an intimate partner, and the image had the strength of memory. That's the only explanation I can find, even now, thousands of miles and millions of dollars later. A unique amalgam of amatory attraction and genuine concern for Savannah Bellington caused her to catch my eye and hold my interest, and the urge to protect her – to shelter and guide her – was as overwhelming as it was unequivocal.

But there wasn't anything I could do about it now. Wherever she might have been when she called, she hadn't been at home. So rather than sit and turn it in my mind until I convinced myself to do something stupid like find her trailer and sit outside of it, I grabbed my keys and wallet and drove down to George's to dilute my shitty day with Beck's.

TWELVE

Savannah calls back; intermezzo

I'd ended up staying at George's that evening longer than I'd planned. I'd gotten there around nine with intentions of having two or three beers, but by the time I'd finished the third the buzz still wasn't settled in as nicely as I wanted. I was looking for that cozy, comfortable spot where the forehead and cheeks tingle just a little and the edges of the day's events begin to dull. One used to do it, and up to a couple of years out of undergrad I could get there with two. These days it was a more involved process, and more often than not led to outright drunkenness.

So I played a few rounds of electronic trivia and ordered another, then another after that, and by then it was eleven. When I was finished with the fourth Beck's I used the payphone to call Marla, dialing her number by memory, wishing I didn't know it, wishing I wouldn't use it. But I knew that I would for as long as she was there. She is a drug, that Marla, and she can make you forget and surrender and lose yourself in the dark and the heat, and each time you do the after-effects – the disgust and self-loathing – grow in intensity.

She'd met me at my place at midnight, without the pie. I doubt there'd ever been a pie; the recollection of the key lime incident in the Appalachian Mountains was simply her tool to get what she wanted. She was always very good at that.

We had a few beers in front of the TV casually bantering back and forth about our lives, the teaching profession, her taste for older, married men. It was meaningless prattling and we were in bed by one, Marla her usual self, which is to say completely unpredictable. She was sedate and calm, eschewing all of the dirty language and elaborate positions of which she was usually so fond.

She pulled me into the bed on top of her, her hands on my hips to keep me slow, lifting her head off the pillow here and again to kiss me as though we were lovers long lost and finally reunited. It was a strange and awkward rhythm for me at first, so used was I to a wholly different brand of sex with her. We hadn't had tenderness since our first few weeks together, years ago. It was unsettling, but it was oddly nice as well. The hollow of her neck, the feel of her hands, the smell of her breath, it was all familiar and comfortable, almost reassuring in its way.

'Leave it in when you come,' she whispered, her deep brown almond-eyes fixed on mine, her mouth open and wet, the skin of her upper chest rushing from pale to pink like a desert bloom. 'I want to feel it spread inside me.'

That I made it through that far without lapsing into memory is commendable, I think. For there were lines that weren't to be crossed, and Dear God I tried so hard to be mindful of them.

But when I found release and felt my body tighten and contract, the muscles in my arms and calves beginning to cramp and burn, I opened my eyes and looked down at Marla. Her eyes were closed, and as her mouth opened reflexively as it always did I watched the muscles and tendons in her neck go as rigid as cords. Then I saw, just as plainly, Savannah looking up at me, her blue eyes wet and smiling, her curly hair bouncing over her neck and breasts like wisps of tinted smoke.

'Come inside me, Mr. Archer,' she whispered, and as I touched her face she lifted her mouth to mine. I sped my pace, held her head in my hands, touching her hair, and as I spilled myself inside Savannah Bellington I kissed her again and again and again.

An hour later I lay there, Marla naked and sleeping beside me. I replayed the fantasy over and over again in my mind, holding and savoring each second before letting it slip into the next.

That's when I decided to get out of teaching. I'd stay through December's payday, which was right before the Christmas holidays, and then I was gone. I'd find another job to keep me in Charleston. I'd wait tables forever before I kept this up. Savannah had gotten to me, and I was beginning to believe I couldn't trust myself around her.

I drifted off to sleep in a fetid cocoon of self-abhorrence, upset with myself for allowing Marla to get to me again, disgusted beyond measure with the willingness with which I allowed myself to imagine one of my kids beneath me, enveloping me, receiving my semen with her body. A dream was one thing. What I'd done that night had implications bordering upon the pathological. Lust was normal. Lusting for teenage girls was mildly deviant but, as any casual net-surfer knows, not all that uncommon. But Savannah was one of my kids, a student of mine, an adolescent in that precarious time of life where the ego and the id are as fragile as cut glass. Unchecked adult lust can forever damage them at that stage, and it can do it in ways that don't fully play out for years.

So I'd find a new job, I repeated to myself as I slipped into sleep. Out of teaching. Into something else. Savannah wasn't an infatuation for me, not yet. She was someone whom I saw on a daily basis and in so seeing found urges and instincts within myself I hadn't known existed. Much easier to simply remove myself from the equation than to try to curb my impulses.

Hours later the telephone pulled me back into consciousness, and I imagine I will always wonder what my life might be like had I simply let it ring.

'Hello?' My eyes still closed, the heat from Marla's naked skin radiating against my bare legs beneath the covers. Brasco was on the pillow beside my head. I could hear him purr at the sound of my voice in the night.

'Mr. Archer?'

'Yes? Who is – Savannah? Is that you?' I sat up, rubbed at my eyes, trying to make out the glowing red numerals on the clock.

'Yes, sir. I'm…I'm really sorry to be calling you this late –'

'– No, no, don't worry about it.' Interrupting. No good. Too eager.

I shook my head and rubbed at my face with my free hand. I was dimly aware of Marla's low groan in the darkness as she rolled to face the other side.

'I'm sorry I hung up on you earlier but I had to go,' she said, and I could hear the sounds of a distant horn behind her, followed by another. She was on a payphone.

'Are you all right?' I asked. 'Where are you? What time is it?'

'A little after three,' she said. 'I'm fine. I'm just stuck downtown and I wouldn't have called but I didn't know where else to turn. I know teachers hate to be called at home by their students, but you were in the book and I'm –'

'No, listen, that's fine. Are you hurt?' When someone needs you, you don't make them beg for it, particularly if you fantasize about them needing you.

'I'm okay,' she said. 'Just a little scared. And it's starting to rain.'

I heard the horn again, and it occurred to me, my head having cleared some, that they weren't cars at all, but boats; she was near the port.

'I'll come and get you,' I said. 'Just tell me where you are.'

'Thank you so much, Mr. Archer. I promise I won't call you at home again. I just didn't… didn't have anywhere…' she'd begun crying, and was trying to hide it from me.

'Listen, Savannah, it's going to be all right. I'm on my way as we speak. Where are you right now?'

'The corner of Calhoun and East Bay. Near the Guillard.'

I stood, flicked on my bedside light, Marla moaning her protest. I found my jeans and pulled then on. 'Is it safe?'

'Yes, sir. I think so. There're plenty of street lights and everything.'

'Ok, listen. About a quarter-mile up East Bay towards the bridges there's an all-night gas station on your right. It's big and well-lighted. Cross over East Bay and go wait for me there. I'm over in West Ashley so I'm a few minutes away, but I'll be on the road in less than three minutes.'

'Thank you, Mr. Archer,' she said.

'You're welcome, Savannah. It's no problem at all. Be careful crossing the street and stay inside the gas station till I get there. Keep out of the rain. We can't have you catching a cold and missing school.'

'No, sir.'

'See you in about twenty minutes, then.'

She sniffed. 'Yes, sir. Thank you.'

'My pleasure, Savannah,' I said, because it was the sort of thing you say at those times, and because it was true. God forgive me but it was true.

I was slipping my loafers over bare feet when she said: 'Mr. Archer?'

'Yes, Savannah?'

'I knew you'd fix it. I wasn't sure how, but I knew.'

'Where are you going?' Marla, awake, lying on her side looking

119

at me, the sheet having fallen off her shoulder and exposing a pale stripe of breast.

'Downtown,' I said.

'It's after three. Don't you work tomorrow?'

'Sure do,' I said. 'But a friend of mine is hammered at a party and needs a ride.'

'I heard. Savannah. New friend?'

I shrugged. 'No. Not an old one, either. Just someone I met a while back.'

'Where does she go to school?'

I was in the bathroom, taking a piss.

'What?' I'd heard her, but I was trying to get out of there without too much of an inquisition. What I was doing didn't need to be known by too many people, and certainly not by any people with Marla's level of discretion.

'I said where does she go to school?'

'What makes you think she goes to school?'

'You said you didn't want her getting sick and missing any.'

I pretended it didn't bother me that she'd heard that. 'College of Charleston,' I said. 'Junior. Majoring in Art. Favorite color is off-teal. Anything else you wanted to know about her?'

'Are you sleeping with her?' She asked.

'No,' I answered dryly. 'Are you?'

She giggled. 'I've never slept with anyone named Savannah, to my knowledge.' She smiled sideways at me from her place in my bed, and for some reason I had the sudden urge to slam her face into the wall until it pulped and bled. Every emotion Marla ever gave me was extreme and on one edge or the other.

'Listen,' I said, sitting on the bed next to her. 'Let me ask you something, all joking aside. Earlier, when we were about finished, you called me Mr. Archer. Why?'

'You mean before you came,' she said.

I nodded. 'Yes.'

She shrugged. 'I don't know,' she said. 'Seemed kinky at the time.'

'Yeah, but you've never done that sort of thing before, and we've gotten kinky together plenty. Why "Mr. Archer?" Why tonight?'

'I wanted to pretend a little,' she said, reaching a hand over and resting it on my upper thigh. 'You've never been a teacher before. I thought it might turn you on. Seems to have worked, I'd say. You weren't even there for a while.'

I looked at her a moment, then stood to leave.

'Did you like it?' she asked from behind me. 'If you did, we can get some bobby socks and pull my hair up in pigtails. You could shave my pussy if you –'

'Do you even know how fucking pathetic you are sometimes, Marla?'

'I know who called whom,' she said, reaching over and turning off the lamp.

I was grateful that I had Savannah waiting for me at a downtown gas station right then; otherwise I would have stuck around to argue with her, and I never won those.

Crossing the border hadn't been a big deal at all; I'd figured as much, but there's something uncannily nerve-wracking about knowing your journey is one-way, that it's illegal, that the very place you now occupy will soon be filled by someone else whose entire reason for being there is to find out where you've gone.

That's what I was thinking as I eased the big F150 up to the guard house, stopping dutifully at the yellow line painted on the blacktop, the engine idling noisily beneath the hood, full and throaty with the sound of metal scraping on metal. I rolled the window down, smiled at the uniformed man with the clipboard and the poker-face, my left arm bent at the elbow and hanging out the window, my right hand on Brasco's neck, holding him still in my lap. I wasn't sure if it was illegal or not to carry cats across the border, and I hadn't allowed myself to consider the possibility of them not allowing me passage because of Brasco's presence. We'd gone through a couple of trial runs back at the motel room, me stuffing him into the duffel bag and zipping it nearly closed, leaving enough of an opening for fresh air and some light, but he hadn't cared for that a hell of a lot. His protestations had sounded akin to a small child being tortured, and I was relatively sure the border guards would be curious if they heard that coming from the cab of my truck.

So I staked my fortune on Lady Luck – knowing she could go either way on me, lying down and spreading her legs or strapping one on and sticking it to me hard – and scratched his ears while I dealt with the Mexican – swear to God, just like in the movies – border patrol. It was four in the afternoon. I'd spent the past three and a half hours sitting on the edge of the motel bed, biting back nervousness-induced nausea, surfing the channels and watching the clock, waiting for three-thirty before I left. I wanted to catch the border-guys at the end of their workday.

'Passport, driver's license, vehicle registration, and one other photo ID.'

I'd taken care of all that before leaving Charleston. I fumbled around in my wallet for effect, then passed him my passport and driver's license. I was, for the moment anyway, Paulwyn Mitchell Bowick.

'Here you go, sir,' I said. 'You need a social security card or anything? My folks said you guys –'

He shook his head. I watched as he rested the documents on his clipboard and began scribbling information from them to his forms. I glanced in the rearview and counted the cars idling behind me. There were seven, the people inside them waiting their turn at the line separating them from whatever world waited across that invisible line we call a border. I wondered briefly if any of them were on a one-way trip like me, running from whatever mess they'd left behind.

'Is the nature of your visit business or pleasure?' he asked, still scribbling from my various IDs, his tone that of a man whose asked the same series of questions a couple thousand times since clocking in that morning, and who had maybe a thousand more times to go before his shift was up.

'Pleasure, I hope,' – smiling here, trying very much for the cheesy, hard-dick college-kid bit I was sure they'd seen a zillion times before.

'Do you have any relatives in Mexico?' He wasn't even looking at me; just checking boxes on his clipboard-attached form.

'No,' I said. 'My roommate does. He's half-Mexican – I mean Hispanic – and his sister's got a little place outside Monterey. She's got business in up in Seattle so we've got the place for a few days.'

Whether this was too much or not enough information for him I couldn't tell; it was just another check on his form.

'You'll be returning on what date?'

'Uh, well, today's the 4th, so tonight, tomorrow … the 10th I guess. Saturday morning, at any rate.'

Check.

'Are you carrying cash or valuables worth ten thousand dollars or more?'

'I wish.'

'Is that a "no"?'

'Yes. It's a no. I'm carrying quite a bit less than ten thousand in cash.'

He nodded. Another check.

'Whose cat is that?'

'My roommate's sister's,' I said, without missing a beat. 'It's a gift. Her last one got hit by a motorcycle.'

My stomach was on fire; my heart was tearing away inside of me like a fan blade. I could feel it hammering in my neck and temples, wondering if Jose there could tell. They'd know to look for that sort of thing. Sweaty forehead, dry mouth, white knuckles on the steering wheel.

The road ahead of me was wide open space, a black-gray cut of lizardskin asphalt unfolding over the brown dirt fields. There was a thin mechanical wooden arm resting in front of me, roughly the level of the truck's grille, letting me know it wasn't okay for me to pass go and collect the 200 pesos just yet. I'd had to face this back at the motel room, this possibility of Brasco being the fly in the ointment.

If they said I could pass but the cat had to stay? That there was some law against transporting domestic animals into their country? Brasco was probably cleaner than ninety-five percent of the people living there, but if they made that call, what choice did I have? I would very shortly be a wanted man in America. All through America. And wanted for some fairly serious shit, enough of which could be convincingly traced to me to more than likely sway any rational jury that I was guilty of the rest of it. I had to leave. There was no question.

But leave Brasco behind? He wasn't a car, like the little Honda I'd sobbed over for forty miles of late-night interstate. He was alive. He could watch me pull away, drive off into the Mexican horizon and leave him behind in the arms of a mustached border-guard, possibly to be stuck into some kennel somewhere until he could be taken to a shelter with God knows how many other unwanted animals. He'd spend his last days and hours watching for me through wide eyes, certain that I'd be appearing soon with a pack of Mousers.

So, if Jose here gave me any trouble about Brasco, pain in the ass that he could be sometimes, I'd decided back at the motel to simply punch it and see how far we got. I know he's only a cat, but he's my pal, and I wasn't going to start my new life off shitting on my pals.

'Are the cat's vaccinations up to date?'

'They are,' I said. 'I've got the papers somewhere in here,' – some more digging around for effect. I knew right the hell where everything was; I'd gone through this scene here a dozen times this morning.

He checked the papers and made some more notations, then returned everything to me, looking me in the eyes for the first time. He held his stare longer than I would have liked. I remember thinking that if he ever had to identify me from a photograph later on, he'd have no trouble doing it.

'Enjoy your stay in our beautiful country,' he said without much enthusiasm. 'Obey all local laws and ordinances. Have a nice day.'

And the mechanical wooden arm rose like the arm of God Himself, and Brasco and I rode the F150 into Mexico and our new life.

THIRTEEN

Cole gives Savannah a lift

I picked her up exactly twenty-one minutes later according to the clock in the Honda. When I pulled into the parking lot of the gas station I saw her through the glass; she'd been inside as I'd instructed, holding a bottle of Evian, looking tired and bedraggled. Her jeans were wet and wrinkled; her pale-gray sweatshirt – two sizes too large and swallowing her whole – had 'Kinerly, Walker, Smith and Herndon' across the front in large black lettering. Written smaller beneath that were the words 'Attorneys at law.' Her curly hair was pulled back into a loose ponytail.

She'd been watching for me and ran outside when she saw my car. I sat, idling, and waited for her. As I'd driven across the Ashley River Bridge several minutes earlier, I'd intentionally refrained from considering the wisdom of doing this, of picking up one of my female students at three in the morning in the heart of downtown, well aware that there was no wisdom involved. But now, sitting here as she ran towards my car, her ponytail bouncing behind her like a child's on the playground, it wasn't difficult at all. Suddenly there was no need in me for the decision to make sense or seem sound. The moment had become enough.

The rain had stopped, but the air was still pregnant with moisture. It clung to her hair like lace as she approached the car.

'Hi Mr. Archer,' she said as she opened the door and sat down next to me.

'Hey there, Savannah,' I said. 'Everything all right?'

'Do you mind if we talk on the way?' she asked, glancing over her shoulder out at East Bay.

I dropped it into drive and pulled out of the neon parking lot and onto East Bay.

'I'll assume that's a no,' I said.

'No,' she said, retrieving her ponytail and pulling her fingers through her hair. She smelled heavily of smoke. 'I just didn't want to stand around any longer than I had to,' she said. 'Some men were making me nervous.'

'Back at the gas station?'

She shook her head. 'At my mother's boyfriend's. That's where I've been. It got ugly – it always gets ugly there sooner or later – so I just left. Walked right out and spent the next couple of hours pacing the battery.'

'What do you mean it got ugly? Did someone try to hurt you?'

'No,' she said. 'They don't ever mean to.' And her tone said there was something final about that statement.

'Nothing's open this time of night, so I found a bench on Market and just sat there, wishing someone would invent a time machine so I could fast-forward these next two years and move a million miles away from here.' She paused. 'Do you ever feel like that, Mr. Archer?'

'Like moving a million miles away? No, I've done all that. Lived in California for a while. Barbados for a while, Virginia too. I kind of like it here in Charleston.'

'I meant fast-forward through your life. Just close your eyes in the middle of all the bad and scared and frustrated and open them somewhere down the line away from it all.'

'Oh,' I said. 'Yeah. Yeah, I guess I have wished that before. I guess probably everybody has a time or two.'

'I think about it every day,' she said. 'And every single night, too.' She paused, opened her purse and began rummaging through it. 'Especially whenever I'm down here.'

'Speaking of down here,' I said, 'where are we going?' I was driving south down East Bay, and there wasn't much more road before we hit the Cooper River. We were the only moving car in a city still with sleep. Charleston is a bustling jewel filled with flavor and culture, but in the early morning hours she's as silent as a church. The only noise is the endless folding of waves on the other side of the sea-wall.

'I live in Winter's Cove,' she said, then handed me a ten dollar bill. 'Here. Take it. For the gas.'

'Savannah, please. Put your money away.'

'No, I'm serious. Take it. A cab costs over twenty from down here. If you don't take it I'll get out at the next red light and walk.'

'Don't be ridiculous,' I said. 'Save your money for Harvard. It isn't a bother at all to come pick up one of my students.'

'Have you ever done this before?'

'Helped a student? I do it every day. I'm a teacher.'

'You know what I mean.'

'Driven downtown at this God-awful hour to pick one up from her mother's boyfriend's? You're my first this week.' I slowed and turned right onto Queen Street, a narrow cut of road that ran parallel with Broad Street and stretched from the Cooper to the Ashley. 'It's no bother, though,' I added. 'Really. I love Charleston at night.'

'Thanks for saying so,' she said. 'But it's pretty obvious I pulled you out of bed. You didn't have to come.'

'Well,' I said, 'I couldn't very well have you stuck down here at this hour, now could I?'

'It wouldn't have been the first time,' she said. 'And one day it will be the last, so there's good in even this, I guess.'

I nodded, primarily because there wasn't much else to do. It was growing clearer to me that I did indeed need to exit the teaching profession as soon as logistically possible. The divide that separates the real from the fantastic had grown thinner for me lately; over the course of the past few weeks I'd allowed myself to walk up to and, while not completely cross, certainly glimpse over certain boundaries surrounding Savannah. And my affection was wholly unilateral, of this I was convinced. Sitting next to me in my old Honda, Savannah Bellington was one of my students, and nothing more. She was a sixteen-year-old girl with a bad home life and a good future who half an hour ago had for reasons beyond her control been stranded downtown at three in the morning. She'd probably run through her short list of people she could turn to before looking me up in the book. And when she'd called me – me, Mr. Archer, charged by the state of South Carolina, The Winter's Cove School District, and virtually any moral code in existence to be a stable and decent adult influence in the lives of my students – I'd instantly begun examining the angles and considering the possibilities. It made me want to puke.

'Alternative Assets,' Savannah said then.

'What's that?'

'That store there' – pointing out the window, her index finger smudging the humidity on the glass – 'It's called Alternative Assets. Don't you think that's funny?'

I shrugged. 'I guess.' We were at a red light, waiting for nothing, the entire city freshly rain-washed and tucked away for the night. The antebellum mansions – narrow and tall and climbing with jasmine, ivy, and honeysuckle – glistened with moisture, their pastel colors brighter in the night air. The air was heavy with humidity that night, and it rolled in off the ocean and settled between the houses, hovering over the blacktop streets and bending what light there was into a hazy orange glow. Wet spots in the pavement caught the reflection from the night air and shone like miniature beacons on a shore.

'Kind of a bohemian place, I think,' I said, referring to the store. I made myself look past her, at the darkened window of Alternative Assets and not at her profile, silhouetted by the lights behind me.

'Have you been in there before?' she asked.

'Only once,' I said. 'A girl I used to date went there to get her navel pierced.'

'They do that there?'

'Yeah. Tattoos too, in the back. Those're illegal here, you know. Illegal to have done, in any case.'

'Did she have tattoos as well?' She was still staring at the window, though there was nothing to see, near as I could tell. 'Your ex-girlfriend.'

'Yes, actually. Two when I dated her. Maybe more now.'

Marla had a wreath of thorns around her left ankle and a tiny German flag above her pubic hair (fairly apropos, I'd always thought, given her love for all things German, cocks included). I'd noticed only a couple hours earlier that evening that she had at some point since our break-up added a small dolphin jumping out of a wave's crest to the center of her left ass-cheek.

'Why all the interest in Alternative Assets? You thinking of a tattoo?'

'No,' she said. 'Not my cup of tea, really. I'd just heard of it somewhere. I can't remember where.'

The light changed to green and my old Honda pushed noisily through the damp night towards Lockwood Drive, which would lead us to Crosstown and then I-26. Winter's Cove was a solid half-hour up the interstate. I glanced at the clock in the dash: 3:54. It'd be another hour before I'd be back to my place. There wasn't much point in my even going back to bed, which meant I'd be going to work on empty, my only sleep the restless hour or so I had between finishing with Marla and answering Savannah's call.

'Everything looks different at this hour, doesn't it?' she said, more to herself than me. 'Are you going to school tomorrow?'

'Listen, Savannah,' I said, dismissing her question, 'I don't want to pry, but –'

'It's probably better that way,' she said. 'That you don't pry.'

'Oh,' I said. 'Okay. Fair enough.' I let it go at that, feeling stung. I hadn't expected her to cut me off like that.

'I don't want to be rude to you, Mr. Archer, but –'

'No no, hey, listen. I was out of line. I shouldn't have even tried to ask. It's absolutely none of my business. I don't want you to think I was implying anything. I'm just concerned, is all.'

'I know you weren't implying anything, Mr. Archer. That's what I was trying to tell you. I didn't mean to be rude, but …well, it's complicated. Have you ever had a recurring dream that was really, really good, only you kept waking up before it ended?'

'Yeah,' I said. 'Sometimes I go back to sleep to try to catch the end of it. Never works for me, though.'

'Me either. I had this one for a long time, where I'm living in this little beige house on a cul-de-sac in a neighborhood somewhere, and I have a backyard and a privacy fence and tall trees scattered all over the place, and between two of the bigger trees – sometimes they're giant oaks, just dripping in Spanish moss – there's this hammock, and I'm lying in it on my back with my eyes closed, and I hear my husband's car pull into the driveway around the front of the house, and I know that sound means he's home from work and we can swing in the hammock together and make shapes out of the clouds, and then I just wake up.'

'That's a nice dream,' I said, because it was. It still is. When I finally stop running I'm going to find some land with trees and tie a hammock between two of them, and I'm going to lie in it with someone special or maybe just someone new. And I might even let myself make shapes out of the clouds, if I think I can do it without thinking of Savannah too much.

'Do you ever get to see how it ends?' I asked.

She shook her head. 'I don't want to,' she said.

'Why not?'

'Because it might end badly. Lots of things end badly, especially

129

things that look like dreams.'

'That's awfully cynical for someone your age, Savannah.'

She shrugged, then smiled at me in the darkened car.

'Just because dreams can turn ugly,' I continued, 'doesn't mean we should stop dreaming.'

'Sometimes it hurts too much,' she said. 'Sometimes it hurts so much I can't bear to go through with it. Can't bear to let the dream reach the end.'

'That's terrible, Savannah. You're too damn —' catching myself — 'you're too young to even know how to think like that.'

'It's not just dreams. Sometimes it feels like it's everything. Like every corner I turn is hiding something ugly that looked beautiful at first. That's why you can't ask me where I was tonight, Mr. Archer. Because I don't want to lie to you. You've been so nice and sweet to me, but if you knew everything about me you might change your mind, and I kind of like talking to you at lunch. I don't have a lot of friends at school, and I don't mind it much, but sometimes it's nice just to have someone who listens, you know?'

I did. Dear God I did.

'Savannah,' I said, selecting my words as carefully as a surgeon selects his instruments, 'I'm not going to judge you. That isn't my job. I don't particularly care where you were tonight except that I want to be sure you're all right.'

'It's nothing I can't handle,' she said. 'It isn't new, and I promise myself every day that it isn't permanent.'

The not knowing was cutting me like a blade.

'Savannah,' I said, trying to sound sufficiently urgent without imploring, 'I wouldn't have come and picked you up if I didn't care.'

'I know that,' she said. 'I knew it even before. That's why I called you. Somehow I knew I could depend on you.' She paused. 'It was nice, knowing that. It was different.'

I sighed, glanced over at her, saw her staring out the side window as if the secrets to every question she'd never thought to ask were written in the passing blurs out there, and finally said, 'Can you just promise me that you're all right?'

She looked at me, then. I felt her look and returned it, and in so doing saw the fire in her eyes that I will until death think of when I think of Savannah Bellington. It was the fire of ambition and fear.

'Would it be enough to know that I'm going to be all right one day?' she asked, her voice clear and full of hope, those pale blue eyes as endless and mysterious as the waters of Cozumel. 'Could you still … could you still be my friend if the only parts of the dream you saw were the pretty parts, so long as I promised that the ugly pieces wouldn't last?'

Before I dropped her off that night – pulling up in front of a ramshackle single-wide with broken redwood steps leading to the aluminum front door, a maze of old tires and orange milk crates scattered around the patch of dirt and grass that separated the trailer from the street – I assured her that her dreams were her own, and that she didn't have to share any parts of them she didn't feel comfortable sharing. I would never push again.

'Friends,' I said, 'real friends, they don't judge, and they don't press for explanations. And for the record, Savannah, our lunch-time talks are the highlight of my day. I mean it. I'd miss them greatly if they ended.'

She smiled at me, and for the second time that night I readily exchanged the reality of the present for the fantastic in the moment. She offered me a nod that said everything I wanted to hear. She understood. If she needed to talk, she knew how to reach me.

If I crossed the line, it was there, outside her trailer, sitting behind the wheel of my old Honda, trying to tell Savannah without having to tell her that I didn't see her as just a student anymore, nor did I want her to see me as just a teacher.

We'd transcended that, which was entirely my doing, which was my first real mistake.

FOURTEEN

Savannah calls again

On the way home from Savannah's trailer I stopped off at an all-night gas station and bought a six-pack of beer and a package of No-Doz. I washed two tablets down with three beers before my shower, then dressed for work.

Savannah missed school again that day – the second day in a row. I didn't blame her, though. The thought of her at home, sleeping in her warm bed, possibly even dreaming a dream she wasn't afraid to see through to the end, pleased me immeasurably. I felt as though I'd done something truly commendable last night; one of my students had been in dire straits, and I'd acted selflessly to see her to safety.

The fatigue didn't set in until lunchtime, and then it hammered down on me without mercy. I was sitting in the lounge (despite Capers' admonition to the contrary, I did have the occasional meal in the lounge, though I had to make it the Social Studies lounge, as the English lounge was missing the couch) nibbling half-heartedly on a piece of school pizza and working on my third can of Coke. I'd swallowed two more No-Doz between first and second periods, but I was dragging nonetheless.

There were a few other teachers scattered around the lounge; Bert Rogers, Teresa Roy, and Clarence Romaine. Bert, perhaps the most grizzled and seasoned of all the teachers at Coosaw Creek, taught economics and Southern History to seniors, and from all accounts could do it in his sleep. The legend rolling around the school about Bert Rogers was that a decade or so earlier one of his more ornery 'prenatal suntans,' as Bert affectionately referred to his black kids, made the mistake of taking a swing at him in the midst of some verbal disagreement over one classroom policy or another. Rogers, no type B personality himself, smashed a Southern History textbook against the boy's head so hard one of his teeth and both of his earrings shot across the room like bullets. The story went that the kid actually had the stuff to stand back up and charge old Mr. Rogers, but that in all his rage hadn't seen the overhead projector cord and consequently tripped, fell, and knocked himself unconscious in the bargain. Whether it all was true or not I'd never determined definitively, but if it wasn't it ought to have been. Bert Rogers – five-eight, hundred and eighty pounds, pushing fifty and sporting a shock of silver hair – wasn't someone to fuck around with. He was connected and irreverent and the closest thing to an iconoclast that Coosaw Creek had on the payroll, and for this I had made it a point to cultivate his friendship from the beginning.

'Long night, Mr. Archer?' he asked from across the table from me. He was reading over the sports page in *The Post and Courier*, his glasses propped halfway down his nose. His tie was loosened at the knot and hanging shriveled around his neck.

'Very,' I replied. 'A buddy of mine got engaged and we went out to celebrate. Hit one bar too many.'

He smiled. 'Had a few like that myself once upon a time.'

I tried to focus on him across the table from me, but the combination of the tiredness and the caffeine and ephedrine I was pumping into my system had begun to blur my vision. My eyes felt like tiny wires were being run through them. All of a sudden I was nauseous.

'Why don't you call a sub, go the hell home,' Rogers was saying. 'You look awful. Damned if I'd stick around after a bender. Don't you have any sick days left?'

I nodded. 'I've already used a couple. I hate to use too many more.'

'No one over at the DO gives a shit about all that, Cole. They're all too busy worrying about how to fuck up the next thing to concern themselves with who's calling in sick and who isn't. Did you donate a day to the bank at the beginning of the year?'

I nodded in the affirmative. 'That plus the two I've taken leave me with six left. And I get the flu every damned winter like clock-work, so I've got to save them.'

He folded the sports page over and set it on the table before him. He was nursing a quart of orange juice from the carton. 'If you gave a day you're fine. That's all the hell that bunch care about. It's logistics. Don't you think if they gave one rat's hairy ass about any of us down here they'd take some measures to improve the conditions? Make the salaries more equitable. Give us tenure. Let us stop wearing the stupid-ass nooses around our necks?'

I shrugged. I didn't know. I didn't give a shit right then, either.

'Hell yes they would,' he said. 'Stay if you want, but the only person who'll know the difference will be you. You sure as hell won't get any medals from that bunch of bureaucrats at the district. You're a paper-function to them. You come to work, sign in, sign out, they shuffle some papers and send you a check. Take a day here and again, they shuffle some more and adjust your leave balance. Go over the limit, they shuffle a few other papers and dock your pay. And that's all there is to it. Sad but true, I'm afraid,' he said, then took another swig of his OJ before returning to his paper.

I stayed, though. I was serious when I told Bert I didn't want to waste the leave. There were so many mornings that I woke up and intensely debated whether or not to call a sub, I didn't want to waste one of my days on a day when I was already out there and halfway through.

It was hard without Savannah, though, and oddly enough it was the few minutes at lunchtime that were the hardest. You'd have thought it would have been the ninety minutes I shared with her during second period, but the presence of the other thirty kids diluted the effect she had on me. Besides, as I may have already mentioned, I was maniacal about not arousing anyone's suspicion or curiosity, and to that end I never made eye contact with her in the classroom.

But lunchtime was different. Lunchtime had become our time, a time when I could scoot my chair closer to hers and smell her breath when she talked, a time when we would talk about things other than verbs and literature and vocabulary assignments. Lunchtime was the time she unveiled herself for me, when she allowed me a closer view of what it was to be Savannah Bellington. It was a time that I could look into those eyes and wonder what thoughts and storms were forming in them, and it was this wonder, I began to understand, this mystery, that called out to me time and time again.

I made it through the rest of fourth period – let's hear it once again for the truly sublime beauty of Sustained Silent Reading – without falling asleep, watching the clock for the final bell like one of the students. When it finally did ring, I was shoveling all my shit into my briefcase, eager to get home and crawl into my bed for the next fourteen hours or so.

I was making my way down the main hall towards Faculty Parking when the intercom blared my name out.

'Mr. Archer, you have a message in the front office. Mr. Archer, there is a message waiting for you in the front office.'

The secretary in the front office – a perfectly rude woman named Ms. Halter who was dripping in wrinkles and faux pearls and who never, ever offered me so much as the slightest 'Good morning' in passing – handed me a folded 'While you were out' note.

Call Mrs. Bellington at home about daughter's missed work ASAP.

Savannah's phone number was written across the top of the note.

'Thank you,' I said to Ms. Halter. She looked at me and looked away.

I was encouraged that Savannah's mother, however pathetically negligent she might be in her rearing of Savannah, cared enough to at least call for her daughter's assignments.

I used the phone in the English lounge to call. It was answered by Savannah on the second ring.

'Hello, Savannah,' I said in my best Teacher-Calling-Home voice. I had colleagues milling in and out of the lounge, and I was trying to shed that raw, skinned-off feeling that comes from hiding guilt.

'We missed you in class today,' I said. 'I got a message that your mother called about your assignments. Got a pen handy?'

'Actually it was me who called,' she said. 'My mother's in Jacksonville with one of her boyfriends at a Harley-Davidson convention.'

'I see,' I said, which of course wasn't true. How could anyone with the slightest modicum of decency leave their sixteen-year-old daughter alone to care for her four younger brothers while she ran around playing biker-girl down in Florida?

'Is everything okay?' I could hear crying in the background, and then, like a chorus of neighborhood dogs set off by the first, another voice joined in, this one louder and closer to the phone.

'Trevor's got a bad fever,' she said. 'I got him to bed a little after noon but he didn't sleep much. I've been wiping him down with a cool washcloth every few minutes, but I'm not sure it's helping much.'

I glanced around behind me to see how much company I had in the lounge. Mitch Landing – one of the few males in the department – was puttering around through the cabinets lining the far wall, ostensibly looking for something, but probably just waiting for the phone to free up so he could Book-A-Meeting. Landing was our resident Amway distributor and he didn't miss too many opportunities to Show the Almighty Plan. I was in my student-teaching internship when he cornered me the first time, drawing little circles all over the grease-board in my room, connecting them like child's dots, showing me the millions that I could make through multi-leveled harassment and all for only five minutes a month of my time. He was an amiable enough fellow though, and seemed to keep to himself by and large. I figured if someone had to be in the room with me while I had Savannah on the phone, might as well be a rabid Amway animal whom people tended to avoid anyway.

'I'll bring over some medicine,' I said, trying to keep my voice low without sounding like I was trying to keep my voice low. 'Is he allergic to anything?'

'You don't have to,' she said. 'I sent one of the neighbor kids up to the Piggly Wiggly to bring back some Tylenol Fever. Gave him an extra five dollars. You'd be amazed what kids'll do for cigarette-money.'

'Are you sure?' I asked. 'It really isn't a bother. I pass you on my way home anyway.'

'No you don't,' she said. 'But you're sweet for lying. But I did want you to stop by for a second. Nothing really serious – I don't want you to get worried or anything. I just – well, I guess I missed our talk at lunch today. I've been cooped up here forever it seems and' – a pause here, as I caught her catching herself – 'I suppose I've said enough, though.'

There were a couple of other teachers in the lounge now, Her Majesty Ernestine among them, so I chose my words carefully.

'I'll have those assignments written up for you in no time, Ms. Bellington, and I'll just drop them in your mailbox on my way home,' I said. 'It's no trouble at all.'

'Crowded room?' Savannah asked, and I can remember thinking how advanced her intuition was. Now, of course, it all makes sense.

There is a brand of wisdom born beyond the boundaries of classrooms and books; I knew this in theory, I'd just never encountered so much of it in someone so young.

'Oh, yes,' I said, my Teacher-Talking-To-Parent voice ringing loud enough throughout the lounge for all to hear. 'Yes, ma'am that's the case. But she shouldn't have too much trouble with it. She's usually very good with her grammar.'

'You'll have to park around back,' she said. 'The front of the trailer faces the road.'

'I understand,' I said. 'That shouldn't be any problem at all.'

All I can remember thinking as I hung up the phone was that whatever happened next, I was clearly not playing the role of conductor or puppet-master. She caught on to my double-speak and directed me to the back, in effect acknowledging that I shouldn't be there, and since I was going to be, I needed to conceal the fact. I'm not blaming her. I could never place culpability on her shoulders; she was sixteen, a high-school student. I was twenty-seven, and her teacher. Morally I'm responsible, and I accept every ounce of that. But in the final analysis let it be known that she was complicit.

FIFTEEN

Cole makes a house call;
what friends do

I parked my little Honda around back as Savannah suggested, my stomach burning with that familiar feeling of embarking upon some illicit act for the first time. I knew that I shouldn't be there, and I sought with as much intensity as I could muster for an alibi I could make myself believe. I was just checking in, making sure she was all right after last night's trauma downtown (though I still had no idea what that trauma was, and was beginning to wonder if it'd been traumatic at all; something in Savannah's tone last night exuded a weary frustration, as if the hours that had preceded her phone call to me were routine rather than exception). Or I was concerned about her brother. I was taking her the day's assignments she'd missed. I tried it all, and it was all bullshit.

I glanced around nervously as I climbed out of the car. I looked into the tiny octagonal and hexagonal-shaped windows of the rickety off-white single-wides lined parallel alongside one another. Tiny plastic ornaments were affixed to most of them. From somewhere nearby I could hear wind chimes. Someone was hitting metal with a hammer somewhere. The sound of babies crying seemed to be all around me.

Three homemade steps led up to the backdoor of Chez Bellington. I took them all at once and rapped on the door. It buckled in the frame beneath my hand.

I could hear the sound of footsteps approaching, and for just a second I was gripped with the fear that someone other than Savannah would answer, that I'd be standing there empty-handed, fumbling for an excuse as to what I was doing at the door – the back door – of one of my student's homes.

But it was Savannah, of course. She opened it and smiled at me, and it was the smile of a lifelong friend stepping off the airplane after so many years. It was a comfortable, established smile, one whose particular qualities had been shaped and molded by an entire lifetime of mutual experience. It was a knowing smile, one which said yes, we both know this is wrong on any number of levels, but neither of us cares.

'Hey, Savannah,' I said. 'How's Trevor?'

'He's settled down a little right now. You better come on inside.'

I stepped into the dim trailer, glancing around at the rattan and pressed-wood furniture, at the carpet riddled with cigarette burns, at the walls stained so yellow they could never come completely clean, just a cleaner yellow. I didn't let myself look for long, not wanting to cause her any embarrassment.

But I'd underestimated her. I would do that consistently for the tenure of our time together.

'It's a hole,' she said, laughing. 'When I don't feel like studying or doing my homework, this is what I think of.'

I didn't really have anything to say to that.

'Want something to drink?' She offered. 'There's milk, and I just made some iced tea.'

'Tea would be great,' I said, standing there in the middle of the living room, feeling a bit like a priest in a bar.

She made her way to the kitchen to pour the tea, and I forced myself to sit down on the couch. A stack of old *Car and Driver* magazines was wedged beneath one of the legs. I sat on the opposite end.

'How long have you lived here?' I asked. 'This close to the school, I mean.'

'Since forever,' she said. 'And I'm leaving the minute I graduate. That night.'

'Yeah,' I said. 'You mentioned that once or twice.'

She handed me the tea and sat down in a chair opposite the couch. 'Thanks for stopping by,' she said.

I shrugged. 'Part of my job,' I offered, as though I might be able to make myself believe it.

'Really? You do this sort of thing often?'

'What? Stop by my student's homes when their parents aren't around?' I sipped the tea, shook my head. 'No. Not hardly. I could lose my job for this stunt, Savannah.'

'I kind of figured,' she said. She looked so small sitting in that chair, her curly hair hanging lazily around her face, cascading over her shoulders like a waterfall. She was wrapped in baggy gray sweatpants and a faded maroon sweatshirt with the logo 'Kinerly, Walker, Smith and Herndon' scripted across the front of it. I recognized the name, then remembered it was from last night. She'd worn a sweatshirt with those names on it last night. A law firm, I recalled.

'I promise not to tell if you won't.'

'I'm counting on it,' I said. I sipped the tea again, more for something to do than for my thirst. I was growing more nervous at my presence there by the minute.

'You look awfully tired,' she said. 'You didn't sleep at all last night, did you?'

'No,' I said. 'But it's okay. I'm used to it.'

'Not sleeping, or being dragged out of bed at all hours of the night by your students?'

'Believe it or not, Savannah, given the kind of night I was having last night, I didn't mind getting dragged out of bed. I wasn't sleeping well anyway.'

'Fighting with Marla?'

That caught me. 'How in the world –'

'Last night,' she said. 'You thought I was one of your friends on the phone. Said Marla had gotten herself all hot and –'

'Okay, okay,' I said. 'Don't remind me.'

'Is she your girlfriend?'

'No,' I said, shaking my head. 'No, she's someone I used to date a while back. She was a mistake.' I began laughing. I remembered once her fifty-something-year-old mother, Caroline, had told me that she and her husband Charles had hoped to remain childless, but that they'd gotten careless when she was in her mid-thirties and Marla had been the result. Marla was aware of her accidental genesis, and it always bothered her. I think it was one of the reasons that she filled her life with so much intentional behavior.

Savannah caught me thinking.

'I'm sorry. I didn't mean to pry.'

'Oh, no, no. You weren't prying. Not at all. You just called up an old memory, but one better left dusty and alone.' I swirled the tea with my finger, heard a car door slam beyond the paper walls of the trailer and wondered if it was one of her mother's boyfriends.

'You're probably wondering why I wanted you to stop by,' she said. 'I know it seems weird but –'

I held up a hand. 'It isn't weird, Savannah. It isn't weird at all. I tried to tell you last night …'

'That's kind of what I wanted to talk about,' she said. 'Last night.' She shifted in her seat, stretched out her legs and refolded them.

'What you said about our talks being the highlight of your day … did you mean that? I mean *really* mean it? Because if you were just saying it to make me feel better about calling you so late, or because you felt sorry for me and it's your job or whatever –'

'I wasn't just saying that, Savannah.' I felt a surge of emotion rushing upwards through me, swelling in my throat and culminating in my eyes. I blinked and fought it back.

'There are a million reasons why I hate my job. I could go on all afternoon about all the reasons not to become a teacher, or at least all the reasons I shouldn't have become a teacher. But the biggest is you, and that's slowly becoming for me a certain kind of hell. If I wasn't your teacher, if I was a brick-mason or a chiropractor or a professional dog-walker or whatever I could be here right now and it'd be all right. Except for your age, there'd be nothing strange about … our friendship. There'd be nothing inappropriate or wrong about any of this.'

'Is that what we are, then?' She asked. 'Are we … are you my friend?'

'I want to be,' I felt naked then, wholly naked and exposed and vulnerable, and it had the dizzyingly intoxicating effect of diving into a cold spring.

'How could it ever be wrong to be friends with someone?' she asked. 'How can something like that be bad or inappropriate, no matter what people think?'

'Sometimes,' I said, 'sometimes just the way something looks –'

'I don't care how it might look,' she said. 'People are going to believe what they want anyway. It's not as though the truth has ever made anyone stop and think.'

I paused. She was right on that one. It wasn't as if the truth ever made anyone stop and think. Even when it came to me, I hadn't let the truth slow me down much. Not really. There I was in her living room, concealing it only partially – the fact that my feelings for this little girl ran deeper than I allowed her to see.

'I need a friend, Mr. Archer. I've never really had a good one, not one I could depend on, and I never thought I was missing anything, but last night' – she hitched, forced back tears with the sheer strength of will – ' … last night I felt … safe. I felt like someone cared, like for just a little while I could relax and not worry so much. That awful, nervous, sick feeling in my stomach wasn't there for a while.' She shrugged, then looked away. 'It was nice knowing you were there with me last night.'

'It was the first real high I've had as a teacher, Savannah, and one of the first I've had as a human being.'

'But what if you got to know me and didn't like what you knew anymore?'

'Don't be ridiculous, Savannah.'

'It's not ridiculous. Friends sometimes share secrets – that's part of the fun of being friends – but secrets aren't always good. Some are ugly and bad.'

'I had a professor in college who was fond of saying that even butterflies have spots. Do you know what that means?'

She nodded, her eyes wide with apprehension. 'Nobody's perfect,' she said.

'That's right. If anyone should be worried it should be me. I'm sitting here trying to think of all the parts of my life I need to extricate from my history before I ever speak of it again.'

'Nope,' she said. 'No fair. If we're going to do this, then we do it right.'

'You mean full disclosure?'

'One hundred percent,' she giggled. 'And to hell with the worrying.'

I laughed at her newfound boldness. 'To hell with the worrying, then.'

'This could be fun,' she said.

'Then we're agreed?'

'Absolutely.'

'Friends?'

'Friends.'

She stood up then, and in reaction so did I, and before I was able to consider the implications she had pressed her small frame into mine and had wrapped her arms around me. I responded in kind, enveloping her torso with my arms, arching my lower body backward slightly to avoid any sort of contact with hers. I could feel her heartbeat against my chest; reaching out had been difficult for her, so accustomed was she to emotional solitude. Her hair whispered alongside my face, and I turned in to her just a fraction of a degree so that I might smell her more closely. I was subtle enough that she didn't notice, though; there were lines that weren't to be crossed, and I wanted to be mindful of them.

'Friends do this,' she said, still holding me, the years of suppressed warmth and love finally finding relief, the heavy longing her arms and hands and body felt for someone to hold, and for someone to hold her back.

'Yes,' I said. 'Friends do this.'

SIXTEEN

The dance begins

The rest of that week passed fairly blamelessly; Savannah returned to school the following day and I dutifully went about the business of pretending she was just another student, just one more name on the roll. We scaled the lunchtime meetings down some; the fact that there was now something inappropriate going on outside of school prompted in me a fairly strong desire to keep up appearances within it.

I spent those next couple of days eating lunch at the computer in my class, surfing every dot-com headhunting firm in existence. More than once I'd be seized with the urge – even now I struggle to avoid the word 'need' – to find her in the library or the courtyard and sit across from her, to find then lose myself in those burning blue eyes and that infectious smile.

Listening to her talk in her voice thick with music filled me with a warm and welcomed easiness. It enabled me to respect myself again. After the moral debacle that was my relationship with Autumn (it'd been the over-endowed check-out girl that had ended us, but there'd been others over the years prior – far too many others) I'd lost most of what I used to enjoy seeing in the mirror. As I slipped out of one clandestine affair and into the next, I'd been able to rationalize and compartmentalize it away. I wasn't hurting Autumn, because emotionally I wasn't cheating. I was having sex on the side, yes, but it was empty, meaningless sex. Sex without purpose, aside from my own physical and psychological gratification. I was merely masturbating, using women in place of my hand. The connection, the bond that came with sex – all that which elevated animal sex to tender lovemaking – I reserved wholly and exclusively for Autumn. Once she walked away from me the illusions were shattered, and the guilt hammered down on me like God's own hatred. It had been only through the copious use of drugs and alcohol that I'd managed to keep myself confused and staggering long enough in the immediate aftermath to avoid suicide.

But being with Savannah changed all of that. When we spoke she smiled, and I'd never seen her smile before. When we passed in the halls and our eyes would meet for one perfect, crystalline second, the satisfaction I could see in her knowing she had a friend in me proved worth all the risk involved in that friendship. Watching the pleasure she took in slowly peeling back the layers of protection she'd so steadfastly wrapped around herself over the years, seeing how visibly relieved and utterly free she became as she gradually let me into her world of guarded secrets and dreams – it made me love myself again because it meant I was, at least on some level, a decent human being again. And all of us need that to some degree.

She'd call when she got the chance. I vowed to myself and explained to her that I would never call her, for obvious reasons. I left her trailer when our hug was through, more for her sake than mine. I could have sat on that rickety couch all day and talked about nothing, or everything at all. But I felt she'd given enough for one day. Climbing out of some hideous darkness and into a blinding light is something which needs to be done in stages. I was older; I'd been there before. She hadn't, so it fell to me to guide her. I was her teacher, after all.

That night she'd called me a little after eight. I was grading papers over beer on my garage-sale couch. Brasco was sleeping beside me, his tail whipping in response to some dream in which he no doubt was chasing an entire pack of dogs.

We'd spoken for almost an hour before she'd had to go; the baby – Trevor – was crying and needed to be fed. I didn't want to get off the phone. Had she invited me over I'd have gone without question. But she didn't. She had homework to do (some for you, Mr. Archer, she'd poked at me laughingly) and needed sleep.

'You need yours too,' she'd added.

'Yes, mom,' I'd said.

'Friends look out for each other,' she'd replied, which is something you might try to keep in mind as you turn these following pages. Examine your own life. Consider your closest friends. What wouldn't you do if they found themselves in need?

So it went as it went, each day meeting and melting into the next until it was Friday. Knowing she was out there and that I couldn't contact her – that I would have to sit and wait for her to call, not knowing whether she'd even have the chance – was tremendously difficult. It made my apartment darker and smaller, made Charleston a little emptier.

SEVENTEEN

The smell of oranges; Christmas vacation; Grey makes a visit

What passes for the Fall in the Deep South passes in about a week and a half. A tiny sliver of days cooled by thin winds smelling subtly of smoke and cinnamon ushers in darker mornings and shorter afternoons. A collection of oak, sycamore, and Bradford pear leaves covers the lawns and collects along the curbs, and before you're aware of it enough to pull your sweaters down from the top shelf of your closet, it's officially winter.

I spent these days in the same cycle as the rest of my colleagues at Coosaw Creek High School, spent them the same way I imagine every teacher in America spends them. I was on the road by half past six with all the other early-birds, following my headlights as they carved the route for me out of the hard dark of Highway 61. Darker than a car full of assholes, my buddy Bill used to say. Never much of a poet, that Bill.

By a quarter past seven I was standing in the teachers' mail-room, pouring myself a cup of coffee courtesy of the Coosaw Creek PTSA, girding my loins for the next eight hours. Another ten minutes and The Kids would be in the halls, wandering aimlessly from one teenage receptacle to another in no apparent order. The cafeteria, the auditorium, the library, the inner court. Just waiting for that first bell.

At 7:45 at Coosaw Creek High in Winter's Cove, South Carolina (and, I would imagine, probably up and down the Eastern Seaboard as well), the first of many bells sounds and The Kids stop their ping-ponging through the halls and begin to resemble something with purpose, a mass of movement now subject to the laws of order and direction.

They flow like huge, twisting worms from hall to hall, turning

147

corners, splintering off into smaller streams, reabsorbing others, leaving behind them a rapid-fire succession of slamming locker-doors and shipyard profanity and the omnipresent smell of shampoos and perfumes. I stand outside my door and sip my complimentary coffee and watch it happen. Precisely eight minutes later the halls, minus a few stragglers, are empty again, and a strange, nearly surreal silence overtakes the school. This – first period, my planning period – is my hour of peace, the totality of my time at work when I am not the property of others.

It soon ends, however, and another bell sounds and the monster moves again through the halls, only this time a portion of it breaks off into my room, where it fragments into thirty different pieces that work both individually and in concert to drain me of whatever energy I'd been able to muster for the day. Another bell sounds shortly after that and the monster reforms in the halls, its presence heralded by the near-deafening chatter it emits. There's a lunch in there somewhere, followed by another class, then a final bell which the students think rings for them, but which really says to the haggard teachers as clearly as a voice over the intercom: you may go now. You are free. This day – this 1/190th of your work-year – has bled from you all it can. Go in Peace. Serve The District. Thanks be to The Board.

So I give The Kids, The Parents, and The Busses time to clear out, and I pile myself into my little Honda and navigate my way home to my little two-room apartment in West Ashley, where Brasco and a can of Vienna sausages await me, where I found a red pubic hair on my toilet when I first moved in, where I can scarcely keep Savannah's voice and smile out of my head.

The next day the alarm clock rips through my world all over again, and Ixion's wheel starts turning once more. October and November proceeded past me like this.

Sitting here, writing this, I try to remember the remarkable parts, the truly significant spots that stand out, and there simply aren't that many. There were nice moments, to be sure. A parent called and thanked me for taking the time to tutor her son during lunch the previous week. Mr. Collins stopped me in the halls to tell me between sniffs he'd heard from reliable sources that I was doing a good job (this could very well have been bullshit, but if Collins was slinging it to make me feel good, it served its purpose just fine). Zack Capers invited me over to his home to have dinner with him and his wife, who was grace and charm personified. Jim Heathcliffe and I managed to sneak off-campus during lunch once or twice to knock back a couple beers at the corner Italian villa. I don't mean to imply there was nothing good about what I did for a living, or where I did it, or who I did it with. There was.

Chief among them, Savannah.

She'd call almost nightly, usually sometime around four or five in the afternoon when her mother and whatever man she was seeing were still out doing whatever the hell it is mothers do when they don't work and don't care enough to rear their children on their own.

Our telephone conversations were unpredictable and relaxed and completely above board. They'd last anywhere from five minutes to half an hour, depending on whether someone came home or one of her brothers needed something. Occasionally we'd talk for an hour or more, and it was during these – these extended journeys through her private places – that I came to truly know her. It was here that she shared with me her dreams of studying obstetrics after med. school, of spending her life delivering babies somewhere in the Pacific Northwest, 'or even Alaska, maybe.' She talked to me about music and movies and all the other stuff you'd expect a teenager to talk about, and it was during these times that she seemed to me so very young, so comparatively innocent and unhurt.

It was also during these times that I felt most that I might be harming her, though I could never fully understand how it was that someone such as myself reaching out to someone such as her could ever be wrong – could ever be anything for her other than positive and beneficial and supportive – so long as I understood that there were lines that weren't to be crossed, so long as I was mindful of them.

During those winter-month conversations that connected my dreary little West Ashley apartment with her even drearier Winter's Cove trailer, I strove to play the role of a teacher encouraging one of his students – though, in truth, there was in this particular student little need for encouragement, so diamond-hard was her focus – to follow through with her dreams, pursue her goals, put off today's gratification for tomorrow's rewards, and all the rest of that tired routine. Savannah saw them for what they were, these comments, which is to say she recognized them as shadow-boxing, the playful bantering of someone dancing around something bigger than he's willing to acknowledge openly. Of course, Savannah wasn't dancing. No, Savannah never danced during our conversations, never parried or dodged or lobbed loaded words my way. That may be why I began to fall for her. I doubt I'll ever understand it all fully.

'There was a time,' she told me during one of our longer conversations, somewhere around eight on a weeknight, 'when I thought about it almost every day. Every day, to be honest with you.'

'That's never the answer, Savannah,' I said, sure that that's what she expected me to say, wondering if I'd failed her in some way for saying it. 'Think of everything you'd miss.'

'There didn't seem like anything to miss at the time,' she said. 'And I'd reached the point where I didn't think anyone would miss me, either. Have you ever been there, Mr. Archer?' – her tone very much that of a student asking her teacher a question – 'have you ever fallen so low that you thought maybe if you disappeared forever, or even if you'd never happened at all, that nobody would care? That it wouldn't make any difference to anyone?'

'We haven't met at age sixteen everyone we're going to meet in our lives, Savannah. Think of all the people still to cross your path one day. Maybe not in high school so much, but college, med. school, your job, your church, your health club, the grocery store. Surely you can foresee a future where someone becomes important to you – I'm talking about center-of-your-world important – and you to them.'

'My, Mr. Archer, what an elaborate attempt to evade my question.'

'What question?'

'I asked you a question. Have you ever reached the point where you thought no one would miss you if you were gone? And you ducked it. That's a point for Savannah.'

'I didn't duck it. And since when are we keeping score?'

'Since just now,' she said. 'And you did duck it. You're still ducking it, which is really just the same as not ducking it, when you stop and think about it.'

I sighed then, a long, affected sigh to let her know I didn't feel like discussing it. She, of course, was unmoved.

There was a pause, one in which I found myself hoping ridiculously that she would break by speaking, before I finally said, 'Yes.

I have. Almost. No, that's not quite right. I have. I wanted to die, no two ways about it.'

'Was it a girl?'

'What else?' I asked.

'Would you like a list?'

'Touché. Yes. It was a girl.'

'Marla?'

'Not hardly. I've already told you, Marla was a mistake. One of those mistakes you make out of boredom and the extended lapse of good judgment. It was a girl named Autumn. Back in college.'

'What happened?'

'We were engaged. Then we weren't. The part that came after the "weren't" is what nearly did me in.'

'How did you get through it?'

'Well,' I said, 'that's a complicated one, Savannah.'

'You're doing it again, Mr. Archer.'

'Doing what again?'

'Sidestepping. I thought we had a deal to be completely honest and up front with one another. Friends do that, remember?'

'You're not going to let me get away with much, are you?'

'Of course not,' she said. 'What kind of a friend would I be then?' She laughed, a high, clear laugh that filled me through with warmth. I don't think it'd be a stretch to suggest that the sound of her own laughter wasn't something she heard much.

'So out with it,' she pushed. 'Confession's good for the soul, after all.'

Another sigh. 'Okay. Here goes. But I'm really crossing the line with this one.'

'Oh, hush with that silly line-stuff. Friends don't have any lines except the ones they set themselves. It's just a telephone conversation. And who's going to know, anyway?'

Who indeed?

'I drank a lot,' I said. 'I consorted with people I probably would have been better off avoiding. I stayed out late, drank a lot more, slept a lot of days away.'

'Did you ever call her?'

'No,' I said. 'I spent a lot of time waiting on her to call. She never did, so I kept drinking.'

'Did she know how badly you were hurting?'

'I imagine she had an idea,' I said. 'We had mutual friends.'

'And still she didn't call,' she said solemnly. 'That must have hurt as much as the break-up.'

'More, I think, on some level. But I knew she wouldn't. The last thing she said to me was "get on with your life". You know, Savannah, I can still see her that day. I can still see what she was wearing, the way her hair was done, everything. I remember staring down at the carpet of my apartment so I wouldn't have to see her face, watching the brown go blurry as the tears started again, and thinking this place could use a good vacuuming.'

More of her crystal, beautiful laughter.

'You thought about housekeeping?'

'Crazy, isn't it? But Brasco's fur must have been half an inch thick down there.'

We laughed together at that, and the laughter was good and real and true, and if I think of that sound even now it still makes me smile, much the way the sunrise splitting the ocean's surface makes me smile, or the feel of my mother's hands against my skin.

'It's not crazy,' she said sometime later. 'Our minds do that to protect us. I've read about it. It's called cognitive re-association. I remember one time I came home from school and found my mother passed out in the living room, naked, one of her ex-boyfriends passed out naked next to her, another one of her ex's passed out naked in his own vomit on top of her bed. I was twelve then, and I thought something had happened and they were all dead. I didn't understand what had been going on, that she'd spent her afternoon entertaining them both at once, and I remember running across the trailer park to get a neighbor and thinking how terribly strong the smell of oranges was just then. I don't know where the smell was coming from, whether it was garbage taken out after collection or someone was cooking with oranges or what, but whenever something like that happens with her now, I can smell the oranges, and it makes it better somehow.'

'Cognitive re-association,' I said.

'Yep.'

'The smell of oranges.'

'It's an amazing thing.'

'You know, Savannah,' I said, figuring what the hell. Friendships had lines only where the friends drew them. 'You are an amazing thing. Sometimes talking with you is like getting punched in the gut, but in a good way.'

'That can't be a good thing,' she said, but her tone said she understood that it wasn't a bad thing, either.

'No,' I said, 'no, I'm not sure that it's a good thing necessarily. But it feels like the right thing, and I have to be honest with you – that terrifies me.'

'Don't be scared, Mr. Archer,' she said mockingly, 'I won't bite you.'

'I may have to hold you to that, Savannah,' I said, making a silent, sacred pledge to myself and my God right there in my little West Ashley apartment that if it ever came to that I would. I would hold her to her promise not to bite.

A couple weeks later and it was December 18 – the final school day before Christmas break that year. No point in trying to teach that day; The Kids weren't going to learn, and who could blame them? They'd looked forward to Christmas break ever since summer had ended, same as the rest of us. Of course, none of this had occurred to me, as I was an Induction Teacher, still shy of my first whisker.

As such, I came to school that morning with a lesson plan I'd spent close to half an hour on the night before – my conversation with Savannah lasting only a few minutes that evening, cut short by Chemistry homework – and was on my way to the English lounge during first period to copy it for Ernestine when I realized, upon passing a succession of classrooms dark as caves, that today was National Movie Day in high schools across the nation. The three classrooms on the left prior to mine were showing, in the following order, *The Last of the Mohicans*, *First Knight*, and *A Separate Peace*. The four classrooms on the right side of my hall were running *Romeo and Juliet* (the one with Leonardo DiCaprio, one of a handful of times Shakespeare has made adolescent girls go moist), *Hamlet* (the Mel Gibson version, another checkeroo in the lubed-up-labia column) *Cheaper by the Dozen*, and *Slaughterhouse Five*.

And it wasn't just the English folks, goodness no. Head down the Foreign Language wing and you had your pick of *Sommersby*, *The Mirror has Two Faces*, *Zorro!*, *La Cage aux Folles*, or *Stalag 17*. The Science people were playing *Frequency*, *Free Willie*, *Invasion from Mars*, and *Star Trek* version 9.2 or whatever. I didn't check, but I'm sure you could have found a fairly broad cinematic selection in progress down the History and Math wings as well, and of course the portly coaches in Phys. Ed. never did anything but show films. 'Push play' and 'push eject' were the first and last steps to all their lesson plans.

So I tossed the lesson plan and dug through the library's selection of movies available to eleventh-grade English teachers, found my options limited to *The Crucible* and *Amistad*. I went with *The Crucible* because I'd seen *Amistad* half a dozen times and didn't think I could take the 'give-us-us-free' courtroom scene again. Don't get me wrong, it was great film, and when I saw it in the theater for the first time it brought my skin to chills, but after a while it loses its heft and comes across as just plain funny. Also, I had a black kid in third period named Amistad – no shit, just like the ship in the movie; her younger sister's named was Shithead, pronounced 'Shuteed' – and didn't feel like dealing with the whole my-roots-are-in-Africa routine today. Ordinarily I'm fairly tolerant of that sort of thing, but like I said, it was just a matter of hours before Christmas break. Besides, there was a quick tits-and-ass scene in the woods at the beginning of *The Crucible*, and I figured since I hadn't brought cookies or candy-canes or anything for The Kids, I might as well throw them a bone. Merry Christmas, kids. Check out the hooters.

The movie went over well, which is to say my sleepers slept, my note-passers passed notes – Hey hoe, I'm just sitting here thinking about my baby he's so sweat I think we might do it this weekend I really love him and I no we'll be 2-gether 4-ever luv ya write back sorry so sloppy – and my students with brains watched the film. A couple of the more studious of the lot actually took notes, ostensibly in case Mr. Archer had designs of spending his Christmas break concocting a particularly difficult pop quiz for their return after New Year's.

I segued from that phase of my day into the next seamlessly. I was walking into my apartment, tossing my briefcase to the floor and dropping to my knees to play with Brasco, when someone knocked on my door.

I hadn't the slightest idea who it might be; I certainly wasn't expecting anyone. I should have been, though. I should have seen her coming from light years away.

'Hello, Cole,' she said, standing before me in jeans and a white, billowy sweater. 'Don't you look yummy in your shirt and tie?'

'Hi, Grey,' I said.

EIGHTEEN

More on bookstores; Grey weighs in; Cole has another dream

It's an amazing feeling, leaving forever. There's a taste in the finality of it, in the undeniable permanence of the act, that I hadn't anticipated. I'd been so consumed with leaving that I hadn't considered what it'd be like having left. Until that moment, until the border when Jose's magical arm rose and my foot found purchase on the big F-150's accelerator, pushing Brasco and me out of America and into Mexico, it'd all been theory, a plan I'd sketched out on paper and spent weeks putting together. Now it was real. Now it was my life. We were out of America forever. Say the words with me.

Out.

Of.

America.

Forever.

Even now, writing countless miles and hundreds of days later, those words still fill me with a sense of awe and fear. People from around the world risk it all for a shot at their dreams inside her borders, and there I was putting it all on the line for a chance to get out.

But it was a long tradition I was following. I thought of this, too, as Brasco and I navigated our way down the cracked blacktop, the border-checkpoint shrinking in the rearview until it disappeared on the horizon like Orion at dawn. How many others had come before me, had made a mess of things in their old life and sought sanctuary on the other side of the mechanical arm, driving down this very road, their reasons for leaving as varied as their histories, but similar to mine nonetheless. Tax-evaders, hardened criminals, economic expatriates, spouses fearful of the fury of ex's and the justice of divorce court. That single wooden arm washes away all those sins, baptizes you on the other side of the line, and lets you start over again. In seeking something different beneath the border I was joining a fraternity as old as time itself – my compeers had fled the tyranny of kings in search of a new world; they'd followed Manifest Destiny in the direction of the setting sun, carving a country out of forest and rock along the way. My own impetus was, admittedly, something less noble, but the common thread remained nonetheless. I wanted to survive. In order to do that, I had to leave.

And for me it began, as I mentioned at the outset, in bookstores. I would spend hours at a time there, entire weekend afternoons. Any bookstore would do, but my favorite was the Barnes and Noble in West Ashley, less than two miles down the road from my apartment. In the corner of that bookstore there was a coffee-shop, one of those trendy, over-priced caffe-latte-grande types that attract everything from businesswomen in smart pantsuits and perfumed twats to transcendentalist college students with nappy hair and unkempt clothes, and the entire gamut in between. I'd walk the rows of books and select three or four novels that had caught my eye, linger around the coffee-shop until the little table in the far corner was available, then settle in with my books for an afternoon of silent bliss. The bookstore is a portal to another world; those who haven't learned this are among the lucky ones.

I was sitting in my spot at that little table when Carr whispered to me of his Alienist, and when Harris's Hannibal forever changed my taste for cold cuts. King, Koontz, Straub, and Saul told me tales of unspeakable evil tempered – but only occasionally – by improbable redemption. Stroud and Leonard and McCammon and Crichton and Greer and countless others peeled back the eaves to their houses and let me visit with them for a time, and for those hours there was nothing in the world save myself and whatever book I held. As the hours passed even the book ceased to resemble a book, becoming instead something of a window through which I watched it all unfold. Now and again – it was indeed a rare event, but was as sweet as furtive sex when it happened – the windows weren't windows at all, but rather doors, and at those times I would leave the little coffee-shop in the giant bookstore and walk through those doors, wandering through the halls and rooms on the other side and walking amongst the people in them. I've said that it started with Savannah – the mess that became my life – and that it was pushed along by Grey. This is true, but it ended in those halls and in those rooms. It ended in a bookstore.

I'd decided to buy a condo shortly after New Year's – Greenspan had dropped the rates again, and although I knew with all certainty that I wanted out of teaching, I knew with equal certainty that I wanted to stay in Charleston – and so was browsing through the financial/business section of the bookstore. I wasn't sure exactly what I was looking for, but there were plenty of catchy titles. *Buy Your Home With No Money Down* looked promising, as did *Real Estate Made Easy*, *Closing On Your First Home*, and *Home Ownership: What Your Banker, Broker, and Realtor Don't Want You To Know*. I grabbed them all and was headed for my spot in the coffee-shop amongst the dilettantes when another book caught my eye. It was written by a fellow named Wolverson, a fellow who had, according to the brief sale-copy on the back, once worked for the FBI, and was now wanted by them.

And now, driving the F150 down the center of the deserted road, the hills rising up out of the earth on either side in giant brown mounds burned red beneath the sun, I know – somehow I'm as certain as I am of my old name, the one I'd used in America before I crossed the line – that Wolverson had come this way as well, that he'd seen these same rust-colored hills, that he'd breathed this same alkali-rich air, that he'd checked off in his head countless times, as I was doing now, all the fine points of his plan, reviewing and rehearsing the next set of hours, of days, of years.

I hadn't purchased Wolverson's book that afternoon – *The Art of the New You: Recreating Yourself on Paper and Becoming Someone Else* – primarily because I wasn't interested in becoming someone else. Not then. What I was interested in was obtaining permanent shelter, so I'd bought the four real-estate books instead.

'Hi, Grey,' I said, as though I'd been expecting her, as though her presence there in my doorway wasn't any real surprise. I hadn't seen her since our evening at the Port City Java, though, and that had been over two months ago.

'Did I catch you at a bad time?' she asked, smiling. She was wearing black sunglasses, and here she removed them and pushed them atop her head.

'No, no,' I said. 'You kidding? Every second away from that school is a good time.' I realized then that I hadn't invited her in, so

I stepped back and opened the door wide.

'What brings you this way?' I asked her as she entered my apartment.

'You, of course. Oh, look! This must be Brasco.'

She dropped to her knees and began scratching Brasco, who, never one to be aloof in the face of physical attention, proceeded to roll over to his back and give her his ample stomach.

'Can I get you something to drink?' I asked, opening the fridge. I had beer and water and one can of Pepsi. 'I've got –'

'Actually, Cole, I hadn't planned on staying too terribly long. I'm usually out of town by this time of year, but I've been moving particularly slowly for some reason. I think it's the divorce. I've been positively elated by the whole ordeal, and elation always throws me off course for a while.'

'Uh-huh,' I said. What the hell else was there to say to that?

'Of course, I've never really thought that people should have their lives too on course, Cole. It makes for a boring existence, and I do hate boredom.'

'Who doesn't?' I said, removing two bottles of Heineken from the fridge, capping one. I held the other one up. 'Sure I can't interest you?'

'Not at all,' she said, still on the floor with Brasco. 'Do hurry up and change, though. Our appointment's in forty-five minutes.'

'Appointment? We have an appointment?'

She nodded, then winked. 'It's an informal one, though. No one will be meeting us there.'

'What kind of appointment are we talking about?'

'Weren't you planning on moving?' she asked.

I nodded. 'I'm trying to scrape the cash together for a condo. Been doing some reading on it lately, actually.' I paused, watched her on the floor, on all fours, hunched over Brasco and tickling his furry belly. Her hair was longer than I'd remembered, and she'd dyed it a yellowish blonde. It made her look younger, I noticed. And wilder.

'I've been meaning to call you but –'

'Cole, please, you must take me for a simpleton. I'm hardly sitting around waiting for you or anyone else to phone, and I'd be utterly disappointed in you if I thought you were watching the clock waiting on me to ring you up. That isn't how these things go.'

No, it wasn't. I knew that. I also knew how they did go. 'I had a nice time that night,' I said.

'Did you?' She turned towards me, still on the floor, still in her prostrate pose, her neo-blonde hair cascading around her head and raining over her shoulder like sunlight, her smile suggesting subtleties words could never voice, and something clicked in my head then – it was the feeling of little windows all aligning themselves for me – and I saw her in her younger years, saw the calculated abandon with which she drew the boundaries in her life. In that moment she was as new to me as a foreign land, and I understood that I would never understand her. She was without metaphor. She simply was.

'I rather enjoyed myself as well,' she said, turning her attention back to the cat. 'Now do throw on something more casual, won't you? Time is ticking.'

I downed a third of the beer and went into my bedroom, removing my tie and tossing it on to the bed.

'Where are we going?' I called into the living room. 'What kind of appointment are you talking about?'

'Just pull on some old jeans and a sweater or something. That little news-fellow over at Channel Five says it's supposed to go below freezing tonight. Can you imagine? Below freezing and me still here in Charleston to see it.'

I grabbed a pair of jeans and a gray sweatshirt that read 'USA' across the front of it.

'Where do you usually go for winter?'

'Depends on the winter, really,' she called. 'I'm heading for Key West this year. I've got a little place I keep down there for times like these.' I heard her chuckle. 'Below freezing indeed.'

'When are you leaving?'

'Tomorrow, probably. Possibly the day after. Are you nearly finished dressing?'

I left my bedroom and went into the bathroom, spritzed a little Cool Water across my neck and chest, and threw back a shot of Listerine, a flavor that never mixes well with beer.

I leaned over and spit, washed the sink and my mouth out, and when I stood up, Grey was standing behind me, looking at me in the mirror, not smiling, but looking as though she were holding the beginnings of one back.

'I wonder if you have any idea how delicious you look right now?'

This made me smile, then blush, then giggle stupidly. 'Thanks,' I said. 'You should see me in a tux.'

'All in time,' she said, then turned and made her way for the door.

We took her car – a new Nissan Xterra that smelled just like her inside – and ended up downtown, in the South of Broad area.

'You said you were looking for a new home.'

She turned off Meeting into a little alley not much wider than the Xterra. Stoll's Alley, the street sign said.

I nodded. 'I don't think there are too many condos down here in the hundred grand range.'

She laughed. 'No, there certainly aren't. But there is this dreamy little apartment on the third floor of that house right there' – she pointed ahead of us, down the alley another thirty or forty yards, to a quaint little three-story brick house. It was typical Charleston architecture, taller than it was wide.

'Isn't it charming?' she asked. 'The top level is the one that's available. Don't you just find all the ivy wonderfully romantic? It's burgundy like that because it's cold; by March it'll be as green as anything you've ever seen. Do you know how long it takes for ivy to cover an entire house? This house is older than most of America's history, Cole. And do you see all those vines climbing the side of it and wrapping over the rooftop? That's wisteria. Once spring arrives the entire apartment is wrapped beneath a canopy of purple-and-white flowers, and Cole you just haven't lived until you've made love all night surrounded with the smell of springtime wisteria in Charleston.'

'Is it completely different than one-night-stand sex surrounded by empty beer cans and the barroom stench of cigarettes?

She winked at me. 'Just a touch.'

I turned my attention back to the house. She was right; the place really was amazing, even in the winter. Hundreds, maybe thousands of brown vines thick as rope and knotted around one another had grown over the building, climbing its sides, branching off and wrapping themselves around the massive oak trees beneath which the house had been built. Standing there, in the dead of winter, I could tell that in the space of a few months – as spring rose from the harbor in the east and pushed away the winter – it would look like something out of a Pat Conroy novel, a regular Prince of Tides kind of place.

'Grey...' I said. 'There is no way in the world that I could ever aff –'

'Look,' she said, brushing away my words. 'Over there,' – pointing at the base of the house, on the far side of it – 'the hedges? Look closely...can you see it?'

I saw the hedges; big and lush and solid as a wall, like someone had taken a huge sword and cut away a swatch of rainforest and situated it here, in a tiny alley tucked away in downtown Charleston.

'I don't see –' but then I did. There, just barely discernible behind the layers upon layers of branches and vines, which would in spring turn varying shades of green, was something a darker hue. I stepped a little closer, treading softly I noticed, as though I were tip-toeing across glass, and saw that it was a big something, running from the ground almost to the uppermost part of the hedgeline, which was a good six feet above the ground. I could see small, scattered patches of it – wood, I could tell now; an aged, dark, cracked, weathered wood – situated helter-skelter behind the skeletal-like branches.

I approached it, stuck my hand out to touch it. The hedge was so thick with branches and vines it covered my hand to the wrist before I struck wood.

'It's a door.'

'Of course it's a door,' she said.

I knocked it with a knuckle. It was a thick door. 'Does it have a handle?'

I could feel Grey standing behind me, could feel her watching me. I was struck then with the particularly strange sensation that she was measuring me somehow, comparing me against some standard I would never know, and for reasons she would likely never share.

'How interesting that you should wonder that rather than where it leads,' she said. 'Most people would ask where it goes before they thought to look for the handle.'

I shrugged, poking my hand in and out of the thinner spots, searching for a handle of some sort.

'No point in knowing where it leads if I can't find a handle to get there, is there?'

'Oh, Cole,' she said, her voice nearer now, 'that's the point of everything. If we want whatever's on the other side enough, we'll find a way to get there. Even without a proper handle. Don't you agree?'

Another shrug from me. I'd found the handle – a small cast iron nugget about the size of a child's fist – and was getting ready to turn it. I glanced over my shoulder, to make certain it was all right.

'I'm not going to get shot or anything am I? You know how these rich Charlestonians can be.'

'Don't be ridiculous,' she said. 'Press on. Besides,' she added perfunctorily, 'I'm sleeping with the owner.'

I looked at her. The handle was like a lump of ice in my hand. 'You're not even kidding, are you?'

'Not at all. But don't worry, he's out of town right now.'

I turned and pushed the door open, listening to it creak on its hinges, ducking and weaving a bit to make it through the branches and vines. I held as many of them up as I could for Grey as she followed, but spider-like tendrils pulled and plucked at her hair anyway. She didn't seem to notice, and I doubt she would have cared in any case. Grey wasn't the type of woman who got worked up over little things like that.

And then I just stood there, more certain than ever that I could work my entire life and not be able to afford even a nice painting of what I was seeing.

'Your boyfriend owns this?'

'I didn't say he was my boyfriend, Cole. I said I was sleeping with him. Boyfriends are constricting. Isn't it magical?'

Magical worked, I guess. A lot of words could have been used to describe the scene behind those hedges, but for my money 'magical' works as well as any other word; when you look at it right it works for everything about Grey. She was – as I began learning that very afternoon, standing within that magical garden hidden behind the concealing hedges – the whispering, smiling, singing incarnation of my will-o-the-wisp.

It was a small garden, a rhombus-shaped hideaway sitting slightly askew off the back of the ivy-and-wisteria-drenched chalet on Stoll's Alley. We'd entered it from one of the two longer walls; the two shorter sides were gray stone, with hedges growing on either side. From here, inside the garden looking out, you could just see the rain-and-time-smoothed surface of the wall because the inner row of hedges was several inches shorter. But beyond the wall was the outer hedge, and it stood a good foot and a half above the wall, so that someone on the outside as I had been moments earlier would think he was simply staring at a row of tall bushes, unaware of the secluded little corner of the world that rested nestled in behind them.

The four corners of the garden each were filled by large, soldierly oak trees planted over a century ago. It would have taken me and two others to wrap our arms around the trunk and be able to touch each other's hands. The limbs reached towards the sky in elegant upward arcs, bending and dipping in places beneath their weight, then turning upwards again and resuming their stretch towards the clouds.

'In the summertime,' Grey said, 'the oaks' leaves are so thick you can't find a single inch of sky. A plane could fly right overhead and you'd never see it.'

'Who keeps this place up?'

'Gardeners, of course.'

'Who pays for it?'

'Steve, probably. I don't know, actually. I've never asked.'

'Steve the non-boyfriend guy?'

She smiled. 'Steve is indeed a non-boyfriend.'

I tried not to think about that too hard. There was an aspect of her that I found as inviting as sleep at times, and I didn't want that part of my brain stepping into things right then.

'It's so quiet,' I said. 'The cars ... it's like all the traffic stopped out there.'

Grey threw her head back and laughed. 'That's part of this city's charm,' she said, stretching her arms out at her sides and spinning around. Her laughter rang in the cold December air like a child's on the playground. 'You can step off the cobblestoned streets into one of her houses or gardens and swear you were in the 1700's.' She stopped spinning.

'Do you enjoy role-playing, Cole?'

'You mean, like –'

She waved it away. 'Never mind,' she said, slightly breathless from her spinning around. 'What do you think about the place? I would have liked to have shown it to you in the warmer months, but you seemed so set upon finding something new that I thought I'd better act now.'

'Grey, I can't afford this place. Look at it, for God's sakes. Places like this aren't rented by first-year teachers.'

'It's the winter,' she said. 'Winter months are a terrible time to show homes.'

'What are you, a realtor?'

She smiled. 'Perhaps I'm getting a finder's fee.'

'Somehow, Grey, I can't see you too worried about money.'

'Not all fees are paid with money, Cole. My place isn't more than a couple of blocks away. If you hung your hat here think how easy it'd be to do coffee.'

'Grey, listen, not for nothing, but if you called me for coffee, I'd drive to wherever the hell you wanted me to drive. I've never let geography interfere with a nice evening.'

'Oh, Cole,' she said, turning away from me then, running across the garden, her hair whispering behind her in the cold air like a little girl's, 'you are positively adorable. Are you incredibly busy over the holidays?'

'I'm a teacher, Grey. The Few. The Proud. We don't work over Christmas.'

'Then it's settled,' she said, standing across the stretch of perfectly trimmed, startlingly green rye grass from me, 'you'll spend it with me down South.'

'Down South,' I repeated.

She nodded. 'Key West. As in Florida? Hemingway? All the cats? You're an English teacher, Cole. Surely you've heard of –'

'Yes, yes, of course I've heard of it. I've just … I don't know …' I was baffled, confused, trapped in the middle of her flurries of words and suggestions and provocative smiles and winks. I was looking reflexively for a reason why I couldn't go, then wondering why I should be looking for any reason at all. It wasn't as if I had plans. I'd probably go back to Augusta for a couple of days, see my mother, but Mom tended to travel during the holidays herself. Not to Key West, of course, but to her sister's house in Oklahoma, a state with more cows than people, if that tells you anything.

She was waiting. She was quite good at that, timing I mean. In hindsight, it's amazing how good her timing was.

'What the hell,' I said, smiling. 'I'd love to go to Key West with you, Grey.'

'Wonderful,' she said. 'We'll leave tomorrow.'

'I can't leave tomorrow,' I said. 'I've got something I've got to take care of first.'

'Well I never travel on Sunday. It's bad luck. It'll have to be Monday, then.'

'Can we make it Monday night?'

'Monday night it is. I'll meet you at the airport at eight. We'll take the late flight. And as far as this' – she was approaching me now, crossing the sea of green, absurdly bright for this time of year, extending her arms to encompass us, the garden, the house and Stoll's Alley – 'don't fret about a thing. If it's money then it's nothing, because money is the least of the world's important things.'

'So long as you've got lots of it, that's probably true.'

'Well I do, and it is. Let's celebrate,' she said. 'Let me take you to dinner.'

'I don't think so, Grey. Key West, the apartment, dinner – I'm starting to feel a little like a kept man here.'

'Nonsense. You're free as the clouds to go wherever you will. It's merely dinner. I let you pay for my coffee the other night, didn't I?'

'Yeah, but that was more like a date, sort of.'

She looked at me crossly. 'Cole Archer,' she said in a tone that was not entirely un-reminiscent of my mother (and, I'm a little ashamed to say, not entirely un-erotic, either), 'I flatly refuse to stand here in the middle of this enchanted secret garden and argue over who's to pay for dinner. If it'll make you feel better, we can go Dutch.'

'It would make me feel better.'

'Fine. Have you been to Garibaldi's?'

I shook my head.

'Are you a fan of Italian?'

'Absolutely. Chef Boy-Ardee is a staple in my pantry.'

She smiled, her face not eight inches from my own. I could smell her cool, minty breath, and wasn't at all surprised to find the smell appealing.

'You'll not order veal, will you?'

I shrugged. 'No, I don't guess so. Is their veal bad?'

'All veal is bad, Cole. It's a baby.'

'Can I have baby carrots in my salad?'

'Smart-asses are not sexy,' she said, and brushed past me towards the door hidden in the branches. As she passed, the fingers of her left hand lingered along my waist for just a second longer than could have been by chance. I watched her walk away, telling myself there was something wrong with thinking the things I was thinking about someone her age, consoling myself with the notion that at least she was old enough not to have homework tonight.

By eleven that night I was home alone, undressing for bed, my dinner with Grey having gone as well as I'd known it would. It's true, she tended to assault one with her barrage of words, but once I resigned myself to the facts of the occasion – that I was indeed out on a date with a woman eighteen years my senior, and that this was all right, even pleasant – it was easy to simply let go and relax, riding the conversation the way a seasoned surfer rides the waves.

In fact, I grew so comfortable with her, so at ease, that halfway through my entrée – flounder, and not veal, per Grey's request – I let it slip about Savannah. It was a mistake – I could see that even then – but an inevitable one. I had to talk to someone about it, and Grey seemed safe. Seemed.

'Does anyone else know?' She'd asked, twirling her veggie pasta in her spoon. 'Co-workers? Any students who might have picked up on it?'

I shook my head. I knew I shouldn't be talking about it, that I was opening the door to that secret room we all have inside, where it's dark and warm and only the most fetid fantasies roam free, but I couldn't stop. I'd become so consumed with the situation, so alienated within it from all that seemed to me to be decent or even rational, that now – across the table from Grey, wrapped within the warm, comfortable coat of her free-wheeling perspective – speaking of it openly with her was an elixir.

'Does she know?'

'Who? Savannah?'

Grey nodded.

'I don't think so. Not to the extent that … I haven't told her how I feel about her. How I think I feel, in any case. I don't think I can. She's … God it sounds crazy,' – lowering my voice here, leaning in slightly over the table, the heat from the candle warming the underside of my chin – 'she's too young to understand.'

'But not too young to be the object of your affection, though?'

'I know,' I said, retreating, picking at my flounder, 'I know how it sounds. I know I've got … issues.'

I felt her smile across the tiny table at me.

'Everyone has issues, Cole. Define normal. You're sharing a table right now with someone who married her step-son, don't forget. Picture the limb-arrangement on that family tree. It certainly doesn't shock me that you fancy yourself smitten by one of your students. I'd imagine that sort of thing happens in America's high schools more than people like to acknowledge, and probably the middle schools, too. It's like the gay thing. Fifty years ago no one was gay. Today nearly everyone knows someone who is. Did everyone just ingest too much chromium or some such and turn all of a sudden? Of course not. It's more accepted now, is all. Imagine if everyone gay had purple skin. We'd be amazed.'

'I'm dying for the point of that. I said Savannah, not Simon.'

'The point, Mr. Professor, is that imagine if every teacher walking around our hallowed halls with a bona fide crush on one of their trusting students glowed. Or had pineapples for hands.'

'I think there'd be a lot of questions at Open House.'

'Indeed there might be,' she said. 'But I for one wouldn't be surprised. Not in the least. People are people, Cole. You can't control who you love. Take it from me. I've loved a great many men, and I've never been in control of any of them, either before or after.'

I sighed. 'Somehow, Grey, I have trouble buying that. You strike me as someone very much in control of most everything you do.'

'Yuck. You must find me incorrigibly boring. Control is such a pejorative term, particularly when one is speaking of one's love life. If you want control, bake a cake. If you want love, cast your line into the sea and wait for whatever happens to happen.'

I thought about that. It was easy to think that way when you were around Grey. Life was one enduring holiday for her, one sustained when-in-Rome trek through a path of lilies and clouds. And, contrary to her assertions otherwise, I thought then and think now that money had everything in the world to do with it. The rich don't have our problems. I was beginning to think that sort of thing more and more lately.

'How old is she?'

'Seventeen. Almost. She'll be seventeen in January.'

'Early or Late?'

'Mid,' I said. 'Why?'

'Just curious if you've checked the date yet.' She smiled.

'I've done so much worse than check dates, Grey. I've sat and done the math, counted out the days until she's eighteen, the days until she graduates, checked into the teaching opportunities in all the cities where she's considering college. I'm telling you, Grey, I'm really fucked up over her.' I took a sip of my beer, held it for a moment, then let it slide down my throat like an oyster. I followed this with another. 'Pardon my French.'

'French doesn't bother me, Cole Archer,' she said. 'Nonsense bothers me.'

'You'd do well to steer clear of me then. It's the coin of my realm, of late.'

'Now, see,' she said, chewing thoughtfully on a piece of ice, 'that's nonsense. That's exactly what I mean. You've got yourself all caught up with this little Savannah princess and you're letting it ruin a perfectly fine meal.'

'I'm just trying to deal with it. Haven't you ever had trouble dealing with anything?'

'Of course I have. But when it comes to romantic issues I've found through my years the perfect solution. I'd simply either sleep with him or marry him. Either way the infatuation eventually subsides. Sex and marriage are wonderful killers of lust.'

'That doesn't help much,' I said. I caught the waitress's eye and ordered another beer for myself. Grey ordered another glass of house wine – her third.

'No,' she offered. 'It doesn't. But maybe your problem is a little smaller.'

'What do you mean, smaller?'

'Well, maybe you aren't out-and-out lusting after this Savannah. Maybe it comes from somewhere else inside you, a little place within that needs to be needed and admired and looked up to. It could be what led you into teaching to begin with, Cole.'

'A deep-seated sense of masochism led me into teaching,' I said. 'That, and an unhealthy respect for penury.'

'Maybe,' she shrugged. 'But it's possible you could get close enough to your problem to defuse it without really having to make matters worse for yourself. The two of you could take a trip somewhere.'

'A trip,' I repeated. 'Grey, she's not even seventeen. She's one of my students.'

'You said earlier that her mother was a derelict.'

'She is. It doesn't mean she won't mind her daughter gallivanting off into the sunset with her English teacher.'

Another shrug from Grey. 'I didn't say it was a perfect idea. Only that it's more feasible than sleeping with her. At least in the long run.'

'It's not even about sex,' I said. 'I don't want to sleep with her. I want to … I want to sleep with her. Just sleep. I want to pull her into me and wrap myself around her and let her know just by feeling me there that everything in the world is all right.'

'You want to protect her.'

'Yes, partly. From all the shit that she's got in her life, yes. But more. I want to smell her. I want to put my hands on her skin and close my eyes and just enjoy that melting warmth that spreads inside you the first time you touch skin you've quietly admired for so long. I don't – it's hard to explain. I don't understand it all myself. I can't put words to it; I just see it in my head. Not even pictures. Just fragments. Little glimpses of maybes and possibilities. When I reach for words I just … I just come up empty.' A quick, sardonic laugh escaped me before I knew it was there. 'Some writer I am.'

I changed the subject then, which wasn't hard to do. Grey was a wonderful conversationalist, and all I had to do to ease us over to different pastures was to ask any of a million probing questions and turn her loose. The running wild part she could do left-handed.

We finished our meal shortly after ten. Garibaldi's is on Market Street, which is only a couple of blocks from the Battery, so we made our way through the cool December air and climbed the old stone steps that led atop the sea wall and separated the South of Broad blue-bloods from the Cooper River. We walked along side by side for a while, looking out across the glassy black water at the lights twinkling along the edge of Mt. Pleasant. Further down, rounding the corner of White Point Gardens at the place where the locals like to say the rivers Ashley and Cooper come together to form the Atlantic Ocean, you could see the mansions of James Island glittering and blinking like fireflies in the night. The air was cold and thin and turned our breath to a whispery vapor as delicate as lace.

I nodded across the Ashley, towards the row of colossal homes.

'What do you think those people do for a living to be able to afford houses like that?'

She shrugged in a manner that suggested she'd never considered it.

'I mean, they can't all be doctors and lawyers and CEO's, can they?'

'I suppose they could,' she said. 'But it's not likely. Most rich people don't actually work.'

I laughed at that.

169

'And most aren't altogether happy, either,' she added.

We crossed the street to the garden, its pebbled path lined with massive, draping oaks dripping with Spanish moss. Shadows danced across the ground before us, and a medley of birds and bats danced through the shadows all around.

By the time we reached the large verandah in its center, her hand had found its way into mine. There was, upon that first touch of skin, a fleeting moment of otherworldliness that swept over me, a dreamlike quality, as if I were watching it happen from some third-person perspective. It passed quickly, though, and when it had gone her hand was in mine. It felt natural and sequential, the logical next step in our evening.

We'd climbed the steps into the verandah – the same steps, according to the city's tour guides, that Edgar Allan Poe had stood upon when he'd been struck with the central theme of 'The Gold Bug', the same steps some twenty thousand blushing brides had over the centuries ascended to meet their waiting grooms, the same steps (though the tour guides weren't likely to mention this one) atop which less than a full year ago I'd dropped to bended knee and promised to be honest and faithful and good to Autumn, garnishing the words with a diamond ring I'd given blood to buy, the whole scene occurring mere hours after my waking up next to Cori, the checkout girl with big tits – and were leaning over the railing. I was staring into the night, through the park and past the river, beyond James Island and the stratosphere above it. Our hands were still together. I could feel Grey beside me, feel the heat emanating off her. I could feel her turn her head and look at me.

'You'll at the very least consider the apartment, won't you Cole?'
I didn't look at her.
'I was kind of looking to buy something.'
'Until you buy, then,' she suggested. She was still looking at me. I wanted to turn to her and let the next few moments proceed accordingly, but there'd been too much said already that night. I didn't want to add to it too much done.
'Well,' I said, pulling my gaze back down from the milky-clear sky, down to the houses running the length of James Island's shoreline, to the lives of the millionaires inside them, 'Why don't we save that conversation for Key West?' I smiled then, but still not facing her. 'You can try to convince me. It'll give us something to do.'

Grey laughed then, a high-pitched laugh of carefree understanding.

'Well it's settled then,' she said. 'And I'm entirely happy with it
all, I must say.'

I was still looking at those houses over there, wondering what
the worries of the people living in them must be. Or what they
mustn't be. It seemed to me that anyone with enough money to
live like that didn't encounter too many things they couldn't make
better through appropriations.

By eleven that night I was home alone, undressing for bed, my
night with Grey having gone as well as I'd known it would. My
mind was a whirlwind of half-thoughts and memories. The apartment, Key West, the hidden garden South of Broad. Grey standing
next to me on the verandah, not more than a few feet from where
Autumn had stood that day. Savannah's laugh on the phone,
the houses across the black of the Ashley, the exquisite sense of
release I'd experienced when I'd told Grey everything, the smell of
Savannah's hair in the high-school library, Grey's hair a burning
firefall as she played with Brasco on my living room floor.

Take a trip with her, Grey had suggested. Just the two of you.

I pulled the bathroom door shut behind me, left the light off
and stepped out of my boxers. I found the exhaust fan switch and
flipped it on, preferring the noise to drown out my own.

I lifted the toilet seat in the darkness and stood above it, leaning
against the wall with my other hand –

– And through it all I kept the image of Savannah at bay; it was
surprisingly easy. I didn't want her – not even the thought of her –
associated with something as base as this. Her soul, in all its purity,
was her own. It was Grey's image I called to mind – the minty
smell of her breath, the suggestion in her smile and step, the feel
of her hand enfolded in mine as we strolled toward the verandah. It
was Grey and Autumn, then Grey and Marla, and finally just Grey
and me and her fiery hair a burning gold in the darkness of my
bedroom, in the darkness of the beach, in the darkness of the dirty,
history-laden boards of the White Point Gardens verandah.

– And this time, when I was finished, there was only a mess left
behind, nothing that couldn't be taken care of with a few handfuls
of toilet paper and a couple flushes of the commode. There was no
guilt, no shattered innocence of Savannah Bellington to contend
with. She was safe at home, in her bed. Unhappy and looking

towards distant horizons for future promises, but safe and at home nonetheless. Only I was here, in my darkened bathroom, my forehead peppered with sweat, my right arm flush and full of blood, the image of Grey already gone.

Afterwards I showered, dried off, closed the bathroom door behind me, and climbed into bed.

I dreamt of Savannah that night, the images rising in my mind like a single, perfect amaranth, and the dreams were innocent and clean.

NINETEEN

Cole writes; intermezzo; Christmas shopping

I was up the next morning at nine, the prospect of seventeen consecutive days free of The Kids, The Bells, and all the rest of it exhilarating. Brasco seemed pleased as well; he was curled into a tight ball on the pillow beside me, his eyes open, watching me awaken, his purr filling the room.

I grabbed him and pulled him to me. 'Morning you furry little fucko.'

His purring went up a notch and he kicked his legs out at me in mock protest.

'Brasco, where're your nuts? What happened to your nuts, boy?' I'd had them removed when I adopted him from the shelter, and from time to time I liked to remind him of it. The first time I teased him about it some years ago he'd promptly leaned over and licked his own dick, then looked up at me triumphantly, as if to say ha-ha, motherfucker. Let's see you do that one. I'd tossed him a few Mousers and had a beer, figuring we'd call it even.

I was scratching his belly. He was purring and squirming around on his back, making sure I had proper access to all aspects of his ample tummy. 'Did daddy's little girl sleep all right?'

Cats, of course, work off tone of voice, not vocabulary. I could have been telling him how it was time for that last ride to the vet's, followed by a quick pin-prick and an eternal cat-nap. It wouldn't have mattered, so long as the tone of voice was right. Cats don't give a shit.

I'd decided to write that morning. It'd been a while – months, actually – since I'd sat down and given it anything more than a half-hour here or there. I'd like to be able to blame it on teaching, on how the stress of a new job into which I'd thrown myself wholeheartedly had regrettably kept me from it, but that wasn't true. I'm not sure exactly what the problem was, only that it was a self-fulfilling one. I'd entered teaching – a job I had no interest in – in order to have time to write. I was now teaching – a job I grew less fond of with each passing day – and hadn't written ten pages in the past four months. Because I wasn't writing, I wasn't happy. Because I wasn't happy, I couldn't motivate myself to write. You can almost hear the voice of Vonnegut: So it goes.

But this morning was different. It was the first day of my extended break. I'd had a rather pleasant and thoroughly interesting evening with Grey the night before, and had capped it off with a guilt-free rub-out session, the remnants of which I'd flushed down the toilet half a minute before falling asleep. And I think I mentioned that even my dreams had been wonderful; the parts I remembered involved Savannah wearing white, walking through that secret little garden downtown, a tiny yellow flower tucked behind her ear, looking almost golden against her hair.

I'd decided somewhere during the midst of that dream that I'd take Grey up on her offer of the South of Broad hideaway.

Having resolved that, I rose and made my way to the fridge. It was too early for beer; to early to begin drinking beer, in any case. I'd had a few benders in college where dawn had caught me by surprise, 9:00 A.M. rolling around to find me in some all-night dive with peanut shells on the floor and Bass on tap, raptly engaged in my fortieth game of darts or shuffleboard of the night. There's not a hell of a lot quite like drinking yourself sober inside some dark, familiar bar over the course of eleven hours, then stumbling out onto the sun-washed sidewalk into a world moving at seemingly twice the normal speed. You feel like you've missed a week, like your entering the bar the night before is something that happened days ago and to someone else. That last beer before you leave is about as good as beer gets. That and the first beer, the one you start by sipping like communion wine it's so good, that smoky-gray ribbon unfurling itself through the bottle-mouth for you like the ribbon off a present, the anticipation not so much climbing as thickening until you tilt, swallow, whisper a little moan to no one but which is understood by everyone there, then set it down on the hard bartop with a satisfying, not wholly unintended thump. The beers between that one and the last are just a bridge to get you from A to B, B being the last sip from the last bottle, a goodbye kiss at the door really, the lingering touch of an illicit lover smiling after a long night with you, making you promise you'll return, promising you she'll be there when you do.

Beer, as my buddy Julian says, is always there for you.

But beer wasn't what I needed now; what I needed was orange juice, lots of it, and my pad and pencil.

For Cole Archer was writing again.

I kept at it for a touch over three hours, churning out what I thought was some pretty good stuff, not entirely sure where it was going, not overly worried about it at this point, though. It's all about the story when you start off. You had to have story, or you didn't have anything other than words on a page. And mere words on the page, Professor Green used to say, isn't much more than owl shit on a hot sidewalk.

The story to this one was fairly complex, inspired by that most perfect of muses, my beloved Charleston. In a bid to make sense of my life of late I'd taken to lengthy solo walks through her downtown streets and alleyways, admiring the architecture and the yards and gardens, basking in the sheer history that seemed to seep from the cobblestoned streets and suffuse the very air around me. You could write a book on the history in Charleston, South Carolina – a city that time seems to have in many ways skipped over – and many have. I've read my fair share, but none which quite captured the feel of the South of Broad area at dusk, the tricks she plays with the broken pink-and-orange light, the sounds she emits from her harbor, the secrets she hides in her ivy and oaks. You simply had to put yourself there, put yourself in the middle of it alone and walk her streets and smell her air; if you ever do you'll come to realize that it is indeed possible to fall in love with an entire city.

It was on one of these walks that I stumbled upon an old church made of massive gray stones, surrounded by tall wrought-iron fencing. The front and side yards were filled with tombstones and other grave-markers large and small, most of the white marble stained a dingy yellow and brown from centuries of rain and decades of pollution. There wasn't much particularly remarkable about the church – Charleston, affectionately referred to by tourists and locals alike as The Holy City for its prevalence of houses of worship, still abided by an eons-old law mandating that no building in the city proper stand taller than the tallest steeple – nothing that would land it on postcards or in the watercolors sold streetside on virtually every downtown corner. But for some reason it looked different to me.

I remembered reading a book on gargoyles when I was a kid; something my mother had picked up at the local library back in Augusta and brought home, thinking I might be interested in it. I couldn't remember much of what the words said – owlshit on a hot sidewalk, apparently – but I did remember this one particular picture. It was an ink sketch of a gargoyle, sitting patiently, his blue-gray membranous wings folded in front of him, his long, finger-like toes holding firmly to the edge of his perch, the nails there as dark and long as rotten banana peels. I can remember staring at that picture a long time, wondering what kind of place something like that gargoyle might live in. I was eight or nine at the time, and when you're that young if it comes to you via a book, you believe it. But now, nearly twenty years later and well aware that gargoyles don't exist, I thought that if they did – these bended, bat-like guardians of ancient secrets – it'd be in Charleston, in that church with the huge gray stones and the wrought-iron fencing.

I began to wonder what it might be like to step back in time then, just to stop everything moving around me that moment and rewind it all two hundred years. I thought how nice it'd be if I had a button or lever or some such that worked like the 'reverse' switch on the VCR, one that when pushed would send the entire fabric of time whirring past me in a sustained blur until I let go of the button. I'd still be standing there, still staring at that church, my feet still on the same cobblestones I stood on in 2000. None of that would change; the church – according to a shiny bronze plaque fastened on the wrought-iron gate by the Charleston Ladies' Club some forty years ago – had been erected in 1677. The road had been there even longer, destroyed during the Revolutionary War, again in the War Between the States, and repaired once and for all in the early 1870's. Things would be cleaner in 1800, from the marble grave-markers to the air itself, but most of it – the lavish homes, the Customs House, and all the churches – would still be there as they are today, as I imagine they'll be in 200 more years. A great many of the people walking along or riding in horse-drawn carriages would be the great-great grandparents of many of the people living here now. Probably more than half the mailboxes in the South of Broad area would still have the same last name on them in 1800 as they do right now. But most importantly, I'd be there, and all my troubles would be safely out of reach, 200 years ahead of me.

It was a nice idea, one I found myself considering more than is probably healthy. And all of that got the wheels turning again – started moving things along up there in that reptilian part of my brain that seems to harbor the stuff of stories for me – so I created a character and named him Mason, gave him an age (34) and a job (literature professor) and a home (NYC), then figured out what he wanted more than anything in the world. It's here that the story moves, if the story is character-driven. An old writing professor of mine back at USC was fond of reminding us that every major character has to want something, and want it badly, even if it's just a cigarette. My guy, Mason, wanted his wife back. She'd died up there in New York, not sure how yet, not sure why. I just knew that she'd died a tragic, early death, leaving Mason behind to deal with her absence and his own slowly growing insanity. He comes to Charleston for reasons still not clear to me, maybe he has a friend here, maybe he visited here once as a kid and needs to get away, maybe it was his and his wife's – Dyanna, I decide – honeymoon spot and he wants to retrace their footsteps before swallowing three bottles of Percocet and taking a warm bath. In any event, here he is, our miserable, lonely Mason, walking along this same South of Broad street, and he sees this church, the same one that had caught my eye, and for reasons that will manifest in the first rewrite he enters it, looks around, then comes back out, stepping, of course, into the year 1800. The church, then, is his rewind button.

There were holes aplenty, to be sure, but I thought I had the workings of a nice start, at least. A skeletal outline of what could turn out to be a good novel, if I handled it properly. 'In the hands of a skilled writer,' as Professor Green always said. I wasn't sure where the gargoyles would fit into the picture, but that didn't matter. Not then. I was writing again. I had a story, had the 'push' back, and I was writing again.

I stopped a little after twelve, hungry and with a headache from bending my neck over for too long. I'd written eleven pages long-hand, a good day for any writer, unless you're Stephen King or Dean Koontz. So I set my big, heavy *Black's Law Dictionary* (the only useful thing I acquired during my brief sojourn at USC Law) atop the pages so Brasco wouldn't knock them off, tossed four aspirin down the pipe, and rummaged through the fridge and pantry-closet to see if there was anything there that hadn't been there yesterday or the day before.

It was a bleak scene – some deli ham I'd bought too long ago, a few cans of tuna, a dozen packs of Ramen noodles, a can of Uh-Oh Spaghettios, and half a hand of browning bananas. I don't know why I even buy bananas; I've never managed to eat them all before the last two or three start to spot, then turn brown, then black, like a collection of human turds sitting on my shelves.

I resolved then to go downtown; my writing had prompted in me a desire to walk around down there anyway, and I figured that since my man Mason was going to be venturing inside the actual church, it would probably be a good idea if his writer were to do the same. There was a pizza joint down on King Street called Doriano's that served the best calzones I'd ever had, and the church – Mason's church, I was already beginning to think of it – wasn't more than a few blocks' walk from there.

Besides, Christmas was right around the corner, and I had people to shop for.

My first night in Mexico was spent, fittingly enough I thought, in a little strip motel 250 miles below her border. I felt no great need to hurry; I still wasn't entirely sure where I was going, but insofar as those who were looking for me were concerned, I was already there. Mexico isn't known for its cooperation with extradition requests.

Jules had told me a story once, about a man who'd murdered his rich wife before absconding with her family's fortune. As I crossed over the border that story kept swirling around in my head. For that man, those on the right side of the law were the least of his worries; it was the high-priced private investigators and mercenary bounty hunters he'd need to look out for, and he'd need to look out for them for the rest of his life.

Of course, I hadn't gone that far – I hadn't killed my wife and run off with her millions. True, there was money missing, and true, there'd been a murder, but one thing had nothing to do with the other. The two events weren't related in any way. Any way, that is, except to me and, I suppose to a lesser degree, Savannah.

But it would take the ubiquitous Them another few days to piece it all together, to fully figure out exactly what I'd done, how long I'd been planning it, how I'd pulled it off. Another day or so after that and they'd likely be through with discovery and onto recovery, the Treasury Department and FBI and who knew how many other agencies mapping out my possible paths, coordinating pick-ups with probable foreign jurisdictions, setting up traps and tails and waiting for my scent.

But they could wait until shit stuck to the moon, far as I was concerned. I'd taken precautions and taken my time, and I had more desire to leave than they'd ever have to catch me. They'd find Elvis before they found me. Guaranfuckingtee it.

The next morning – my first as a Mexican – Brasco and I were back in the Ford, back on the road, still working our way south in a sort of zigzag pattern I'd mapped out a month earlier from the comfort of my community library. Amazing the stuff you can find in the public library, if you're willing to put in the time. Libraries and bookstores – between the two of them, you could find almost anything. Throw the Internet into the deal and you've got every bit of useful information ever written down anywhere in the world right there at your fingertips.

Two days later – at just past noon, Mexican time – the massive, jutting edge of Mexico City began to grow in my windshield. Above it, hovering overhead like a rain cloud ready to burst, was a blanket of smog so dark you wondered how the sun managed to break through it at all. Traffic was busy now; I was on an interstate full of city-bound cars, their drivers all looking impatient and irritated at the existence of everyone else. I was beginning to understand. The stop-and-go, gas-brake-gas-brake of the traffic coupled with a never-ending cacophony of horns was enough to drive anyone batshit. I did my best to ignore it, telling myself not to get jumpy this close to the end-zone. This, the Mexico City part of my plan, was integral to everything else. The rest of my life was riding on it, you might say. If I failed here, I'd be nothing more than another gringo looking for work south of the border. I'd have the few bucks left in my pocket, an old truck on her last legs, and a cat with a big belly and no nuts. Not your ideal resumé for Central American success.

It took me another hour and a half negotiating my way through the city's lunch-hour traffic before I found what I was looking for. I'd done my homework at the bookstore weeks ago. I'd printed up maps of Mexico City off the Internet at the local library – maps of the city as a whole, maps of its various sections, maps of every major road leading into and out of the city limits in every existing direction – and taken all of them to my little chair in the café in the big Barnes and Noble down the road from my apartment, where I spent hours upon hours studying them, committing every last detail to memory. I'd marked various specific landmarks on the road I intended to come in on, the road I had indeed ridden right into the center of the world's most populous, polluted – and for me, for now – beautiful city.

As I drove through the city, foot alternating from brake to gas with frustrating regularity, I saw the Marriot on the left, followed by the Embassy Suites. Weeks ago I'd found these on my map and circled them in red. Next would be the Coca-Cola bottling factory, I remembered, and ten minutes later there indeed was the massive, Nafta-inspired Coca-Cola bottling factory, where minimum wage was $1.09 an hour and the minimum age for employment was zygote. If my maps had been correct – and so far they'd been dead-on – I'd come in another few miles upon a Royal Crown Hotel on the right, followed by a tobacco factory on the left, and a clock company, also on the left. I'd need to turn right two blocks past the clock company, follow that road through the textile district and out the other side, take another right at the first intersection beyond the textile district, then travel about a block or so. It'd be there on the right. The Mexico City International Bank and Loan.

If my plan worked out, the rainbow would end for me there.

'I'll pass,' Julian said. I was in the lobby shitter at The Omni downtown – a massive mega-hotel in which the likes of Bruce Willis and Mel Gibson stay when they're in town making movies – tapping the old hogleg off with one hand, holding my cellphone to my ear with the other. I was trying to convince Jules to meet me downtown for a few beers.

'Pass? You can't pass. You pass and it's three in a row. Three in a row and you're on Cole restriction.'

'Three in a row? How d'you figure?'

'Racquetball last Wednesday…?'

'I was sick.'

'You weren't sick. Don't give me that.'

'I was so sick I couldn't fucking stand. I had snot the color of ripe piss pouring out my nose. I'm not kidding, man. Thicker than come. I was puking blood, for God's sake.'

'In any case it's Christmas, and I know you haven't finished your shopping any more than I have.'

'Right. I'm getting you a box of tampons for that pussy of yours

'Dude.'

'Why can't you shop alone?'

'I thought we'd knock a few back afterwards.'

'You can do that alone, too. I drink alone all the time. It tastes just as good. Buzz comes the same time, too.'

'Are you coming down here or not?'

'Can't do it.'

'Fucking hell, Jules.'

'Sorry, Colon.'

'Come on. First round's on me. And no cheap stuff. Guinness. Beck's. The good shit. All dark.'

'No can do, bro. I'm fucking exhausted. I got in at six this morning.'

'Big night?'

Yawn. 'Big enough.'

'Jules –' letting his name hang in the air like that, hoping shame might work where verbal coercion had failed. It didn't.

'What the hell are you doing up so early, anyway? Isn't this the first day of your big stretch?'

'Yeah. I guess I'm inspired. I started writing again today.'

'Hey, good deal. Congrats. Any good?'

'Good enough for now. Good to be writing again, in any case.'

'I'm happy for you, bro. I really am. But right now I'm also hung-over like a whore and I need another ten hours' sleep. What are doing tonight?'

'Dunno.'

'A couple-few folks at the station are having a party. Interns, production assistants, all sorts of young ass. You interested?'

I wasn't leaving for Florida with Grey until Monday; I had plans for tomorrow – more on that in a bit – so tonight was wide open for me.

'Yeah, sure. What the hell? Your little Baptist letting you out?'

'We're having problems. She bumped into me at tango last night.'

'She see you drinking?'

'It was between rounds. I was puking at the bar.'

'Imagine that didn't go over real well, huh?'

'Like Nazis in Palm Beach. She was a little stifling, man. What the hell. Probably for the best. Oh, yeah, before I forget. Something you might want to know. Marla.'

'Jules, before you finish, let me get it on record for the fifty-fucking-fifth time that that girl could chug every cock in Charleston and email me jpegs of all the money-shots and I wouldn't care enough to sprout a hard-on.'

'All right, man. Just wanted to let you know. She's tight with one of the producers there. Hangs out at the station all the time.' Another yawn. 'Not like I didn't see enough of the bitch when you were dating her.'

'She's a devious, calculating sociopath. I pity your pal.'

'He's not my pal. He's just some guy I work with. It doesn't make a fuck at any rate. I just didn't want you to be there and get Pearl-Harbored. You know how old ghosts can do that.'

'I appreciate your thoughtfulness, Julie. Now, you coming down here or what?'

'Yeah, sure,' he said. 'I'll be right down. Hold your fucking breath.'

And the line went dead.

It was just as well. I had my Christmas shopping to do, and while I might have tried to wrap it all behind the veneer of buying gifts for my mother, my boss, a couple of my co-workers, even Grey (I couldn't very well tag-along with her to Key West empty-handed, and, truth be told, I really did enjoy myself when I was with her), my main purpose in being there was in preparation for tomorrow. I'd begun assembling the idea last night during dinner with Grey, then some more as we strolled hand-in-hand through White Point Gardens. It had probably been present in some form during my white-and-gold dreams of Savannah last night, and it was definitely there now.

All it would take, as Grey was fond of saying, is money. I had none, but I had something just as good, at least short-term. And the intro. rate was only 9.9%, to boot.

So I sidled up against the crystal-clear glass case inside the King Street jewelers shop, leaning my weight into it a bit as I gazed down into all the gleaming diamonds and gold. When the saleswoman made her way to me I pointed out the piece I was looking at.

'The locket?' She said pleasantly. 'A lovely item, sir. It's eighteen-carat gold, hand-crafted right here on the premises in our lab, and inlaid along the perimeter with fourteen tiny individual diamonds measuring more than three-quarters of a carat.'

'Does it open?' I asked as she removed the golden locket from a bed of forest green velvet.

'It does,' she said, opening it. 'Your sweetheart can keep a picture of the two of you together in here. Is it for your wife?'

'No, no,' I said. 'I'm not married.' I didn't offer any more than that.

'Well, whoever she is, she must be very special. That's one of our more valuable pieces of neckwear. She'll be the envy of all her friends when she's wearing it.'

'She is very special,' I said, holding the locket, turning it over in my hand. It was flawless; smooth and delicate and seemingly perfectly made. I'll spare you the comparisons.

'I'll take it,' I said. The saleswoman's face brightened into a well-practiced smile.

'Wonderful,' she said. 'Will this be cash or charge?'

I dropped my credit card – $5,000 limit, $200 balance, give or take – atop the glass jewelry case and smiled back at her.

'Credit, of course.'

'Shall I wrap this for you?'

'Please. And do you have any of those nice velvet boxes?'

'Of course,' she said, and disappeared into the back with Savannah's Christmas present.

It occurred to me then that I hadn't even bothered to look at the price, which was probably a good thing. When she handed me the receipt I read the numbers with a kind of resigned euphoria. Thirty-one hundred dollars. Over three grand. On one Christmas present. For a student. An underage student. It was ridiculous and irresponsible and probably on some level quite sick, but it was also liberating as well. I was dropping three grand on a piece of jewelry on a whim for a girl I carried a secret crush for – a crush, incidentally, that would cost me my job were it ever discovered. But none of that mattered right then. I was buying the necklace. Money wasn't stopping me. Price wasn't an issue. For just a few seconds now, and for a few hours once I gave it to her (provided my plans for tomorrow worked out) I was living like those folks across the Cooper lived, the ones whose houses you can see twinkling through the vapor of your breath on cold, clear nights downtown, the ones whose mansions lined the coast of James Island like monuments. For just those few moments I tasted what it'd be like to be rich, to purchase without adding and figuring in my head, to buy without rationalizing, to spend as though money really was just paper and plastic, and I found the taste agreeable.

The rest of the afternoon went along fine. I walked from the jewelry store – the absurd sense of euphoria, purchasing the necklace having dwindled some, but only some – to Mason's church and spent the better part of an hour skulking about the premises, breathing in the ambiance, studying the specific angles and planes and contours of the building itself, the surrounding graveyard, the age-old iron fencing running its perimeter. How would Mason feel as he came upon this church, memories of his cherished Dyanna careening through his mind like razors, cutting the viscera of his soul?

I would move worlds for her, he'd think as he stood here, staring at this church, pulling the humid sea-air into his lungs, his face beginning to burn and his eyes filling.

I would move worlds for you, Dyanna. I would murder children and steal blood from God for just one more day with you.

And it is here, in his moment of greatest despair, that he'd decide to venture into the church, pushed along by forces unknown – perhaps the spirit of his beloved wife, nudging him from some other world.

I was struck again with the urge to write, to simply sit and write and write until my hand cramped and my head throbbed with eyestrain. Mason's story had me under its spell, and it's there, as any writer will tell you, that the really good stuff starts to happen. When a story grabs and holds and refuses to leave the writer alone, it's almost as though he's merely along for the ride, just another watcher as the players and events unfold themselves before him the way the secrets of the sunset unfold for those who take the time to watch.

So I left Mason's church and my downtown and went back to Brasco and my little apartment, on fire with a hunger to see where the story would take me. I spent the next seven hours hunched over my tablet. Twenty-one pages later and I'd written Mason, Dyanna, and their wonderful history into existence. When I finally slid my chair back and stood from the table, I understood both of them – the Kirkleys – as well as if I'd grown up with them. I knew how they met, how they lived, how they loved. I was there for their wedding, for Dyanna's graduation from grad. school, for Mason's appendectomy. I watched them become a them.

I could have written for hours more, but Jules called with directions to the party, and I felt it best to leave them – Mason and his cherished Dyanna – for now; I didn't want to overstay my welcome and run the risk of their tiring of me.

And too, Jules had mentioned something about Marla being at the party tonight, and some part of me that I've never been terribly proud of was hoping she would be. It'd give me the chance to show my indifference, which was important to me. Of equal importance is the fact that I really did want to be indifferent to her, though by virtue of that wanting I guess it's pretty obvious that I wasn't.

TWENTY

Party with Jules; intermezzo; Marla and Cole catch up

The party went well, as parties are meant to go, but there are specifics from that Friday night that bear mentioning.

Jules and I pulled up in his fire-engine-red convertible Del Sol – a little pig-tail of a car, the type you might expect to see twin blondes zooming by in on their way to the beach, their fiery yellow manes whipping in the air behind them, their skin a copper bronze, the edges of their pearl-white tan-lines glowing beside their spaghetti-string straps – at just after ten that night. We'd stopped off at a little place down the street from my apartment called Rpub, the R having one of those clever cross-slashes like you see on prescription drug containers, the message here apparently being that whatever it is that ails you, come on in, we've got enough beer to fix it.

Jules and I had only had a couple before making our way over to the party at Mt. Pleasant. It was being thrown by one of the directors at the news station where Jules worked – someone was having a birthday or had gotten promoted or had taken a really nice shit or somesuch. That bunch didn't need much reason to get together and drink. Newsies love to get tanked. They love to fuck, too, which is the main reason Julian counted himself among their numbers. He'd been a copy-editor for Peachtree Press in Atlanta briefly, right out of college, then had gone back to pick up his Master's in Journalism. I remember when I asked him why once, he'd said through his big Mexican grin, 'Lots of pussy in TV, amigo. Lots of it.'

He'd been right, too. For a brief time after Autumn I dated one of his colleagues, a cute, perky little weekend anchor fresh out of college and ready for the world. It was doomed from the start for a number of reasons, but her ego and attitude were near the top of the list. You've never seen an industry of people more consumed by their looks, or more willingly seduced by their own image on screen, convincing themselves as they held their microphones or scripts and enunciated their names ever-so-clearly into the camera, that yes, they really were famous and talented and heads above the rest of the class when it came to everything that made one matter. They had shiny faces and shiny resumés and anyone they happened to suck, fuck, or simply wave hello to on their way to a top-20 market they were doing a favor. Most of them had shit for salaries, worse even than teachers, but it wasn't money that pulled them in. It was the juice, the electric buzz they generated and fed upon and believed could be seen by others. Kiss them and you could taste their self-importance like dried perfume or deodorant; lick their skin and it was as distinct as crystallized urine not fully wiped from the pudendum.

But man could they throw a party. Jules and I made our way through the front door of someone's trendy Mt. Pleasant condo, edging our way on a zigzag course for the kitchen, Jules stopping every second or third person to hug or be hugged by someone he either worked with or used to. That's another thing about the news-crowd; they go through jobs like condoms.

We finally reached the kitchen and navigated our way towards the sink. Someone had dumped in a few bags of ice and what looked like forty or fifty bottles of beer. It was domestic, but it was free, so I two-fisted a couple and proceeded to mingle. I bumped into a girl I'd met through Jules a couple months ago at a hip little appetizer-only restaurant over on East Bay called Meritage. She'd been with her husband at the time, I thought, but as far as I could see she was flying solo tonight.

As she recognized my face in the crowd and began approaching I racked my memory for her name. A-something. Ann, maybe, but not.

'Cole?' – long, affected scream here, as if I'd just come back from war and had been presumed KIA – 'How are you?' She threw her arms around my neck and gave me a hug. I wrapped each of my beer-filled hands around her back and tried not to look as awkward as it felt.

'It's been so long,' she said. 'What have you been up to?'

I shrugged. I always hate that fucking question. What are folks looking for with that one? Hey, you know, curing cancer, breaching racial divides, feeding the hungry. How 'bout you?

'Oh, you know, little of this, little of that.'

She laughed, again laying the affectation on nice and heavy.

'God,' she said around a mouthful of bluish smoke, 'we haven't spoken since, what, –'

'Meritage –'

'Meritage, right –'

'You were with …' snapping of the fingers here …

'Oh, Elliot,' she shook her head and stuck her tongue out in a way that made me think of a little girl biting into her first lemon. 'That's totally history.'

'Sorry to hear that.'

She waved my condolences away. 'You and my mother both. He was just so phony, though. Everything was him him him. His beachfront house, his stock portfolio, his next big thing. I don't know why we ever got married. Never do that, Cole,' she said.

'Get married?'

She nodded. 'It's not all it's cracked up to be.'

I nodded. 'How long were the two of you together?'

'Six, seven months I guess.'

'They're calling those starter-marriages now,' I said. 'Like starter houses. Kind of a holding zone until you trade up.'

She laughed again, and it didn't bother me as much this time because I was sort of trying to be funny. That starter-marriage bit was pretty good, I thought.

I took a long pull from my Bud Light and followed it with another, longer one. What was her damn name?

'Did you ever get that novel of yours published?' Puff, hold, blow out.

'Not yet,' I said. 'Got a few decent leads. A couple of agents are reading it; one of them looks pretty promising. It's a long process on both ends, though, the writing and the publishing…' I'd lost her at this point. She was still standing there in front of me, still holding her cigarette between her thin, manicured fingers, but her eyes had ticked over to my right a couple clicks, at whomever it was moving his or her way behind me. She was negotiating for better real estate.

'– and that's when I decided what the hell,' I said, 'I'll just fuck the little hamster right in his furry little ass and see if he calls me in the morning.'

Her eyes found mine again and she nodded understanding, as

if to say yes, hamsters did indeed have furry little asses, and they can be particularly ornery when it comes to calling after you fuck them in it.

'Cole, would you excuse me for just a second? It was great seeing you again. Don't be such a stranger and good luck with that book …' She trailed off, whatever her name was, to repeat the routine with someone else. Old Ann but not. Sure am glad I got to see her.

As I was meandering towards the living room I saw Jules chatting up some blonde chick I recognized from the evening news, Priscella Ravenel – of the Charleston Ravenels, case you give a shit – and apparently doing fairly well with it. They were tucked away into a corner of the dining nook, the both of them smoking and laughing and carrying on over their beers like the Masters of the Universe they were certain they were meant to be. He saw me and threw me a nod of the head; I returned it, finished off one of my beers, started in on the second one and began looking around for something stronger.

There was a girl walking around, big and meaty looking and therefore definitely not on camera – maybe a director or producer or something – carrying a tray of twenty or thirty multi-colored Jell-O shots like they were hors d'oevres. Hands appeared from all over like fluttering little birds over breadcrumbs in the park. I reached in, grabbed two and sucked them back, and grabbed two more. I was on my way towards the couch when Jules appeared in front of me – no sign of Princess Ravenel, as the other newsies liked to call her – with a joint the size of a small cigar.

He was holding in a mouthful of the acrid smoke, passing the blunt to me.

I shook my head. He shrugged, let the smoke out. I heard someone off behind me call his name. He glanced over in their direction and nodded.

'You all right?'

I nodded, and killed the other two Jell-O shots. 'My fly open or something?'

'You were talking to Angie,' he said. 'Thought maybe you were working it a little there. She's recently divorced, you know.'

'Angie. That's her fucking name. I kept wanting to say Ann.'

He took another pull off the joint. People milled past, behind him, behind me, a few pushing their way between us. A medley of voices rose like heat off hot pavement and meshed into one another, into sounds as incomprehensible as foreign music. I saw Angie Ann-but-not talking to the Jell-O shooter girl, and wondered if I could get her attention. The Jell-O shooter girl, not Angie.

'How you making out with the Princess?'

He shrugged. 'Hey, you know how these girls are. Every one of 'em's got a honey-lined cunt and tits made of sugar.' Another couple tokes on the old lettuce-log. 'They operate off their own agenda.'

I nodded. That they did. Off to the left, in the living room that I was trying to reach before someone else lowered their ass into my spot on the couch, the stereo cranked on. Pink Floyd for a second, followed by the Grateful Dead, then Led Zeppelin as whoever choosing CD's finally found one they approved of.

'Remember Lynn?' he asked. 'Long brown hair, green eyes. You used to ask about her whenever you saw her on.'

I remembered. She had arms like steel pipes, and wanted you to know it. She was always doing the news – that's the industry term, 'doing the news,' as if the news simply wouldn't have happened had they not deigned to get out of bed that morning – in these sleeve-less blouses so you could see her arms ripple and pulsate when she squeezed the mike just so. I always kind of liked watching that.

'She's around here somewhere,' Jules offered. When I nodded noncommittally, he blew a hefty plume of pot-smoke into my face.

'What's the matter with you lately?' he asked. 'You get your mojo back and all of a sudden it's this Thomas Pynchon anti-social routine.'

My turn to shrug. 'I don't know, really. I'm not into it for some reason.'

'You're probably sick. It's going around, case you hadn't heard. I tried telling you that this morning.'

'Just sort of blah. Not really down, but not not, either.'

He looked at me. 'Fucked up, dude. There's tons of pocket wandering around this place and you're blah. You're queer as folk is what you are.'

'Don't let me hold you back, bitch,' I said, finishing my second beer. I wanted more, lots more, and right now. I wanted to skip the drinking and just mainline it into my veins, like the boys from Motley Crue back in the 80's. Help me relax, stop thinking about Savannah and what I had planned for tomorrow.

'You worried about the whore?'

'Dude,' I said, 'why do I have to keep telling you –'

He held his hands up. 'Fine, fine, I wasn't implying anything. You're just acting like a kid who watched Old Yeller for the first time. Cheer up. Have a couple beers.'

'Now you're talking,' I said. 'Why don't you stake out some real estate in the living room and I'll scrounge up enough alcohol to make the ugly pretty.'

I scooped ten beers out of the sink, stuffing one into each of my front khaki pockets, two down my pants next to Amadeus and the doorbells, and three dangling like ripe fruit from each hand. Five minutes later I'd reached Jules and the couch. He'd managed to get a couple more Jell-O-shots, and we flicked those back with the cursory twist of the wrist that said you're in this one for the long haul. You didn't pile seven beers on top of five Jell-O-shooters and plan to leave anytime soon. It wouldn't be enough to get me drunk – the night I'd graduated college I had thirty-two beers in one wonderful sitting at a tittie-club called Tailspins – but it'd do the trick I was looking for. Rub the edges down a bit, smooth things out some.

And it was working famously, too; Jules and I kept our spot on the couch and listened to the Zeppelin on continuous play, drinking the beers and talking to whoever passed by. I'd smile, raise my beer a bit, make idle chit-chat for a while, finish my beer, start another, and the whole cycle would repeat itself. We progressed through the evening like this for several hours; when the ten beers were gone I returned to the kitchen for another round. They were out of singles and had tapped a keg, so I filled four plastic cups with whatever cheap pale ale was pouring out the tap and moseyed back towards the couch. My buzz was here, and it'd brought enough luggage for a respectable stay. Hiya, Cole. Been a while. Glad to be back. Where's my favorite chair?

'Good to see you again, too,' I said aloud. Some dude thought I was talking to him, nodded hello to me as he tried to figure out where he might have seen me before. I ignored him and concentrated on getting back to the couch. My face was tingling, and my chest was feeling warm and full, which happens every time my buzz shows up at the door, dropping its carry-ons and making itself comfy.

I was ten paces from the couch, smiling and buzzing and just as content as a cat on a sunny windowsill, when I saw Marla on the couch, sitting next to Jules.

*

It'd taken the good folks at the men's wear store nearly three hours to finish with my suit. I had neither the time nor the cash to have one tailored for me, so I'd carefully gone through the racks until I'd found one that did the trick. It was a Brooks Bros., charcoal gray, pinstriped. The gentleman helping me – a tall, erect man with an Errol Flynn mustache and skin that looked as tough as rawhide – selected a dark blue shirt and matching tie, then completed the ensemble with the undershirt – Hanes, made in America, ironically enough – socks, shoes, and belt. When he was done he stood behind me, towering over me by a good five-six inches, looking at me as I looked at myself in the tri-paneled mirrors in the middle of Mexico City, looking entirely different than I'd ever seen myself look.

While the in-store tailor hemmed the pants and took out some of the fabric in the groin area, I browsed through their accessories. I found an imitation-alligator wallet and briefcase and bought them with the suit. At first blush, the imitation alligator looked more expensive than the real leather; it wouldn't stand up to any serious inspection, but for my purposes they'd work just fine.

I also bought a ten-pack of plain white athletic socks. The total bill cleaned out the rest of my money. I was left with exactly eleven dollars and forty-one cents, American currency. Not enough to fill the truck up with gas. Not enough to rent even one of the city's seedier motel rooms for the night. Barely enough for a couple of Happy Meals.

I remembered reading somewhere about one of history's great explorers – Cortez, or maybe Ponce de Leon – destroying all of his soldiers' boats once they'd reached their destination, the idea being that his men would work harder if they knew they had no option, that there was no Plan B.

I felt like that, just then. I'd reached my destination, and had destroyed my boat.

My scheme had to work. There was no Plan B.

I'd found a McDonald's – when they finally land a man on Mars, I have all confidence that he'll take his first Martian shit in a McDonald's toilet – amid the shops, strip-malls, fast-food restaurants, and auto dealerships, and pulled in long enough to change in the bathroom. As I left the place – the only ready-sign that I was not in America the fact that all the kids on the McSlide and McMonkey Bars were chattering away in Spanish instead of English – I felt a little silly, climbing up into that clunker of a truck in my spiffy new suit. I thought maybe the folks at the bank might think so too, if they happened to see me climbing out of it before walking in to do the sort of business with them that I was intending to do.

So I parked the truck in the space furthest from the street, knowing it was for the most part a useless gesture. There was no way they'd have traced me here, not yet, and if they had, it wouldn't matter where I parked.

Brasco had settled into a semi-sleep state. The nearly three straight days of traveling hadn't done much for his disposition, but he was adapting as well as I could expect. Provided I stopped every four or five hours so he could piss along the side of the road – always with me holding his hunched shoulders, always with him whining hatefully beneath his breath, his mouth closed and ears back the way cats do when they're really pissed – he was generally okay. He'd taken a shit in the floorboard on our first day as Mexicans, but I'd kicked it out and dumped a box of baking soda – Arm & Hammer, just like in America, only a hell of a lot cheaper – there to soak up the smell. It worked, for the most part.

I rubbed his back a bit, careful to work that soft area between his shoulder blades he was so fond of. I resolved several minutes earlier not to get out and do this until I'd gotten him purring. It took a couple minutes longer than it would have under ordinary conditions, but again, how much could I expect right now?

'Daddy'll be back in just a sec, okay boy?'

I waited another two minutes, my stomach twisted into knots and burning, my bowels feeling like they were on the verge of emptying into my Wal-Mart boxers.

'Calm down, Archer,' I said aloud. Then, remembering, repeated, 'Calm down Stevenson.' This part of the deal was known throughout law enforcement circles as the name-game. The idea is to bounce from name to name, laundering each one along the way, until you get wherever it is you're going. Then you change it one final time and live out your days as whoever you are at that point, your new name squeaky clean, the path that got you there non-existent. For my part, I figured I'd need to leapfrog at least three different times in Mexico alone; I'd started out as Cole Hammer (my mother's maiden name – cool, huh?) Archer, a handle which would by now be eight degrees hotter than hell. He disappeared in Charleston; I'd neither signed nor put my name to anything since leaving three days ago. The Honda/van exchange had been without paperwork, the dealer no doubt pocketing the grand I gave him with my Honda, both of us happy enough to have it that way. No paper trail, no questions asked. I disappear with the clunker of a van and he gets his big-screen TV.

It was much of the same in Brownsville, where the salesman hadn't even bothered to ask. At the hotel I'd had to use the Paulwyn Mitchell Bowick ID, and if they did their research – and I was betting it all that they would – they'd catch on to that one before too long.

But Paulwyn Bowick didn't last long. He crossed the border, and then his IDs were summarily buried a foot and half deep in the Mexican dirt, hundred yards or so off the tiny back road I was traveling that day. Philip Roth Tellerman finished burying Bowick's effects in about an hour, climbing back into that truck and picking up where Paulwyn had left off. Brasco hadn't seemed to notice any difference.

So far Tellerman was on record for staying at two different roadside motels; the Feds were likely to catch on to that one before too terribly long, though. They'd do what they had to do to get the guest registrar from every roadside come-'n'-go on every Mexican back road all down the country. It'd take them a while to sift through it all, but the government's a big animal, with lots of patience.

Tellerman was gone now, his driver's license (Seattle, Washington), passport, birth certificate, and social security card destroyed and flushed down the toilet of room 304 of the Casa Serena Motel and Lodge this morning.

Now, in Mexico City, there was only Brasco the cat, and his sidekick Marcus James Coker. I sat there behind the wheel and thumbed through the appropriate papers. Driver's license, (Irvine, California) passport, professional documentation, and birth certificate (born in March the same year as I). I'd memorized the account information weeks before, and calmly took a moment to review it in my head again. And again. I could do it drunk, upside down, under duress, in my sleep. I could even do it backwards, if they wanted it that way.

I opened the pack of athletic socks and stuffed them into the briefcase, one pair at a time. They gave the case a respectable bulge, *as if it were full of important papers and documents.*

I then organized Marcus James Coker's identification into his new wallet, folded the wallet, and slipped it into the inner coat pocket of his new suit. The gesture had a refined feel to it, a touch of that je ne sais quoi I was counting on. That was half the reason for all the pomp; the other half was fulfilling the implicit expectations of the people I'd be dealing with inside.

I examined the briefcase one last time, checking for any store-tags, checked myself in the rearview, steeled my nerves, and let out a long, heavy sigh.

'Here goes, boy,' I said, and climbed out of the truck, one Marcus James Coker of Irvine, California, vice-president of Outland Capital and Casualty Insurance, dressed to the fucking gills.

'Well don't you look nice?' – Marla, sitting next to Jules, closer than I would have thought, Jules not appearing to mind, though. He was holding his bottle on his knee with one hand, a fresh cigarette – tobacco now, not marijuana – in the other.

Marla was wearing a black skirt made out of some material I couldn't quite place. Her shirt was as white as your grandmother's wedding dress.

'Evening, Marla,' I said, lowering myself on the coffee table across from them so I could see. She was like a beautiful, deadly creature from the ocean, that Marla, fascinating but dangerous, both reasons to keep your eyes on her.

'Have you been working out, Cole?' she asked. She was holding a sweating glass of something mixed. I couldn't help but notice there was a diamond on her wedding finger.

'Yeah Cole,' Jules chimed in, 'have you been working out? You're looking buffed, baby.'

I shrugged. 'You know. A little here, little there.'

'Me,' Jules said, 'I work my right arm a lot. Nothing like the ol' dirty handshake to help you fall asleep. You wanna feel my right arm, Marla.'

'I'll take your word.'

'Nice rock you got there,' I said, nodding at her finger. 'Kicking things up a notch?'

She smiled. 'Greg asked me to marry him. In Paris.'

'You're getting married in Paris?'

'No, silly duck. We were in Paris when he asked me.'

'Atop the Eiffel Tower, no doubt,' Jules said.

'The base of it, actually. Greg's afraid of heights.'

'Congratulations,' I told her, and for the most part – the very most part – I meant it. Her being happy wasn't a notion that upset me. Just her being with me.

'Son of a gun,' Jules said around a mouthful of beer. 'Didn't take the old boy long to figure out you were the one, did it?'

She shook her head, still smiling. 'We've been inseparable for over a month, now.'

'Well in that case...' Jules let the rest of that sentence die in mid-flight.

'When's the big date?' I asked.

'We haven't set one yet. Greg wants summer. I'm hoping for something a little later but there's sweeps.'

'Ah, yes,' Jules said. 'Sweeps. The all-mighty sweeps. The Second Coming's going to have to work around sweeps, I'm afraid. Local news lives and dies by it, God bless.'

'Well congratulations, Marla,' I repeated, aware that I was repeating it, not particularly concerned about it though. I felt that my sincerity insulated me.

'Thank you, Cole. Of course it wouldn't be the same if you weren't there. I've already mentioned it to Greg and he agrees. We do hope you'll plan to attend.'

'I thought there was a lake at the bottom of the Eiffel Tower,' Jules said.

'Have you ever been to Paris?' Marla asked, and you could tell she was irritated that he interrupted her in the midst of her charity. If you were Marla Grossman, to invite someone to share time with you was the act of giving a gift away.

He shook his head. 'Cole, isn't there a lake at the bottom of the Eiffel Tower?'

'Guess not,' I shrugged.

'In *European Vacation* there was a lake down there. Little dog fell into it, remember? Chevy's doing the whole "I want to paint, I want to sculpt, I want to create, where's the bathroom?" Remember?'

Marla said, 'I think that was just a movie,' and she patted his shoulder in a wonderfully condescending fashion that made me admire her even then.

'Marla,' Jules said without missing a beat, his eyes a little glassy from the booze and the dope, 'I have to know, if Cole's invited, may

I come as well?'

She looked at him, expressionless. 'To tell you the truth, Julian, we haven't finalized the guest list. That's the kind of thing you do during the engagement. We just got back from Paris, the Eiffel Tower and the dry land beneath it, two days ago.'

I smiled.

'Well, you just asked Cole to come. Said it wouldn't be the same if he wasn't there. Cleared it with the groom-elect and everything.'

'That's a little different, Jules.'

'Tell you what,' he said, 'I'll even bring a gift. Not a serving spoon, either. Something you have to fucking plug in and dismantle when you're through in order to have room for the toaster or whatever. Big ol' sumbitching George Foreman grill, maybe. Drain that fat right the fuck off those steaks, huh?'

'We'll see, Jules.'

'Is the wedding here in town?' I asked, trying to steer the conversation away from Jules' chances for attendance. He wanted to be there about as much as he wanted pubic lice. He just liked needling her. When he found out she'd been cheating on me, he'd wanted to steal her car and set it on fire on Kennedy Street downtown. Said he'd even cover it on the next morning's news.

She nodded. 'Either St. Philip's or St. Mary's, we haven't decided yet.'

'I just don't understand why Cole gets to go and I don't.'

'It's not a trip to the state fair, Jules,' she said.

'Then what's the big deal? Do you specifically not want me there?'

'Greg might be a little uncomfortable, actually. The two of you working together and all.'

'Greg? My Greg? Channel Fucking Five's own Greg Robinson? No way. He and I are like, like what Cole?'

I shrugged. 'Cat and nip.'

'Yeah. Cat and nip. Suck and swallow. Big Oil and the GOP. We've been tanked together I can't count how many times. Why, Marla Grossman, not two weeks ago – that reminds me, are you planning on taking his name?'

'We haven't discussed that.'

'Marla Robinson,' Jules said, smacking his lips as though tasting the name. 'Kind of Waspish, you don't mind me saying.'

'I like the sound of it just fine,' she said. 'I'll be sure and take your opinion into consideration though, sweetie.'

'No, hey, sounds great. Just doesn't have that German ring to it that Grossman does. You like German names, Cole?'

'Lighten up, dude.'

'No,' Marla said, waving it away, 'don't worry about it, Cole. Jules always amuses me when he drinks too much and fancies himself intelligent.' She turned to Jules. 'Tell me, Jules, does this oh-so-evident resentment of me stem from the fact that your prick is shorter than your thumb, and I was forward enough to comment on it? Because if it does, you should know that length really isn't the issue.'

'Ouch,' Jules said, lighting another cigarette. He inhaled, held it, and blew a long, blue-gray arrow of smoke up towards the ceiling. You could tell he was enjoying the hell out of this little repartee. He lived for this sort of shit.

'It's width that gets us off,' Marla continued. 'Which admittedly leaves you coming up a little, well, short, but still, personality can make up for that.' She turned, winked at me, then said, 'Personality goes a long way.'

'*Pulp Fiction*,' Jules said, finishing off his cup of beer. 'Breakfast scene. Black guy to white guy. Black guy's eating a muffin.'

'Very good,' Marla replied. 'If only movie trivia and character were synonymous.'

'Character?'

She nods.

'You just said character, right?'

'Right. Character. As in what you have none of, presuming your pedigree and face on the television bright and early every morning to be sufficient substitute. Character. The sort of thing men like Greg have. The kind of thing you'll likely never have.'

'Marla,' Jules said, looking at her now, taking her all in, 'you seem to forget, sweetheart, that I know you. I've known you for a good long while. I could tell your delicate Greg a thing or two to make his eyes water and his asshole pucker.'

'Greg knows me,' she said.

He shrugged. 'You're probably right.'

There was a pause then, an awkward, uncomfortable pause that reminded me of so many of my evenings alone with Marla. You were always alone when you were with her. Usually it was better once she left; at least then you got you back.

'Then again,' Jules continued, 'changing the name does have a nice cleansing quality to it, doesn't it? Sort of wash away the old checkered past and trade it in for a brand new one, eh? Quick walk in a church on proud daddy's arm wearing a white dress and poof, it's off to Hawaii or the Poconos. New name, new trousseau, new you and off you go.' He laughed. 'I made a rhyme, Cole.'

'Be cool, bro,' I said.

'I'm cool,' he said. 'I'm king of cool. Here's one for you, babe. "You're so cool. You're so cool. You're so cool." Gorgeous dame, loose-cannon dude, briefcase full of coke and a trip down to Mexico. Little note written on the napkin.'

'*True Romance*,' she said. 'We saw it together.'

'We did, didn't we?' Jules was on a roll now; he was throwing jabs for both of us at this point. He'd find Marla to be a tough target, though.

'At that theater in Columbia, right?'

'Yes,' she replied. 'As I remember you made a complete ass of yourself. Nothing new for you, unfortunately.' She sipped her own drink. She was a picture of control on that couch, as cool and confident as anyone I'd ever seen before or since. 'Poor Julian,' she said, 'always either too immature or too premature.'

'I'd had a lot to drink,' he said, looking at me. 'She was blowing me and I came too soon. Right in the "Sicilians-are-spawned-by-niggers" scene.' He laughed. 'The whole rest of the movie was kind of sedate for me after that.'

'You always did love good dialogue,' I said. '*Glengarry Glen Ross, Swingers. Beautiful Girls.*'

'*Things to Do in Denver When You're Dead,*' he added, then snapped his fingers. 'Hey Marla,' he said, 'I just thought of something. Is that why our sweet Greg's not too keen on my being there when he lifts the virginal veil? The whole bit about us fucking back then and all?'

'Probably. I wouldn't want all of his ex-flings there, either,' she said.

'Hell,' Jules chuckled, 'that would be a problem. Imagine if you'd munched rugs with any of them. Think how confused some of them might be, not knowing which side of the church to sit on.'

'That's a good point,' Marla said, standing, smoothing her skirt – short and tight enough that she doesn't need to smooth much; what wrinkles there are pressed out against her thighs and rear as she stands – leaning over in front of Julian, nice and close, her white shirt unbuttoned up top, giving Jules a nice view down her shirt, over the smooth, cream-white skin of her lower neck and upper chest. He refused to take it, choosing instead to lock eyes with her, an act which always reminded me of trying to stare down a cobra.

'You take care of yourself there, Julie,' she almost whispered. 'I'll see what I can do about sending you an invite. Greg and I might just throw pretension to the wind and invite everyone either of us has ever slept with. In fact, that might be nice. You could sit with your sister.' She stood. 'At least you would know which side of the church to sit on.'

And with that she was gone.

Some segment of time later – it was getting difficult to gauge now – Jules, in his same spot, fresh beers in our hands, said, 'I really do hate her, Cole.'

'It's an understandable emotion.'

'She's evil,' he adds. 'She's the fucking devil through and through.'

I sighed. 'I've had my share of days when I agreed with you, bro.' I took a nice, long swig of my beer and couldn't even feel it go down.

'She didn't have to throw that in there about Angelina.'

'Dude, you knew she dated Greg.'

'I never knew she dated Marla.'

He was dazed. I reached a hand over and tousled his hair. 'She's what, twenty-four, twenty-five now? She's growing up. It was probably just a phase. You know how girls are about that shit.'

'Twenty-three.'

'What?'

'She's twenty-three.'

'Twenty-three, then. Same difference. Angelina's a wonderful girl.'

'That Marla is a bleeding fucking cunt.'

'That she is, Jules. That she is.'

He looked at me then. 'Cole, you never fucked my sister, did you?'

'What do you mean?'

'What do you mean what do I mean? I mean did you ever fuck my sister. There's no qualifier there. It's not ambiguous. Has Angelina ever seen your dick?'

'Seeing my dick and my banging her aren't necessarily the same thing, bro. Maybe she just came over and nibbled a while.'

'I'm in no mood to play right now, Cole. I just found out my baby sister's a carpet-chewer and I'm not too fucking pepped up about it.'

'Lighten up, man. There's no guarantee Marla's telling the truth. She probably just said that to ruin your night. Lucky for us it didn't work, huh?'

'My night, my month, my beshitting year.' He sighed. 'How could she do that? My little sister.' He was shaking his head.

I shrugged. 'You did. I did.'

'That doesn't excuse it. I'm a man. You're a man. My sister's a little girl. Yesterday she had braces and was cheering for those sadistic penguins at Sisters of Mercy. Last week I watched her being born. Now she's licking lilies with my ex-slut.'

'And mine.'

'And yours.'

We sat there in silence then, drinking and thinking and making a point not to talk about it anymore. Julian was stuck with the knowledge that his sister was a wild one; the rest of us already knew that. I hadn't been aware that Angelina had had a thing with Marla, but I didn't doubt it. I didn't believe it as a matter of course, either. That's how it was with Marla. Lies and truth were all the same to her, depending on her mood. It was kind of like deciding which perfume she was going to wear.

Sometime later Jules and I stood from the couch, and I can remember walking unsteadily through the crowd in the living room, exiting the condo through the back door onto the porch. There was another keg back there, and I vaguely recall allowing Jules and myself to be talked into a keg-stand by someone I'm fairly certain I'd never seen before in my life.

There were three or four grills fired up on the back porch, and music, and lots of beer, and row after row of oysters on the grills. I ate somewhere around a million of them; much of that evening's fragmented memories for me are of me knifing open the shells, shaking Tabasco onto the meat, and dropping it down my throat without so much as a chew. It seems I did this for several hours. Jules did a second keg stand, I think – I can remember him falling over, laughing, burping, beer spilling from the tap all over his face and hair and neck, and I'm pretty sure – though not definite – that

I didn't. I know I drank a good bit more, ate more oysters, and spoke in what must have been anything but sequential fashion with any and everyone who might have been out there with me. I was not aware of the passing of time.

At some point I realized Jules had left, back into the house or upstairs to one of the bedrooms or out to his car for a drunken drive home, I wasn't sure. I remember not caring. I also remember Marla being out there on the porch with me; there were words, none of which I remember. I can recall tones though, and when you're as drunk as I was that night – when you can barely stand and your face has gone numb and everything inside your skull feels loose and lubricated and decidedly fluid – tones are all that really matter. Just like with the family dog; you can tell him you're going to kill him and so long as you do it in a nice tone his tail will wag itself into a blur.

Marla's tones were nice; I do remember that, and whatever I had that passed for a tail had begun to wag. I can remember Marla leading me out of the porch and down the soft grassy embankment, around the condo, and under a deck. It was cold and dark down there, the noises from the party above sounding distant and softer somehow, like they were coming to me through water. I can remember thinking very distantly of Greg, then figuring what the hell. I remember Marla unzipping my fly and pulling me free, her hands cold but warming quickly.

I fell over at some point, I know that, and I also know that I had managed to remove myself fully from my clothes. Everything save my socks and shoes, which were loafers, and which for some reason I had decided to leave on. Maybe in case Greg happened upon us and I had to run. That would've been a sight, me running drunkenly through the condo complex, naked and shriveling fast, nothing on but my goddam black socks and loafers.

As I recall – though my memory of that night is not now and will likely never be complete, and not merely because of the beer – Marla was not entirely naked; she had her skirt hiked up over her lower back, and had situated herself on top of me.

What's my name, bitch? I thought absurdly, and started to laugh.

'What's funny?' she asked.

'We are.'

Marla was looking down at me, her smile never fading, her hand gripping me tightly down there, her arm a piston that never tires, never slows. I tried to focus on her as she lowered her head down my frame, but it was pointless. She was shimmering, a dull, hazy blur shimmering all the colors of the rainbow around her edges.

I felt her breath on me, then the teasing flickering of her tongue, then an enveloping warmth that I'm pretty sure made me cry out.

'Sshhhh,' she said.

She stopped, then lowered herself over me, that place inside her body as smooth as exotic oil.

'We shouldn't,' I managed.

'That's half the point.'

'Greg,' I managed, but my heart wasn't in it.

'He's upstairs,' she'd said, rising, lowering, rising. 'They're passing the bong. He'd never leave.'

Good enough for me. I don't think either of us said anything for a while. I just lay there, staring up at her, having forgotten temporarily that we were outside, in the dirt beneath the very floor upon which her fiancé was standing, looking high and low for his date, for all I knew.

I wasn't thinking that at the moment, though, and, if it had occurred to me, it wouldn't have been important to me in any case. One doesn't multi-task when one is fucking, particularly when one is drunk beyond coherence.

Her arms were hugging herself beneath her breasts, her head lolling back so that I could see the long, pinkish-white curve of her neck, the subtle arch of her soft Adam's apple. Everything around me had begun spinning rapidly, and I felt as if I might puke.

At some point we'd switched positions, with Marla on all fours in front of me, me on my knees behind her, little bits of gravel and rock digging themselves into my knees and shins hard enough to make me wince, but not hard enough to make me stop. I remember thinking how cute the little dolphin leaping out of the wave in the center of her left cheek was.

Then, as abruptly as an arrest, she said, 'Put it higher,' and I knew what she meant. Of course I knew what she meant. Marla Grossman had during our ill-fated relationship taken me in her bed to the razor's edge of mordacity numerous times; I'd learned more about raw physical pleasure, pure as a clear flame, from her than I ever wanted. A great deal of it was involuntary, in fact, and very nearly against my will, very nearly not pleasure at all.

'Put it in our spot, Cole,' she said, her voice throaty and rasping.

'Our special spot.'

'Sweet spot,' I remember saying, pulling out of her, looking down at myself, all shiny and wet in the cold December night, realizing then how incredibly cold I was. I'd been shivering through most of it.

'Yes,' she said, wiggling her bottom around some. 'Our sweet spot.'

Things were going blurry for me then but I managed to angle myself, the normal coordinates plus half a click northward, and she backed into me, softly, hitting resistance at first.

'I want to feel you in our sweet spot,' she said, and leaned her head back towards me. I was on autopilot; I'd been there before. I grabbed her hair in my hands like a bridle and pulled her head back hard enough to make her neck crack. She moaned a low, guttural moan, and pushed herself back into me harder.

The first half-inch was always the most difficult. After that it's easy, different, dryer, more open and spacious, as if you're in a room with no walls at all, only a single door which opens nearly all the way for you, but never quite, and never quite all at once. You have to push, pull back, push again. It's a progression, a dance of degrees, further this time, further next time, always further.

'Yes,' she said – something between a moan and whisper. 'Fuck it, Cole. Fuck me.'

My hands on her hips, pulling her into me. Me pushing forward, getting stuck, pushing, pushing, pushing –

'Yes – yes, Cole. Yes –'

– pushing pushing pushing –

'Call me a whore.'

I withdrew, pulled her hips and pushed my own forward again.

'You are a whore,' I said, meaning every word. 'A dirty fucking cock-loving whore.'

I pushed again. 'All you do good is fuck.'

'I'm a slut,' she said, grabbing handfuls of dirt, hammering her fists on the ground before her – 'your slut' – her head thrashing wildly in front of me, her hair flailing about in a kind of comic-fantastic theater I'd seen played out by her a hundred times before.

She was grunting, moaning between clenched teeth, making noises deep in her chest and holding them in her throat.

Pushing, pushing, pushing, past the resistance, past the tenseness of muscles unaccustomed to this direction of travel, then finally fully in, past her surrender and through the earthen, fecund smell of desire and pain and dirt dirt dirt –

– I'm not proud of it, and if sitting here now I try to quantify my displeasure with the fact that I'd allowed myself to sink to that level with her, it simply pales next to how profoundly displeased Greg appeared to be as he came down that grassy embankment towards us, a stick the size of Rhode Island in his hand.

His eyes were wild and wide and his arms were up, and that stick came round in a perfect, surreal arc that sounded like a sigh.

TWENTY-ONE

Savannah takes Cole home; intermezzo; that which is sweeter than water

I awakened at the hospital, my entire head bandaged, the meat on the side of my face radiating a warm heat like something raw.

It took me a minute to realize what had happened, then pieces of the memory made their way to the surface even as I struggled to keep them at bay.

I realized almost instantly that it was daytime, and that I was in a hospital; everything was either stainless steel or white, and the entire room smelled like sterile fabric that had been sitting too long in the sun. There was a silver television protruding from the wall before me on a long steel arm. The walls beyond that were a calming off-white; the ceiling was white, the bedsheets were white, the little empty swivel chair to my left was even white, albeit dingy with age.

(You motherfucker! –)

Yeah, he'd been pretty upset. Understandable, really. I don't know what I'd do if I stumbled upon my fiancé with some guy tagging her in the –

A horrible, numbing thought occured to me then, and the skin along my spine tightened. Instinctively, I reached a hand beneath the antiseptic-smelling white sheet and felt for my unmentionables, made sure all three members of that particular boys' club were present and accounted for.

They were, which was a relief. Everything else would heal. I wonder obliquely if Marla was okay. I'm no great fan, but I hate to think Greg had taken after her with whatever the hell it'd been he'd clocked me with.

'You're alive,' she said from my right side, the bandaged side, which was why I hadn't seen her earlier.

I tred to turn, and found the move too painful. My neck felt as if everything vital in there had been ripped apart, stomped on, and stuffed back in.

'Who's that?' My voice sounded foreign to me, strained and hoarse.

No words this time, though. Just a touch, a feather-like fan of fingers on my wrist, and suddenly I knew who it was.

'Savannah,' I said.

'Hi, Mr. Archer.'

'What – how did you ... who called you?'

She was still out of my line of sight, still off to my right. Her hand was still on my wrist.

'Julian,' she said. 'He made me promise not to tell you, but you and I promised no secrets, and I don't even know him.'

'Jules? How in the world did he get your number?'

'He found it in your wallet.'

'I never told him about – '

'That's why he didn't want me to say anything to you. He knew you'd be upset.'

'I'm not upset ... Savannah, are we alone in here?'

'Yes. There's a nurse that comes in every couple of hours to check on you and fill in her charts. Julian was here earlier, but you were still a good ways gone then.'

The fingers on her hand had begun moving softly, almost imperceptibly. I wasn't sure if she knew she was doing it, but its effect on me were unequivocal either way. I felt a rush of warmth and safety and, oddly, gratitude towards her.

'How long have you been here?'

'A while,' she said. 'They asked me to leave earlier this morning but I told them you were my brother and I lived with you, so they let me stay. You've been sleeping pretty hard.'

'Did I snore?'

'Some,' she said. I expected a giggle but didn't get one.

'I can't see you,' I said. 'Slide around a bit.'

'No,' she said, her fingers still rubbing across the skin of my wrist, the way a child might rub the silken edge of her favorite blanket, although if there was a child in the room at that moment, it wasn't her.

'Not right now,' she said. 'Just lie there and rest. It's been a long night. You don't need to strain yourself.'

'I want to see you.'

'And I want to touch you. If you're watching me, you might tell me to stop.' Her fingers drifted up my forearm, nearly to the sensitive, fleshy spot of my inner elbow. I could feel her weight leaning into the side of the bed. I closed my eyes and concentrated and found the scent of her hair. In my mind's eye her smell was a pool of golden pearls on a bed of black velvet.

'You might say something about boundaries, and the need to be mindful of them. This way, you can pretend you're sleeping. We both can.'

There was the sensation of something breaking inside me, of a great, rushing tide of water that has been hammering away at a strong but small dam that's beginning to give way as I watch from some disembodied third-person perspective, no longer believing the lie that the dam will hold, merely resigned now to learning how to live after the flood.

'I don't want to pretend to be sleeping.'

She didn't say anything. Her fingers continued down my forearm, hesitantly it seemed, as though she was afraid I'd stop her at any moment.

'I dreamt of you,' I told her, and it was the truth. I'd never stopped dreaming of her, and doubted I ever would.

Still she said nothing, and still her fingers continued down my arm, reaching my wrist, then my palm. I felt her thumb on the underside of my hand, her fingers, delicate as rose petals, in my opened palm.

This is it, I hear a voice inside telling me. You do this, and you're officially on the other side of the line. Everything up to now has been a little questionable and maybe even unethical, but if you enclose her hand in yours you're a bona-fide criminal in the eyes of the Almighty District, and maybe even the law.

Yes, I knew that, and yes, that mattered to me, but it didn't matter enough. There wasn't much I knew for sure about tomorrow, or tomorrow's tomorrow, and even less I could control. Babies are born addicted to crack every day in this country. Nations go to war over oil and warm-water ports and the right way to spell God. People hit possums and raccoons on the road and don't care enough to so much as turn around and finish the job. I can't do anything about any of that. It is what it is and so it goes. What I knew for sure at that moment was that Savannah's hand was in mine, that the dam was giving and the deluge was coming, and I couldn't control that, either. All I could do is find a way to live after the flood, so I slowly folded my hand closed, holding hers inside it, and everything made sense right then, everything I'd ever been through and everything I knew I'd have to go through later, it all fit together just fine at that perfect second, and I had to close my eyes to hold back the tears.

Savannah drove us to my apartment a little after noon that day, Saturday, still less than twelve hours after Greg had had his way with me beneath the condo. She stopped off at a Kerr Drug to fill the two prescriptions the doctor had called in for me, during which time I reclined the passenger seat and tried not to pass out from pain.

The backseat of her car – an early nineties Celica bought for $500, she told me, and fixed up for her by the man her mother'd lived with two boyfriends back – was filled with her textbooks, pens and pencils, a ruler, compass, and protractor, and a couple novels I saw were from the Coosaw Creek High library. Under normal circumstances I suppose it would have all served quite nicely as a reminder as to how taboo and forbidden my being there with her was; as it was, I simply shrugged it off. Things changed after the flood.

She laid me down on my garage-sale couch, pulling the shades closed on the one window in my living room. She kept the lights off, and pressed a cold washcloth over my forehead. She brought me a glass of ice water to wash down two of the aspirin-sized painkillers the doc had prescribed. Aside from the missing skin on that side of my face, the doctors said I had a fairly severe concussion, and that I needed to stay off my feet as much as possible for the next few days. He said there'd likely be some lasting hearing damage to my right ear as well, but that it was still too soon to know for certain.

So I laid there on my old couch with my head bandaged and a cold washcloth across my brow as Savannah removed my shoes and elevated my feet and covered me with the comforter from my bed. I was extraordinarily dizzy, and my head was hurting in a way I'd never felt it hurt before. The pain seemed to roll in from some unknown universe in waves, filling my skull to the breaking point before ebbing and subsiding, throbbing dully for a minute or two, then returning in waves again. I could feel my heart pounding in my temples, at the base of my neck, around the joints of my jaw. Each time that pain returned I thought I would black out. I welcomed the idea. Anything to impede the pain.

Savannah sat on the floor next to the couch and laid her head on my stomach, looking up at me. I took my left hand and did the thing I'd dreamt of since nearly the beginning, the thing that called me in the halls and in my class the way the bottle must call the drunk: I ran my fingers through her hair.

I awoke sometime later; it must have been hours, because the apartment was nearly pitch-black. What little sun had managed to drip in past the closed shade earlier was gone, and the previously cool washcloth on my head was room temperature now, and nearly dry.

I was still on the couch, still on my back, still covered by my comforter. I felt around in the darkness for Savannah but she was gone. I considered rising and looking for her, but my head was swimming and felt full of gauze, so I closed my eyes again, and found sleep.

My eyes opened to complete darkness, as though they weren't open at all. Brasco had spread himself over my ankles. The washcloth which had been on my forehead had at some point been replaced; it was cold again, and damp. Drops of water trickled down the sides of my face, over my ears.

I remained motionless, closed my eyes again and listened. From somewhere very near I could hear Savannah breathing.

Spears of daylight stabbing through the edges of the window past the lowered shade woke me. When I opened my eyes Savannah was sitting on the couch next to me, holding a glass of ice water and two more pills. She looked as delicate to me as finely carved ivory; she seemed then to be all that was important in the world. I can remember thinking as I looked up at her that nothing beyond the door of my little apartment had any worth at all next to her.

'The pills make me groggy,' I said.

'They're supposed to. Take them.'

'I need to go to the bathroom,' I said.

She helped me up, guided me towards the bathroom, waited outside the door, then helped me back to the couch.

'Take the pills,' she said.

I did. And slept.

*

Again I awoke, and again it was dark. At some point I'd shifted in my sleep, turning from my back to my side. As I realized this it came to me that Savannah was lying beside me on the couch, her small frame spooned into mine, my arm draped over her stomach and curled under her, her arm wrapped around my own.

I lay there and listened to her breathe in the darkness, then lowered my face into her hair, and asked God to take me now, for I understood then that the rest of my life would always be an attempt to reach this level of peace once more, and that no matter how good it may get for me, everything would be judged a failure next to this.

'I remember once,' I was saying, still lying on the couch, Savannah having risen at some point during my sleep, sitting at the far end of the sofa Indian-style, my legs curled to make room for her, 'I walked into my mother's bedroom and found her holding on to her pillow, holding it while she cried. That's when I learned how to hate. I hated my father. I could have killed him that day as easily as I might have killed a mosquito or a gnat. I hated him for leaving us – for leaving my mother, leaving her behind to hold her pillow and pretend she's not alone.'

'Did you know him well before he left?'

I shook my head. 'I was four. I remember little glimpses, broken pieces of stuff. I remember him reading to me on my bed once. I can't remember what he looks like, and mom threw out all the pictures when he went.'

I was wearing sweats; gray pants and a garnet USC sweatshirt. I hadn't had them on when Savannah had brought me home, I was sure of that.

'My dad was a stage-hand,' she said. She was in sweats as well, blue, the same baggy sweatshirt with the law firm logo pasted across it in black lettering.

'You mean like in an acting troupe?'

Shaking her head. 'A band. *Illegal Cargo*. Far as I know they never made it. Never even made an album. Isn't that pathetic? I'm the product of seed from a roadie with a traveling beer-band that sang covers.' She laughed. 'Mom happened to be at the swill house where they were playing one night, then bang, here I am. She had a boyfriend, too. Black guy. He was pretty sure I wasn't his.'

211

I felt a laugh coming and suppressed it.

'Don't fight it,' she said. 'What else can you do with that except laugh? She didn't even make him use a condom.'

'Good thing,' I said. 'Otherwise where would we be?'

'Your life would a lot simpler.'

'Less interesting, in any case.'

She smiled. 'Let's hope so.'

After some time in which neither of us said much and there was no awkwardness in the silence, I said, 'Thanks for being there yesterday. At the hospital. You didn't have to come.'

'It was Friday,' she said. 'And of course I came. We're friends. You keep forgetting that.'

'Friday? What's today?'

'Sunday. Morning. You've been – '

'Sleeping for two days ...'

'You were in and out a good bit. The medicine had you delirious. For a few hours last night you alternated between sweats and chills.'

'Did I say anything?'

'You did a lot of mumbling.'

Mumbling. I'll bet I did. My whole life I've been a prolific sleep talker. I can only imagine how chatty I'd be in a doped-up delirious state.

'Did you change me?' I asked. 'My sweats – ?'

She blushed a little. 'I promise I didn't peek.'

'Well, that settles that,' I said. 'I'm going to jail.'

'And I'll be the laugh of the lunchroom.'

'You're handling this rather well, all things considered.'

'I'm happy,' she said. 'I'm happier than I've ever been. You make me happy.'

I looked at her.

'Yes,' she said, her skin a glowing radiant, like morning sun off a fresh snow. 'Is that so hard to imagine? You make me feel good. You make me like things I used to not like. The sound of the telephone ringing. The rhythm of sleep's breath in a pitch-black room. Conversations about everything and nothing. I like being with you. I like you.'

I reached a hand out and grabbed her foot, holding it. 'You set me on fire, Savannah. You make me feel so good it's scary. I've never met anyone like you. It's just ...how can you be only –'

'– Sixteen?' she finished. 'It's just a number.'

'It isn't fair,' I said.

'It isn't relevant,' she replied.

'You were a fetus when I was ten.'

'When you're forty I'll be thirty.'

I considered that. 'Not that big a deal when you look at it like that, is it?'

She shook her head. 'I'll be out of high school in a year and a half, sooner if I go to summer school and carry an overload next semester. I can be done in a year. A year from right now.'

Out of cowardice, I said nothing. She was doing fine on her own, going exactly where I would have led, had I had the courage.

'I can graduate in January.'

'A couple weeks later you'll be eighteen.'

'That's right. You could wait. One year. Then we could walk through this world together.' She wrinkled her brow. 'How'd you know when my birthday was?'

'Jan 11. I checked.'

'You checked my birthday?'

I nodded. 'You're not the only one who's thought of this, Savannah.'

She smiled at that, then abruptly leapt from the couch.

'Hungry?' she asked.

'Starved, now that I think of it. There isn't much over there.'

'There wasn't. I don't know how you and Brasco survive. I went to the store, though.'

'You went grocery shopping?' I asked, pulling myself to an upright position on the couch. Both knees popped in unison in protest. My face was beginning to hurt again, too, but no way was I taking any more medicine. I didn't want to waste time being groggy around her. I would rather deal with the pain.

She nodded, opening the refrigerator and cupboards, removing items and setting them on the small counter.

'I hope you don't mind,' she said. 'I didn't know what you liked so I got a little of everything. We've got deli, some pasta salad, chips and dip, and ice cream for dessert. If you're in the mood I can fry us some chicken.'

'You know how to fry chicken?'

She nodded. 'I raise four brothers, remember.'

'Oh, shit.'

213

'Don't worry. They're with my mother. She's sober this weekend.'

'Where does she think you are?'

'She doesn't ask many questions.'

'She lets you wander off for days at a time?'

'She lets me do whatever I like. She's terrified I'll move away from Charleston when I graduate and never return.'

'Which is your plan, of course.'

'Absolutely.'

I smiled, then stood and stretched, reaching my arms for the ceiling. My spine cracked several times, loud as pine knots exploding in the fire.

'I haven't had homemade fried chicken since the last time I went to Augusta to visit my mother.'

'Well sit down and rest your feet. I'll get the grease going and fix us some salads to start.'

I loitered in the kitchen while she mixed the salads and breaded the chicken. Watching her hands, watching her move through the kitchen in patterns and rhythms that suggested a woman much older, I felt myself falling for her. It'd been happening for a while now, I knew that. But it was in the tiny kitchen of my West Ashley apartment that I crossed the Maginot Line. There would be an 'us' out of all of this. I would do whatever I had to do to make it so.

It'd gone as good as I could have hoped at the bank. I'd walked through the lobby with the self-assured, foot-and-a-half-cock confident swagger befitting a vice-president of an offshore insurance company, a twenty-six-year-old millionaire with worries no greater than deciding whether to bang a blonde or a brunette that night, and on which yacht.

I'd practiced that walk for weeks in my living room, a full-length mirror and Brasco my only audience, lugging my canvas briefcase back and forth for practice.

I'd spoken to the receptionist in the accounts maintenance department, informed her of who I was, and retreated to the waiting room chairs with my sock-stuffed imitation-alligator briefcase resting between my feet like a faithful dog. I casually glanced down as if to examine my shoes for scuffs, made sure I'd zipped the case completely closed. It wouldn't do for a pair of athletic knee-highs to come tumbling out anytime soon.

They didn't keep me waiting long. I'd folded my legs at the knees in a show of patience, reading through one of the periodicals – in Spanish – so as to keep my hands occupied. I was intensely nervous, my mouth dry and my stomach reeling, and I didn't want them shaking.

A gentleman who introduced himself as Renaldo Regencia approached me five minutes into my not-nervous dot-com whiz-kid routine and invited me into his office, which was small but impeccably neat.

'And how can we be of service to you today, Mr. –' His accent was light and pleasant.

'Coker,' I said. 'But please, James.'

He nodded. Smiled his business smile.

'My firm' – removing my imitation-alligator wallet in a fluid wrist motion I had practiced some thousand times back in Charleston – 'has recently begun maintaining an account here for the purposes of tax avoidance.' I smiled, removed the identification card that declared me Vice President of Outland Capital and Casualty Insurance. 'As you're well aware, Mr. Regencia,' – sliding the card across his desk for his examination, knowing it was a useless gesture, that accounts the size of mine were opened and closed with nothing more than numbers and physical description, 'it's an unfortunate fact of doing business in America that one must contend with such a punitive, onerous tax structure.'

He was nodding agreeably; he'd heard all this before. According to my research – bookstores, bookstores; it all comes back to bookstores – the tax system I spoke of accounted for over forty percent of The Mexico City International Bank and Loan's business. It was one of the reasons I chose it.

'My company's board has recently decided to expand its operation. We believe the US economy is on the verge of a significant change, and that the current administration is likely to take aggressive steps in the direction of further deregulation of the laws governing non-life-insurance companies, specifically in regard to low-premium-writing companies such as ours.'

Renaldo Regencia nodded politely, his face a perfect picture of neutrality.

'Of course, an expansion of this size – we've recently acquired majority shareholder status in two other offshore companies whose names I'm not at liberty to disclose at this time, though I can tell you that one is in Bermuda and the other in Grand

Cayman – requires liquidity, which brings us to why I'm here with you this afternoon.'

'I see,' Regencia said, his demeanor unchanging, his black hair shining a midnight blue beneath the harsh fluorescent lighting of his office. He turned his attention to the monitor on his desk, placed his hands atop the keyboard.

'Your account number, sir?'

'Certainly. It's 9031971-09291979-0-595-09399-X. Registered to a male, five feet nine inches, aged late twenties to early thirties, brown hair, medium build, tattoo on the left shoulder.'

He tapped away on his keyboard for a minute, stared intently at the screen, then glanced across his clean, organized desk at me.

'This is a very large balance, Mr. Coker.'

He said it with finality, as if that was why I was there in his bank, to hear him confirm for me that the balance in my account was indeed large.

I nodded. I tried to look a little impatient, the way someone with a very large balance in a foreign bank account might act when the bank told him he had a very large balance.

He stared at me for nearly half a minute. I stared back, trying to time my blinks with his.

'I'll need to inspect your left shoulder, Mr. Coker. You under-stand. It is policy.'

I nodded again. 'Of course. I'd expect no less from a bank of your repute.'

I stood, removed my coat, loosened the tie, unbuttoned my shirt. I rolled up the cotton sleeve of my undershirt, showed him the tattoo. He looked at it for several seconds, then nodded.

'If you'll excuse me for a moment,' he said, and left me in his office in my undershirt.

The next fifteen minutes were long ones; I spent them sitting in my chair, my shirt and tie and coat back on. I kept my eyes closed; in my head was an entire universe of memories I could retreat to at will. I recalled the one of Savannah on that day some four months ago, in the little kitchen of my West Ashley apartment, her hands covered in flour and the air hanging heavy with the smells of frying chicken and the sounds of grease popping, the entire world outside having dwindled down to nothing.

'If you had a million dollars what would you do with it?' she asked.

'I'd buy you a fur coat, but not a real fur coat; that's cruel,' I sang.

She laughed, which got me laughing, and the laughing was as good and real as anything I'd ever experienced.

'I know what I'd do,' she said. We'd finished the meal an hour ago, and had migrated back to the living room, where we'd propped against opposite ends of the couch, facing each other, our legs intermingled beneath the blanket. The space between us was occupied by Brasco.

'Tell me.'

'I'd buy a house in Oregon. On one of those cliffs high above the frothy ocean so I could sit and watch the sunsets over the water. I'd move my brothers in with me, and I'd raise them right, and I'd go to college and medical school, and at the end of every day I'd come home to watch the sunset. I've never seen a real sunset.'

'There's one every night,' I said. 'News'll even tell you what time.'

'We get the sunrises on this coast. You have to be on the other side to get a real sunset.'

'You're hooked on this West Coast thing, aren't you?'

'I'm enamored with nearly anywhere but here. It's one of my chief flaws.'

'I have an idea.'

'I'm rapt.'

'You're a smart-ass,' I said.

She smiled, and I knew why. The barriers were coming down, one at a time. 'What would you really do with a million dollars? Besides singing lessons,' she asked.

'I'd buy my idea.'

'What idea?'

'The one you're rapt about.'

'Your idea's worth a million dollars?'

I nodded. 'I think so. It could be, at least, if it went well. Want to hear it?'

'If it's that valuable, it might be the type of thing you shouldn't share.'

'How can anything be valuable if you don't share it? All the money in the world is just paper if you don't have anyone to spend it with.'

'Then tell me,' she smiled.

'Not now.'

'Why not?'

'Too much build-up.'

'Fair enough. Have you had a lot of girlfriends?'

'Define a lot.'

She shrugged. 'More than ten.'

'Define girlfriend.'

'Someone you were with a while. Six months at least.'

'Less than a lot, then.'

'Fewer.'

'Huh?'

'Fewer, not less. Girlfriends are countable nouns. I think English teachers are supposed to know that sort of thing. What were their names, besides Marla?'

Hearing Marla's name reminded me of Friday night, the parts of it I could bear to remember, in any case. It occurred to me then that had Marla not been so incorrigible I wouldn't have had the opportunity to be on the business end of Greg's wrath that night; I wouldn't have been in the hospital for Savannah to visit. We wouldn't be sitting here now, she and I, which meant Marla had done for me perhaps the greatest favor of them all. Ironic, but there it is.

'Marla wasn't really a girlfriend. She was kind of –'

'No need to explain. I'm not a simpleton. Before the non-girlfriend?'

'Girl named Autumn. The one I was engaged to.'

'Did you love her?'

I took a moment with that one. 'I thought I did at the time.'

'Even when the two of you broke up?'

'Probably even more, then. It always hurts more once you know it's gone for good.'

She nodded, as if this made sense to her, which it shouldn't have, but which by now I know it did. Perfect sense.

'How did you know?'

'That it was over?' I shrugged. 'Just knew, really. We didn't seek each other out as much. My eyes started to wander some.'

'That can be a problem,' she said.

'Yes,' I agreed. 'It can. It definitely can.'

'I take it there was a non-girlfriend or two in there about that time?'

'Maybe,' I laughed. 'I don't remember.'

'Probably for the best. Before her?'

'Before Autumn?'

She nodded.

'Girl named Jenna. Nice girl. Weird taste in clothes.'

'What was weird about it?'

'She didn't wear them much. She was a naturist. It caused a problem in public places.'

'Interesting. Who else?'

'A couple others in high school. Nothing serious. High-school things.'

I realized how that sounded.

'Then this is a first for both of us,' she said.

'What is "this", exactly?'

'For me this is wonderful,' she said. 'Beautiful and wonderful and tingling with potential.'

'Potential,' I repeated.

She nodded. 'Lots of it.'

'You want to hear my idea now?'

'Only if you have the million dollars to make it come true.'

'I have something better.'

'Better than a cool mill? Now I'm really intrigued.'

'Yep.'

'Do tell.'

'Tomorrow we can go to a little town I know – same name as present company, interestingly enough – and see the sights. We can eat and shop and walk unafraid of being seen. When the sun goes down we can make our way to the river and pretend we're on the Pacific and watch it disappear, and if I'm feeling full enough of myself and drunk enough on the moment I might take a stab at the thing I'd buy for my million bucks and hold your hand.'

'Savannah,' she said. 'You want to take me to Savannah?'

'If you can't go, I'm willing to try to pretend it's just a want.'

'I can go,' she said.

'You can go,' I repeated.

She nodded. 'I can go,' she said, her eyes and face and entire body blossoming with a happiness you could tell she hadn't felt in years, if she'd ever felt it at all. 'Yes yes yes I can go. A thousand times yes.'

'That's wonderful,' I said, overflowing with words for the moment, afraid to give voice to any of them, afraid if I opened my mouth they'd just fall out randomly.

'I'll have to use the phone first.'

'Who're you going to ask?'

'No one. I have to call in sick for work.'

'I didn't know you had a job. Where are you working?'

'Nowhere important,' she said dismissively. 'It's just a waitressing thing I picked up for a little extra money.'

'Oh. Will they let you off?'

'I think so. I can get one of the other girls to cover for me.'

So she used the phone and called her boss and told him she'd be sick tomorrow, that she'd caught that cold that was going around, which almost always works, because there's almost always a cold going around somewhere. Everyone knows someone who has a cold right now.

Once she was off the phone – telling her boss goodbye, signaling me the thumbs up as she dropped the phone in the receiver – I remembered Grey.

'Oh, hell,' I said. 'I've got to make a quick call, too.'

Grey was terrific about it, which is to say she was just Grey.

'I feel terrible about this, but I'm going to have to cancel on Florida.'

'Whatever for, Cole? I hope everything's all right.'

'No, no, everything's good. Everything's really good, Grey.'

'Is it her? Your angel? It is. Tell me it is.'

'Yes. It is.'

'Then you should stay, Cole. Stay and don't let a single second with her get away from you. There's ample misery in this world to go around, and from just the little bit of time we've spent together I can tell you've seen your share. If she makes the air around you crackle with energy then do everything you have to do to hold on to her. Defy the world, if you must.'

'It might come to that.'

'Probably not, darling. Few things ever do. People are too busy with their own lives to worry much over yours. It just doesn't look that way from inside our glass houses. Why don't I send you a ticket for next weekend? You can join me for the last week of your break.'

'Can I call you?'

'Anything but Mother,' she said. 'It reminds me of my mortality. Enjoy, sweet Cole. Give me a ring if I can fly you down. I really would love to see you, and I promise to do my best to behave.'

'I doubt that.'

'As you should,' she said, and was laughing as she hung up the phone.

Savannah and I lay stretched out across from each other on my living-room floor and filled the rest of that afternoon with conversation – hundreds of thousands of words upon words. It was liberating and rejuvenating and it was exactly what I needed from the person with whom I needed it, the fulfillment of all the fantasies I'd fostered from my corner in the library, from behind my teacher's desk, from behind her in the crowded, deafening halls.

Hours later it was dark; I wanted her to stay the night, but I was afraid of what might happen if she did.

I took the coward's way out again: I left it up to her.

'It's late,' I said, glancing at my watch. It was twelve after ten. 'Should I go?'

'Are you asking?' I said.

'I don't know. I think I'm afraid to.'

'Won't anyone expect you?'

'Not tonight. Not until tomorrow morning, when I'm supposed to get off work.'

I let out a long, heavy sigh I'd been unaware of holding.

'If you ask me to stay,' she said, 'you'll be crossing the line. That's what you're thinking, isn't it?'

'No. I was thinking how far behind I left all the lines some time ago. I was thinking how deep the shit is I'm already in.'

'I've been here the past two days.'

'I was unconscious. And drugged.'

She nodded.

'Do you want to stay?'

'Are you asking me to?'

I tried to make myself say it but couldn't.

'Because if you're asking me to stay –'

'With me,' I managed, interrupting her.

She nodded. 'With you tonight. Here. The two of us. Alone. All night. Are you asking me to do that?'

Yes, I thought. 'No … I'm asking if you want to.'

'If you ask me to, I will. I wouldn't if I didn't want to. You wouldn't ask me if you didn't want me to, would you?'

I shook my head.

'So if you ask, I'll stay, and it'll be what we both want, which means it'll be a good thing, a good thing that's completely good. Maybe even better.'

'Your staying would be better than good,' I said.

She nodded. 'We could rent movies,' she said.

'And order pizza,' I added.

'And curl up with Brasco under the blankets and stay up all night and pretend there's no one else in the universe except the three of us.'

'And when I woke up you'd be there,' I said. 'That would be the best part.'

'Then ask me to, Cole,' she said, and my name coming from her like that was as startling and crisp as the sound of breaking glass. 'Ask me and I'll stay.'

I was pulled out of the memory as sweet as jasmine by the entrance into the office of Renaldo Regencia's apparent supervisor. He stepped into the office, a full head shorter than Señor Regencia, with sharp facial features and piercing brown eyes flecked through with green. I stood, shook his outstretched hand, then retook my seat.

After all, there was a lot of money in my company's account, and vice-presidents of multinational companies don't wait for bank managers to tell them they can sit.

'Mr. Coker,' the man said, smiling, his face even sharper for it, 'I am Gilbert Patrillo. It is a pleasure to meet you.'

'Likewise,' I said.

He maneuvered his way around Renaldo's wiry frame and took his seat at the desk. Renaldo remained standing.

'I trust Señor Regencia has been accommodating?'

I nodded. Said nothing. No need to speak when I could listen and let them do the talking. The money was there, everyone in the room knew it. It was mine, I was me – James Coker – so it was just a matter of time.

'The account you mention –'

'My company's account,' I interrupted, because it was the sort of thing done by the wealthy, the young, the impatient, and I was all three that afternoon. 'Outland Capital and Casualty Insurance.'

'Yes, sir. It's a rather unusually large amount, so we must take every precaution to ensure the complete integrity of any transactions.'

'As I'm sure you would for any lesser account,' I said, offering them a semi-smile. 'As I told Mr. Regencia, I would expect nothing less from a bank of your reputation.'

'We appreciate your patience,' he said, then began tapping the keys. Renaldo slid over a few feet to get a better view of the monitor. I uncrossed my legs, smoothed my pants, removed one of Brasco's hairs from my thigh, and recrossed them. I wondered what Savannah was doing just then, and forced the thought away. I didn't need my concentration divided right now.

'Could you confirm the account number for me once again please sir?' Patrillo asked.

I nodded. 'Of course. 9031971-09291979-0-595-09399-X. Registered to a male, approximately five-nine, brown hair, late twenties to early thirties, medium-build, tattoo on left shoulder.'

Tap-taptaptap-tap on the keyboard.

'The tattoo has been confirmed?' – Patrillo to Regencia.

Regencia nodded.

'The spelling is identical?' Patrillo.

Another nod from Regencia.

Patrillo looked at me.

More tapping on the keyboard. I waited. I counted to a hundred in my head, slowly, then backwards down to one. I waited some more until Patrillo said: 'Can you confirm the balance for me, Mr. Coker?'

'Of course. Is that necessary?'

'It is preferred,' he said, his cheekbones and nose looking sharp enough to cut paper.

'There was a single transaction by wire in early June – '

'Early June, Mr. Coker?'

'June second, to be precise. The origin of the transfer was the National Bank of Antigua.' I quoted him the balance.

Patrillo nodded. 'There is a maintenance fee on this particular type of account – where discretion is of the highest level – of one half of one percent of total deposits. We must charge this in order to maintain our policy of absolute secrecy, you understand. Your American government is not fond of foreign banks who do not comply with their disclosure policies. Staving them off is not a cheap undertaking.'

'It is because you do it so well, Mr. Patrillo, that my company chose this bank. Half a point is a bargain.'

He nodded. 'And what is the nature of your transaction this afternoon, sir?'

At this point I removed a piece of plain stationery from my inner breast pocket and slid it across the desk to him.

'There are three. I'd like one half of the balance wired immediately to the first bank listed there,' – a casual nod at the piece of paper, now in Patrillo's exotic brown hand – 'and the other half, minus ten thousand dollars, wired to the second. The accounts are already established, their routing numbers written next to them. The ten thousand I'd like to withdraw, in twenties and fifties if possible.' I smiled. 'This is my first visit to your beautiful country and I'm told there are many sights to see.'

'Certainly, sir. It will take a few moments. May I offer you a café while you wait?'

'Actually a restroom would be nice,' I said, standing.

Regencia fielded that one. 'Right this way, sir.'

Savannah had gone to get the movies and snacks; I'd stayed behind for obvious reasons. I didn't have many students who hung around the West Ashley area, but I couldn't risk it. All it would take would be for one person who recognized either of us to see us together and it would be like a brush fire, spreading past the point of containment with exponential speed.

She'd been gone less than five minutes when the phone rang.

'Cole,' she said when I picked up. Marla. Her voice let loose an assault of memories from two nights ago and I nearly doubled over with revulsion.

'Marla,' I said without inflection. 'Now's not a good time.'

'No, I didn't think that it would be. I'm terribly sorry about Greg. There's no excuse for his temper.'

'Yeah, well, he had a right. We were way out of line.'

'No one ever has a right to resort to violence. It's a total turn-off. I wanted to make sure you were all right.'

'You mean my face? I'm fine. I hear doorbells ringing every couple seconds but I'll heal. Like I said, I deserved it.'

'Nonsense, Cole. Greg's impossible when he drinks. I spent most of the night trying to convince him that it was nothing more than a fond memory-fuck, but he's hopelessly abstruse.'

'Obtuse.'

'What?'

'You mean obtuse. Abstruse means profound.'

'Whatever. That's the other thing I called about. It's probably best that we not see each other anymore. I know we've said that before, but Greg does in all his ranting have a point. I am engaged, and you know as well as anyone how destructive an emotion jealousy can be.'

'This is true,' I agreed.

'Besides, I don't really care for you Cole – certainly not enough to have any sort of relationship with. I think you're basically a sensitive guy, and you were always very cooperative when it came to eating lots of fruit; I really did appreciate that. Most men have such low fructose levels. And they wonder why we spit into the sheets.'

'If you can't drink orange juice for your girlfriend, who can you drink it for?'

'And I do hope our little tryst beneath the condo didn't lead you on. It's just that occasionally I find myself overwhelmed with the desire to eat you.'

'It's understandable,' I offered.

'Good, then,' she said. 'No hard feelings, then?'

'Marla?' I said calmly. It was time to tie this end off once and for all. If I didn't do it now there'd be another night beneath some condo or in some bar's bathroom somewhere, another goodbye-for-good call down the line.

'Hmmm?'

'There's something I've wanted to say to you for a long time now. I should have been fair to both of us way back when I caught you in the sack with that Deutscher-dyke roommate of yours, but … well – '

'Just say it, Cole. It isn't as if we haven't disagreed before.'

'I know, and I don't want to disagree anymore. I would have cut things off long ago, but to put it bluntly you've always had one hole or another just begging to have a dick thrown in it, and I've discovered that I am at heart a very weak person when it comes to that sort of thing, at least in your case, so I've put it off.'

'It isn't like you to lash out verbally like this. I'd always thought you more sophisticated.'

'You aren't a nice person, Marla.'

'You never complained before.'

'Yes I did. I complained constantly. You just couldn't hear me

225

because you were always listening to yourself talk. You're selfish and greedy and probably psychopathic. I'm sure a lot of it can be traced to your cold-fish parents, but whatever the reason you lack all semblance of a conscience, which means you aren't much more than a shell. A pretty, curvy shell with cooperative holes in it, and for my sake I need to get shut of that sort of thing.'

'I don't remember you fighting me, Cole Arch – '

'Marla?'

'What?' she snapped.

'I have to go now. I've got a life in progress. Goodbye.'

With that I hung up, and she was out of my life forever.

I felt clean and redeemed in some way, though I knew it would take more than simply cutting Marla loose and hanging up the phone to acquire redemption. But it was a start. That, and a hot shower, was at least a start.

Savannah had my keys and could let herself in, so I climbed into the shower and scrubbed myself down beneath the hot water. I got out, climbed into a clean pair of sweats, and set about situating the blankets on the floor just so. I grabbed the comforter from the couch and spread it out in front of the television. I then laid the pillows next to one another, stepped back and surveyed, then decided to leave a few inches' space between the pillows' edges. I didn't want the scene to appear too intimidating.

I spread two other blankets out atop the comforter, then cracked the single living room window an inch to let in some of the cold December air. I didn't want to freeze the place, but I wanted the atmosphere right for blankets.

Twenty minutes later she returned, a large Papa John's pizza in one hand, a Bi-Lo bag of ice cream and a two-liter root beer, and two movies in the other.

'Sorry it took so long. It was two-for-one night at Blockbusters. I got *Midnight in the Garden of Good and Evil*, since we're going to Savannah tomorrow.'

'Clever, clever,' I said, sticking the ice cream in the freezer and pouring up two glasses of root beer. 'What else did you get?'

'Something called *Lawn Dogs*. The back said it's about a rich lonely little girl who meets a down-on-his-luck, older lawn boy and forms a fairy-tale friendship with him. I don't know if it'll be any good or not, but the irony was too rich to pass up. Which one first? You pick.' She was holding them both up in the air, and in that moment – standing there in my living room in her baggy sweats and her hair pulled back behind her ears and her face expressing all the possibilities of the road we were starting down together – in that moment she was more beautiful to me than she'd ever been. I was so comfortable with her like that, so free and willing to allow the evening to simply unfold on its own, that I was seized with a nearly irresistible urge to run to her and grab her and hold her body flush against my own, to squeeze hard enough to make the rules of the world outside go away, hard enough to make the choices I was making be as right as I wanted them to be.

I didn't do any of that, though. I think if I had, she would have returned it. I'm nearly positive of that. I think I would have found peace in her arms right then, peace and meaning and purpose in the fact that someone as smart and sincere as she, however unformed she still might be, had chosen me to open up to. I think I could have felt good about that for the rest of my life, as a man and as a teacher.

Instead I pointed to the movie in her right hand, which turned out to be the one about the lawn boy and the little girl, and we ate pizza and root beer floats and crawled under the blankets and watched the little girl and the lawn boy create their own magic world to keep the pain out, and somewhere in there I realized she'd fallen asleep, her head on my chest, the scent of her hair and skin filling the room with all the smells of a sunset on the Oregon coastline.

Brasco and I left the parking lot in our beat-up Ford F150 with ten thousand dollars cash in my socks and underwear, and an everloving shitpile waiting for us Out There. All we had to do was go and get it.

I found a convenience store and changed out of the suit, figuring the best way to get mugged in a place like Mexico City was to walk around dressed like you were carrying cash, asking directions in English.

I filled the truck's twin tanks up and bought a shrink-wrapped turkey sandwich and a large orange-juice, a can of tuna for Brasco, a pack of Chesterfields for me, and a hundred-minute phone card. On the payphone outside I dialed up the first of the two banks listed on the sheet I'd slid across the desk to Patrillo. I spent five minutes on hold watching Brasco in the truck, situating himself in the crook of the dash and windshield, keeping a watchful eye on me. When the woman came back on the line, her Bermudan accent oddly comforting in this land of foreign tongues, I recited by memory the transaction number Patrillo had given me, followed by the receiving account's number, and tried to remain calm as she confirmed the balance. I thanked her and hung up. It was all I could do to keep from dropping the phone.

I stood there for a few seconds, catching my breath. The truck and Brasco in it faded in and out of focus, everything going blurry around the edges like a telescope lens gradually closing in on itself. I had to hold myself up against the side of the convenience store.

I opened the orange juice and downed a third of it, then dialed the second bank, this one in Aruba. The man's accent on the other end of the line was a crisp Dutch and extremely heavy. He asked me for the transaction number. I gave it to him. He asked for the number of the receiving account. I gave him that, too. He spoke for three or four minutes about transaction fees and wire policy and institutional privacy regulations, a lot of which I missed. I got the important part, though. The transfer had been received by them via wire some twenty minutes ago from Mexico City International Bank and Loan and deposited into said account. He said it as casually as if it'd been fifty bucks.

Brasco and I left then, driving around in circles for half an hour until we found a mid-range hotel where we checked in and spent the next three days sleeping, eating room service, and watching our story on CNN.

I opened my eyes to see her opening hers. I'd fallen asleep during the movie and now it was over and the VCR had turned itself off, leaving the room trembling in the gauzy, liquid blue of the blank television screen. I had no idea what time it was, and I didn't care. I didn't want the sun ever to come up. I wanted to live the rest of my life right here, on my comforter across from her, both of us protected from the world by the safety of blankets.

She'd moved during the night. Her head was off my chest and over on her pillow, facing me. I allowed myself to run my eyes over the outline of her shape beneath the covers. Down her side, dipping in at her small waist, rising up with the sloping arc of her hips. I could feel her watching me drinking her in. I looked into her eyes for a reaction – embarrassment, repugnance, arousal, surprise – but got nothing. Her countenance was stone.

Heat radiated off of her beneath the blankets, pushing against my legs and stomach like a force. She wasn't more than a foot away from me, twelve inches of warm dark air separating our bodies. Tiny beads of sweat had formed along her hairline, and they shimmered like bubbles in a pond. I had the urge to lick them and press their saltiness against the roof of my mouth.

Her breath smelled peppery, hot and terrifyingly close. She was still looking at me. I kept waiting for her to say something, and I know the reason she didn't is because she knew I needed her to.

My stomach started to burn and it got tough to breathe, as if all the air in the room had suddenly become too thin and light to pull in. My senses grew extraordinarily keen. I could hear her heartbeats reverberating through the floor and my pillow. I heard the sound of her ribcage rising and falling beneath the blanket. I heard my eyelids click with each blink. From between my ankles I could hear Brasco's short, steady breaths. From within my ears I heard my blood whispering through my veins like silk rubbed against smooth wood.

'Do you want to kiss me?' Her voice split the night like a wedge.

Every part of me responded, screaming in whatever way it had. My throat constricted and burned with bile.

'Savannah.' It was all I could say.

'Because you can.' Soft, like rain falling on a garden. 'I want you to.'

I'd gone hard beneath the blankets and I wondered if she'd change her mind about kissing me if she knew.

'I can't.'

'Why not?'

I slid a hand out from beneath the blankets, across the twelve-inch expanse separating us, brushing it through her hair.

'I love your hair,' I said.

She smiled. 'No one's ever told me that and meant it.'

'They meant it.'

'What part of me do you like the most?'

I remembered reading in one of those Oprah Club books that men who fantasized about women's rears were closet fags. Men drawn to legs secretly wanted to be women. Breast men were yearning for their mothers. And no man, the book said, was attracted to the pussy proper because deep inside we were all afraid of it.

229

None of that applied to me, though. I knew exactly what part of Savannah it was that held dominion in my dreams. I'm not sure what it said about me.

'Your voice.'

'That's not a body part.'

'I don't care. I could listen to your voice forever. Your voice could make me forget to breathe.'

She inched toward me. One inch.

'Do you want to know what my favorite part of you is?'

'I didn't know you had one.'

She nodded in the tourmaline blue light. 'Your hands.'

'My hands? Why?'

'They're safe. They look like hands that could never hurt anyone.'

I moved my hand from her hair and touched my thumb to her cheek. If she noticed it didn't show.

'They've hurt people before.'

She shook her head. 'I watch them while you teach.'

My thumb ran up her cheek as though her skin was a razor that would cut me if I pushed too hard.

'You talk with your hands when you lecture, and the girls in the back talk dirty about you while you do.'

Ordinarily this would have been vaguely interesting to me. Tonight I didn't care.

Tonight I fought to keep the images out, images that set every nerve-ending on fire, images that skinned open every sense and left them weeping and raw. The feel of her hands on my body, burning and freezing me all at once. The smell of the hollow of her neck, the night's sweat sprinkled over her throat and shoulder. The low, brassy sounds I knew she'd make when I touched her down there, touched her with fingers that spoke of love and safety and worship.

The taste of her saliva, sweeter than water.

'Chessie says you make her hips tingle.'

'N'Sync makes Chessie's hips tingle. Chessie's a doof.'

She slid closer again. Another inch.

I thought how good it was that she couldn't see my thoughts; I had a fear that she and I were seeing this same scene played out from different perspectives. Every cell in my body had gone hard; my hands were shaking and my mouth felt like I'd been sucking on cotton all night. I was channeling all my energy into not slipping my hand behind her head and pulling her into me, running my hands down her side and under her sweatshirt, licking and tasting every inch of her.

'Kiss me, Cole.'

I'd wanted her to say it so badly I wasn't sure if the voice had been real or not.

'Kiss me,' she whispered again.

I moved forward even as I begged myself to back away.

Her eyes were big and watery and looked almost electric in the blue light.

'Savannah, if we do this everything will change.'

'Everything's already changed.'

'It'll change forever.'

'I want it to.' Her mouth found my thumb and kissed the tip. I thought there'd been the softest hint of tongue there, but I couldn't be sure.

'Don't you?' she asked.

Another inch. Then another.

I moved my hand to her throat, touched a gathering of dust-like freckles in the center that I'd first noticed the day she'd stayed after class to thank me for being her teacher.

She moved closer still, her lips parted. I could barely tell her breath from mine.

'There are things we can't predict,' I said.

'Good.'

'I could hurt you,' I said, and there were a thousand ways that could be true.

'That's what makes it so good,' she said. 'Because I know you never will.'

When I allow myself to recall the trip to Savannah with Savannah it is always in the same sequence that the events replay themselves for me. They never vary or waver, as many of my recollections do, and they never break apart and reassemble in any new order, as most strands of remembrance will beneath the weight of time. In the canon of my memories they are unique in their immutability.

Sitting alone on the side of my bed in the apartment listening to the water splash as she washed herself in my shower, humming a familiar tune I had trouble placing. Opening her door for her in my little Honda for the first time. The seamless conversation on the drive down. The way her hair played tricks with the sun in the open-air café as she lowered her head to study the menu. The twist of her face when she bit into a wedge of lemon. Walking along the cobblestones of Bay Street, popping in and out of every sort of store. Stores that sold candles, chocolates, taffy, t-shirts, books, tobacco, leather, knives, Swarski's crystals, bamboo furniture, always in that order, the order of that afternoon. Giving her the necklace, her crying as she realized I'd bought it before she touched me in the hospital. When the sun dropped into the Savannah River I touched her hand with mine. She leaned her head against my shoulder and let out a little sigh I'd meant to ask her about. I'd been opening my mouth to speak words we never heard because she put hers over mine and kissed me while the daylight died and told me I was her savior.

TWENTY-TWO

Cole gets a lesson in Winter's Cove history; Savannah's new job; Taryn the cheerleader

Zack Capers called me the night of Dec. 31st. I'd been watching television alone on the couch with Brasco, wondering if Savannah was going to be able to slip away long enough to give me a buzz on her break. She was working at an all-night Huddle House downtown on King Street, and didn't clock out until two tomorrow morning. Her manager had told her personal phone calls were an absolute no-no, so I'd been thinking about slipping down there to surprise her when the phone rang.

'Hi, rookie,' his strong, deep voice boomed. 'I'm not interrupting your grading, am I?'

'As a matter of fact –' I trailed off, shooting for ironic. I doubt he got it, though. I knew Zack Capers had spent a number of Friday nights toiling over lit. crit. essays and research papers and discussion-question tests and all the rest of it. He wrote comments all up and down the students' papers, and I'd bet the back half of my prick most of them got tossed in the can without so much as glance.

'I've got an interesting piece of news,' he said.

'Good or bad?'

'For you?'

'For starters.'

'Neither,' he said. 'It concerns me. You knew Ricke was leaving us, didn't you?'

'Ricke?' The name didn't do anything for me.

'Collins.'

'Oh, right. I don't ever –'

'I know, I know. You never felt comfortable calling him Ricke. Looks like you won't get your chance, now. He's moving up. He got the superintendent's spot in Greenville.'

233

'Wow.' I knew that was probably meant to impress me, but it was like listening to white noise on the tube. Just about anything else would have been more stimulating.

'Which means the District's in a frenzy to fill the principal's spot at The Creek.'

The Creek was short for Coosaw Creek High School, which for me was short for House of Pain, Shop of Horrors, Shower Time in the Turkish Prison, take your pick.

'You up for it?' I asked.

'Not exactly. I was wondering what your plans were for the next couple hours. You have a big date lined up or anything?'

I checked my watch. It was a quarter after ten. Savannah didn't get off for another five and a half hours.

'I was going to wash my cat,' I said. 'What did you have in mind?'

He laughed. 'Want to meet me for a couple beers? Tamela's got a kitchenware party going on and I've got to make myself scarce before I drown in estrogen. There's a little pub not far up 61 called The Red Wolf Inn. Ever heard of it?'

'Been there many times. It's one of the few that stays open past two.'

'That it is,' he said. 'I'll be there in half an hour.'

Capers had to come from Winter's Cove, which was twenty miles up Highway 61, which was more of a two-lane cut of blacktop through the trees than a highway. I'd been there fifteen minutes and two beers when he came in. His eyes caught mine across the way and he threw me a mock-salute. I nodded, thinking how I'd have to go home and shower the smoke out of my hair and off my skin if I was planning on surprising Savannah. I didn't want to show up stinking like a bar.

He swung by the bar first, said a few words I couldn't hear over the noise to the girl serving drinks with one hand and wiping spills with the other. The girl smiled in that way people smiled when they knew each other professionally or had fucked in the past. I didn't know the case with Capers, and would never be close enough to him to ask.

'Mr. Archer,' he said collegially, sitting across from me. 'Thanks for coming.'

I shrugged. 'No problem. I'm always up for a beer or ten.'

He nodded at the bandage taped over the side of my face.

'What the hell happened there?'

'Fell of the back of a buddy's motorcycle.'

He winced. 'No helmet?'

I shook my head. 'No common sense, either.'

He was looking over the menu. 'I'm surprised you're not out with the boys tonight: this the last Friday of the year and all.'

'I wasn't up to it. I think I'm coming down with something. Besides, after the millennium, they're all pretty much the same.'

'Do you remember where you were?'

'When the millennium turned over? Sure. I was drunk. Weren't you?'

He nodded. 'Tamela and I had some friends over and the six of us got blitzed on boxed wine and watched the comedy shows on HBO. It was pretty grim.'

'My then-fiancée and I were in DC. I'd just proposed and she'd just said yes and we were locked up on the dance floor in one club or another when the ball dropped. It was a good night.'

'Bad break-up?'

'Probably the worst in human history,' I said, ending it there.

'Sorry to hear that,' he said in a tone that suggested he really was. Capers was one of those rare birds you stumble across every now and again who doesn't seem to have the capacity to lie. What he says isn't always too fucking pleasant to hear, and it's never sugar-coated, but it is always the truth as he knows it.

'No, it's okay now,' I said as much to myself as to Capers. 'I couldn't have said that six months ago, but there's no pain anymore. It's kind of like a cut that gets infected but eventually heals up and after a while you forget even where it was.'

Jennie the waitress arrived with two more beers – another Guinness for me and a Rolling Rock for the Caped One. Jennie the waitress was a redhead with a silly smile and a tongue-stud the size of a railroad spike. She was also at least eight months pregnant.

That bothered me.

Capers took a long sip of his Rolling Rock, and I started in on the Guinness.

'How are you coming with your Long-Range Plan?' he asked.

'I'm working on it,' I said, which was a lie. I wasn't like Capers in that department. Or a lot of others either, I bet.

He nodded. 'Be sure you do. That bunch at the District blow their fair share of hot air, but they are serious when it comes to the

Long-Range Plan. You know we lost a good teacher last year simply because he wouldn't finish his.'

The Long-Range Plan was a document every first-year teacher had to generate. Its stated purpose is to walk its reader through the entire academic year, instructional unit by instructional unit, week by week, educational strand by educational strand. It covered everything from Short-Range Planning to Communication with Parents to Creating an Environment Conducive to Learning, to Materials Used in the Classroom, and so on and so forth, *ad nauseam, ad infinitum*. The second-year teachers I'd spoken with who'd all gone through it last year likened it to a root-canal/enema combo, with the dentist and the proctologist fighting over who could go deeper.

Most of my fellow first-years were well into theirs, which was a good thing, since they were due the first of May. A few of the more eager beavers had already finished and turned theirs in. I was planning on beginning mine over Christmas break. Now all I could think about was Savannah and the way her tongue had tasted like strawberries. Cataloguing the number of pencils and rubber bands I use in my class just didn't seem terribly relevant.

'They just fired him?'

'They don't call it firing,' he shook his head. 'They call it not renewing your contract. They can do that the first two years, you know.'

I knew. They told you all the time your first year. You're an induction teacher. You can go at anytime. It's like having pancreatic cancer. Tomorrow's never a guarantee.

'You'd think with the national teachers shortage they'd stop threatening us with that sort of shit,' I said around my beer bottle. 'Like you said, if I get hit by a bus tomorrow there isn't an English application on file for them to choose from. You think they'd really can me because I didn't type up some first-year playbook?'

'Yep,' he said. 'In a minute. And you're right. They wouldn't have anyone to replace you with. They need you more than you need them. It isn't hard for you to turn around and go find a job paying you what you're making now. Hell, Becka behind the bar probably makes more than either of us.' He took a slug from the Rolling Rock and looked across the table into my eyes with an intensity I had long ago come to associate with him.

'But they'll let you go anyway, because they're stupid, and

they're insulated, and they don't have to be either efficient or productive. If they were in the business world they'd have been out of business a long time ago. But they're not. They're in education, and as you've probably already begun to see, in education the stakes are low.'

'Then how do they keep their jobs? Who puts them there?'

'The Board.'

'How do the Board Members get their job?'

'They're elected officials.'

'Then it's the voters.'

'Yes and no.'

'I don't understand.'

'The voters put them there to begin with, but after that it's all but a sure thing. Every once in a while you get someone who really pisses everyone off, and someone will come along and bump him out of his seat, but that's rare. It happened with the uncle of that shit for brains who slept with his student, but that's only because he fought it so hard. He didn't leave anyone much choice. Before that was almost a decade ago. Before that, who knows.'

'We've had the same Board for ten years?'

He nodded. 'Longer. You've got the famous basketball coach, who'll get re-elected after he's dead –'

'Delaney?'

'Chopper Delaney, yes sir. Most winningest high school basketball coach in America. There's not even a close second. Folks in Winter's Cove go to church Sunday morning to pray to God, and back again Sunday night to worship Chopper Delaney. People who weren't even born when he retired vote for him because it's all they know up there. No one's even run against him in the last fifteen years.'

I raised my glass in a mock fashion. 'Three cheers for the Grade-A good ol' boy system,' I said. 'Our test scores are low, but we can by God reward an old Winter's Cove family.'

Capers was nodding. 'You're more right than you think. If you had time enough and cared to do some digging, you'd find plenty where that sort of thing came from.'

'What do you mean?'

'Swing by your local library sometime. Better yet, hit the town planner's office up in The Cove. It's all public information. All available for anyone who wants to look. Check the land purchases, the residential developments, the construction permits, the zoning board, the police department, the credit union's board of directors, the school board, the newspaper's private shareholders, and so forth. Check all the names of all the District's superintendents from the past. Go back far enough, you'll keep running across the same ten or so names.' He chuckled to himself. 'Family ties are a wonderful thing.'

'How far is far enough?'

He shrugged. 'Hundred years ought to do it.'

'And it's their kids now?'

'Not exclusively, no,' he said. 'They wish. But it's the next best thing. It's their kids and their kids' kids. And it's those kids' in-laws and their business partners and their lovers and their country-club buddies. Those ten names have had to spread out and diversify a bit as the town has grown, but they've kept things pretty well in check.'

'How?'

'I just told you how. Marriage, nepotism, mergers, sponsorships, fucking. It's like any other small town; it's got a closet. Just the way it is.'

I shook my head. If every one in Winter's Cove paired off and took turns tail-piping their chocolate lab it wouldn't change one aspect of my life, but still the idea intrigued me.

'Sounds like a good idea for a book,' I said. 'Anyone ever do anything with it?'

'No,' Capers said. 'Maybe you should. Hell, there are some pretty interesting stories. Who knows, in the hands of a skilled writer –'

'That leaves me out,' I said. 'Besides, I can't finish my Long-Range Plan and play Pat Conroy at the same time.'

Jennie the pregnant waitress came back and took away our empty bottles and replaced them with two more of the same. I noticed her hand stunk of cigarette smoke. It disgusted me that she'd smoke while pregnant. It also made me want a cigarette.

'Did she smell like smoke to you?' I asked.

'She works in a bar.'

'Yeah, no, I mean her hands. I thought I smelled smoke on her hands, like she'd burned one on her break.'

'Who knows? Fifteen years from now that kid'll be in your class, and if his SAT scores aren't what they should be, it'll be your fault.' He raised his glass. 'Hell of a job we have, isn't it?'

'Yeah,' I said, swallowing enough Guinness to hurt my throat.

'Hell of a job.'

'Which actually serves as a nice segue into why I wanted you to meet me here. I mentioned Collins took the superintendent's spot up in Greenville, leaving an emergency vacancy at The Creek.'

I nodded. 'You interested in it?'

'And get demoted from teacher to professional educator? Not in this lifetime. But my brother-in-law, Tamela's brother, pretty much has a lock on it.'

'What do you mean lock? Have they even listed the spot as available yet?'

He shook his head, a small smile emerging on his face red with windburn. 'Welcome to Winter's Cove. It's all being done in-house.'

'Is that legal?'

' "Legal" is a technical term. The Board's going to hire who the Board wants to hire. Olin's going to get it because he's a good man and a known quantity and he's been loyal to the district his entire life. He went to school in Winter's Cove. Married a Winter's Cove girl three decades ago and stayed here to raise his family. All six of his kids go to school here. He's paid his dues to the District, and the District takes note of that.'

I finished the last of my Guinness and glanced around for Jennie the orally-enhanced waitress. I couldn't find her. She was probably out back toking up, the kid in her belly getting stoned again, a couple weeks shy of this world and already hamstrung by forces beyond its control. It made me ill. I wondered what it'd be like punching Jennie in the face, hard enough to dislodge that dick-sucking tool she had in her mouth, hard enough for the blood and snot to run out of her nose like water from a cut pipe. I could do it. I could excuse myself from Capers here, go out back, find her standing around the broken-down piles of beer-boxes smoking and thinking about whatever shit trash like that thought about while they abused their kids, and smash my elbow into the meat of her face a couple times. I'd come sit back down without breaking a sweat or tweaking my conscience the slightest bit. They'd find her when enough customers complained their beers were empty or their sandwiches were still missing.

'So good deal, then. You'll have connections in the big guy's office.'

He shook his head. 'See, here's where the hypocrisy rears its head. I got a call from Olin a few nights ago. He wanted me to hear it from him first before it trickled its way down into the classrooms. They're not going to be able to keep us both at The Creek. If they're moving him in, they'll be moving me out.'

'What the hell for?'

'Nepotism, Mr. Archer,' he said. 'The District has a firm policy against nepotism.'

'Nepotism? You've got to be kidding me. I've been there five months and I can give you half a dozen examples of nepotism running around. Alicia in Spanish? Her father-in-law is Walker, an assistant principal. Briars in English? Her husband is in personnel at the District. He's one of my evaluators. And Bangmore in PE? Come on. That nimrod's old man is on the Board, for crying out loud. Even I know that. That means he votes on the size raise his kid gets each year.'

Capers was nodding. 'That's why I called you tonight. There's going to be a hearing shortly after we get back. I think you should go. It'll give you a feel for the way things work on paper, and the way they work in practice. The earlier in your career you learn the difference the better off you're apt to be.' He took a long, pensive swallow on his Rolling Rock. 'It'll be an education, I'll guarantee you that much.'

'Who called the hearing?'

'No one yet. First Olin'll have to be hired officially, which'll be sometime next week I'm betting.'

'Before we get back to school they'll do it?'

'Oh, you better believe it. They'll announce it in the paper and Olin will release a brief statement thanking everyone from God down to the janitor. Sometime over the summer they'll stencil on the office door "Pepperidge" where it says "Collins" and that'll be the end of it.'

Jennie finally returned from her cigarette or crack pipe or whatever it was she was doing while she was gone, and Capers ordered us two more beers.

'Once that's done – the official announcement – I'll be notified within a day or two that I'm being transferred to somewhere else within the district.'

'A middle-school,' I said with finality. No one wanted to teach middle-school, least of all high-school teachers. Most of them would rather be transferred to Kosovo than step foot into a middle-school classroom.

He nodded gravely. 'The hour I get notice I'll file a grievance; under the rules of the district I'm entitled to a public hearing. I intend to make it very public, very informative, and very cathartic. They'll have to give me fifteen minutes of unabridged speaking time during which I will summarily rip the Board and their hypocritical policies a new set of assholes. It won't work, but it'll make me feel a hell of a lot better. Then I'll go over to Berkfield county.'

Capers and I stayed at The Red Wolf another half hour before I began feeling my buzz and decided I ought to shut off the spigot since I was heading down to the Huddle House to see Savannah later. Showing up with a buzz wouldn't be much better than showing up stinking like a bar.

We each dropped a five-spot on the table for Jennie so she could buy more cigarettes, and we left. He didn't speak to the woman – Becka, he'd called her – behind the bar on the way out.

'You know,' Capers was saying, climbing in behind the wheel of his faded blue Jeep Cherokee, 'I might play it another way and hire a lawyer to argue my case for me. Do the digging you and I were talking about and build a case for discrimination based on the rampant nepotism that goes on in the District.'

I whistled. 'You sue your employer, you better not lose. Biting the hand, and all.'

He thought about that for a second, sitting there in the driver's seat, the engine idling loudly. He looked big and imposing hunched over the wheel like that, the lines and angles of his face all shiny and smooth and red from the endless hours he spent sailing the Ashley and Cooper.

'They'll more than likely settle,' he said. 'The District's had some bad publicity lately. It'd be worth a couple hundred thousand just to shut me up, particularly when they know I'm right. I'll buy myself a sailboat and name her WINTER'S COVE.'

I laughed. 'What about your family? Won't that make Christmas kind of awkward, you suing your employer because your brother-in-law's getting hired caused you to be transferred?'

He shook his head. 'Fuck 'em,' he said, and off he went, leaving me standing there in the middle of the parking lot of The Red Wolf Inn, picturing the most dedicated teacher I'd ever met – a man who spent hours each night grading papers and reading student essays because he cared so much – relaxing in his cut-off khakis in the middle of the Cooper River, catching the currents beneath the bridges with the wind blowing through his graying hair and his face a shiny metallic red, a couple hundred thousand of school district money earning ten percent for him while he sailed along in a boat named WINTER'S COVE.

I was pulling out myself two minutes later when I was struck with an idea I felt compelled to see through.

I left the Honda idling and climbed the four wooden steps into The Red Wolf Inn. It took me a few seconds, but then I saw her, wiping down a table in the opposite corner.

'Jennie,' I said, approaching her from behind.

She turned and looked at me, then smiled when she recognized me from one of her other tables.

'Oh, hey. Did you forget something?'

'You shouldn't be smoking while you're pregnant,' I said. 'It can hurt the kid.'

She looked at me funny, like she hadn't understood what I said.

'Is it a boy or a girl?'

'Huh?'

'Your baby,' I said, nodding at her belly. 'Do you know what it is?'

'Little girl,' she said.

I nodded. 'A little girl. You know you're hurting her every time you light up, don't you?'

Her hands made her way to their hips, and her mouth hung open a bit the way women on Jerry Springer hang their mouths open when they're going for that victim look.

'I don't see how it's any of your –'

'It's my business because I'm a teacher, and I have to deal with the mess people like you make. You can't just go around fucking and smoking and doing whatever the hell else you want to do and pretend it's not going to affect your kid.'

That really bothered her, which for some reason pleased me.

'Isn't it enough that you're bringing her into this tits-up world without a father? Do you have to make sure she's born smaller and weaker and less intelligent than she might have been had her mother not been a barmaid who can't kick the habit for nine lousy months?'

'I think you better leave,' she said with a clarity that surprised me. 'You don't know anything about me.'

'I know you smoke. I know you're pregnant. I know you have a nail through your tongue the size of a fucking pool cue. Tongue-studs are for chugging cock and licking clit, and you don't need to be doing either while you're pregnant. Later, after she's born, if that's what rocks your socks, fine. But not now. You've got a child inside of you. It isn't the uterine lining and it isn't just a bunch of blood and snot all rolled together. It's a little girl. She might grow up to do good things, Jennie. She might turn out to be a beautiful person on the inside who makes this planet that much nicer. Can't you even give her that chance?'

'Either you leave, asshole, or I'll have my manager toss you out on your ass. Fuck you for telling me how to live my life, you fucker. Who the fuck are you to judge me?'

I stood there a second, looking at her, seeing her entire life up to this moment and the life of her child up through high school, seeing the disappointments that'd been had by her and that would be had again by her progeny, and I couldn't make myself be mad at Jennie anymore. I felt sorry for them both. I hoped there was someone around like Zack Capers when her little girl got to her adolescence and needed someone to help her through it. There wouldn't be, because people like Zack Capers didn't stick around in the classroom long. A pension wasn't part of their plans. They gave it ten, fifteen years tops, then they left because they had no more to give. Or they got bumped out by a nepotistic district that didn't believe in nepotism.

It probably wouldn't have mattered, anyway. Most of who we are was established before we were born, before we'd even formed fingers or toes.

Besides, she was right about one thing. Who the fuck was I to be judging her?

'You could at least stop smoking,' I said, then turned and left.

By a quarter after one I was riding through the velvety night down 61, heading towards the Ashley River Bridge and across the water into the city of Charleston. The city really is remarkable at night. The jagged skyline shimmers and glows the colors of uncut gems; steeples jut up between the centuries-old buildings like calcium and coal stalagmites under ground. All around you're aware of the presence of water, of its gentle, insistent, perennial lapping against the marsh and pluff-mud, and it reminds you that you're very nearly on an island, the center of something, which makes perfect sense once you've lived in Charleston long enough. For those who call it home, Charleston is the center of the world.

The Huddle House where Savannah was working was on the corner of King and Courtney Streets. I got there at twenty to two and parked my car along the curb. I checked my teeth in the mirror and popped two pieces of Wrigley's Spearmint in my mouth. The windows to the place were full-size, floor to ceiling numbers that ran the entire length of the restaurant. I could see people milling around in there, heads bent over plates covered in piles of varying shades of brown, yellow, and red. I counted two, three, then a fourth waitress going back and forth, moving quickly the way waitresses serving drunken revelers with early-morning munchies have to move. None of the four was Savannah.

Their uniforms were pink, patterned over with white squares and rhomboids, cut above the knees. I was looking forward to seeing Savannah in it, the pink pinching in at her waist, then flaring just a little at her small, young hips. When she got off at two and saw me waiting for her she'd smile and blush both at once, a medley of expressions that made my insides turn to water.

By five till two the last of the drunks had stepped awkwardly out onto the sidewalk, joining the steady drizzle of others just like them, making their way down King Street in search for somewhere open after-hours. They were all hugging and talking and holding on to whoever happened to be standing next to them. Lighters lit cigarettes, cigars, and joints. Bottles of liquor appeared from coat pockets. A few of them were still wearing 'Happy New Year' hats. Someone twirled a noise-maker. Their voices were loud and seemed to carry forever in the cold, clear night. It'd been next year for nearly two hours now, and everyone was happy.

On any other New Year's Eve I might have been one of them, drinking and laughing and stumbling along Charleston's down-town streets looking for the next party. But tonight the year had ended without my even noticing. I'd caught the time as I'd climbed into the shower; it'd been 12:30, which meant that at midnight I was lying on my back on the floor of the living room, Brasco on my chest, the two of us staring absently at one another, and at least one of us thinking of nothing but Savannah.

So now I sat behind the wheel of my little Honda and waited, watching for Savannah, wondering if she'd have time for a walk along Waterfront Park before having to go home. I wasn't going to ask her. I didn't want her to feel bad if she couldn't. It would be enough to simply see her for a few moments, to hear her voice as she called my name aloud.

By ten after two the waitresses were beginning to file out. I saw the four I'd watched earlier, followed by two others I hadn't seen. I watched the last one, a woman in her late fifties or so, set her purse and a white Styrofoam To Go box on the sidewalk as she reached in to turn the lights off, casting the entire place in darkness, the wall of windows becoming one giant mirror against the night.

I was out of my car in one half of one second.

'Excuse me,' I said, approaching the woman. She was stooping over to retrieve her To Go box. She looked at me quizzically and took a step in my direction.

'Has Savannah already left?'

Her look softened.

'Who?'

'Savannah Bellington. She's new. Just started a couple days ago. Young girl, curly-brown hair...'

'I don't know of...' – she looked at the others, clustered together like sheep for warmth. 'Does anyone named Savannah work here?' She asked them.

I turned my attention to them.

'She just started,' I said again. 'Tonight was only her second night.'

They were all shaking their heads.

'Maybe she called in sick,' I said, wondering why, if that was so, she hadn't called me. Even if she had to stay home to watch her brothers, surely she would have had the chance to find a phone.

A terrible thought washed over me then. Something had happened. Her piece-of-shit car had left her stranded on the interstate. Or one of her brothers had gotten hurt and she'd had to rush him to the hospital. Or whoever was fucking her mother this week could have lost it and hurt her.

'We haven't hired anyone new for close to three months now,' one of the sheep said. She was younger but grayer and was also taking home leftovers.

'I've been here seventeen years,' she continued. 'I'd know if anyone new had come aboard.'

'You're sure?' I asked, trying not to plead, the looks in their eyes telling me I'd failed.

'I'm sorry, young man,' the door-locker said, and she looked like she probably meant it.

'Thanks,' I said. 'Sorry to have bothered you.'

'No bother,' one of them said.

'Happy New Year,' a different one offered.

I got in my car and considered calling her even though I knew I couldn't. There were rules, and that was one of them. I could never call her house. It'd been Savannah who'd established that, but of course I'd known she was right. I had to keep reminding myself that I was her teacher, she my student, and that no one else on the planet – with the possible exception of Grey, who didn't count – would look upon what we were doing with favorable eyes.

'Fuck,' I heard myself whisper. It was getting difficult to breathe. My stomach had started burning.

'Fuck.' My hands were shaking. 'Fuck fuck fuck fuck fuck.'

I drove to Capone's half a mile down King Street, struggling against the urge to floorboard the Honda through one of the plate-glass windows that lined the street.

Capone's was still kicking. The air was thick with smoke and phero-mones and the sound of glass striking glass. I shoved my way to the bar, the floor vibrating from the music, and ordered a Killian's. Capone's doesn't carry Guinness, which is their primary flaw.

I was sitting in one of the old reclining chairs in the corner, nursing my beer, when it occurred to me that Capone's second flaw was that Marla worked here. She was absolutely the last person I wanted to run into, now or ever again. The last time I'd seen her I'd ended up unconscious, left with a concussion and bits of her shit on me. It was a pretty good metaphor for our entire relationship, now that I thought about it.

I was standing to leave when I saw Jules. He'd seen me, and was making his way my direction.

I sat back down. He found a chair and pulled it into the corner next to mine.

'Glad you're all right,' he said, slumping down into his chair. 'Your face looks like shit.'

'Yeah.'

'Hurt?'

I shrugged. 'Only when I blink.'

'Drink more. It numbs the pain.'

I nodded. 'Thanks for getting me to the hospital,' I said.

'I didn't. Marla did. I didn't know where the hell you were.'

'Thanks for telling her I was there,' I said.

'Marla? To hell with her.'

'Not her.'

'Oh,' he said. 'Her.'

I nodded. The music was a techno-mix of Aerosmith and Four Non-Blondes. I was almost done with my beer.

'How's that going, by the way?' he asked.

Another shrug. 'If I say good, it's bad. If it's going bad, you'd tell me that's a good thing.'

'Hey, Cole. I don't judge you, man. If she's old enough to brush her own teeth, then by all means. You know me. Grass on the field, old enough to play, all that shit. I just worry about you.'

'I know,' I said. 'I appreciate it.'

Neither of us spoke for a while.

'That where you were earlier? With her?'

I nodded.

'You fuck her?'

'Jules.'

'What? It's a legitimate question.'

'It's a fucked-up question.'

'No, it's a fucked-up situation. Fucking her's no worse than spending weekends with her. Better, actually. Long as you don't send any salmon spawning upstream you can fuck and just fuck off. That's not what's going on here though, is it?'

'No. It's not.'

He nodded slowly. 'I didn't think so.'

I finished my beer.

'How long we been pals, Cole?'

'Long time.'

'Since freshman year at Carolina, right?'

I nodded.

'I've always been straight with you, right?'

Another nod.

'So you know what I say I say out of concern.'

'Yeah. I do. And I appreciate it, Jules. I do.'

There was another stretch of silence. I wondered where Savannah was. I wondered if she was all right. I wondered why I felt like I'd been lied to, and I felt guilty for the wondering.

Jules stretched his back and yawned.

'This one's going to get more complicated before it gets easier, isn't it?'

'Yeah,' I said. 'I think so.'

'Anything I can do?'

'You can drink with me,' I said.

'I can do that.'

'You can never ask me again if I'm sleeping with her.'

'Fair enough. Doesn't matter much at this point, anyway.'

'And you can promise me that if any of your fellow jackals over at Channel Five get a tip about anything hinky going on at The Creek you'll give me notice before the story's assigned.'

'You don't even have to ask that,' he said. 'I got no loyalty to them.'

'I know how you newsies get pissed when things leak.'

'Fuck 'em.'

'They hold grudges.'

'Fuck 'em and feed 'em fish.'

I nodded.

'You want to get out of here?' he asked.

I did. But it wasn't Capone's. I couldn't sit still. I had to keep moving. If I sat around in one place too long I started thinking, and the thinking led to wondering, and the wondering never led to anywhere good.

'Chasey Lain's over at The Belle tonight.'

'No shit?' I said.

'None at all. New Year's extravaganza. She came by the station today for an interview with Greg. Looked almost plain without the makeup. Except for the tits.'

'How's his arm, by the way? Hope he didn't hurt it trying to take my head off.'

'I think you're off the wedding-guest list,' he said. 'He wasn't happy that night. Marla insisting on taking you to the hospital didn't help things.' He smiled. 'I really do hate her, dude.'

'There's no need,' I said, standing. 'She hates herself enough for both of you.'

We were at The Southern Belle by a quarter after three. The place closed at four. The lady taking the ten-dollar cover told us Chasey had left right after midnight.

'She did her New Year's show with Jenteal at twelve and left afterwards. You boys should have been here. Place was packed.'

'Did they eat each other's assholes?' Jules asked. He looked at me. 'Chasey loves a good asshole, dude.'

The woman – girl, actually, and maybe twenty-one if you were generous – gave Jules a hard stare.

'Don't you work on TV?'

He shook his head. 'I get that a lot,' Jules said, and we walked into the belly of The Southern Belle.

It was the same as any other tittie bar you've ever been to, at least now that Chasey and Jenteal had packed their bags and scattered off to whatever hotel they were spending the night in. Now it was nearly 3:30, a half-hour before quitting time, and the remaining girls were tired, you could tell. New Year's Eve was probably their biggest night.

We'd taken a seat at the base of the T-shaped stage, Jules counting out a handful of ones, me sitting there trying to get my mind in front of me and away from Savannah.

A girl in a cowgirl outfit came out and spent about ten seconds gyrating to Madonna's 'Papa Don't Preach' before taking every last stitch off. Her pubic area was shaved. Both nipples and her bellybutton were pierced. The ten or so men still lingering around whooped and hollered a bit, but you could tell it was late and they'd been there a while.

'Look at the size of those ta-ta's,' Jules said, lifting a dollar and waving it around in the air before him.

'I'm not gonna give it to her yet,' he said, his eyes fixed dead-ahead on the action. 'She's gonna have to earn it.'

The girl had jet-black hair and silicone tits and a pair of ass cheeks that suggested life had been hard at times. She probably had a couple kids at the neighbor's apartment, sleeping on the floor in their PJ's waiting for mommy to come home from work.

'Guarantee you she's a lily-licker,' Jules was saying, the dollar in his mouth now. 'Most of these chicks are big-time cock-haters. Cokeheads, too.'

'You love your lesbians, don't you?'

He nodded, the bill bobbing up and down in his mouth. 'Only kind of porn I'll watch.'

'Something wrong with you, Jules.'

He laughed. 'You gotta admire their work ethic. Could you bring yourself to munch some joe's balls for a paycheck? Fuck no, me either. But the Vivid Girls do it. Every day they get up and go to work and give it their best. Heart like that is what made America, brother.'

'You gonna give her the dollar or what?'

He threw an arm around me, signaled the topless waitress, old enough to be the dancer's mother, and ordered four Coronas.

'All out of the foreigns, fellas. Just Bud Light left. Sorry.'

'Six Bud Lights, then,' Jules said, the dollar back in his hand. 'And how much for a table dance?'

'Twenty for one song, forty for two.'

'How much for a private dance?'

'We don't do private dances.'

'Right. Right. Let's do it this way, then. How much for me to go sit in one of those rooms you've got in the back, you know, the ones with the couches and the black curtains over the doorway and all the neon shit on the walls and ceiling, with one of your girls back there rubbing all over me?'

'Are you a police officer?' she asked.

'Nope.' The dancer had noticed Jules, seen the dollar in his hand, and begun crawling on all fours in his direction. She had her mouth twisted up in this half-pucker, half-grimace in an effort to appear horny. It looked to me like she was getting a tetanus shot.

'If you're a cop and I ask, you have to tell me. Otherwise it's entrapment.'

'I know, professor.' He handed her ten bucks. 'You guys close in half an hour. I'm not a cop. I'm a randy car salesman with money in my pocket. How much is it for two girls?'

'For how long?'

'Till I'm done, baby. Done and done.'

The dancer leaned forward on her elbows, flicked her tongue out at Jules like she was trying to catch a moth, and grabbed the dollar with her teeth straight from Jules' mouth. She had silver fillings over her bottom molars.

'It's $150 per girl, per half-hour. That's all you've got left, so it's $300.00 for two girls.'

'You got any black ones working tonight?'

She nodded. 'Stephanie. She's gorgeous. Very popular.'

'Yeah,' Jules said. 'She'll do. Her and another one. Shaved if you got it. Bushy as hell otherwise. I don't care for that indecisive Mohawk thing you chicks are into now.' He handed her another ten and said, 'And see if you can get those beers here double-time, huh?'

The woman took the money and disappeared behind the bar.

Three minutes later – I marked the seconds on my watch – Stephanie the black girl, who was indeed gorgeous, came and sat on Jules' lap.

'You looking for a good time, sweetheart?'

'You know it, baby,' Jules said, then threw me a wink.

'What's your name?'

'Beavis,' Jules said. 'I sell stationery. Very big deal.'

The girl ooohed wide-eyed like he'd just said he was Governor.

'Who's your friend?' she asked, looking me over.

'He's my friend. Where's yours?'

'Waiting for us, sweetie. All we need to do now is take care of the business end and then we can get down to the fun.'

Jules nodded, stood.

'We ordered some beers,' he said, rummaging through his pocket, pulling out a wad of cash. 'They gonna bring 'em back to us?'

'Baby, you won't be worried about no beers back there.'

'That a fact?' He counted out fifteen twenties into her upturned palm.

'Cole, you want some of this? I'm buying.'

I shook my head. 'I'll wait. You gonna be long?'

He looked at Stephanie, who was wearing a hot pink little bikini that glowed against her black skin beneath the black lights. 'Shit no. You sure you don't want to come with?'

'I'll pass,' I said. 'I got six beers coming.'

'Fucking-A,' he said. He looked Stephanie up and down and put his hand on her flat stomach. 'Tell you what, angel. You and your friend get along real well for me, like you haven't seen each other in a while, and I'll toss in an extra hundy for each of you.'

Stephanie giggled, her teeth a neon white in the lights, and led Jules by the hand toward the rooms in the back.

The beers came a few minutes later – Bud Dry, as it turned out, and not Bud Light – and I decided to see if I could drink all six of them before Jules got back. I figured that and the case I was planning on picking up once we left here ought to get me through the night.

After the cowgirl came the secretary, dressed in a men's white button-down and black slacks, black high-heels and carrying a briefcase. She did her thing to AC/DC's 'Shook Me All Night Long' and Motley Crue's 'Girls Girls Girls'. She spent a lot of her time hanging upside down from the steel pole. By the time she was finished I'd made my way through three of the beers. Even though she'd paid me a good bit of attention, I hadn't given her any money.

All the lights went down for a second then, and the music stopped, and I was aware of the sound of empty bottles being thrown atop one another back behind the bar. They were closing up shop.

I was wondering how much longer before Jules wrapped things up, starting in on beer number four, when the DJ's voice boomed over the ceiling-speakers.

'That was Nina the Paralegal, folks, on loan to us from Atlanta. Put your hands together to show her your Charleston hospitality.'

I tapped my free hand on the edge of the stage. Someone off to my left whistled. Someone else screamed 'We love you, Nina,' in a voice that suggested it wasn't love on his mind.

'And now, for our final dance of the night, you boys behave for Taryn the Cheerleader. Her homework's done and she's ready to play and guys, she brought her pom-poms just for you …'

The stage grew gradually from dark to light as Billy Idol's 'Cradle of Love' started thumping through the speakers. Taryn's leg slipped out from behind the black velvet curtain, then an arm, then the rest of her. The guy a few chairs to my right screamed out, 'Come to Daddy, baby,' and turned to high-five all his buddies like he'd invented the phrase.

I glanced over towards the doorway in the back that led to the private rooms. No sign of Jules. I thought about going to get him, but I knew the gorillas that more than likely passed for management in a place like this wouldn't care too much for me moseying back there to hurry him up. Knowing Jules, there wouldn't be that much action going on, at least not with him; he was a talker, the original Mr. Question himself. He'd have them doing things to each other while they narrated it in graphic detail. The first time we ever went to a tittie-bar together he'd dropped forty bucks on this little honey of a blonde for talk. That's it. Just talk. No table-dance, no dark-corner hand-job, just Q+A. She'd sat on his lap and smiled all doe-eyed while he played with her nipples and threw her every perverted interrogative he'd ever wanted to ask. Ever had a girl sit on your face? How old were you the first time you took a load of spunk down the hatch? Do you like it in the ass? Are black cocks really bigger than white cocks? Old Jules, he was born to be a reporter.

I knocked back the rest of the fourth and was reaching for the fifth when Taryn caught my eye. It was Taryn's ass, actually, covered by her little red bloomers, which she was currently wiggling out of in time with Billy Idol's syncopation. She'd already removed whatever top she'd had on. That shows you how distracted I was that night; I didn't even remember that happening.

She was still giving what passed for the crowd her backside when the bloomers came off, leaving her wearing nothing but a glittery, silver thong which I didn't imagine would be on for too much longer. Her hair was done in matching pigtails looping out from the sides of her head. All she needed was the Power-Puff lunchbox and the middle-school motif would be complete.

Jules emerged from the back rooms then, alone. His thick black hair was disheveled and his shirttail was hanging out of his jeans. Apparently it hadn't been all talk.

I stood and handed him the last beer.

'You ready?' I asked.

He nodded, blew out a breath. 'Came three times,' he said. His cheeks were flush and rosy. 'Third one damn near killed me but five hundred balloons is a lot of cabbage.'

'Five? Guess they got along well?'

'Like wild animals,' he said. 'Freaks of fucking nature, those girls.' He was breathing hard through his nose as he tilted the bottle back to his mouth.

'I can't even talk about it right now,' he said around a swallow. 'I feel filthy.'

'You are filthy, bro.'

He nodded. 'I need to floss.'

'Let's head,' I nodded towards the door. Jules nodded in return, held up his beer to show me he only had another gulp or two, and poured it down his throat, twin streams missing his mouth completely and riding his chin down his neck and chest, glowing beneath the neon lights.

He wiped his mouth on his shirtsleeve and set the empty bottle down on the edge of the stage.

'Wow,' he said, motioning towards the girl on stage. 'Nubile little thing, isn't she?'

I turned and glanced at Taryn the Cheerleader once more. She was sitting on her rear, leaning against the center-stage steel pole that had been used so creatively by Nina the Court Reporter or whatever. Her thumbs were hooked into the elastic band of her silvery glittering thong. Her body was facing my direction, but her head was turned to a trio of middle-aged men to her right. It was then that I first realized something was wrong. Either that, or I was losing my mind. I'd have preferred the latter.

She turned her face away from the men teasingly, and our eyes met, and everything I ever believed in or held holy crumbled into dust beneath the force of a rushing tide of frigid water that left me unable to breathe.

'Savannah,' I tried to say.

TWENTY-THREE

Watching Savannah

I never went home. It had never been home for me, and wasn't now, except that it was there that I first touched Savannah's hair, first smelled the hollow of her neck and touched the small of her back. None of those memories were true now, and I had no home.

I'd run out of The Southern Belle because I knew that if I didn't run I'd fall. I'd barreled through the side-door, past the ALARM WILL SOUND IF OPENED sign and into the freezing night air, my breath a puff of vapor before me. I ran and ran until my knees gave, and then I fell. I landed on the sidewalk, tearing the skin off the heels of my hand. I pulled my knees up under me and hugged them, my face pressed hard into the cement. I realized I was crying and didn't care. I hoped someone would find me and kill me so I wouldn't ever have to stand and confront reality again.

I don't know how much longer it was before Jules found me and got me into his car. I remember the sound of his talking as he drove – speaking in conversational, placating tones – but I don't remember the words. I stared out the window and pretended I was someone else and somewhere else. I thought of my mother and wished she was here to hold me. I thought of the Savannah I'd fallen asleep beside on my living-room floor and I reached out to her in my mind, but she pushed me further and further back until I fell over the edge and down into the darkness, staring up at her image getting smaller and smaller as I fell away, her hair in looping pigtails and pom-poms in her hands.

I woke up with a scream and a kick and had no idea where I was. There was a Post-it note stuck to my forehead. I pulled it off and read it.

COLE – HAD TO GO IN TO WORK FOR A FEW. THERE'S

PIZZA IN THE FRIDGE. WAIT UNTIL I GET BACK AND WE'LL TALK ABOUT IT. I TOOK YOUR KEYS SO I COULD FEED BRASCO ON MY WAY BACK – JULES.

I was on Jules' couch, in his living room, not much different than mine except it wasn't mine, which right now was enough.

I stood from the couch on tremulous legs and was heading for the kitchen for some ice-water when a wave of nausea swept over me and dropped me to all fours. I puked bile and blood all over Jules' linoleum. It splattered up into my eyes and face. The tears came and I bit my lip to stop them. The pain was sharp and stopped when I stopped biting, which made it the best thing in my life at that moment, the only thing I could control.

I left the puke and climbed into the bathtub, filling it with cool water. I puked twice more into the tub and didn't bother to empty it. I drifted some, and dreamt of Savannah. When I came to the puke-water had gone from cool to cold and I remembered she'd been wearing the locket I'd given her around her neck. That, and the silvery thong had been all she had on, and the thong had probably come off before I'd made it to the door.

After the tub I slept. I don't know what time it was when I woke up, only that Jules was back and the sun was going down outside. January 1st was almost over. Happy New Year.

I'd finally convinced Jules I was well enough to drive around six that evening, January 1st, eleven days before I was supposed to go back to school and teach ninety-plus kids, among them Taryn the Cheerleader. I apologized for puking all over his apartment, explained I'd done the best I could cleaning it. Jules understood. He'd puked on me and my shit plenty of times. You aren't really good friends until you've puked on each other, or shared a whore. I read that somewhere once.

He dropped me off at my car at Capone's. I watched him drive off, then turned and began walking down King Street, towards the water. I spent the next three hours wandering around downtown. I went down East Bay and back up Church, down Broad and all over Meeting. I finally stopped at the Waterfront Park where I sat in one of the porch swings and stared out over the Cooper River and watched the seagulls fight the winds on their way to Mt. Pleasant. It began raining. Sometime later when it was dark and I was so cold I could no longer feel my face, I started back for my car.

Brasco was waiting for me when I got home. He rolled over onto his side, pulling his paws up in front of his face, next to his cheeks. I leaned over and picked him up, threw him over my shoulder and tried not to look at the phone.

I made it almost all the way to the refrigerator before giving in and picking it up. The dial-tone was stuttering, meaning I had messages. I punched in the code and listened to the automated voice tell me I had seven messages. I set Brasco on the table and sat down as the voice began to go through them.

Message #1, 5:44 this morning: Cole, please call me. I need to talk to you. Call and let it ring once and I'll drive to a payphone and call you back. Please call, Cole. Please.'

Message #2, 6:01 this morning: 'Cole, it's me. Please call me. I'm worried about you.'

Message #3, 6:17 this morning: 'It's me, Cole. Please at least give me a chance to explain before you give up on me. I told you I had secrets and not all of them were good. I told you you might not like everything you came to know about me. Do you remember? Do you remember what you said to me? You told me even butterflies have spots. I didn't want you to have to learn this way. I was going to tell you later, after I was finished with it. If you'd just give me a chance to explain it all to you I know I can make it better. Call me when you get this, Cole. Please.'

Message #4, 7:15 this evening: 'I'm worried about you, Cole. It's been an entire day. If you don't call me tonight I'm coming to your apartment.'

Message #5, 8:11 tonight: Click. Dial-tone.

Message #6, 8:51 tonight: 'Cole? It's Grey, sweetheart. We're having a swimmingly good time down here. There are so many wonderful people I'd love to introduce you to, all sorts of stripes and variations. If you find a few spare days and would like to come down, I'm leaving you my number –'

Message #7, 9:05 tonight: 'I'll be home all night with my brothers. I'm not going to call you anymore because I've already called too many times and I don't want to bother you if you've begun to see me as a bother. My mother is gone for the night and I'll be up late reading. You can come around back and tap the door. I'll let you in. Or you can ignore me and pretend nothing happened between us this past week, and I'll try to do the same. But that will break my heart, Cole. If you come tonight I can show you that, how much losing you and us would break my heart.'

I deleted them all and hung up the phone. I checked my watch. It was a quarter after ten. Savannah was up at her trailer with her brothers, curled up on the couch with a book hoping I'd come by so she could show me how she felt about me. Show me how much she cared and make everything all right. I was certain she could do it, too, but I wasn't going to let her.

I called Grey instead.

My plane left for Key West at 1:00 a.m. It was 10:30 p.m. when I hung up the phone. I spent the next hour packing. Grey had said it was a pleasant low-eighties at her place – 'nubia weather, darling' – and the forecast was calling for sun for the next several days.

I left a message on Jules' machine telling him I was getting out of town for a few days and that the key'd be atop the door jamb. I was leaving Brasco enough food for three days, and I filled both the bathroom and kitchen sinks with fresh water, but I didn't want him to be all alone while I was down in Florida soaking up the sunny weather on the beach, watching Grey prance around in a nubia, whatever the hell that was.

'If you don't mind,' I said to his machine, 'you can crash at my place so he has someone to sleep with while I'm gone. And if you fuck in my bed, make sure she doesn't let him out when she leaves. Thanks, bro. I owe you.'

At a quarter before midnight I left. The airport was a ten-minute drive from my apartment. I'd be there an hour early if I went now.

So I decided to take the long route, via Highway 61 through Winter's Cove.

I reached Savannah's road twenty minutes later and pulled my car off onto the shoulder. Except for the light from the moon and stars it was dark. Her trailer park was a hundred yards or so down on the left. It glowed a gentle orange against the blue-black of the night like something radioactive.

I walked into it silently, careful not to allow my feet to scrape the pavement, watching for toys or pieces of trash lying around so as not to kick them and get myself shot. That would be a nice headline. LOCAL TEACHER SHOT TRYING TO PEEP IN TRAILER PARK WINDOWS. STORY ON PAGE 4.

I approached her trailer from the back just as I had before, the time I'd told her that even butterflies had spots, and that real friends didn't judge or press for explanations. The back end of the trailer was dark, but in the front part, the end nearest the street, the lights were on. The window, about three feet higher than my head, had blinds on it but they weren't closed. I could see the top of the paneling in her living room.

I looked around and found a few orange milk crates strewn about. I grabbed two of them and stacked them on top of each other. As I stepped up on the second one I had the unshakable feeling that the Bubba in the trailer behind me was bearing down on me right that second with his shotgun, the same one his pa used to shoot peepin' toms with, and his grandpa before him.

No shot came, however, and I lifted my head slowly above the edge of the sill and could see very plainly the entirety of Savannah's living room. It was there that we'd hugged and I'd come away knowing a part of me was falling for her. And now here I was outside her window at midnight, knowing that the rest of me had as well.

The room looked the same as it had that afternoon I'd stopped off ostensibly to give her assignments to her mother. The furniture was in the same place. The same stains were on the wall. Savannah wasn't in there, but I could hear her footsteps reverberating through the thin trailer, and I knew she'd appear soon. It was the only light on in the place.

She came into the room from the far end, the dark part where I assumed her four brothers were sleeping in the tiny bedrooms. She was wrapped in a stark white towel that covered her from the tops of her breasts to just above her knees. Her hair was dark and straight with moisture. The color was high in her cheeks and forehead from the heat, and a thin layer of steam still clung to her upper chest and shoulders. In her hands she held a brush and a book.

She sat down on the couch and opened the book in her lap, pulling the brush through her long, wet hair while she read. I watched her and wondered what would happen if I got off the milk crates and tapped on her door like she'd asked. She'd invite me inside. I'd spend the night with her, and she'd show me how much we meant to her.

She'd find it an easy task; her smile was a baptism. All it would take would be for me to hear her whisper my name and look into me with those cornflower-blue eyes, and all the shit from the previous two days would be washed away.

A moment later she set the book and the brush down and stood, walking across the room and disappearing from my line of sight. Two seconds later I could see her again, holding a couple of folded pieces of clothing. She was turned, unknowingly giving me her profile. I was glad. It seemed less obscene than seeing her head-on, the way I had at the strip joint.

I knew what was coming and knew I should look away. I'd been invited but my presence was unknown; watching her dress seemed a violation. I watched, though, mostly *because* it was a violation. I felt I was owed.

She undid the towel and let it fall to the floor. She was naked. There was a bruise the size of a quarter on her left calf. I watched her step into a pair of white denim shorts one bare leg at a time, pulling them up her thighs, arching her back slightly as she lowered her hips into them. Then she stretched her arms out over her head and slid into a light blue tank-top the color of her eyes. Standing in the center of that single-wide living room she was the flawless, ephemeral amaranth of my dreams. Her lines made me ache.

Once she was dressed she returned to the couch. She pulled her legs up and folded them in front of her. She held her book against her calves and read.

I left her like that.

TWENTY-FOUR

Grey in the Keys

My plane touched down in Key West at 3:30 A.M. The airport was virtually empty. I told myself as I walked through the concourse, following the Pick-Up and Drop-Off signs to the outside, that I was not going to think or talk about Savannah while I was down here. I also wasn't going to sleep with Grey. I'd come to that conclusion on the plane. The idea intrigued me, and if I considered it for too long all the familiar responses began to take shape. I had no doubt she could do things to me in bed that would defy the laws of gravity, but I didn't need the emotional baggage that I knew would come after. For Grey it would be no more complicated than taking a shower and sipping something over ice, but for me it would be more. It would be like cheating.

Grey had said she'd be waiting for me in the Pick-Up/Drop-Off zone. I'd asked her what her car looked like and she'd said she wouldn't know until she was in it.

I stood out front with my lone carry-on draped over my shoulder. The weather down here was much warmer than Charleston's. Even then, at nearly four in the morning in early January, I could stand outside without a coat.

I waited for about five minutes with no sign of Grey. I had her cell number in my wallet, and was considering going back inside to call her, when I heard a man's voice calling my name.

'Cole?' From my left.

I turned and looked for anyone I knew. It was silly. I'd never been within three hundred miles of here in my life.

'Cole Archer?' It was a man, in his thirties or so and completely bald. His head was a deeply tanned bronze, like an oblong leather orb floating through the air. He was coming towards me with his

261

hand out. I shook it instinctively.

'I'm Bartholemeu Pell, friend of Grey's. She asked me to meet you here. Get your bag for you?'

I shook my head. 'I can manage, thanks. It's just this one.'

'Well enough,' he said. 'I've got a car this way.' He nodded his Coppertoned head toward the direction from which he'd come. He was dressed nicely, slacks, white button-down with French cuffs. His eel-skin belt glistened beneath the fluorescent streetlights overhead. He appeared to have been in the middle of something formal when he'd had to excuse himself to come get me. It was a strange look at four in the morning, particularly on a bald guy. White bald men always look funny to me, like chemo patients or bassists in underground bands.

I followed him. 'How did you know it was me?'

He spoke without looking back. His pace was brisk.

'Grey said I'd know you when I saw you.'

'What the hell does that mean?'

He laughed. 'You know Grey.'

And at that point, I still thought I did.

'Is this your first time in Key West, Cole?' Bartholemeu was steering his Lexus with both hands together at the top of the wheel, in the twelve o'clock position. His nails were manicured as pretty as a girl's.

I nodded. 'I almost didn't come.'

'Why ever not?'

Shrug. 'Effort, I guess. Plus, you know – I don't know, really. It's just easier to stay than it is to leave.'

Bartholemeu nodded. 'Sometimes it is,' he said. 'But you'll be glad you came. Key West is one of the most epicurean localities this side of the equator.'

'Sounds like Grey.'

Bartholemeu let out a little giggle that I'd heretofore thought to be exclusive to young girls. 'If you don't mind my asking, what happened to your face there?'

He touched the side of his own face, in case I wasn't sure where mine was, I guess.

'Battery acid,' I said. 'I was jumping a friend's car off and got the cables crossed.'

'Goodness. Lucky it didn't reach the eye.'

'Yeah. Lucky.'

The road made its way down the coast, riding next to the ocean for about ten minutes before Bartholemeu reached over me with a polite 'Excuse me, Cole' to the dash and retrieved a cell phone. He punched in a series of numbers, waited, then handed me the phone.

'Put that back in the glove box for me, won't you?'

I did. I thought about asking him who he'd called, but figured it wasn't any of my business.

'Where are we going, exactly?' I asked instead.

'To a party, of course,' he said, slowing the Lexus, turning left onto a single-lane road. About fifty yards ahead I could see a massive chain-link gate with barbed-wire trim sliding back off the road, allowing us to pass.

'Party?' I whistled. 'At four a.m. No wonder Grey loves it down here.'

'The party,' he said, slowing the car, watching the gate re-close in the rearview, the stainless steel bathed over in the bloody red of the brake lights, 'is for you. Grey arranged it in honor of your arrival.'

I looked at him. He looked at me and said, 'It's a sunrise party, of course. What residents of the Caribbean call a dawn-to-dusker. It won't begin for another few hours yet.'

'Uh, Bartholemeu, I don't mean to sound rude or ungrateful, but I haven't slept well the past couple days and I'm really pretty beat.'

'Oh that's no problem at all,' he said, his hands still at the top-center of the wheel, as prim and demure as a young lady-in-waiting. 'You don't actually have to be there,' he said. 'Your arrival merely gives everyone an excuse to gather and socialize. Of course, you should probably put in an appearance sometime, for Grey's sake.' He glanced over at me. 'And yours. Relieve yourself of that burden you're carrying and enjoy yourself for a time.'

'That obvious, huh?'

He smiled. 'It's always in the eyes.'

He made an abrupt turn to the left and all of a sudden we were traveling over hard sand. I glanced out the window past Bartholemeu and saw the ocean, still and black with a milky, moving center beneath the moon. We were on the beach.

'See the lights up ahead there?' He nodded forward. Up what looked like maybe a couple hundred yards there was a series of yellow twinklings, like falling stars that landed in the sand and never lost their light.

The shape of the house became clearer as we neared. It was a large, single-story house; not monstrous, as I think I had expected, but plenty large enough, considering that for nine or ten months out of the year it sat empty. It was perched atop a small precipice that overlooked the sand below. At the base of the precipice, I saw as we approached, there was a group of jagged rocks standing tall like sentries manning a post. The waves pounded against the rocks and sent white froth shooting into the air like foam spewing from a giant can of beer.

'Is that Grey's place?'

Bartholemeu nodded.

'Marrying well sure does pay.'

'Divorcing well pays much better,' Bartholemeu amended.

We veered to the right and caught a narrow, hard-earth path bumpy with roots and rocks that looped us around and emptied out onto a concrete area in front of the house. There were no other cars there.

Bartholemeu pulled in front of the door and left the car idling.

'Get some rest, Cole,' he said. 'Grey's been beside herself with excitement since you called. I'm quite sure your stay won't be boring.'

I looked at the house. It was completely dark inside. The only lights on were the yellow external house-lights I'd seen from the beach.

'How long have you known Grey, Bartholemeu?'

He smiled. 'Hard to say, really. She seems to have always been there.'

I knew what he meant.

I was getting ready to ask whether Grey was actually here when the front porch light came on. The door opened, and out stepped Grey. She was wearing peach-colored silk pajamas. She was barefoot. Her hair was pulled back behind her. She was smiling.

I climbed out of the Lexus and leaned my head back into it.

'I guess I'll see you around, Bartholemeu,' I said.

'Oh, I should think so,' he laughed. He was still laughing when he drove away.

I watched the Lexus for a moment as it drove off, then turned and looked at Grey. She was still on the porch, still smiling.

'Hi, Grey,' I said.

'Hello, Cole.' She gave me a look full of warmth and compassion that reminded me of the way my mother looked at me when I did something that made her proud. It was a smile not just with her mouth but with her eyes as well, her entire face lighting up as though she were admiring intently whatever it was I'd just done, even though I hadn't done it all that well. I remember my mother looking at me that way when I learned how to tie my own shoes.

'Was your trip tolerable?'

I nodded. I was still standing where Bartholemeu left me. I could hear the sound of the water hammering the rocks beyond the house. There was no wind. 'I got bumped to first class.'

'Did you drink?'

'I slept.'

'You still look tired.'

'I am. Bartholemeu tells me you planned a party. You didn't have to.'

'Bartholemeu's silly. It's just a little get-together. People should start arriving shortly. But I want you to sleep first. There's a bed waiting for you down the hall.'

She looked at me. 'What happened to your face?'

'Fishing accident,' I said.

I still hadn't moved. I wondered how long she was going to let me stand there, waiting for me in her peach pajamas and her bare feet in the almost ninety-degree January morning air.

'You love her, don't you?' she asked.

'I don't want to talk about it,' I said, walking towards her, feeling absurdly like I was conceding something by doing so. I felt profoundly out of place until I reached her. Then I felt like I was home.

'Of course not, darling,' she said, leaning forward and kissing my mouth before I saw it coming. 'We don't have to talk about anything at all.'

TWENTY-FIVE

Grey's friends; Gatsby's green light; calling Autumn

I slept without dreaming for what felt like days. When I woke up the sun was well into its routine outside. The shade in the room was pulled, but the light slipped in around the edges in bright, golden daggers. I could hear the waves beating the rocks outside my window. They never stopped; the rocks never got a break. It reminded me of something a psychology professor said back in undergrad: It's not the little problems that become big that push people over the edge. It's the little problems that never go away, never stop grinding, never stop at all that do the trick.

It's being the rock that can't catch a break.

I laid on my back for a bit, listening to the white noise of the surf beyond the window, sprinkled over with the sounds of gulls carried by the wind. I watched a patch of shadow work its way across the ceiling as the sun followed its arc in the sky. I could hear voices from somewhere else in the house. Laughter. Groups of people all talking at once.

Grey's sunrise party.

I was still in my clothes, except the shoes. My watch said it was half-past noon, which would explain the hunger pangs I was feeling. I told myself Charleston didn't exist and that even if it did it'd be there when I got back. I'd come here specifically to relax before going back to work in a couple days, and it wasn't going to do me any good to sit here and wish I was there.

I forced myself off the bed and trudged down the hall towards a bathroom I remembered passing last night. The voices grew louder. There was music coming from the living room. Classical. Brahms, or Haydn.

I spent half an hour in the shower. I adjusted the water until it was so hot it almost burned, then sat down in the tub and let it pour over my head and neck and shoulders. Steam surrounded me. It opened my sinuses and stung my eyes. I closed them and pretended I was in the enchanted little garden downtown on Stoll's Alley, where everything was wrapped in ivy and jasmine and wisteria and all the noise of the rest of the world passed by unheard. I tried hard to keep Savannah out of it, but she showed up there anyway, wearing a pair of pure white denim shorts and a sky-blue tank-top that brought out her eyes, and on her left calf was the quarter-sized bruise I'd noticed last night, and around her neck was the locket I'd given her.

She'd kissed me after I'd placed it around her neck. I'd been starting to speak when she'd stretched up on her tip-toes and touched her tongue to mine. I sat there in the shower of Grey's winter hideout and tried not to remember that.

I didn't fight the tears, though, which I thought was probably progress.

I ventured into the living room where I heard all the laughing and talking and saw fifteen to twenty people standing around, sipping drinks and nibbling crackers and cheese, miniature sandwiches without the crust, bits of colorful fruit on toothpicks. They were all dressed in expensive clothes that looked scalpel-cut and hugged their bodies like mist. They looked like they were leaving here for an evening at the opera. Like Bartholemeu last night, it was a strange look for early afternoon.

I scanned the crowd for Grey but didn't see her. I was wearing jeans and a half-sleeve gray knit shirt I'd borrowed from Jules' closet. My hair was still wet. I was barefoot.

An incredibly skinny woman in a black evening gown saw me and smiled.

'You must be Cole,' she said warmly. She'd been speaking to a man and woman who were apparently a couple, but now she excused herself and approached me. She reminded me of what a praying mantis would look like as it morphed into a human.

I nodded. 'You don't happen to know where Grey is, do you?'

'I'm Madeline,' she said, extending her hand. I shook it. She looked like she might be in her late thirties and resented it immensely. The skin of her face was pulled so tightly I waited for it to tear with each blink.

'Grey's on the beach. She asked me to point you the way if you woke before she came back.'

I nodded again. I was getting very good at nodding. 'I didn't mean to be rude,' I said. 'I'm just getting up. It's been –'

She waved it away. 'Nonsense. You're just as precious as Grey said you were. Now, if you go on through the living room past the Kleinfeld twins there, then through the kitchen after that, you'll see a door in the breakfast nook. It opens out onto the deck. There're steps leading from the deck down to the beach below. Be careful. They're nearly always slippery.'

'Thanks,' I said. Madeline looked at me like I was something furry she'd brought home from the exotic pet store.

'It was nice meeting you, Madeline,' I said.

She touched my shoulder briefly before turning back to her friends.

I found Grey sitting alone on a green blanket spread over a stretch of dry sand. There was an opened bottle of champagne sitting in a bucket of ice on the blanket next to her. She was wearing jeans rolled up at the ankles and a billowy white sweater. She was holding an opened book in one hand, staring out over the water. The temperature was cooler now than it'd been when I'd arrived.

'Some view you've got here,' I said, descending the final steps and landing on the sand.

'It never gets old,' she said, looking at me. 'Sometimes I envy it that.'

'I wouldn't worry. You look half your age.'

'You're sweet.' She tapped her hand beside her on the blanket. I sat without hesitating.

'Did you sleep well?' She asked.

'Well enough. I didn't dream. These days that's an answered prayer.'

'Do you want to talk about it?'

I shrugged. 'Not much to talk about, really. I'm in over my head.'

'Which is a wonderful place to be, if you ask me. Anywhere else would be impossibly boring. Think of the memories you'll have, regardless of how it turns out.'

I stretched and laid back on the blanket. The sky was overcast and the air was salty and cool. I closed my eyes.

'Easy enough for you to say, Grey. You've got places you can go.'

'Don't you?'

'No,' I said. I kept my eyes closed. The sand beneath my back was lumpy and hard. 'I've got to go to work the next day. Always will.'

'A lot of people work, Cole.'

'You don't.'

'No, that's true, I don't.' She paused, and I could tell even with my eyes closed that she was thinking about whatever it was she was getting ready to say.

'What would you do if you didn't have to work?'

'What, as in ever?'

'As in never ever.'

'Like retired people,' I said.

'Exactly, except not old. If you could be the baby you are now and not have to get up each morning merely because personal finance necessitated it, what would you do then?'

'Have an orgasm.'

She laughed. 'Then what?'

'Get cleaned up and have another one. What'd you do when you found out you were out of the rat-race?'

'That's a good question,' she said. 'I can't ever remember picturing myself *in* it, to be honest with you. It just never seemed my style.'

'No,' I agreed. 'It doesn't.'

'It doesn't seem yours either, Cole.'

'No?'

'Not at all. You're a writer, Cole, and writers are creatures of the mind. You're students of the human condition. People work for money and money isn't what the writer needs. He needs time. Time to read poetry and walk through cities at midnight and meet mysterious people in insensible places. Time to make glorious mistakes and life-affirming decisions, to endure new pains and pleasures and everything else. A writer needs to hurt others in love and be hurt as well. How else is he to have anything to write about? Our writers are the keepers of our souls. They're society's vampires and recorders of our history all at once. We should treat them like the treasures they are and forbid them from working in jobs that don't inspire them.'

'If you ever run for President, Grey, you've got my vote.'

She chuckled. 'How is the writing going, by the way?'

'Shitty.'

'Writer's block?'

'No. Writer's block is when you can't think of anything to write. I've never had that. My problem flows the other way. I'm teeming with ideas and I can't find time to put them down on paper. Sort of creative constipation, I guess.'

'What idea are you working on now?'

'Trying to figure out a way to sleep for a hundred years so I can wake up and realize all my problems are dead.'

'Cole. Don't be morbid.'

'Sorry. I'm working on something that deals with obsession.'

'How apropos.'

'Isn't it? It seems I'm obsessed with the topic lately, pardon the pun.'

I felt her lie down beside me. The edge of her bare foot was touching mine.

'Is our hero a teacher?' she asked.

'I don't know yet,' I said. 'Probably not. Teachers are boring. I can't imagine trying to write a book about one, much less reading it. This guy's probably an engineer or a lawyer or something. He's lost his wife and –'

'What's her name?'

'Whose? The wife? Dyanna, why?'

'The Goddess of Passion. Very nice, Cole. Keep going.'

'He's lost his wife, finds himself in Charleston, plans on killing himself to end the pain. And somewhere in there there's a colony of gargoyles and a church that doubles as a gateway between time-periods.'

'Ooohh, sounds spooky. Will you tell it to me?'

'I just did.'

'I mean the whole thing. We can come back down here tonight and you can tell me all of it. Who knows? I might even get scared and need to be protected.'

We lay in silence for a while then, and I was grateful for it. I gradually felt myself sinking into the blanket, hovering in that no-man's-land between sleep and consciousness, where you're aware of your surroundings in the concrete world but your mind takes liberties with them nonetheless. The sand beneath me became the sand of Sullivan's Island. Grey's body beside mine became Savannah's, even as I knew it was just Grey, even as I knew the words 'just' and 'Grey' never belonged together.

'Want me to tell you about our trip together?' I asked some time later. I kept my eyes closed.

'If you'd like,' she said. I felt her weight shift next to me as she turned to her side. I felt her looking at me. 'But I don't want you to think you have to.'

'I told myself I wasn't going to talk about her down here.'

'That's a silly thing to tell yourself, Cole.'

'I know. I think about her everywhere. Everything reminds me of her. I see her face when I close my eyes.'

'There's nothing wrong with that. You'll think about her all the time until one day you won't have to anymore because she'll either be yours forever or none at all. Either way you'll be at peace with it. That's just the way it goes.'

On the inside of my eyelids I saw her through the trailer window as she pulled the brush through her wet hair in long, smooth strokes. I saw her sitting on the couch reading, waiting for the quiet tapping on the door that never came. I imagined her climbing into her bed that night worried that she'd lost whatever part of us we had, worried that her spots had proven too big or dark for me to handle, just as she'd told me they would, even as I assured her they couldn't.

'I took your advice,' I said. 'We took a day-trip to Savannah.'

'The city of the same name,' Grey said. 'Was it exquisite?'

'It was more.'

'Tell me, Cole,' she whispered, her fingers touching my face now, tracing softly over my eyebrows, my closed eyelids, down the bridge of my nose and over my lips. 'Tell me all of it.'

We stayed out on the beach until the sun went down. I watched it drop into the ocean and thought of Savannah, and how she wouldn't have considered it a real sunset because it wasn't on the West Coast. I thought of all the sunsets she had in her future, how many of them she'd watch standing along the edge of the Pacific somewhere. I wondered if I'd get to see any of them with her, and then I thought of Moses and God's penchant for irony, so I stood and told Grey I was getting cold and we walked back to her house.

By seven that evening a new batch of revelers had replaced the ones who'd arrived at sunup. These were a less formal lot – a moving sea of slacks and earth-toned knit shirts and Capri pants and open-toed sandals. They looked the same as the previous bunch, though, all shiny and neat and punctuated with gold in all the right places. They acted the same, too. Lots of laughter and nodding heads and watching of others to see who might be watching them. All the men looked wealthy and all the women looked aware of it. I felt about as in-place as Larry Flynt at Mass.

Grey maneuvered me through the crowd and made the introductions, behaving like something between a proud mother and a smitten schoolgirl. One moment she was refreshing my glass or brushing a stray hair from my forehead with a thumb, and the next she would hold my hand as if we were lovers, or whisper possibilities into my ear that, another time, would have left me embarrassingly erect.

They'd all heard of me, Grey's guests. They'd all heard I was coming and were glad I could make it, as if I spent my days holed away in some lab searching for a cure for Ugly, and here I was on sabbatical, walking among The Beautiful Ones to remind myself why it was I strove so mightily to end the scourge of the unfortunate face. They were beautiful, too, every one of them. And not just physically. They had about them the same air as Grey, that sense of self-actualization that came with years of carefree days filled with sun and smiling and sin, and nights much the same minus the sun. Even the men were attractive, some of them prettier than the women.

'Grey tells me you're a writer,' one man said as I shook his hand, holding my third Bloody Mary in the other. He was a chisel-jawed specimen with salt-and-pepper hair. He was wearing a burnt-pumpkin turtleneck with a black blazer unbuttoned over it, like a mannequin that just stepped out of the Sak's bay window.

'Trying, in any case,' I said. 'It's a lengthy process.'

'Well you simply must tell me, what is it that a writer does to suffer facial trauma?'

'I was helping a friend move and spilled down the steps with a sofa on top of me.'

He made a face. 'Ghastly,' he said.

'The ghastliest.'

'I'm curious, have you published anything I might have read?'

'I wrote a monograph on the prevalence of zoophilia amongst modern-day university academics you'd probably find interesting,' I said, figuring what the hell. 'It's entitled *Bookstore to Barnyard: A Case-Study.*'

He set his jaw and angled his eyes upwards, as if trying to recall the titles of all the monographs he'd recently read.

'I can't say that I've heard of that one. What else?'

'There was an article on the dangers of dihydromonooxide in its liquid form.'

His eyes widened. 'I've heard of it. Is it really dangerous? Wasn't the California quake of the early nineties tied to that?'

I nodded. 'Oh, you bet. Its mere presence is responsible for most of the planet's erosion. A single teaspoon inhaled will kill a grown man if not expelled immediately. It's the most prominent compound in our sewers. Symptoms of over-exposure include bloated abdomen and increased urination.'

He was shaking his head in the affirmative. 'I did read that. *The New Yorker*, right?'

'Reprinted there. Originally published in *The Dartmouth Review*.'

'You know,' he said, shifting to himself, a topic with which he was clearly enamored, 'I dabble with the old quill and scroll a bit myself. In fact, I've recently begun a novel.'

'Really? I'd love to hear about it.'

So was the scene for the next few hours. I made the rounds, Grey on my arm for much of it, and did the grip 'n' grin with everyone in the room. They were situated in little clusters of three or four apiece, and I moved from one to another with ease, slipping into their conversations, picking up pieces of their pasts, listening to stories about their kids, their investments, the problems they had in finding good, quality help for their yachts.

'So Cole,' a blonde woman with a year-round tan said, 'where did you earn your money at such a young age?'

She'd been introduced to me as M.J., and according to Grey she spent her time island-hopping around the Caribbean. I wondered what someone like that did for a vacation.

Before I could open my mouth another woman – Darcy, formerly of Detroit, now a passport-carrying resident of the Honduras – answered for me.

'Cole's a bibliographer,' Darcy said to the group, which was comprised of herself, M.J., and their dates – Ned and Ted, or Ted and Ned, I wasn't sure – and myself, Cole Archer, bibliographer *extraordinaire*.

'I heard Nan mention it earlier,' she explained.

Darcy threw me a look I'm pretty sure her date wouldn't have approved of. 'How'd you hurt yourself there, Cole?'

'I was sodomizing my ex-girlfriend, Darcy, and her fiancé found us and tried to take my head off with an oak limb.'

Darcy smiled an understanding, people-can-be-so-silly smile.

'Is it exciting, Cole?' M.J. asked.

'Anal sex?' I asked, shrugging. 'It has its moments.'

Everyone got a real kick out of that.

'Oh, Cole, you really are a treat. But of course I meant being a bibliographer.'

'Oh. It has its moments, too. Fewer head injuries, in any case.'

'I never would have thought it paid particularly well, though,' Ted or Ned – Darcy's date, in any case – said. 'Although I must say it's rather useful work. One often needs a good cataloguing of important texts.' He smiled at me. 'A damned underappreciated calling, too. Good show, Cole.'

'Thanks. The trick is to specialize,' I continued.

'And what's your specialty?' M.J. asked.

'The concomitants of drink,' I said. 'Books which deal primarily with them.'

'Really?' Ned/Ted piped up. 'I'm something of a collector myself. Ancient or modern?'

I shrugged. 'All of it. Pins, firkins, hogsheads, faucets, spiles, spigots. Not to mention the kilderkin, the tierce, and the puncheon. Whole gamut, really.'

They seemed to all like that, especially Darcy. She kept glancing down at my crotch, her eyes swimming up my frame and back to mine before offering me a smile full of moist, pink gums.

I was getting ready to really sling some top notch bullshit but Grey swooped in out of nowhere with a fresh Bloody Mary for me.

'Darling,' she said, lacing her arm through mine and kissing my cheek, 'how are you getting along?'

'Cole was just regaling us with the details of his work,' Ned/Ted said. 'Very interesting, I do say.' There was general agreement throughout the group. I glanced at Darcy, who was staring at my mouth. She didn't even try to look away.

'May I borrow him for a moment?' Grey asked, already leading me away. I felt like a puppy who'd stayed in the neighbor's yard too long. 'There's still someone I need to introduce him to.'

'It was nice meeting you,' I said, smiling to them all. They returned the smile and fell back into their previous pattern, everyone talking and flitting their hands and showing each other their teeth.

She led me out to her deck without a word, down the wooden steps and onto the beach. It was darker now, and seemed louder as well. The waves smashed against the base of the still, sentinel rocks and exploded upwards like geysers. Above them, just out of reach of the foamy tendrils, Grey's House in the Keys bustled with the bullshit of millionaire expatriates. You could see the squares and ovals and rhomboids of orange-yellow light pouring through the windows.

'Interesting bunch, your friends,' I said. 'Not a lot of calluses on their hands.'

Grey laughed. The wind carried the sounds and her hair behind her, twirling them together. The blonde looked almost red beneath the starlight.

I was several paces behind her, walking at the place where the sea and the sand come together, letting the cold water wash over my bare toes. I watched her move. She was wearing a blue sarong which clung to her hips and shimmered softly with each of her steps. She moved to an unheard music. If it weren't for the little puddles her bare feet left in the wet sand, I might have mistaken her for a moonbeam.

She turned to me, a single arm outstretched, the fingers on that hand fanned.

'Catch up, Cole. I won't bite.'

'So you keep telling me.'

I reached her and allowed her to take my hand in hers. It occurred to me then that my life was one whose ebbs and flows were controlled by women, of all ages and degrees of purity. My mother raised me with soft hands and softer words; my sister fucked the senior class her freshman year and liked it so much she quit high school to do it for pay in New York. I'd been nearly killed galloping through the Land of Sodom with Marla as my guide, and I was here now, with my mother's lusty contemporary, seeking respite from the suffering heaped upon me back home at the hands of my sixteen-year-old student.

Except I knew Savannah wasn't part of all that. She didn't fit into my life the way these other women did. She hadn't raised me like my mother. She hadn't decided like my sister, shortly after her first period, that her sole asset was her body, and that it might be easy but it would never come cheap. She wasn't Marla, sullying herself in search of her soul, and she wasn't Grey, aging and wealthy and trying to make the latter stave off the former. Savannah existed for me beyond my realm of experience. She was what might have been had the deal in Eden not fallen through. Trying to understand it was like trying to understand what was there before time, or how God created God. It just was.

Denying it didn't change anything.

We walked along in comfortable silence for a while. I watched the ground before us, milky in the moonlight. Grey watched the stars.

'You don't have to worry,' she said, sometime later.

'About what?'

'Me,' she said. 'I know you love her.'

'I never said I love her.'

'You don't have to say it, darling. You wear it.'

I didn't say anything.

'It's no secret that monogamy has never suited me well,' Grey said. Her hand in mine was surprisingly warm. 'I've never seen the virtue in it, to be honest.'

I shrugged. 'Seems a good enough idea to me.'

'I'm sure it's wonderful, but it isn't me. It's you, though, I can see that.' She looked at me. 'I thought you might want to know that I see it.'

I laughed at that. 'Grey, ordinarily…' I drifted off. Out on the glassy black water a lone green light shone. I thought of Gatsby, whose ending was anything but Great.

'Ordinarily we might have carried on terrifically for days at a time,' she said. 'I won't lie to you, Cole. Young men have an effect on me. I find their brand of virility quite titillating. It brings out my adventurous side. I suspect it's much the same with you and Savannah.'

'Savannah's not particularly virile.'

'No, but she's young. The world hasn't hurt her yet, even if she thinks it has. Nearly all men find that inviting. It awakens forbidden yearnings in them. Paternal, incestuous …'

'I don't think of it that way.'

'Nor should you. You've over-thought things enough as it is. Have you discovered this evening's common theme?' Grey asked.

I remembered reading somewhere that Zelda Fitzgerald complained publicly that F. Scott's crank was too small.

'Sure,' I said. 'They're each the center of the world.'

'Many of them are, yes,' she laughed.

'And shit-rich,' I added. 'World travelers, most of the ones I spoke with.'

'All of them, actually. You and I were the only ones there tonight who hold exclusively American citizenship. Many of the people you met tonight renounced theirs years ago.'

'Are they criminals? People don't just give up their citizenship for the hell of it. It's impossible to get back once you do it.'

'Criminal is such a caustic term for those people,' Grey said. 'But they are here illegally, technically speaking. Most of them, anyway. They come in once or twice a year for a few days. Sometimes they stay here. Sometimes they stay elsewhere. They're wonderful people, though, once you get past the ostentation. And they're not all criminals. Some of them are just very wealthy and have an aversion to taxes.'

'That makes them criminals.'

She shrugged dismissively. 'Have you given much thought to the downtown apartment?'

'Some,' I said. 'Why?'

'Nothing,' she said, in a tone that implied much more than merely nothing.

'Nothing,' I repeated.

She squeezed my hand. 'Well, I was thinking the other morning how much you seem to dislike your job.'

'You too, huh? I think about it every day.'

'What do you hate about it? The kids?'

'Some. Not the good ones. The good ones are great. They're the only reason I can bring myself to shave and put on that fucking tie each day.'

'Then it's the bad kids?'

'It's the whole thing, Grey. It's the administration who'll butt-fuck you to save themselves a hassle from The Board. It's the pettiness of my department chair. It's the parents who don't give a shit about their kid's grade until report cards come out and all of a sudden it's my fault I didn't call and tell them little Johnny can't read a comic book, much less a novel. It's the black ones who act like apes because it's all they know, and the athletes who fail with impunity because they can hit a curve ball, and the greasy pubescent little fucks who think being laid a couple times makes them my equal. It's the Emotionally Disturbed kids who act like idiots in the hall and can't be disciplined because legally, on paper, according to the government, they're as cracked as a shithouse rat. There're days it's all I can do not to rip some mouthy piece-of-shit's spleen out through his throat and feed it back to him. I come home so juiced some days it takes twelve beers to get me to sleep. Other days I'm so drained I nearly pass out in the car on my way back to the apartment. It's just the wrong job for me. That's all there is to it. Some people are suited for it, and I salute them. But I'm not one of them.'

'What if you didn't have to work?'

'Haven't we had this conversation?'

'I'm serious,' she said, turning to me, walking backwards over the sand. The wind blew through her hair and tasseled it. Her toenails glimmered silvery beneath the moon. 'Would you write?'

I was reminded of the first time I'd met Grey, on the Isle of Palms beach, when I'd been trying to look at her without looking like I was. I was doing that now. But I could tell she knew, and I could tell she didn't mind.

'Sure.'

'A lot?'

Shrug. 'As much as I could.'

'Every day?'

'If I didn't have to work?'

She nodded, slowed her pace. 'At all. Like me. Like those people back at the house, with their hands free of calluses.'

'I imagine I'd write all the time. I could probably bang out a book every year or so. Why?'

'Well, I was thinking,' – slowing even more, moving backwards one hip at a time, her eyes never leaving mine.

'Yeah,' I said, 'you mentioned that. Thinking what?'

She stopped walking. Even though I'd seen it coming it still caught me off guard, and I nearly bumped into her. Our faces were three inches apart. I could smell the citrus on her breath.

'Thinking how badly the world needs writers.'

'The world needs a lot of things.'

'Everyone needs something,' she said, and she was on her knees before me. It happened too quickly for me to follow. One second she was speaking, her mouth inches from mine, and it seemed that in that same second she was lowering herself in front of me, lowering my fly, fumbling me free.

She held me in her hand.

'Tell me what you need, Cole.'

'We can't,' I said.

'I could be your patron.' Her breath mixed with the cool night air and turned my dick to steel. 'Every good artist needs a patron.'

'Grey ...' there was a deep, rolling ache down there.

'I could take care of you while you write. You could live in the little apartment downtown and write at all hours and never have to worry yourself with anything but words. Part of the year I'd be gone. The other part I'd be there when you called.'

'It wouldn't work,' I said, refusing to look at her, staring out across the ocean instead, looking for Gatsby's green light. It was gone.

'You're tense,' she said, moving her hand back and forth.

The wind smelled like salt and cinnamon, heavier and warmer than in Charleston.

'I can help.'

My knees buckled. 'I'm begging you not to.'

'You could close your eyes. Listen to the wind. Give me your tension.'

'It's not right.'

'How could it be wrong?'

'Grey, I need ... I have to ... I have to not do this.'

'Let me have your tension, Cole. Let me take it from you. I want to.'

Her other hand moved with practiced fluidity back and forth, cupping the rest of me down there. Every part of my body tightened.

'Grey ...'

'Close your eyes and relax and give it to me, Cole. Just let me take it from you.'

I looked back down at her. Her mouth was half an inch from the tip. If she slipped out her tongue ...

'Please ... Grey, no –'

She released my balls. 'Tell me you love her,' she said.

'What?'

Her hand stopped moving. Part of me was disappointed. I tried to focus on the part of me that was relieved.

'Tell me you love her and I'll stand up.'

'I don't understand,' I said, fighting the urge to push my hips forward, past her parted lips and into that wellspring of pleasure which is always so brand new and so familiar. 'Why do you want me to say it so badly?'

'Tell me you love her and that's why you have to keep your stress and pain and angst inside with you. That you're keeping it so you can remember what it's like without her, that you're remembering so you'll know why you have to have her.'

And I understood then. Everyone needs something. I needed Savannah. Grey wanted me to say it so I could make it real. She knew how badly I needed her; she wanted to be sure I knew it, too.

'I love her,' I said, nodding, closing my eyes, fighting back tears, biting the inside of my lip. 'God help me Grey … I love her.'

She stood up, kissed my cheek, then hugged me as though I were her son. 'You should put this scene in a book someday,' she said, then resumed walking down the beach.

Grey didn't mention the incident; to sit atop the sand and talk with her that night was to believe that it'd never happened at all. In her mind it was solved. I'd admitted loving Savannah. And even though there were questions I'd never think to ask, I already had all the answers. She'd shown me that.

So we talked about everything else: my writing, her daughter, the future and all it held. She was most interested in Dyanna, and how her Mason pined for her after she was gone. Grey wondered if it was possible to want something into existence.

'Is he going to find a way to bring her back?' she asked.

'I don't know. Maybe not so much that as find a way to join her.'

'In Heaven?'

'Maybe in some level between here and Heaven. I'm not sure yet. And I've no idea where the gargoyles tie in.'

'No, me neither, but they must tie in somewhere. Gargoyles and antebellum Charleston are too good a match to pass up.'

Time turns to elastic on the beach at night. You can sit there and close your eyes and listen to the sounds of the gulls overhead and the waves before you and the wind all around and get lost among whatever clutter exists in the corners of your mind. When you pull back into the moment again it seems it's been ten minutes, and perhaps it has. But if it's been an hour you'll accept that, too, because there are holes in the fabric of things at the edge of the world at night, and sometimes we wander through them.

At some point Grey rocked forward on her butt and stood.

'Are you coming back?'

'Not just yet,' I said, stepping out of the hole, entirely unaware of how long I'd been sitting there next to her. 'I'll be along in a bit.'

She nodded. 'Mind you don't catch your death of cold,' she said.

I nodded, watched her walk off. Half a mile past her, twinkling high in the night, I could see her house.

She turned back to me. 'Are you hungry? I can have something waiting for you.'

'That'd be nice.'

'Anything in particular?'

I shook my head.

She smiled. 'I'll surprise you,' she said.

'I've no doubt,' I said, but the words were lost in the wind.

Midnight found me back at Grey's, the revelers still reveling. They were comprised of all shapes and sizes and accents and skin-tones. Everyone knew my name and greeted me warmly; one woman congratulated me on my latest movie, and I thanked her, told her I was surprised she recognized me, the camera putting on ten pounds and all. She giggled at something inside her head and moved along towards the bar.

Which, of course, is where I remained for most of the night. I was drinking Crown and Cokes for a while, until Grey ran out of Coke and then it was Crown and soda, then Crown and Crown. Somewhere in there I migrated to the deck, where I stretched out in a reclining chair and drank and watched the boat lights twinkle white and red in the distance and listened to the waves hammering the giant rocks below.

I know I fell asleep because a hand on my shoulder roused me. My first thought was that the hand was a masculine one. My second thought was that it was just barely so.

'Freshen your glass, Cole?'

The ocean had gone blurry while I slept. Looking out at it now was like looking into a well filled with pitchblende.

I nodded, turned my head. It felt heavy and lopsided.

'Bartholemeu. Good to see you 'gain.'

He smiled, a slice of white in the middle of a smooth, tanned face, and handed me another glass filled with Crown and ice. I tried to fish the ice out but my fingers weren't cooperating, so I made do.

'Mind if I sit a spell?'

I motioned towards the chair beside me. 'Be my guest.'

He sat at the edge of the chair, fiddling with a silver cigarette case.

'Care for a smoke?' he offered.

I shook my head.

'Gave it up once,' he offered. 'Years ago. I don't remember why I ever picked it up again. One day I was standing on the starboard bow off the Ivory Coast and I realized I was smoking again, and had been for a while.' He shook his head around his first drag. 'Wretched habit.'

'I used to smoke dope some,' I said. 'Back in college, mostly. Gave that up.'

'Good thing, too. Bad for the pills.'

'Pills?'

He nodded. 'Testicles. Turns them black from the inside out. Fellow from my university years had pills like lumps of coal by the time he graduated.'

'Where did you go to school, Bartholemeu?'

'Oxford,' he said, staring out over the wooden banister into the blackness beyond. The moonlight poured over his head and tinted it silver. 'Eighth generation.'

'What'd you study?'

'Philosophy of course. Eighth generation for that, too. Never had much choice in the matter, looking back.'

'Philosophy,' I repeated. 'What the hell do you do with a philosophy degree, besides get a graduate degree in philosophy?'

He shrugged. 'Whatever one likes, I suppose. I myself took up with a man twice my age and set about sailing most the world over.'

'A man, huh?' I wasn't surprised.

'Physically, at least. Not much more than a boy at heart. And a certifiable cur in the personality realm. But, that's as they say …' – a delicate waving of his hand through a cloud of cottony smoke – 'ancient history. What about you?'

'What about me what?'

'Oh, come along now Cole. You're walking beneath the proverbial weight of the world. It's the first thing I noticed about you at
the airport. The second was your shoes.'

'What's wrong with my shoes?'

'They've been resoled. Resoled shoes have the unfortunate
side-effect of looking resoled. It becomes their prevailing charac-
teristic.'

I poured half the Crown down my throat and chewed on a couple
ice cubes. 'Fucked-up world,' I said.

'Yes, it very often is. But I'd wager a kingdom that I'm a fair
lot older than you, and in all my years it's come to me that there
are only two things out there that can drag a man to the point of
honest depression. Two things only – and perhaps just one.'

'Love and loss,' I said.

He chuckled. 'Dear boy. Those are one and the same. To love is
to fear loss, and to feel loss is to have loved. No, the first is love,
and the other is money. And though I've never cared to test the
theory, I've heard people in positions to know swear that enough of
the first renders the second irrelevant. I have not, however, heard
anyone convincingly argue that enough money can inoculate one
against the necessity of love, or the pain of its absence.'

'Have you ever been in love, Bartholemeu?'

'Oh yes, countless times. Beautiful men from beautiful countries,
all. And each time it ends the same, which is to say with tears and a
journey. The person crying and the nature of the journey change a
bit, but it's really all the same when one looks back upon it.'

'Why does it have to end?'

'Because it does,' he said. 'Everything ends.'

'Not everything ends with tears.'

'Everything that matters does,' Bartholemeu said. 'If it isn't
worth crying over once it's gone, what's the point in having it at
all? Where's the worth in that?'

I finished the rest of my glass. 'Fucked-up world.'

'Yes,' he chuckled. 'You mentioned that. Is she promised to
another?'

'No. How did you know she was a she?'

'Really, Cole. Eat enough apples and one learns the smell of
apples, even amongst the oranges and pears. Does she fancy you
the same way?'

I nodded.

'Then it's you who's dallying? I might have known. Grey said you were a heartbreaker.'

'It's nothing like that,' I said. 'She's young.'

He shrugged.

'And she's one of my students.'

'You're a teacher?'

I nodded.

'Fancy that. What do you teach?'

'English. Eleventh grade.'

'That's not so young,' he said. 'It isn't as if you're skulking about the grammar school hallways handing out peppermint sticks.'

'It might as well be.'

'Nonsense.' He shook his head. 'You're a typical American, Cole. All of life's pleasures are mitigated by inherent guilt bred into you by the miserable puritans. Jonathan Edwards has done the lot of you a kicking bad disservice. It really is a tragedy. American youth are taught that A is good and B is bad and there's very little in between. Life is a series of grays, Cole. The men who wrote your rules had to take time out from boffing their slaves in order to pick up the quill. You could do yourself the favor of getting shut of their sanctimony. Perhaps it'll have some ripple effect throughout your culture.' He sipped his drink. 'One finger in the dike, as it were…'

'It's not that easy.'

'It sounds precisely that easy. The great harm I think is in not seeing it. You're in love with a woman who's young and happens to be your student. Where's the wrong in that?'

'I could lose my job.'

'Do you favor the lass or the job more?'

'I hate my job.'

Bartholemeu looked at me as though I'd just asked help with two plus two. 'I'll never understand Americans. You allow this nebulous middle-class morality to befuddle you into want and sadness when all the while the object of your desire is sitting right there before you, desiring you in return.' He shook his head again. 'Makes as much sense as baseball to me.'

'It's not even that, really. I mean, it is that, but it's not. I could give a shit what people think. I could quit my job tomorrow and walk away a happy man. The money they pay me I could make doing twenty different things, all of them rewarding enough to keep me at it.'

'Then what, pray tell?'

I wrestled with how to say it, and realized I'd never actually said it aloud. 'She's a stripper.'

'A dancer?'

'If you want to call it that. She takes off her clothes for money. I saw her doing it.'

'And this bothers you.'

'I know it shouldn't, but –'

'No, no. Not at all. I can see where that would. Even a stoic might grimace a bit at that. Have you spoken with her about it?'

I shook my head. 'No. I just left. I couldn't stay.'

'Does she know you saw her?'

I nodded.

'Well,' he said, 'every man's got to set about the course he sees best in this world. If her stripping for money ruins her in your eyes, there's no shame in telling her. It is a bit seedy.'

'A bit.'

'But consider her reasons. I've no idea, of course, but judging by your feelings for her I'll hazard the assumption that while her vocation is seedy, she likely is not. It may even bother her more than it does you. And if that's the case, she must really need the money badly, and needing money badly is not a condition in which one customarily makes sound judgments.

'That said, it's possible she's a wanton little tramp who thrills to the moment and is never more happy than when she's on stage beneath the lights. That's your call to make, Cole, but I suspect you've already made it.'

He stood. 'In any case, I've begun to ramble and I must be getting back. Claude will be wondering if I tarry much longer. He's a bit of a paranoid, and you haven't lived until you have a queer paranoid on your heels. Rather like having an unreachable itch in the small of your back. Best of luck to you, Cole.'

'Thanks, Bartholemeu,' I said. 'I appreciate the advice.'

'Mostly prattlings' – sipping his drink, pausing, looking at something beyond the black horizon. 'If I may –'

I nodded.

'I think I know something about being different. A good bit, actually. And I can tell you that it's never an easy thing to pretend to be something you're not. It wears away at one's sense of dignity and self-respect and wounds deeper than any weapon man has ever produced. If your young woman-friend is denigrating herself in your eyes because you thought more of her, it's entirely possible she's doing the same in her own eyes as well, because she knows it's beneath her, that it's merely an unsavory means to an end. If it's that, then she's probably confused, hurting, and now that you know, even more ashamed than she already was. If you loved her before, the last things she needs now is to lose that, too.'

I looked at him, but he was still staring past me, out at the ocean, at the stars above it burning like candles through black velvet. 'Just a thought.'

I finished my drink alone beneath the soft black sky, listening to the sounds of Grey's never-ending party behind me. I thought about what Bartholemeu had said. He was right. I knew it before he told me. I knew it after. I was going to act on it once I got back to Charleston, too.

But there was something I had to do first.

'Grey.'

She was in the foyer, a long, wide brick room filled with brass and cherry furniture, clucking away with three other women, all of them carved of gold and ivory and dripping sensuality from their pores. A tall, middle-aged man with dirty-blond hair going white around the temples was standing next to her, his arm around Grey's shoulders. Grey turned and smiled when she saw me. The scent of possibility hung in the air like mist.

'Cole,' she said. 'You look positively piqued.'

'You got a phone?'

'The bedroom. Is everything all right?'

'Yeah. Fine. I just gotta use the phone.'

She nodded. 'Last room on the left. Take your time.'

'Thanks.'

I fell on the bed and stared at the ceiling, the room spinning, clockwise or counter, I couldn't tell. I kept one leg posted on the floor to anchor myself. It didn't help much.

I dialed the number from memory. She answered after the third ring. The sound of her voice ripped me some place deep.

'Autumn,' I said.

'Who – ? Cole? Cole, is that you? What in the world are you doing calling here?'

'I need to talk to you.'

'It's three in the morning.'

'Yeah. Sorry about that. I need to talk to you, though.'

'You're drunk.'

'I know. Sorry about that, too. I've been drinking for two days.'

'You'll have to call back tomorrow, Cole. I've got to be at work early and –'

'Autumn, please. Give me just a second –'

'Call back tomorrow, Cole –'

'Please Autumn. Don't make me beg. It hurts too much to beg. Just give me two minutes and I'll never call back again. I promise.'

'I've heard your promises before.'

'I know.'

Dead silence. For a second I thought she'd hung up.

'Well?'

'How've you been?' I asked.

'I'm hanging up, Cole.'

'No, no! Don't. I'm sorry. I just – I don't know what to say.'

'Then why'd you call? It's been two years. I haven't thought of you in a long time.' Pause. 'I didn't mean that to sound so mean.'

'It's all right. You're just...I wish – I wish I had more than two minutes.'

'It's one and a half now, Cole. I'm sorry, but I really do have to get up early.'

'You a pharmacist?'

'Yeah.'

'Good. Good deal. I knew you'd do it. I'm not surprised. I'm really not. Which one?'

'Which one what?'

'Pharmacy?'

'Why does it matter?'

'It doesn't. Do you ever think about us, Autumn?'

Pause. 'I did for a while.' She sighed. 'We had some good times, Cole. You don't just forget four years of your life like that.'

'There were bad times too, though, right?'

'There were lots of bad times. Too many. We held on too long.'

'Did I ever apologize for hurting you?'

'I can't remember. It doesn't matter now. I've moved on. You should too, Cole. This isn't good for you.'

'No, no, I know. I have. Moved on, I mean. I just – I just wasn't sure if I ever told you I was sorry for... the way things ended.'

'I know you didn't mean to hurt me. I knew it then. But I don't think –'

'Why'd I do it?' I asked her. I had my eyes closed, and they were dry.

'Why'd you do what?'

'The check-out girl.'

'You called me at three in the morning after two years to ask me why you cheated?'

'I know it's weird, but you knew me better than anyone.'

'I didn't know you. If I'd known you were going to sleep around on me, I never would have gotten involved with you.'

'I didn't want to do it.'

'I'm not even going to respond to that. Your two minutes are up. Take care of yourself, Cole.'

'I meant I never saw it coming. When I asked you to marry me I meant every word of it. I meant I'd never hurt you or lie to you or treat you like anything other than a princess. I wanted to do that.'

'Goodnight, Cole.'

'I'm sorry, Autumn. Sorry I couldn't be the man you were looking for. I know I ruined it and it's my fault but I also know I'm not dead yet and there's still time for me to do good things, to be the man someone's looking for, and I'm just looking to get it right before I blow it again.'

'Then don't fuck other women,' she said. I tried to remember if I'd ever heard her swear before, and I couldn't think of an occasion. 'Don't lie to them. Don't scream at them and say you'd like to smash their face through the windshield.'

'Did I ever say that to you?'

'Which month?'

'I was a real shit, wasn't I?' She didn't answer. 'Why'd you stick around as long as you did?'

'Truthfully?'

I nodded to the empty room. 'Yes.'

'I gave you my virginity,' she said. 'I didn't want to be the kind of girl that slept with half a dozen men before she got married. I loved you and believed you and let you inside my body, and I thought I should marry you because of it.'

'That's a pretty good reason,' I said.

'I've grown up since then.'

'Are you in love with anyone?'

'I'm not discussing my life with you.'

'Because I am. I am so much it hurts. So much I bleed on the inside when I'm not with her. And I don't want to do her wrong the way I did you. I don't want to flush it the way I flushed us. Because when I'm with her she makes all the hurt losing you put me through worth it and more.'

'Cole –'

'I used to cry in the shower, Autumn – did you know that? No. No reason you would. But I did. I used to cry in the shower and cry in my closet and cry when the wind blew wrong, but I'd go through our break-up again every day if I could just kiss her one more time. I don't know why I called you to tell you that – I know I'm weak – but I needed to wrap it up with you. I know you wrapped it up the day we split – before, probably – but I didn't. I harbored it a long time and let it fester and rot inside me and push me into relationships with all sorts of wrong people but I'm out now and I'm okay and I'm going to be okay. I just wanted to tell you that. I don't think you care either way but I wanted to tell you just the same.'

'You called for *closure*? Now? After all this time?'

'No. I called for starters. I'm starting the rest of my life right now, and I'm going to do it right. Everything before was the prologue, and I'm warmed up now. I'm going to do what's best for her, because she needs it and deserves it and because she'd do it for me. And because I love her.'

'I'm happy for you, Cole.'

'I know. I knew you would be. I think that's part of why I called.'

'I have to go now.'

'I know. Are you happy?'

'Cole –'

'I'm not pressing for details. I just want to know – just to know – that you're happy. It'd make me feel good to know you're happy.'

'You mean it'd ease your guilt for finally being over us.'

'No. I cried the guilt down the shower along with the shame and my pride. I want to know because I'd like to know you're happy out there. I'm never going to call you again, and I know I'll never see you, so I thought –'

'I'm happy, Cole. I got married last year. He's a wonderful man.'

'He better be. Anyone I know?'

'Goodnight.'

'I was only kidding. Goodnight, Autumn. Take care.'

'I will, Cole. You do, too.'

'Yeah,' I said.

There was silence.

'Cole?'

'Yeah?'

'Are you still writing?'

'Some. Why?'

'Well, if you ever publish anything, stick a copy in my parents' mailbox. I'll eventually get it. You remember where they live.'

'Yeah. I do. And I will. Goodbye, Autumn. Thanks.'

When I woke up Grey was sitting at the foot of the bed, wearing a heavy white terry-cloth bathrobe that stopped short of her knees and showed lots of thigh. Her hair was wet and pulled back. In her hands she was holding a mug of something steaming. The logo Kinerly, Walker, Smith and Herndon was scripted across it in thick, sturdy lettering.

'You've decided, then?'

I pushed myself to a seated position and rubbed my eyes.

'Good. I'm proud of you, Cole. Proud, but not surprised.'

'You mean Savannah?'

She nodded. 'You and I spoke some last night, after you got off the phone.'

'We did? I don't remember.'

'No, you wouldn't. You were fairly well gone.'

'Yeah. Sorry about that.'

She held up a hand. 'No apology needed, Cole. I'm delighted you came down.'

'How much longer are you staying?'

'I don't know,' she shrugged. 'Philip has asked me to go to sea with him for a while. Did you get a chance to meet Philip?'

Aside from Bartholemeu, none of the people I met at Grey's stood out.

'He one of the expatriates?'

She nodded. 'They've been looking for him for years now.'

'They?'

'They,' she nodded. 'The FBI. They've even got his picture on their website.'

'How much did he steal?'

She shrugged. 'I've never asked. His yacht is always sufficiently stocked for a twelve-month sojourn at sea, though, so it must've been a good bit.'

'He keeps it all on the boat?'

She laughed. 'It's not real money, silly. Only lights on a computer screen somewhere. You push a button or two and it moves from this account to that. Just little lights blinking and blipping. Only poor people really handle cash anymore. Are you leaving today?'

I nodded. 'After a shower and a cup of whatever that is you're drinking.'

'To make her yours forever?'

'To tell her how I feel.'

'Splendid,' Grey said, standing, twirling in the middle of the room, then leaving in a flash of terry-cloth and skin. 'Splendid.'

TWENTY-SIX

Intermezzo; Cole reaches clarity

I got back Monday afternoon, the 4th of Jan., at half-past twelve. I'd decided on the plane what I was going to do, and what I was going to do was this: I'd get back to the apartment by one, shave and grab a shower, then call Savannah. If she answered I'd ask her to meet me somewhere, whenever she could. It didn't matter. I'd wait.

If she wasn't there, I'd get in the car and drive up to Winter's Cove, where I'd wait. Eventually she'd come home. Eventually I'd speak to her and make things right. Eventually we'd have forever. I understood that now.

She'd beaten me to it, though. When I got home Brasco was waiting for me as usual, sprawled out in the center of the living room. I fell to the floor and loved on him for a while, then went into the bedroom and began stripping off my clothes.

The note was in the center of the made-up bed. I never make up the bed, so that in itself was a dead give-away that someone else had been here. I knew Jules had been in and out to check on Brasco, but I didn't see him taking a nap while he was here, much less bothering to make up the bed afterwards.

But the note answered it all, even before I read it. It was a single piece of lined white paper that looked as if it'd been removed from my tablet by the computer. It'd been folded once, width-ways.

cole,
julian told me where you'd gone and when you'd be back. i asked him for the key to take care of brasco. don't be mad at him. he's sweet. he cares about you a lot.
i understand you had to leave that night. i told you in

the beginning there were things about me you might not like. if you want to forget there was ever anything between us i'll find a way to understand that, too. but i wish you'd give me the chance to explain it to you. our time together was special enough to deserve at least that.

i'll wait for you tonight in that little garden beside the big methodist church down off king street. i'll be there from eleven to twelve tonight. i hope you'll meet me there, cole, but only if there's still a chance for us. not just to tell me you can't forgive me, or that we're through. if that's the case i'd rather just sit there by myself and get used to missing you.

i'll be there waiting for you, on the bench in the garden where we walk in my dreams at night.

yours,
savannah

I didn't leave the hotel room in Mexico City for the three days. I'd checked in and paid cash for two weeks in advance as Wallace Webster, taking care to destroy all of Marcus James Coker's documentation once I reached the room. American driver's license, American passport, employer ID, social security card, all of it. I ate room-service, ordering large enough amounts to last for several meals and always during separate shifts so as to avoid having the same bellhop twice the same day. When they arrived I'd slip a five-spot beneath the door and instruct them to leave the food. Five dollars was enough of a tip to keep them from complaining to the others about the cheap gringo on the fifth floor, but not enough to warrant them jockeying to serve me.

When housekeeping came by I was always either in the shower or standing before the mirror with a face full of shaving cream. My old face was all over the television now, and while I was comfortable in its dissimilarity to my new one, I wasn't taking chances.

In preparing for this, I'd spent countless hours in my chair in the West Ashley Barnes and Noble, researching expatriation and all the particulars of the paper chase that followed once those who'd be looking for me began their search in earnest. According to what I read, the people who got caught usually did so in one of two ways: they left a trail, or they ignored old Wolfe and tried to go home again. That's rule number one when it comes to disappearing *successfully. You can't go back. Period. End of story. Done and done. Next question.*

I knew I was never going back, so that wasn't a problem for me. Their only shot at finding me was to find my trail, so to that end I disappeared with enough different identities to keep them guessing forever.

James Coker had done a good job at the bank, but I didn't need him anymore. I was Wallace Webster now, and all Wallace Webster wanted to do was hang out in his room and eat room-service, pet his cat, and watch the international news on CNN.

And crunch numbers. Wallace Webster was hell on a calculator.

On day four, Wallace Webster rose from his bed at ten that morning and rode the elevator down the five floors to the lobby, where he walked outside into the overcast Mexico City day. He wore a plain brown ball cap and sunglasses. He was right handed so he turned left, because he had read once in a novel somewhere that when people were in unfamiliar surroundings they tended to choose the direction of their dominant hand.

He walked down the road, passing the street vendors, the suit-clad commuters, the university students traveling in groups. He traveled two blocks, found a pay phone, and, using his prepaid phone card, dialed a number from memory. Twenty seconds later and he was speaking to someone in Bermuda, listing off account numbers, and instructing the gentleman two thousand miles away on the other end of the phone to direct the contents of his account into two others. Half to the Royal Bank of Scotland in the Channel Islands, the other half into the International Merchant Bank, Ltd., in the Isle of Man. The accounts had already been set up, Wallace Webster informed the gentleman. The gentleman put Wallace Webster on hold for most of a minute, then returned to inform him that the transfer was complete. He gave Wallace Webster the transfer numbers and bid him a nice day.

Webster hung up the phone and redialed. His fingers shook a bit, but not as much as Coker's before him. He'd had four days to play with the calculator and stare at the numbers; four days to watch the story of his old life unfold before him on the hotel television screen before him. He was in it for real now, and he knew it. If he was caught, he'd go to jail forever, and possibly worse. Murder is a capital crime in South Carolina. So the money was less a wonder to him now than a means to preventing his capture. That's rule number two of disappearing. Running is cheap, but hiding is expensive. Often exorbitantly so.

Rule number three is cash makes no enemies and leaves no trail, so you'd better have lots of cash.

Once the man in Aruba had accessed the account, Webster directed him to transfer it to Citco Fund Services, Ltd. in Barbados, and Santader Investment Bank, Ltd. in the Bahamas, in equal portions. Again, the accounts were already established, and again they were awaiting the transfer.

Fifteen minutes later Wallace had called all four of the new banks, verified the account numbers and the balance amount, and begun walking back to his hotel. As he walked, he silently recited the four separate account numbers, for Wallace Webster didn't write anything down. His memory was his key.

On the evening of the fourth night, Wallace Webster and his cat lay in bed and nibbled tuna salad, both of them eating around the little bits of onion. They were watching the evening news. CNN was covering their story. There were shots of the West Ashley apartment, of the school where Cole Archer had taught, of the trailer park where Savannah lived. There was also a shot of the big hotel in downtown Charleston, 'site of the murder,' the reporters seemed to like calling it.

Wallace Webster and his cat, Taco, watched for anything new, just as they'd done the three previous days. It was essentially the same thing each time. Occasionally the order was varied. First-year teacher. Underage student. Illicit affair. Rape. Obsession. Millions of dollars disappeared. Wealthy lawyer murdered in downtown hotel. This time there were a couple of addenda, however. First, the FBI, which had officially taken over the case two days ago, was formally speculating that it was possible Cole Archer had created a new identity and might soon attempt to flee the country, if he hadn't already.

Second, border guards at both the Mexican and Canadian borders had been notified to be on the lookout for any male traveling with a cat.

Of the two, Wallace Webster appeared more interested in this fact than Taco the cat beside him, who was concentrating heavily on the remains of the tuna salad. The cat, who didn't answer to Taco particularly well, had been noticed when he'd crossed the border; the FBI would be aware of this shortly, if they weren't already. It was entirely possible that the Feds, anticipating his watching the news, would leak their information when it was several days old. They could have located the border-guard back in Brownsville as long as three days ago. If that was the case, they'd be in Mexico City by now. There would be extradition issues, matters of international diplomacy that would make the logistics of removing him – if they found him – more complicated, but the FBI was a big machine and it wanted him badly. You don't steal the kind of money Cole Archer stole and expect no one to come looking for you.

Which meant it was time to leave.

Two hours later Taco and I were a hundred miles away, heading south, driving a used mini-van bought for two thousand American dollars, cash. I'd left the television on, the truck in the parking lot, and I hadn't checked out. I left a couple shirts and a pair of jeans in the closet. I'd even put in a request for a wake-up call at nine the following morning, and room service at eleven that night. Our days of being Mexicans were through.

I reached the garden a quarter before eleven. She was already there, but I didn't let her see me at first. I stood in the shadow of a massive oak and watched her sitting there on the little cement bench, nearly lost in the darkness of the little garden, only her hair and patches of skin catching the moonlight and turning it silver. She sat and stared up at the stars, and from where I stood I thought I could see her mouth moving silently. Like she was counting them, perhaps. Or praying.

It was a mild night. The city surrounding us was quiet. The harbor breeze wisped through the tops of the trees and scattered leaves along the ground. Savannah was wearing jeans and a sweater that looked maroon in the moonlight but might have been black. She sat there motionless, a young girl waiting beneath a milky golden moon for her love to come and tell her he still needed her, that she still had worth in his eyes.

I watched her shimmering like a jewel beneath the moon in the center of that silent garden and knew I'd never write anything as beautiful as what I was seeing, and that no one else would either. In that moment the realization that nothing either of us had ever done up to this very second had any bearing on the future – hers, mine, or the one I wanted us to share together – settled over me with perfect clarity. Ours was tomorrow.

'Hi there,' I said, stepping out from the shadow.

'Hi,' she said, and her voice was like the touch of someone familiar.

I took several steps toward her. 'I was watching you.'

She looked down at her crossed ankles.

'You were beautiful,' I said.

'I knew you were there.'

'No you didn't.'

She nodded. Smiled. 'The breeze carried your scent.'

'I should have showered.'

'You always smell good. I noticed that in class the first day.'

'What does it smell like?'

'Like you.' She paused. 'There's room on this bench,' she said, patting the spot to her left, 'if you're interested.'

I sat down beside her and took a long breath. I leaned over my knees and placed my hands together and sighed. There was a lot I wanted to say and I wasn't sure how to start.

From somewhere off in the distance the sound of horse-hooves clip-clopping over cobblestones echoed through the garden. It reminded me that I was in the most beautiful city in the world, next to someone I was madly, passionately in love with, and all of a sudden I didn't have anything to say to her at all except that.

'Savannah – '

'– It's for the money,' she said. 'I don't do it for any other reason than the money.'

'I don't care,' I said. 'It doesn't matter to me. All I want –'

'It matters to me. I told you once I graduated I was getting out of here forever. Anything I made squirting mustard on subs or selling shoes at the mall my mother would take on payday. With dancing she doesn't know how much I make. With dancing I can keep some – a lot – for myself.'

I nodded. Distant voices rode in on the wind. The air was turning cooler.

'I work two nights a week and after a busy weekend I can take home close to five thousand dollars. I tell my mother two and she takes it all, and even though she tries, not even she can drink two thousand dollars' worth of liquor in a week. My brothers have the food and medicine they need and she even bought them some clothes from Wal-Mart last week. They've never had new clothes. Not even from Wal-Mart. It's always been either hand-me downs or Goodwill.'

I didn't say anything. I thought about leaning over and kissing her, but I didn't want to cut her off.

'That still leaves me three. That's three thousand dollars, Cole. Do you know how long it would take for me to make three thousand dollars at minimum wage? I'm doing it in a weekend at the club, weekend after weekend after weekend.'

'Five grand?'

She nodded. 'I'm never coming back to Charleston. Ever. I'm going to college some place far away and I'm taking my brothers with me and none of us are ever stepping foot in this city again.'

'Five yards? How in the hell?'

She laughed. 'Alcohol and testosterone. The stuff of births and deaths. On a good night I'll do twenty private dances at $200 a dance. Half goes to the house and half to me. I'll do twenty-five, maybe thirty table dances if we're busy; each of those is forty, twenty of which is mine. Every girl's on the stage twice an hour and there's always at least thirty to forty dollars to be made in a two-song routine. I get all that, and any tips I get from bringing drunk men drinks are mine, too. It's disgusting and ugly and immoral and I hate myself for doing it, but there isn't any other way. I've got almost twenty thousand dollars saved up. When I have fifty I'll quit.'

She nodded with finality. 'Fifty will be enough to get me out and keep me gone.'

'Fifty thousand dollars,' I whistled. 'It'd take me almost two years to make that, and you'll have it a couple months.' I whistled. 'Are they hiring down there? I can line dance like a bastard.'

She laid her head on my shoulder, and neither of us spoke for a long time.

After a while she said, 'Thank you, Cole.'

'For what?'

'For being so sweet. I was afraid you'd never want to see me again.'

Her head was still on my shoulder. I could smell her hair, and it burned everything beneath my skin. I wrapped my arm around her small shoulders and pulled her close to me.

'I did a lot of thinking down in Florida. Virtually everything about this relationship is unorthodox. The world uses the word "wrong" for this sort of thing. If we're caught, I'll lose my job. I might be charged, depending on how far they wanted to push things. And it'd be no picnic for you, either. And the reasons are as simple as they are temporary. I'm twenty-seven and you won't be seventeen for another week. So because of this we have to sneak to other cities and hide out in my apartment and meet in dark gardens –'

– She touched my hand, slid her thumb beneath it. 'I think it's romantic here.'

'So do I. But in another week we'll be back in school and then I'm your teacher again and you're my student, out there with thirty other students, and I'll be honest with you Savannah, I hate teaching about as much as I've ever hated anything at all. I want to just get through the rest of this year, make it to June without anyone figuring anything out, then seven months later you'll be eighteen and graduated and then we can go wherever you want.'

She lifted her head.

'We?' – almost a whisper, as if afraid she might have misheard me.

'Yes,' I nodded. 'We. I'm through with defeatism. I want to be with you. I know it now. I've known it for a lot longer, I think, but I was afraid to admit it to myself. I was too busy listening to the world. But a good friend in Florida helped me realize that all I was doing was making excuses as to why we shouldn't work, instead of focusing on all the reasons why we would.'

I took her small hands in mine and pivoted on the little cement bench, straddling it between my legs. Her face was inches from me.

'I want to be with you, Savannah. I want us to be together. Forever. To hell with all the rest of it. We'll work that out as it comes. We can go to Oregon or Alaska or the University of Mars, for all I care. What matters is that it's us going there.'

A single tear fell a burning silver down her cheek. I touched it with my thumb.

'That we fall asleep beside each other and that we watch sunsets together –'

'And curl up beneath blankets with Brasco,' she said. 'And listen to it rain outside the windows –'

'And go outside and dance in it whenever we want, knowing it won't matter who sees us.'

'It rains all the time in Oregon,' she said. 'Kiss me, Cole.'

I kissed her. In the corner of the little garden on King, South of Broad, I kissed Savannah Bellington. It was the first time I'd done it as an honest man, all my safeguards and pretensions stripped away before her.

'Again,' she said. 'Kiss me again.'

Sometime later she said, 'I love you, Cole. I love you I love you I love you a million times I love you. I've loved you since the hospital and before. For the first time in my life the idea of forever sounds wonderful, and it's all because of you.'

I kissed her again.

At some point I asked, 'Have you ever been in love before, Savannah?'

She smiled. 'Lots of times.'

I stopped. 'Really?'

'Of course,' she nodded, the night around us a dark, velvety blue. 'But every other time it was with books.'

TWENTY-SEVEN

The me-room; intermezzo;
Cole before the Board

So it's official,' Jules said. He was lying on his back on the couch in his living room, balancing a bottle of Corona on his stomach, working the remote up and down the stations with his other hand. 'You and the embryo are an item.'

It was Sunday afternoon, the 24th of Jan. Aside from school, I'd seen Savannah only twice since our night in the park, once for a midnight meeting along the Battery, and once more at my apartment, two nights ago. She'd slipped in after dark and stayed the night. The next morning my apartment was replete with her intoxicating scent.

Her mother thought she was working, and her mother's boyfriend – who managed the club where she danced – thought she was home with a sinus infection. When I asked her what would happen if her mother's boyfriend mentioned her absence to her mom, she just shook her head.

'It isn't that way with my mother and her boyfriends,' she said, stretching out on my garage-sale couch, laying her head in my lap. 'They show up drunk whenever they feel like it and if she's sober enough she has sex with them and then they leave. They don't talk much.'

Now, at Jules', I was currently stretched back in Jules' favorite recliner – a can of Dasani water, and not beer, in my lap – watching the channels flip every two or three seconds. Jules had close to two hundred of them, and I can't remember ever seeing him settle on one for more than a minute.

'I wouldn't call it official,' I said.

'What would you call it then?'

'Settled.'

'Settled?'

'Right. There's no longer any conflict or confusion. There's only clarity.' I took a sip of the water. 'Settled.'

'Right. You don't think any of the other kids have noticed in class?'

'Nope. I'm stone in there.'

'You better be. A year's a long time to keep something hidden. Especially something that's been settled with such … clarity.'

'Don't fret, Juliet. This time next year I'm an Oregonian and no one'll know the difference.'

He finished his beer, rose, retrieved another from the fridge, and tossed me a can of water, my third of the afternoon. Capers' grievance hearing was scheduled at the District Office for seven tonight and I needed to be sober. I was planning to speak on his behalf.

Jules was back on the couch, the channels flipping as quick as ever. ESPN. ESPN 2. HBO's 1-5, STARZ, the locals.

'You think you and a set of pig-tails running around Oregon with four pints of half 'n' half might raise an eyebrow or two?'

'Not sure what's going to happen on that front, actually. Savannah's pretty set on getting her brothers out of there.'

'I don't blame her. But Oregon isn't exactly the South. They had a black person there once and he moved away back in the seventies. You guys'll stick out like oral herpes.'

'I'm touched by your concern. How's Alicia, by the way?'

He shrugged. 'I finally got her to come home with me. That's progress, I guess.'

'Maybe you should go a little slower with this one. I thought she seemed nice.'

'None of them are mean, bro.'

'No, but plenty aren't nice. Remember Jan?'

He whistled. 'Do I! What a Slavic-K grade-A cunt. That bitch sucked the rigid cock of Satan, didn't she?'

'And to think you almost married her.'

'I didn't almost marry her. I bought her a ring. There's a hell of a big difference. I didn't even give it to her.'

'You gave it to her.'

'Yeah, but I got it back two weeks later. There's a gray zone there. It's like food on the floor. It's still edible as long as it doesn't stay down there too long.'

'Whatever. I like Alicia. You should take it slow.'

'You don't even know her.'

'I met her at Meritage that night, same as you.'

'I don't know her, either. All I know is she's got a big pooper and she doesn't like my room.'

'Don't take this the wrong way, bro, but not many girls are going to dig the Me-Wall.'

'Hey, fuck 'em. Fuck the lot of them if they don't dig the Me-Wall. That's the first test. If the Me-Wall scares them, then they sure can't handle me. Somewhere out there there's a woman who'll love the Me-Wall. When I find her, I'll make her my queen.'

The Me-Wall was Jules' shrine to Jules, a carefully crafted, years-in-the-making, floor-to-ceiling collage of pictures of Jules on all his vacations. It was comprised of hundreds of shots, from Polaroids to professional portraits, all solo, each having as its subject a posing Jules by some significant landmark. The giant Caesar in Caesar's Atlantic City. On the edge of the Grand Canyon. In front of a café in Las Cruces. The deck of a cruise ship. The beaches of Hilton Head. Next to the Liberty Bell. On the steps of the US Capitol. There were never any other people in his pictures. Ever. To look at the Me-Wall you'd think Jules traveled everywhere alone, grabbing some helpful tourist to snap his picture for posterity. It wasn't so, though. I'd been with him for half a dozen of those trips, as had buddies from Channel Five, his parents, various girlfriends, name it. Jules just cut everyone else out before sticking the shot on the Me-Wall.

Whenever he brought a new girl home to his place, he'd take her back to his room, show her the Me-Wall the way a lot of guys will show you their new sports car.

'This is me in Times Square,' he'd say, tapping the picture, emphasis on me. 'And this is me in Barbados. Me in Ft. Lauderdale. There's me riding a horse on the beach. Here's me in Vegas for a buddy's bachelor party. Me down on Market Street. This one is of me in Puerto Rico, visiting my grandparents. And here's me in the hospital holding my little niece the morning she was born.'

If the girl had the nerve to ask where the hell the grandparents or the newborn niece were, he'd just look at her like she'd said she's fond of boiling eggs on Tuesdays. If she pushed the point, chances were Jules wasn't calling her back.

He had a helluva healthy self-image, old Jules.

'You heard about Doug Feldstein, I assume?' Jules was saying.

'Who the hell is Doug Feldstein?'

'Station manager at 5.'

I shrugged. Checked my watch. I had another hour or so before I had to go home and put on a tie for Capers' thing tonight.

'He got caught with his hand in the cookie-jar.'

'He was stealing?'

'Fucking-A. Couple million is what they're saying. Feds blew through the place and everything today. Scooping up hard-drives, file cabinets, expense reports, whatever. He's already been placed on administrative leave, and supposedly they've got him on suicide watch down at MUSC.'

'How the hell did he get his hands on millions of dollars?'

Jules shrugged. 'It's not all out yet. Apparently he'd set up phony companies to sell the station airtime we never got, then just dumped the fees into his own account, or something like that. I don't know all the ins and outs yet.'

'Damn,' I said. 'You never liked him anyway, did you?'

'You know how that sort of thing goes,' he shrugged. 'He was a real assbag but he hired me when those douches over at 2 and 4 wouldn't, so I hate to wish the bitch too bad a ride. I think he's pretty much corked, though. Tell you the funny part. After his arraignment they were leading him down the courthouse steps and Hart Jeffords was the first one to stuff a mike in his face.'

Hart Jeffords was a middle-aged, bald reporter at Channel 5 who'd been hired and groomed by Doug Feldstein himself some two decades ago. Over time he'd grown legendary around Charleston for his willingness to go anywhere and ask anyone any question he thought was newsworthy. 'Our viewers have a right to know' was his big line, and he'd hammered it home through the TV's of those viewers for the past twenty years.

'Doug hadn't been out in the light more than ten seconds before old Hart stuck the microphone under his nose and snapped out a quick "Our viewers have a right to know, Mr. Feldstein, if you were stealing from your company." Two days earlier Feldstein signed Hart's paycheck.' Jules belched and laughed. 'Life's an ironic little slut sometimes, isn't she?'

'He was that close,' I said, more to myself than Jules.

'Who's that? Feldstein? Fuck him. He's on his way to being Bubba's girlfriend.' Jules winced and shook his head. 'They're going to have a high old time with his tight little Jewish asshole.'

'Why didn't he leave before they caught him?'

Jules shrugged. 'Why doesn't anyone quit before they're caught? He got greedy.'

He took several swallows of beer, savoring it the way a parched man might savor water.

'But he had to have known he was going to get caught eventually. You don't just pull something like that off without someone somewhere noticing something.'

'Someone somewhere always notices something. It's the law of the land.'

'Then why stay? If he was stealing money, how much would have been enough?'

'Fuck do you care, bro?' Jules said around a belch. 'This kind of shit happens all the time. You remember my first story as a reporter, don't you? The Wellington murder?'

'I know this is hard on your ego, Jules, but I don't actually make a point of watching the local news.'

'Whatever,' he said, rising for the fridge again, leaning over the door. 'It went national a couple days after I had it. You sure you don't want one? I got a couple Beck's back here.'

'I'd love one. Can't, though. I'm talking at this thing tonight. Shaved and everything.'

'Suit yourself,' he said, grabbing two Coronas. 'It won't go to waste.' He popped the cap and took a long pull from the bottle.

'Anyway, this Wellington fuck lived up in Myrtle Beach with his rich wife. Her family owned an ass of hotels up and down the Eastern seaboard, as well as half a dozen casinos in Atlantic City. One day he got tired of her shit and shot her and her kid – hers by another marriage, his step kid – and rode his yacht out into the horizon.'

'Seems drastic.'

'If he'd divorced her, he'd have been giving up the nice lifestyle he'd grown accustomed to. So he started moving money out of the country a couple months before he popped her. He pulled it out of various corporate accounts and wired it into a Cayman bank and back out the next day. The Feds had a record of the transfers – Big Brother has records of all outbound transfers over ten grand, you know – but by the time they could gather enough evidence he was playing shuffleboard out on the great big blue somewhere. And of course they had no idea where the money went once it left the Caymans. The banks down there are pretty good at keeping secrets.'

'It's that easy?'

'I don't know about easy. I don't think it'd be too fucking easy to shoot my wife and her nine-year-old son while they slept, but people do some strange shit when money's on the line. He liquidated everything he could get his hands on. At least five million dollars in the few weeks before the murders alone, and maybe even as much as ten. Probably bounced it in and out of a dozen different banks before finally stashing it someplace safe. Doubt we'll ever know, though' – another swig of Corona, another run through twenty channels – 'motherfucker's long gone by now.'

'Just like that.'

Jules nodded. 'Just like that.'

'You don't think they'll ever catch him?'

'Lots of places to hide if you're rich,' he said.

'How long you think they'll look before they give up?'

Jules shrugged. 'Imagine they've given up already, the law, anyway. There're always crimes being committed, and they'll have to redirect their manpower if they aren't getting anywhere with Wellington. The Coast Guard'll keep his description on hand, and they'll monitor all his old friends' phone lines, but provided he doesn't screw up and send his mother a card for Mother's Day or renew his subscription to *The Robb Report*, he's probably free as farts.'

'So it's the first six months that are the hottest, then. Survive those, and you're in the clear.'

Jules considered it. 'Clearer, maybe. But that's from the law. The legitimate law. Someone like Wellington pops a casino heiress, odds are the family will hunt until they find him. And the sort of folks that deal in that business won't be there to arrest him, either. Five years from now he might be sipping single-malt in a Hong Kong high-rise and accidentally fall off the balcony. Or he might catch a gaff through the neck while snorkeling in Fiji, or choke on his swordfish and mango sandwich in Brazil. Lots of ways to die if someone wants you dead enough, and can afford to chase you long enough. It all comes down to money.'

He belched again, then added, 'Course you don't have to get your tits all twisted up over it, Cole. No one's going to come looking for some rookie teacher who ran off with an underprivileged student.'

But I wasn't listening at this point. I was still stuck on the last thing he'd said: It all comes down to money.

And of course he was right. It all comes down to money.

I drove straight through to Guatemala, crossing the border as Jonathan Curtis, loyal subject of Great Britain. I'd purchased the British passport – along with four others, each listing a different name and registered to a different country – from a Panamanian company I'd found on the Internet. Effective immediately, I was no longer an American, at least on paper. Any crossing of borders I did now I did under a forged and foreign passport, a crime egregious enough to land me in jail in whatever country it was that caught me.

It was a risk, but one I had to take. Americans traveling abroad stand out, particularly when the American authorities are looking for them. But you have to be careful when you hop from one identity to the next. Border guards aren't stupid. They ask your name, date of birth, occupation, home address, etcetera, and then they check your documents. If you're running under half a dozen different names and histories, it's easy to get tripped up. In order to avoid confusion you have to have a system. Mine was simple. I had a different identity with different supporting documentation for each country I passed through. When I crossed over into the next, I'd become someone new. The old stuff got tossed, burned, or buried.

Guatemala was stunningly beautiful but still too close to all that I left behind. It was only a ninety-mile plane trip to Miami, and the Guatemalan government didn't have any problem turning over felons to the United States government. I stayed long enough to sell the van and purchase another truck, this one only a few years old and painted a nondescript brown. I rented a room in a little villa for two nights, and spent most of my time drunk. I tried not to think of Savannah. I tried not to picture her that last night before I left, in the hotel room in downtown Charleston, amidst the smell of pain and feces and bleeding flesh.

I told myself if I ran long enough, if I ran far enough, I might be able to outrun the events of that awful night, when I became a murderer and in so doing murdered my dream.

On the morning of the third day in Guatemala, Jonathan Curtis and his hangover began making his way towards Honduras.

*

That night in the downtown garden with Savannah became a line of demarcation for me. I drove away from it with a new perspective on everything that had begun to assemble and assimilate around me with such hurricane-like ferocity. Before The Garden I felt as if I had no control over any of it. After The Garden it seemed that things stopped simply happening, and began to occur as a result of my actions. There was purpose. An end had been established – Savannah and I leaving together for someplace far away – and I'd set about determining the means.

During the immediate days after The Garden, everything looked simple enough. We'd lie low until the school year was through, at which time I would be finished with my teaching career and would find some other way to make a living. I'd save as much money as possible over the summer and fall months, and once we knew where she was going to college, I'd go a couple weeks ahead of her and find myself a job and us a place to live. I could support her while she was in college. The tuition she'd already taken care of. I wasn't exactly thrilled with the way she'd done it, but, after The Garden, even that became a necessary component to our plan. Virtually anything, I felt, was justifiable, if it got us closer to being together.

I mapped everything out on my calendar. From the night of The Garden – Jan. 4th – to Coosaw Creek's December Graduation was a total of 342 days and 342 nights. Once she walked that stage she would literally be walking out of a world that would condemn us at every turn, into a world which wouldn't know any better, and wouldn't care if it did. Until then, my days were filled with rote routine and my nights with dreams of Savannah and me on the Pacific coast, dancing in the darkness beneath a silvery moon.

I was good at ignoring her at school. She was good at accepting it. Both of us understood the game. Each day she walked into my class and issued a polite 'Hello, Mr. Archer,' and each day I'd respond, without glancing up from my desk most mornings, with a detached 'Morning, Savannah.' I sailed through the days without incident or difficulty because I knew each one brought me closer to Dec. 12, when Savannah would walk across the stage and, her hand in mine, out of Coosaw Creek High, Charleston, and South Carolina for good. I stopped spending time with her at lunch. I didn't smile at her in the hallway anymore. I had her routine memorized long ago, and made certain that our paths didn't cross between classes. I was a picture of rectitude, a young English teacher toiling away, teaching outside the box, meeting the standards, encouraging creativity and all the rest of it. My lesson plans were turned in on time, my tie was always straight, and I never missed a meeting – including Capers' grievance hearing, which is probably one I should have skipped.

It was informal enough, held in the boardroom at the District Office, with the members of the Board fanned out across the front of the room behind their big, ostentatious, altar-like bench. They sat up there in their Sunday best behind their shiny nameplates and sipped sweet tea and waited on the commoners to take their seats and hold their tongues so Capers could have his fifteen minutes. You could tell they weren't too happy about his asserting his right to a grievance hearing. Winter's Cove, I was learning, had a preference for spills that were easily swept into cracks and beneath rugs. Capers airing his beef for the community – read: voters – to smell had them struggling to hide their consternation.

Capers was up front, sitting next to his wife, Tamela, an attractive redhead who was a terrific cook. They'd had me to dinner twice since the beginning of the school year, and each time I'd driven away at the end of the evening fighting back a tinge of envy; Zack Capers had the perfect life, far as I could tell. Nice house, well-behaved dog, adoring wife. I had Brasco, a dump of an apartment, and an inappropriate relationship with one of my students.

There were another forty or fifty people in attendance, enough that the custodian – who in this non-union state would be making the same six bucks an hour for working Sunday night that he made during any weekday – had to bring in extra chairs for all the additional asses, anatomically speaking, of course. I positioned myself in the back, so that when I spoke – which I'd decided to do a couple weeks ago, and so had spent hours upon hours in the County Records room researching the amazing and intricate world of family ties in lovely little Winter's Cove – anyone who wanted to see me would have to turn around and look at me.

It went the way I imagine most grievance hearings go. Superintendent Charles Waters made a few opening remarks, talked about the collective mission of Winter's Cove's employees, about how the term 'grievance hearing' was a misnomer, that Winter's Cove was a Family of Educators and that all families occasionally had issues which needed to be discussed and resolved. He pledged his personal confidence in Mr. Capers, in the esteemed members of the

Board, and assured all in attendance that everyone up and down the District Office's roster had but one thing in mind when personnel decisions were made, which was of course the best interest of the children. Somehow he got through it all with a straight face.

Capers got his fifteen minutes, standing strong and sturdy up front, discussing the good he'd done at Coosaw Creek High, how without his presence the Advanced Placement program would fold, and that this couldn't be in the best interests of the kids. He discussed his role in the debate program and the moot court program, both academic clubs founded and still sponsored by him. The esteemed members of the Board listened and nodded and sipped their tea and said they understood, but that in order to avoid the appearance of impropriety in the eyes of the faculty at Coosaw Creek, Capers couldn't continue to teach there if his brother-in-law, Olin Pepperidge, was going to be the principal.

Capers took exception, explained that the principal's position, according to the Winter's Cove handbook, was an administrative one with no direct oversight of teachers, this task being delegated to the assistant principals instead. The Board said they understood, but, for example, in the case of a teacher-to-teacher dispute, Olin Pepperidge would act as the final arbiter, and the fact that he was Capers' wife's brother would inherently – though probably unconsciously – disadvantage any teacher with whom Capers had a dispute.

There wasn't much Capers could say to that, except that he felt the Board's enforcement of the nepotism policy was selective and specious at best. At this point Superintendent Waters jumped in and thanked Mr. Capers for his comments. He then allowed 'concerned members of the community' to stand and be heard. A number of parents stood and talked about how Capers 'taught my child to write' and 'got my daughter into college' and 'gave my son the discipline and guidance he needed at such a crucial stage in his development.' Plenty of former students followed – everything from doctors and accountants and English PhD's and published poets to kids who'd graduated just a couple years ago – and sang his praises, and while it was clearly gratifying for the normally stoic Capers, it all missed the point.

The point was nepotism, and it was nepotism I was there to discuss. Capers had tried, but he'd been cut off. His fifteen minutes were finished and, after all, he was still an employee of Winter's

Cove and didn't need to push things too far. I on the other hand was under contract until June, and had no plans of returning afterwards, and so could speak the truth with relative impunity.

I stood, feeling a little as though I were jumping off a very high precipice, but reminding myself that in another couple of hundred days I'd be with Savannah and all of this would be a story we'd talk about cuddled up beneath blankets on the living room floor of our apartment.

'Mr. Waters,' I said, raising my hand, already standing. 'Mr. Waters, I have a few comments I'd like to offer.'

Waters was making a show out of checking his watch. 'I'm afraid our time is running short,' he said, then added with an affected chuckle, 'It is a school night, after all.'

I was ready for that line of defense, though.

'According to the Winter's Cove bylaws, sir, any employed individual under contract with Winter's Cove has a right to be heard at a grievance hearing for an uninterrupted period of time to be determined by the superintendent or his designee, but not less than five minutes.'

Superintendent Waters nodded his head solemnly. 'I commend you on your understanding of the bylaws, Mr. – ?'

'Archer, sir. Cole Archer. English teacher at Coosaw Creek High School.'

'Very nice, Mr. Archer,' he said happily, even friendly. He was a consummate politician, and was ever-mindful of the number of 'concerned members of the community' that were present.

'I think we can certainly afford you your five minutes, Mr. Archer, particularly if you feel you can offer something useful here tonight.'

'Yes, sir. I hope to.' A few people had turned in their seats to see who was talking. The Board was sipping its tea and waiting patiently.

'If I may address the Board,' I said, focusing in on Mr. Bangmore, second from the right. 'Mr. Bangmore, isn't your son a P.E. teacher at Coosaw Creek?'

'He is,' Bangmore said.

'Which means that each year, as a member of the School Board, you have the opportunity to vote on the size of the pay raise your son receives, correct?'

Waters jumped in. 'Mr. Archer, this isn't a trial. I'm afraid both your question and the tone in which you asked it are a little inappropriate. Mr. Bangmore is – '

'Is one of nine men and women who voted to remove Mr. Capers from Coosaw Creek High School under the excuse of nepotism. I simply want to know why nepotism isn't a problem for Mr. Bangmore and his son.'

'I'm afraid you're out of line, Mr. Archer.'

'Mr. Waters, the bylaws read that my five minutes are to be uninterrupted. Can I assume the clock isn't ticking as long as I'm responding to your statements rather than airing my concerns?'

'The airing of your concerns is certainly appropriate, Mr. Archer, but singling out members of the Board quite clearly is not.'

'It's not my intention to single out members of the Board, Mr. Waters. It is my intention to examine this policy against nepotism this Board seems to be so fond of if the occasion is right. Mr. Bangmore is, I feel, a glaring example of nepotism, given the fact that his son is a teacher at Coosaw Creek.' I paused, removed from my front pocket a stopwatch, and pushed a button.

'I have according to this chronometer another four minutes and forty-two seconds, Mr. Waters. I feel my questions are legitimate, and judging by the tenor of the letters to the editor published in the *Winter's Cove Journal-Scene* this past week, I'm not alone with my concerns.'

Waters nodded. 'Proceed with due respect, Mr. Archer.'

'Yes, sir. Mr. Bangmore, your son is also the head football coach at Coosaw Creek, a position voted on by this very board, correct?'

'That's correct, Mr. Archer, a vote I abstained from.'

'True, but your eight colleagues voted, didn't they? One would imagine that Mr. Pepperidge could abstain from any direct decision involving, say, a teacher-to-teacher conflict involving his brother-in-law, Mr. Capers?'

'I'm afraid the relationship is different, son.'

'I agree. Mr. Capers and Mr. Pepperidge have no genetic relationship, unlike yourself and Coach Bangmore.'

I shifted two board members to my left. 'Ms. Andrewson, you're currently dating – living with – Mr. Rollings, band director at Beach Mountain Middle School, aren't you?'

She flustered for a moment, then straightened in her seat. 'I hardly see where my personal life is relevant to tonight's proceedings, young man.'

'What's irrelevant, ma'am, are my age and gender. How is it that your personal life isn't relevant but Mr. Capers' is? He's married to the new principal's sister. You're dating the band director at one of the schools you as a board member oversee.'

'We aren't married, Mr. Archer. We aren't family.'

'True, though I think that's a technical point at best. We're told every day that we're all a Family of Educators here in Winter's Cove. Our faculty meetings over at Coosaw Creek are euphemistically referred to as Penguin Family Gatherings. You and Mr. Rollings have been involved for a number of years now. Is Mr. Capers' wrongdoing that he is married to his wife? What if they were just dating and living together like you and Mr. Rollings? Is it the marriage license that renders their situation different?'

'It is a different situation, Mr. Archer.'

'Is that the lesson we want to send to our kids, Ms. Andrewson? That marriage renders a relationship less appropriate?'

Waters piped up again. 'Thank you for that enlivening repartee, Mr. Archer. While you've certainly made your point, I'm afraid your comments do little to further these proceedings. We all appreciate your devotion to Mr. Capers and – '

'This has nothing to do with Mr. Capers, Mr. Waters. This has everything to do with the district in which I work. As a new teacher I'm on the front end of a thirty-year career, and therefore have a vested interest in seeing to it that the district in which I teach administers its policies in a judicious and equitable fashion. Now, I still have three and a half minutes.'

Virtually everyone in the room was looking at me now. My heart was pounding away and my hands were sweating, but I was just getting warmed up.

'At another of Winter Cove's middle schools, Owl Creek, James Thermon is the head of the Social Studies department, and his wife – both on paper and in spirit, Ms. Andrewson – is a teacher at the same school, same department. This means he gets to determine her teaching load, her lunch period, and her planning period, which has been fourth every year that he's been department head. I'll add for the benefit of those here tonight who aren't teachers that fourth is by far and away the most coveted planning period. His is also fourth, and a cursory look at sign-out cards will render some interesting if not surprising information. I'll assume that a Board so diligently consumed with the prevention of nepotism is aware of the number of times husband and wife signed out early together in the previous academic year?'

'How did you get this information?' another Board member, Judith Walker, blurted out.

'It's public record, ma'am. We are all public servants, as you are well aware. But I would think of more importance to the Board than the origin of the information would be the accuracy of the information. Can the concerned members of the community count on this Board to determine if nepotism in the halls of Owl Creek Middle School has led to husband-wife teams flagrantly violating district rules regarding sign-out times? After all, regular early sign-out is a fringe benefit not afforded those of us not fortunate enough to have a spouse as department head. This would, it seems, be terribly interesting to this Board.'

There was a rolling, hushed whisper in the boardroom which started near the front and made its way back toward me. I glanced over at Waters, who was visibly seething. I checked my stopwatch. Two more minutes.

I thought about putting on the brakes then; I'd made my point, and I'd made my bed a bit rougher, as well. That I didn't anticipate being around long enough to sleep in it was my chief consolation. That, and the fact that I was right. They – the Board, the crooked, back-patting, good-ol'-boy, wink-and-handshake Board – were sticking it to a good man because it was the expedient thing to do. Because not doing it would take a modicum of balls, and this Board checked their balls at the door.

I looked at them sitting up there, each of them quite pleased with what they saw in the mirror each morning. Waters was standing up front, too, his little birdlike hands clasped together, his chief concern getting through the hearing with as little difficulty as possible, when it should have been making sure Capers got a fair shake.

Fuck 'em, I thought. Fuck 'em and feed 'em fish.

'Two years ago the married principal of Glenview Elementary School was caught having sex with a second-year teacher, age 23, in the library of that very same school. That teacher's name was Sandy Allen. They were caught by a fifth-grade girl whose father threatened to sue the district. The district replied by settling, which I'm sure surprised no one. None of this is news, and yet the district's policy against nepotism was MIA on that account, as well. That principal, Mr. Stanley, was promoted to a District Level job, and has since been promoted again. I understand that it isn't nepotism to sleep with your staff, however unsavory it might be to do so at work, but again, it seems to me that Sandy Allen in her role as mistress was at least – if this Board will pardon the pun – in a position to be looked upon more favorably by Mr. Stanley than the other teachers at the same school. And yet there was no issue of nepotism ever mentioned by this Board. Once again it seems that Mr. Capers' offense would be that he has made the mistake of marrying Mrs. Capers. Had she remained Miss Pepperidge his position at Coosaw Creek would be secure and they would have been allowed to carry on wherever they might have liked, Winter's Cove libraries included.'

There was a rising tide of laughter with that, which I'd hoped wouldn't happen. It ate into my time.

'I think we've heard enough,' Bangmore chimed in.

'No sir. We're still another minute and four seconds from having heard enough.'

I dropped my voice several levels, speaking in a flat tone and punctuating the words with my finger in the air.

'This is a witch hunt, plain and simple. Anyone who cares enough – and judging by the sounds of some of the moving testimonies given by many in this room tonight there are a lot who care – can obtain and verify the things which I've spoken of this evening. It's all public record, and it's all been brushed aside by a District Office who'd prefer to avoid rather than solve conflicts. There are countless other examples, but I don't have time to go into them right now. It's instructive, though, to consider the possibility that Mr. Capers is being transferred out of a school where he and his students have flourished, where his auriferous instruction has benefited every single student who has chosen to embrace it, and where virtually every faculty member there will be the lesser for his absence, because of a personal vendetta. Even those who never bothered to open a book or take a note in his class will stand here and tell you that in Mr. Capers' classroom there were rules, boundaries, and expectations, and that they were meted out fairly and without prejudice. And it's true that, if he was such an asset to Coosaw Creek High, he'll be an equal asset wherever he goes; but it's entirely and pathetically disingenuous for this District Administration and this Board to hide behind the spuriously enforced policy against nepotism as they take him from your children.'

I checked my watch. Twenty seconds.

'This is a witch hunt. Not against Mr. Capers, but against Mr. Pepperidge, and this Board' – I paused, met each of their nine sets of eyes, pointed at each of them – 'knows it. He was selected as principal of Coosaw Creek without much real deliberation at all, with the same intensity of purpose one might imagine this Board employed when selecting the head football coach of Coosaw Creek High, a man who, by the way, comes to work after lunch most days, a man who can barely spell PE but had the good sense to be born into an old Winter's Cove family. Now I know that isn't a nice thing to say about someone. But this isn't a nice business we're gathered here to discuss. It's an ugly business, where the rules are made up on a whim and followed and enforced with no consistency at all. If anyone cares to review the qualifications of the other finalists, and one in particular, they might find that a Mr. Spader from neighboring Berkfield County was passed over, despite his two PhD's, despite his thirty-three years in education, despite his endless number of national awards, despite his seven children and eleven grandchildren all either current or past Winter's Cove students. What Mr. Spader is missing I'll never know. What he has, in addition to those qualifications, is black skin. Whether that's why this esteemed Board passed him by for a favorite son is probably only known for sure to the nine men and women you see sitting there before you. But at least one other saw the process and smelled the stink and decided to punish Pepperidge and, to a lesser degree, this Board. Mrs. Jefferson, twenty-seven year veteran of Winter's Cove, and my colleague in the English department – it was her lone complaint that set this claim of nepotism in motion, and this Board caved. They caved the way they've caved so many times before, the way they caved when faced with the lawsuit from the father of that little fifth-grade girl who stepped into her elementary library and stumbled upon the primal scene; the way they caved when Bangmore's kid eked out of college and needed a job. They're caving into Mrs. Jefferson's misguided complaint now because caving is easier than taking a stand.'

'Your time is through, Mr. Archer,' Mr. Waters said. Every trace of diplomacy was gone from his tone. He looked embarrassed and intensely angry.

'There is but one rule governing this Board, ladies and

gentleman,' I continued. It didn't matter what Waters was saying at this point. I had the full attention of the members of the community, concerned that they were.

'Whatever it takes to get re-elected. That's it. It would do for all of us to remember that when election day rolls around next.'

'And that's quite enough!' Mr. Waters said, his voice raised. 'Impugning the integrity of the members of our School Board is beyond the pale and entirely inappropriate for these proceedings. You've done yourself, Mr. Capers, and the community members here in attendance a grave disservice …'

But you get the point.

TWENTY-EIGHT

Collins' office; intermezzo;
Cole and Savannah

here's a saying in education, Archer,' Collins was saying, which is an irritating way to start a sentence. There's a saying for everything. It was Monday afternoon. When I'd checked my mailbox during lunch there'd been a note in there, 'Cole, see me during your planning. Ricke Collins.' I recognized his handwriting and knew immediately what it was about. I hadn't seen him at the grievance hearing last night, but Winter's Cove is a small place. News travels fast. And shit rolls downhill.

'Nothing is black and white in education,' he continued. 'Except black and white.'

He paused. I sat with my hands folded in my lap. He and I were alone in his office. The door was shut. I was not having a good time.

'Nothing,' he repeated, 'is black and white in education, except black and white.'

'Yes, sir.'

'That mean anything to you, Archer?'

'I think so, yes sir.'

'Tell me.'

'Even though there aren't any absolutes in education, race is one of them.'

'Not just race, Archer, but the perception of racism. Do you understand the difference?'

'Yes, sir.'

He nodded from behind his big, nearly empty desk.

'We had this trouble with you a while back' – sniff – 'with the little Jew kid.'

'This trouble, sir?'

He nodded. Sniffed. 'The racist thing.'

'I'm not a racist, sir.'

He shook his head. 'Doesn't matter if you are or not.' Sniff. 'What you believe in your own time is your own damn business. What matters is perception. Members of the Board are pretty unhappy with you, Archer. That's bad for someone in my position. For someone in yours it can be' – sniff – 'disastrous. Do you enjoy teaching?'

'Sir?'

'Teaching. Your job. Do you enjoy it?'

'Most days, yes sir.'

'Because,' he said, shaking his head, sort of holding back a chuckle and sort of succeeding, 'for someone on an induction contract you sure did step on your dick last night. What did you hope to accomplish, other than piss off the nine most powerful people in this district?'

'The dissemination of the truth, I guess.'

'The truth?' Sniff. 'The truth is perception. If you don't learn anything from this, learn that. People believe what they want to believe, what others make it easy for them to believe. The folks who live in Winter's Cove are small-town people living small-town lives, Archer. They go to work' – sniff – 'go to church, raise their kids, have barbecues, walk the dog and watch TV. They don't want problems and they don't want issues. That stunt of yours last night has everyone talking. I was on the phone with Charles Waters for over an hour last night.' Sniff. 'An hour, devoted exclusively to you. He didn't have much good to say about you.'

'Yes, sir.'

There was an extended pause at this point that I filled by counting the little golden circles running through his tie.

'You knew that going in though, didn't you?'

'Yes, sir. I made peace with it a while back.'

'I see. Have you had your evaluations yet?'

'Three of them. I've got two more.'

'You had two more." Sniff. "You'll have at least one a week now. They'll call them drop-ins but they'll be looking for any reason in the world not to offer you a contract next year.'

'Yes, sir.'

'If I were a betting man I'd say they'll find one.'

'Yes, sir. Me too.'

He studied me for a second, then leaned back in his chair. He folded his hands across his belly and nodded softly. He had the look of one who'd solved life's more difficult problems long ago, and was simply enjoying the ride now.

'Do you have a back up plan for next year?'

I thought about that. 'I've got some things in the works.'

He nodded again. 'Probably a wise idea.'

Savannah came over at seven that evening. I'd called her just before six, told her I'd had a shitty day and needed to see her. She said she had to fix supper for her brothers but that she could get away for a few hours afterwards. I was so happy I thought I'd explode.

I rented a couple flicks – *The Untouchables* and *The Edge* – on the off-shot she could stay the night. I wasn't going to push the point, but if she could I'd call in sick tomorrow and she could skip and we could get up early and go to the farthest point of Folly Beach. No one but the surfers and fisherman go there and we'd have the dunes to ourselves. We could take a blanket and some food and stretch out next to each other beneath the pearl-gray sky and make shapes out of the clouds.

She knocked at seven on the dot. I'd spent the previous hour making the bed and cleaning the kitchenette counter and vacuuming Brasco's hair out of the carpet and off the couch. I'd also showered and brushed my teeth.

When I answered the door she was standing there smiling, and the day I'd had melted away like snow before the gaze of God.

We spent a couple hours curled up on the couch, her small frame spooned into mine. I didn't mention her staying the night because I didn't want her to have to tell me no. So instead we talked about Oregon.

'We should get an apartment up high,' she said.

'Makes it tough on grocery day.'

'I don't care. I want to be up high so we can open the windows and listen to it rain.'

I ran my hand through her curly auburn hair and kissed the back of her head.

'High it is, then. As high as they come.'

'We'll have to have a separate room for me to study in. I'll have to study a lot.'

'I can write while you do.'

'And we'll take breaks for other things,' she said, nestling backwards into me a bit.

'Lots of breaks.'

It went on that way for the next hour, the sound of her voice – of that music that had become my purpose – filling my little apartment …

… and even now, sitting here on an old, splintered bench along the Honduras coastline, I wonder if it might have turned out differently had I been content to simply lie there and touch her hair and smell her skin and listen to the music in her voice that night. Had I not asked her about work, is it possible she might be sitting here next to me now? Might she and I have slipped away together as I had alone, swapping out cars and dyeing our hair and playing musical passports?

The possibility haunts me. I dream of it every night, and it is my Hell. I can reach back into the thousands of days which are my history and point out to you the single second – the cardinal moment that stands in agonizing relief against the others – that I ruined my life forever. Until then I had a choice. Afterwards, I was no longer in control. It was all just reaction from that point forward.

It is a living hell for me that no amount of running or money or alcohol will ever temper, because I might have avoided it all had I just not asked.

'You don't have to ask me about it, Cole,' she said. 'I know it makes you uncomfortable. I'd be worried if it didn't bother you.'

'It's a means to an end. That's all. How can it bother me when it's buying you your dream? It isn't as if you're sleeping with them.'

She shook her head. 'Don't sound so worried. Some of the others do. But there's not enough money in the world to turn me into a prostitute. If it came to that I'd give up college and content myself with working in a Wal-Mart somewhere.'

'Do the men there push you?'

'They ask. I tell them no. They don't have to push. They're plenty of other girls who want the money.'

'You wonder what goes wrong in someone's life to make them do that sort of thing,' I said.

She laughed. 'You could ask them yourself tomorrow at school.'

I looked at her.

'You know Chessie?'

'Chessie from class?'

She nodded.

'Chessie's a stripper?'

'She does more than strip.'

'Chessie Singleton? Perky little Chessie with braces and bows in her hair? Chessie the junior class vice-president?'

'There's a whole world pulsing out there beneath the surface of things, Cole. That's the only reason I dance – to make sure I never have to see it again once I get out of this place.'

'Chessie … I can't believe it. She's going to Palmetto Girls State this year.'

'She's going into the private rooms at Southern Belle this Saturday night.'

'Chessie Singleton has sex with strange men for money at the Southern Belle. You're sure of this?'

'Well if you'd like you could always grab three hundred dollars and swing by this Saturday and see for yourself.'

'Three hundred … if I'd had a gun to my head and someone had asked me if Chessie was a virgin or not, if my life had depended on the answer, I would have said yes. I swear to God. I would have said yes.'

'Well,' she said, turning over on the couch and facing me, kissing my mouth, 'let's be glad it didn't come to that. You're much cuter alive. Chessie's virginity has been gone a while.'

I set aside my awe long enough to pull her into me and kiss her lips, neck, and ears. I pulled the scent of her hair deep into my lungs and wished I could breathe it forever.

'If you really want to be surprised,' she said, 'I'll tell you who her best regular is.'

'Best regular?'

'Customer,' Savannah said. 'He's in there two, three times a month. Sometimes more. And she hasn't ever told me, but I'm pretty sure they've got a side thing going on, too, even though it's against the rules.'

'Do I want to know?'

She shrugged. 'You might find it interesting, in light of recent events.'

'Tell me.'

TWENTY-NINE

Geist drops a bigger dime;
Savannah teaches Cole

Iate lunch that Friday – fish sticks, hushpuppies, and coleslaw all served in neat little school-house portions – with Kevin Geist, master linguist, in his classroom. It was just the two of us; he had his door closed to keep the kids out so that we could eat and drink in peace. Lunch lasted thirty-eight minutes, a sliver of time barely long enough to buy and eat your food, much less take a shit afterwards. To this end caffeine and chocolate were no-no's on lunch break.

Alcohol, however, was not, and many was the time, today included, that Kevin and I would cloister ourselves away inside his room or mine and pass a flask of Wild Turkey or – Kevin's favorite – Beam back and forth.

'You get your car tax bill yet?' he asked, swallowing a mouthful of Beam from his flask. Droplets of the stuff collected on his beard and he wiped them away with the back of his wrist.

'Last week,' I said. 'Forty bucks.'

'Be thankful you've got an old car. Adrienne decided a few months ago she just had to have the new Excursion. Assessment came yesterday. Care to take a guess?'

I shrugged. 'Hundred bucks?'

'Try seven hundred. Due all at once, in two weeks.' He took another swig from the flask, passed it across his desk to me. 'Motherfuckers.'

'That's a pretty good pop.' I took the flask and poured the Beam into the back of my mouth. It burned going down but the burn was comforting because it was familiar. And because it was a constant.

'Got no industry in Winter's Cove,' he said, cracking the small window beside his desk. 'No tax base. Other than the Krauts over at Bosch there isn't anything.'

'I thought they were trying to do away with the car tax.'

He shook his head. 'They talk about it every few years. Maybe once in a while a legislator will offer a bill to eradicate it, but it'll never happen.' Another swig. 'Taxes are like herpes. You can dress 'em up or call 'em something else or turn the lights off, but they're still there. They never leave.'

'That's the money they use to pay our salaries with, right?'

He opened a desk drawer and produced a pack of Marlboros. 'Took these from a kid in first period. Lighter too.' He flicked the top up and down a few times. 'Nice. A Zippo.' He lit one of the cigarettes and took a long, almost lustful drag.

'I took the little reprobate out into the hall and talked to him a bit,' he said around the smoke, 'preached the evils of smoking, all that. Kid's got no motivation, no direction. He's failing every subject and his rich parents just keep throwing money at him.'

Another drag, another ten-count while he savored the smoke filling his lungs.

'I asked what he wanted to do with his life – he said nothing. I asked about his interests, hobbies, aptitudes – know what he said?'

Geist let out a long breath of smoke.

I shook my head. 'No telling.'

'He said he likes to pretend he's in Iowa, walking through crowded rooms, bidding everyone goodbye. Now Cole, you tell me what in the hell does that mean?'

'It's the television,' I said.

He shivered. 'Whatever it is it gave me the creeps. I made him take his desk out there for the rest of the period.' Another drag. 'Pretend he's in Iowa,' Geist muttered. 'God save the lot of us.'

After a time which I filled by finishing my slaw and Geist filled by finishing another of the Iowa kid's cigarettes, he piped up, 'The counties assess the tax and send the payments to the state. The state takes its cut and sends the rest back to the school districts every June. That's why we never know what our salaries'll be until the last few days of summer. It takes them that long to figure out their budget.'

He blew a plume of smoke out the window and took another drag. 'You asked about our salaries.'

'Right,' I said.

'Richer counties pay more tax, so their districts get more money.

That's the problem with your Republican friends in the legislature. Long as they're around' – exhale, drag, hold – 'the rich'll keep getting richer and the poor'll keep getting it in the ass.'

'Sounds like anyone with a car gets it.'

He nodded, crushed the cigarette on the bottom of his shoe, and tossed the butt out the window. He produced a small vial of cologne from his desk drawer and sprayed himself and the air around his desk.

'It'll always be that way, until the tax structure's set up more equitably,' he was saying. 'You got your third quarter grades done yet?'

'No. We've still got a few days.'

'You'll want to make sure yours are perfect. They'll be watching.'

'The district?'

'Everyone,' he shrugged. 'Lot of Theys out there. That bit of yours at the DO made you priority numero uno to a lot of pissed-off people. Have you retained a lawyer yet?'

I shook my head.

'You should think about it.'

'Lawyers make me nervous.'

He shrugged. 'Even so,' he said, reaching for the flask, grabbing one more nip before the bell sounded and fourth period came rolling in, 'you'll likely need one. They're probably not going to offer you a contract this April, and South Carolina is a right-to-work state, which means you aren't much more than a nigger on the plantation. And the massuh is pissed.'

'I'll manage. They wire this money?'

'What money?'

'The state. The money for the school districts.'

He shrugged. 'Don't imagine they mail it down.'

The bell rang, signaling the fourth and final period of the day. Geist was squirting breath-spray into his mouth and dabbing at his forehead with a handkerchief.

'One more to go,' I said, standing, crossing his room for the door.

'Think about what I said,' he said, his bushy black beard bobbing up and down with the words. 'About the lawyer.'

'I will,' I said, but I didn't.

I thought about the State Department of Education, instead. And all that money they'd be sending down to Winter's Cove this June.

The phone ripped through my apartment at ten after midnight. I'd been lying on my bed in the dark, Brasco on my chest, drifting between sleep and not, when someone somewhere punched in my digits and shattered the silence around me like glass.

'Hello.'

'He's here.' It was Savannah. I could hear the heavy thump-thump of music in the background. The mingled chatter of voices. She was at work.

'Who is?'

'Chessie's favorite. I thought you'd be interested.'

'You're kidding me.'

'Nope. I watched him walk in ten minutes ago.'

'Has he seen you?'

'I waited on him. He tipped me a twenty and told me to be careful going home.'

'What a peach. Imagine he's there for Chessie?'

'He's got her schedule memorized. She's on stage now. When she's done they'll probably disappear for a few hours.'

'I'm coming down.'

'What?'

'I'm coming down. I want to see this.'

'That's not a good idea, Cole. It could be dangerous. Remember our plan.'

'It's not dangerous. I'll be disguised. You won't even recognize me.'

'What if he figures something out?'

'Then the four of us can double-date sometime.'

My disguise consisted of a Gamecock ball cap and dark glasses. I brushed my teeth and squirted on some cologne and promised Brasco I'd see him in a bit. I stopped by the ATM long enough to get some cash, and I was in the Southern Belle by one that morning.

The girl behind the register – different one than the last time I'd been, when Jules had done his thing in the back and I'd discovered Taryn the cheerleader – took my ten-spot and stamped my hand and bid me a good evening before returning to her book, the title to which I didn't catch.

The place was packed. Bodies – ninety percent of them male – were situated everywhere, packed together at tables, perched on stools and hunched over the three different bars, lining the T-stage like buzzards over road-kill. Every couple minutes small jets along the tops of the walls would hiss and emit a shower of steam, filling the entire club, sending shards of strobe and shadow ricocheting off the countless mirrors.

I stood there and let my eyes adjust to it all. A topless waitress with enormous tits approached me through the steam with a tray of beers and a Vaseline smile.

'Beck's,' I yelled over the music. *Love in an Elevator*. She nodded, handed me the beer.

'Four dollars.'

I gave her the five and she turned and left, apparently assuming the fifth buck was her tip.

Lovin' it up while I'm goin' down...

I found a stool in a far corner and sat and drank my beer, scanning the room casually, keeping an eye out for Savannah, Chessie, or her best regular, two of whom I would rather not be seen by. If he saw me I'd be just another guy drinking beer at a tittie-club. A little awkward embarrassment, maybe, but nothing too bad. It wouldn't be the kind of thing we'd talk about at work the next day.

But if Chessie recognized me, well, that could conceivably be a problem. In that single, frozen-in-amber moment she'd realize I knew she was a tittie-dancer and I'd know she knew Mr. Archer the English teacher patronized such places, and we'd both have won and lost something in the trade-off. My guess is neither of us would say anything about it. She'd continue to come to class and I'd continue to teach her, and we'd both pretend we didn't know anything. If that was as complicated as it got, I could handle it. I'd grown quite used to pretending in class.

Just the same I kept my hat pulled down low and tried to blend in with the shadows in my corner. I counted seventeen naked or near-naked girls of all shapes, sizes and color, but no Savannah. No Chessie, either. And no best regular, which, I thought, probably explained the no Chessie.

Then there she was, not Taryn the cheerleader this time, but Savannah – my Savannah, my flawless rara avis, working her way towards the Oregon coastline. The get-up was the same as last time, but the emotions inside me were not. I understood now. I'd figured it out with finality lying on my bed this evening, the sunlight receding beyond my window as my apartment succumbed to darkness.

Both of us had to get our hands dirty if we were to get where we were going. I knew what I had to do – Kevin Geist had tipped me, quite by accident to be sure, at lunch today – and though I hadn't figured out exactly how to go about doing it yet, I knew where I could find the information.

'Hi,' she said when she reached me. She was wearing the little cheerleader skirt, her hair pulled back into twin ponytails.

I tried not to look like I was judging her.

'Are you all right with this? Seeing me here. Like this?'

I nodded.

'I like your sunglasses,' she said. 'They make you look mysterious.'

I nodded again. It occurred to me that she couldn't see my eyes. Without moving my head I lowered my vision to her legs.

'Have you been seen?'

I shook my head.

'Will you say something please? This is hard enough for me. What are you thinking?'

'I was wondering if you'd be bringing that outfit with you to Oregon.'

She smiled. Took my hand.

'I can go you one better. Wait here.'

She turned and crossed the club. She stopped at the bar and leaned across, said something to one of the men back there. He was big and fat and wearing denim and leather. I saw her look my direction, saw him do the same, then saw him hand her something. They spoke back and forth for another minute, and then she was coming back towards me.

'What was that all about?' I asked.

'Follow me,' she said, taking my hand in hers.

I did. I let her lead me to the other end of the club, through a set of double doors, down a hallway, and to a large metal door that looked like it belonged in a bank somewhere. She took the key the fat guy had given her and inserted it, unlocked the door, and ushered me in.

She pulled the door shut behind us. We were in another hallway – this one illuminated by a single blue light bulb dangling overhead – which dead-ended fifty feet in front of us. On either side of the hall were five black doors, each of them as big and heavy looking as the one we'd just come through. From behind them you could hear what sounded like muffled moans.

'The private rooms,' I said.

'Chessie's in that one,' she pointed, her voice low. 'Room 7. He rented it for an hour. Five hundred dollars.'

I shook my head. 'I never would have known. She blushes when I call on her in class.'

'Maybe that's why he likes her so much,' she said. 'Old men love innocence.'

She took my hand and brought it to her mouth. Touched my fingertips with her tongue. 'What do you love, Cole?'

'You,' I said, feeling myself responding. 'I love you, Savannah. I love our dream.'

She smiled, her eyes a burning black beneath the Prussian blue light. The music on the other side of the door hammered through the walls and vibrated the floor. Her breath, I remember, was cinnamon chewing gum.

My hands were on her hips, then, and I was pulling her into me. When I opened my mouth to speak she slowly shook her head.

'For the next hour,' she said, her eyes never leaving mine, her hips moving in slow circles against me, 'we're in room 8.'

THIRTY

Dunlap's curse; intermezzo

Sunday night, the last day of January. The last January of my life in Charleston. The last January of my life without Savannah.

Tempus fugit. Time flies. Whatever sage put pen to parchment for that little gem was probably dying, looking back on all the things he'd never done and thus could not regret. When you're waiting for something, though, waiting for it as if it were air itself, tempus doesn't fugit at all. Tempus dragass.

Savannah and I were in a little café in Mount Pleasant, tucked away from the window in a corner table. It was a good half-hour's drive from Winter's Cove and The Creek, but we were still taking a chance. It was half past seven, dark as midnight outside, and she and I clearly weren't involved in a conference about American Literature.

But we'd made a deal the afternoon after the Southern Belle to have one evening a month together, out of my apartment, like regular people. Getting spotted was something we'd simply have to deal with if it happened. The closer I got to the end of the school year, the more I could feel that Oregon sunset on my face and shoulders, the more I could see Savannah's silhouette walking barefoot through the sand and sun in cutoffs and a bikini top, and the less I cared about those around me. Everything was centered around her and our plan. It became all I needed.

'What're you thinking about?' she asked, reaching across the table and touching my wrist.

'Honestly?'

'Always.'

'The Southern Belle.'

She blushed. 'Should I be embarrassed?'

I shook my head. 'Small wonder you'll be a millionaire by next month, though.'

'It's different with the others,' she said. 'With them it's just work. It wasn't that way with you.' Pause. 'I wanted to do it for you.'

'You don't do all that for the others though, do you? You know, what you did with me?'

'Most of what I did with you I'd never do for anyone else. For them it's strictly look but don't touch.' She smiled. 'With you I like the touching.'

'What do you think about during it?'

'With you I thought about you. With the others I think about you.'

'And before me?'

'Before you I wasn't alive.'

After a while she said, 'I did some surfing on the net last week. College stuff.'

I sipped my Coke. 'And?'

'Seattle has a really good pre-med program.'

'Seattle's supposed to be beautiful,' I said.

'You'd be all right with it?'

'I'll be all right wherever you want to go. I wonder, though, have you given much thought to after college?'

'Med. school somewhere. Probably.'

'But not definitely?'

She shrugged. 'There isn't much out there that's really definite. Except getting out of here. Why?'

I shook my head. 'No reason, really.'

'Cole...'

'I was thinking, is all.'

'Care to share?'

'Well, say I said I found something. Something that had the potential to change the rest of our lives together.'

She squinted her eyes a bit. 'I'd be interested.'

'Well, let's pretend I had a great aunt who died and left me a bunch of money.'

'How much is a bunch?'

'Lots, let's say.'

'Lots,' she repeated.

'Would it change anything?'

'Between us?'

I nodded.

'You mean would it make me love you more? That's silly. Girls hungry for money don't fall in love with teachers.'

'Would it change our plans any?'

She shrugged. 'I don't see why. I like our plans. Don't you?'

'I love them. I wouldn't change a thing, unless maybe ...'

'...unless?'

'I don't know. What if we could accelerate things? What if my aunt left me enough money –'

'I'd probably be curious as to how your aunt got all this money.'

'Maybe she invented a new quiche recipe or something. The point is, what if she left me enough money to take care of you, me, your brothers, and anyone else who might happen along?'

Her eyes smiled across the table at me. 'Like babies?'

'I didn't say that. Stay on task here, Ms. Bellington.'

'Yes, sir, Mr. Archer.'

'I guess I'm trying to see how important it is to you to be a doctor. If you were independently wealthy, would you still follow that path, or would you be willing to just disappear into the sunset on a yacht or something and spend your life spending money with me?'

She tilted her head a bit, looked past me.

'I never really thought about that,' she said, still touching my wrist. 'I've been poor all my life, Cole. All I've ever wanted for as long as I can remember wanting anything was to go to college and be a doctor so I could take care of myself and my brothers. Doctors make lots of money. Everyone knows that. I like the idea of helping people, but if I already had a lot of money, I don't know if I'd still want to be one or not. It's never been a choice I had to make, really.'

'What if it was?'

'Cole,' she said, '*do* you have a great-aunt who invented a new quiche dish and left you all her money?'

'No.'

'Then why are we having this conversation? Is this one of those what-if scenarios you like to do in class so much?'

'No.'

'What, then?'

I glanced around, saw no one I'd ever seen before, and leaned closer to her, lowering my voice instinctively. 'I might have found something just as good.'

'As good as a rich great-aunt leaving you her fortune?'

I nodded.

'Well goodness, Cole,' she said, 'stop playing these silly games and tell me.'

I stood, dropped a five-spot on the table for the Cokes, and said, 'Come take a walk with me on the beach.'

I had a literature professor back in college named Dunlap – smartest man I've ever met. He was one of those lecturers you didn't mind getting out of bed to go listen to. He got one of his ten or twelve doctorates in Ireland, talked about that place a lot. He met his wife during his first teaching job in Florida but the stories he regaled us with never involved her. They were all about the one that got away, this willowy Italian exchange student with whom he'd first discovered true bliss in an open Irish field along the banks of the river Shannon. I remember sitting there in that classroom as Dunlap spoke, and the sincerity of the emotion behind his words was so strong I could almost feel the grass beneath me and smell the apple blossoms all around.

Dunlap said something that morning that stuck with me, something about the permanence of imagery.

'Once every few lifetimes,' he said, 'we see something we'll see forever, something for which the passage of time is irrelevant. It will be there tomorrow, and the day after that, and all the days that follow. It will seem to have been there for every yesterday we've ever seen, for we'll catch glimpses of it in every memory and see hints of it in every future hope or wish.'

For Dunlap, the sight of that Italian exchange student lying next to him along the edge of the Shannon was still ringing through his senses some forty years after the fact, through the courtship and marriage to his wife, through the raising of their children, through all the various lives we live over the span of four decades. He was still catching glimpses of it in all his hopes and wishes. My guess is they always fell short.

For me it's the image of Savannah on the beach in the midst of winter, walking along the edge of the receding tide, her jeans rolled up her ankles, bits of ocean foam clinging to her smooth skin. It's something I saw before I ever saw it; she and I walking along the Oregon coastline was the end of the rainbow for me.

And so the first time we actually ever stepped through the sand together it was simply a matter of the pieces falling into place. I knew then, though, that Dunlap had been right. I'd be seeing this forever.

We were out on the Isle of Palms, far down the beach from the popular stretch. It was February now, and Charleston's various beaches were cold and gray, the air infused with that salty mist that leaves a thin film over your skin and lips. Savannah and I were walking north, the black ocean to our right. It was similar to where I'd been and what I'd seen in Florida with Grey, but only on the surface. I'd been lost down there, casting about in search of direction and purpose, struggling to stave off Grey's siren-song. In another life that might have been an entirely different vacation – I had no doubt that Grey could do remarkable things with that mouth, that its abilities to relieve a man of whatever stresses or pressures that ailed him were without rival – but it wasn't another life I was leading. It was mine, the only one I'd been apportioned, and I'd already spent enough of it as though there was no tomorrow. My days of wild abandon were through. Planning was the coin of my realm now. Long-range planning.

'Someone's quiet tonight,' Savannah said. 'Must be considering all the ways you'll spend your great aunt's-zillions.'

Her small hand was in mine, her fingers interlaced through my own. I didn't say anything, but instead squeezed her hand a bit and listened to the waves pouring over the shore. The silences between us were never awkward; they were the places chance and possibility were born.

'I would go with you wherever,' she said. 'Whenever. As long as my brothers were taken care of.'

'They could come.'

'Would people follow us?'

I kept my stride steady, though I know my countenance changed.

'For a while, maybe.'

I felt her smile. 'Must be an impressive quiche recipe.'

'It's a doozy.'

'A big one, too, I bet.'

I nodded. 'Lots of ingredients. Some hard to find. Others sitting right there in front of me all this time.'

'Who has them now, these ingredients?'

'No one who can't replace them.'

'And you're sure you know how to get them without getting

yourself caught? Or worse?'

'No. But I think it's worth the risk.'

She was quiet for a while. The ocean rushed over our feet and she splashed it on my legs with her foot.

'I trust you with my life, Cole. And all I want now is to be with you. It's all I think about anymore. If you say you found a way for us to have that, and if you're sure my brothers will be taken care of, then I believe you.'

I stopped, took her face in my hands. 'It'll mean having to run for a while. Then disappearing for a while longer after that. We'll be leaving more than just Charleston.'

'It's a big world out there,' she said. 'Lots of places to hide in it.'

'We'll have to change identities, appearance, and we'll have to sever all ties to the lives we lived before. Are you prepared for that?'

'I live in a single-wide with four brothers and a mother who sells her body for drugs and money. I work as a stripper to buy diapers and medicine and lunch at school. I've been preparing for this since I learned to crawl. If you hadn't come along I'd be doing it without you.'

'You'd have been going away to college and medical school, but you wouldn't have been doing this. This is permanent, Savannah. This is the rest of our life. Once we get where we're going, if you decide you made a mistake with me, you can't go back. You're stuck.'

'No. Stuck is what I am here. What I am with you is happy. Happy and whole and not afraid to dream. I'm seventeen years old, Cole. I don't know what's out there. All I know is what's here, and that I'm leaving it as soon as I get the chance. It's why I take my clothes off for disgusting old men for money. But I trust you. If you think this is something that can work, I believe you. I believe in you. I'll go with you and be your best friend and your lover and your confidante and it won't matter at all where we are as long as there's a sunset and a sunrise and you and me between them.'

The dunes were behind us, dark and rolling in the night, covered with sea oats and saw grass. An hour later, lying next to her behind them, I could hear the breeze whispering through the sand around us, and our future together seemed as clear as the stars that burned holes in the night above.

I was drinking, and lonely, and that combination's never worked well for me. I'd been thinking of her endlessly lately. There've been moments I've considered going back because being away hurts so bad.

Talking about her, about our time together, dulls the hurt some, but there isn't anyone to talk to. Not usually.

But there are others down here, others who speak my language and understand my pain, and occasionally I talk to them.

So my fourth month in Roatan, sitting outside a small sidewalk café less than a hundred yards from the ocean, I suspended my better judgment and gave into the pain and said:

'It begins in the graveyard. Of course, the joke is that it eventually ends there too, but that's not something you're likely thinking about when you take your pen and pad and walk amongst the tombstones and the vases filled with artificial flowers. You've made your decision to leave, and all you're doing is digging the dates of those poor bastards unfortunate enough to have predeceased you.

'You go at night, on a Sunday, because you know most graveyard traffic happens during the day. Something about keeping company with the dead in the hour of the wolf that bothers most folks. It bothers you a bit, too, but there's not much to do about that. It's past three in the morning, you're in a North Florida graveyard four hours from your home, and you've got work to do.

'So there you are, walking up and down the rows, trying not to hear the scuttling and rustling that issues forth from the surrounding foliage every few minutes. A little mammal, you tell yourself, searching for berries. A fox chasing that little mammal. Nothing interested in you.

'You finally come across the headstone for a boy born the same year as you. He died when he was three, which is a tragedy that isn't lost on you. The potential of it isn't, either. Three-year-olds back in the mid-seventies usually didn't have social security numbers yet. These days hospitals take care of that sort of thing at birth, but that's a relatively recent phenomenon. And until you have a social security card, you aren't in the government's database. On paper you aren't alive, and if you aren't alive you can't die. So the kid's name is clean.

'You jot it down – Paulwyn Mitchell Bowick – and his birthday and date of death. Then you leave the graveyard, because graveyards aren't fun places at night.

'A couple days later you send off – using a downtown Charleston Mail Boxes, Etc., because it looks and acts like a street address, "fronting" is what The Kids call that these days – to the Social Security Administration for a social security card. It takes them two weeks to respond, and when they do it's a letter asking why it has taken you until now, when you're in your late twenties, to finally get around to applying for a social security card. You wait a few days and write back that you've been out of the country since you were three, traveling with your missionary parents, and haven't needed one until now.

'Six weeks later it comes in the mail, and it's become clear that you're cooking with gasoline at this point. Paulwyn Mitchell Bowick, resurrected in death by bureaucratic oversight, has a social security card. His very own number. He's legit now, in the system. Welcome back, Paul.

'Over the next few weeks you go about the business of acquiring that which will prove needful later on. The social security card makes it easier. Florida's Department of Vital Records uses it to issue you a notarized copy of Paulwyn's birth certificate. South Carolina's DMV looks at both and, once you pass the driving test, gives you a valid driver's license, good for the next five years.

'It's odd, at first, looking down at your picture on the license next to Paulwyn Mitchell Bowick's name, but it gets easier with each new one. You repeat the process five more times, and before long have five more social security cards, five more birth certificates, five more driver's licenses. The driver's license, a $98.00 fee, and a trip to the local post office gets you the passports.

'You've no intention of going this alone, so all the while you're doing it for her, too. North Carolina graveyards, Tennessee graveyards, Georgia graveyards, even a trip to Virginia just to be safe. You're a firm believer in the incompetence of institutions, particularly governmental agencies, but you're also a believer in the adage that Satan works in mysterious ways. The possibility of some gum-smacking civil servant in some windowless public building wondering why five different girls from Charleston, South Carolina, all roughly the same age, all need copies of their birth certificates after extended missionary stays abroad isn't something you're willing to chance. So you become accustomed to late-night trips up I-95 and I-26, and you choose from five different states.

'The international stuff is easier. Once you're out of the country you'll need to travel in and out of foreign countries as something other than an American. They've got companies that sell that sort of peace of mind, but it doesn't come cheap. Fortunately, in America credit does. You get at least half a dozen offers a week, and lately you've begun filling them out, sending them in, putting the little piece of magic plastic that returns two weeks later into your wallet.

'There's a company in England that specializes in international passports. For three thousand dollars they'll send you one, along with ancillary documentation. You supply the picture and any name you want.

'Criminals, especially new ones, walk around feeling thin-skinned and raw, as if their crimes are showing on their sleeves and faces. There's an aura around them – or at least you feel as if there is, but this is probably because you're on the verge of becoming one yourself. And along with that feeling comes paranoia, massive amounts of it. Everyone suspects you, everyone is whispering about you, everyone is watching for your next move. Intellectually, of course, you know this isn't the case, but you also know that a lot of your decisions aren't made with intellect. Balls are what put your plan in motion. Gut is what will see it through.

'And it's your gut that tells you not to use your new credit cards to buy your new passports, that somewhere out there in the vast wherever there's an office with a computer in it that keeps track of those sorts of transactions. Americans buying new passports from offshore companies specializing in foreign, false documentation might raise a red flag on that computer in that office, so you use cash instead. Cash makes no enemies and leaves no trail.

'So you tap the credit cards for cash advances – fourteen of them in all, with advances ranging from $500.00 to $4,000.00, for a total of $37,500 – and stash it under your mattress. You open a new account at a new bank – using one of your aliases, of course – and wire the money to them from there.

'The two of you spent hours together curled up beneath blankets in your living room, on the beach, in your bed, making up your names. She chose names like Carolina Reese and Kinsley Wexford. You've always liked Irish beer so you go with Jonathan Curtis and Roary Rua.

'Twelve thousand dollars later you each have your IDs, foreign and domestic. Now it's just a matter of time.'

'And you had to leave without her, after all that,' one of my two companions that afternoon – the girl, blonde and tanned and always touching her male companion's arm or shoulder or thigh – said.

I nodded. 'Things went bad near the end,' I said. 'Two nights ... no, two hours earlier we could have left and she'd be sitting here with me now.' I sipped my beer, leaned back in the chair and looked at the cloudless sky.

'We'd be here breathing this air like the two of you,' I said, ignoring the bitter taste of envy.

'A lot can happen in two hours,' the guy said.

'Yes,' the girl again, whose name is false but which I can't remember anyway, 'whole lifetimes can come and go.'

THIRTY-ONE

Cole's girl; Grey, Philip, and the taste of honey

Once we'd made the decision the rest came easy. Savannah's agreement sanctioned my plan, what we'd come to call our quiche talk. The rest was simply a matter of timing.

Our self-imposed moratorium on in-school contact was going fine – I was able to keep myself busy planning lessons and working on the hallowed Long-Range Plan – but the after-school stuff was getting harder to manage by the minute. We continued speaking on the phone every night, but our evening and night liaisons increased in frequency. I began meeting her after she got off work every Friday and Saturday night, usually just long enough for an early-morning breakfast before she had to head back to Winter's Cove, but occasionally more, and it was during these occasions that we ran the greatest risk of being discovered. It was these times that I let the moment – the ethereal qualities of those hours between two and four in the morning, when time seems to slow and everything around you is strangely and subtly muted – overtake me and cause me to lower my guard.

'It isn't as if anyone could prove anything,' she'd said once across her plate of Huddle House hash browns, which she ate, disgustingly enough, with mustard and hot sauce. 'Not actually prove it.'

'It wouldn't matter to me if they could,' I said. 'I haven't made many friends at the District Office anyway. No way I'll be getting a contract next year.'

'Just imagine how thrilled with you they'll be after we're gone, run off with one of your students.'

That made me laugh. It made me laugh so hard I thought I'd popped something somewhere in my gut.

I walked her to her car in the cold clear Charleston night air,

340

my arm draped over her shoulders like a shawl, her small frame pressed against mine. She started her car and slid her arms inside my jacket and around my waist while she waited for it to warm. Her lips found their way to my chin and rested there.

'You need to shave.'

'You should see my legs.'

She kissed me. 'I have seen your legs.'

'When do I get to see yours again?'

'Soon,' she smiled, tightening her arms around me. 'This week sometime.'

'You won't be able to stay the night though.'

'I was thinking the day. We could cut. Do you have any days left?'

'A couple,' I nodded. 'One or two.'

'We could take Monday. You could wait for me in bed. I'll leave home my normal time and come slide beneath the covers with you and Brasco. We'd have all day.'

She kissed my chin again, then my mouth. I'd just watched her eat a plate of fried potato wedges smothered in mustard and Tabasco sauce and still she tasted like strawberries.

'I've been meaning to talk to you about something,' I said.

'Oh, pooh,' – kissing me again, softly, her tongue sliding over mine and giving me chills – 'you're ruining the mood.'

'Your grades are falling.'

She shrugged.

'This doesn't bother you?'

'Some, yes. But it's a moot point, isn't it? If we leave in June I won't even graduate.' She brought her hands around from behind me and slid them under my shirt, up my stomach and onto my chest.

'I'll be a helpless uneducated love struck schoolgirl and you'll have to take care of me.' She gave my nipples a playful twist.

'Savannah,' I said, taking her wrists in my hands and removing them. 'I'm being serious here. You've been a straight A student since birth. Everyone knows that.'

'Hardly anyone even knows me at that school. I'm the quiet girl in the back with the old clothes.'

'Teachers know you. Teachers always know the good ones. They talk about them in the lounges all the time, particularly when they start doing not so good. And the administration might not know your name but they're going to notice if a student who was pulling straight A's across the board is now barely scraping by. The computers flag that kind of thing.' I paused, tried not to sound too preachy. 'Have you just stopped trying?'

'Maybe some. I'm working more trying to save money – '

'Well that's the first thing you can do is quit that.'

'I can't quit. I have to give my mother $500.00 a week.'

'Or what? She doesn't get her nightly ration of Beam?'

'No, she never misses her nightly ration of Beam. My brothers miss meals before that happens. If I don't give her the money it'll only end up hurting them.'

I did the math quickly in my head and said, 'There're roughly seventeen weeks until we disappear. That's eight and a half, nine grand of income you need to replace if you quit, right?'

She nodded.

'I'll take care of it.'

'How?'

'Don't fret over it. I'll figure a way. I'll give you the first five hundred Monday when you come down.'

'Cole, that's sweet, but you really don't have to do that. I'll bring the grades up. It's just a matter of – '

'It's not just that. I don't want you working there anymore.'

She gave me a wry little smile. 'It makes you jealous, doesn't it?'

'No.'

'Yes it does. It makes you jealous.' Her hands were on her hips. 'Why can't you say it? It doesn't make you weak. I think it's kind of cute.'

'You and I made a decision to be together, right?'

She nodded.

'Then you don't need to dance for strangers anymore. The 500 balloons a week I can float until we leave, and once we leave we'll never worry about money again. So there's no reason for you to keep doing it.'

She looked into my eyes. 'You really do want to take care of me, don't you?'

I nodded. 'Of course I do. You're my girl.'

As she drove up Meeting Street towards the interstate, I stood there, watching her one functioning taillight glowing a receding red like an eye moving backwards through the night.

My girl, I thought. She's my girl. And I was right. She deserved everything in the world she'd ever been afraid to want, and all I wanted now was to give it to her.

I was troubled the entire drive home. Savannah's sudden willingness to let go of everything she'd striven so hard for and against such odds surprised and scared me. It hammered home with all finality the fact that she'd put herself entirely in my hands, placed all of her faith and trust in me and who I was, without any real concern or doubt that I could pull it off.

But I had plenty of doubts, enough for both of us. Savannah's unshakeable confidence was gratifying, but it was terrifying too. I knew more than she about who I was. I'd seen my failure before.

I'd spent an hour behind the Isle of Palms dunes a few weeks ago explaining to her parts of my plan – parts, not all; not where the money was coming from, or how I planned to get it – what I'd seen after our night together at the Southern Belle. None of it surprised her, which made me kind of sad. Seventeen-year-old girls shouldn't be aware of all the bad that goes on out there.

As I had left the Southern Belle that night three weeks ago, stepping out of the private room hallway into the bass and strobe and smoke of the rest of the club, I had seen Collins slinking out the front door, like a chinchilla that's escaped its cage. I'd turned to kiss Savannah goodbye, but she'd simply kept walking, brushing her fingers softly along my lower back as she passed. Over to my left, behind the bar, I saw why. That big son of a bitching bouncer was watching, and probably wouldn't take kindly to one of the girls kissing her boyfriend goodbye.

I would have liked to walk across that club and kick the shit out of him, but it would have taken three or four of me to do it. He was built like an oak, with hands the size of waffle irons, and didn't look as though causing some stranger a great deal of pain would ruin his night much.

I hadn't dwelled on it. Instead I hastily made my exit, the way I imagine most men leaving the private rooms head for the door, their steps the quicker and lighter steps of men who've left behind several hundred dollars and a few ounces of semen.

'Come again,' the set of tits reading the book behind the ticket counter said as I hurried out. I considered asking her if that was an intentional pun, but didn't have time to explain the term so instead I nodded and walked out into the night. She never looked up from her book. *Martin's Rules,* or something like that.

It'd begun raining. Not real rain, but that light, steady drizzle that's more like a mist falling from the sky. I stood beneath the bright pink awning as it sprinkled over my face and arms, and I watched Collins cross the parking lot, climb into his Jeep Grand Cherokee, and pull out onto Calhoun Street.

He turned left. Towards Mount Pleasant.

Not much of note there, except that Collins lived in West Ashley. West Ashley was to the right. Nothing was to the left except a bridge, which led to Mount Pleasant. You went that route you were either planning on jumping off the bridge into the Cooper River, or there was something on the other side you were trying to get to.

I wondered where Ricke Collins, married father of five, was trying to get to in Mount Pleasant at two in the morning.

I wondered how long he'd been banging Chessie, forty-plus years his junior, and I wondered what other pies the man was fingering. I don't know why I wondered it. Perverse curiosity, perhaps. Or maybe just human nature.

Whatever it was, it was enough on that particular night to cause me to follow him. I knew nothing would come of it, but I was lonely and had nothing better to do. I couldn't see Savannah until the next day, if then, and I wasn't ready to go back to that empty apartment alone.

So I got in my car and proceeded to follow my boss, Mr. Ricke Collins of Coosaw Creek High School, just to see where it led.

'Cole? How wonderful to hear your voice! However did you find me?'

'Hey Grey,' I said. 'A mutual friend. How are you?' I was sitting in my little kitchenette, working my way through my third Beck's of the afternoon. In front of me was a stack of essays I told The Kids I'd have back to them tomorrow. There were ninety-one. So far I'd graded three. The fourth in the pile was currently serving as a coaster.

'Bartholomeu. Isn't he a doll?'

'He's a good fellow. Where are you?'

'Oh, darling, you've no idea how complicated that question is. As of late last night we were somewhere in the Adriatic Sea. Then Philip decided he wanted a bowl of chilled shark's fin soup so we sailed into Rimini for the evening to this delightful little chateau called Hotel Levanti. We'd planned to stay a few weeks but Philip has an overwhelming urge to play games with the International Date Line.'

'What kind of games?'

'Oh, you know men, Cole. He wants to make love on one side of it, then the other, then back to the first side again, all so he can say we did it on the tenth, then the ninth, then the tenth again. Then, as if that weren't eccentric enough, he wants to map out precisely where the line falls, place one of us on either side of it, and have sex while I'm in Tuesday and he's in Wednesday. He said he's always wanted his penis to be in two days at once. I told him I wasn't sure his equipment was long enough for time-traveling copulation, so he's angry at me now. How are you and Savannah, sweetheart?'

'That's sort of what I was calling you about.'

'Wonderful,' she said breathlessly. 'Tell me everything. Did you take my advice?'

'Yeah,' I said. 'I told her how I felt.'

'And – '

'And she feels the same way.'

'Of course she does. I never doubted it. Has it been Heaven?'

'It's going to be,' I said. 'In time. There're a few things we have to take care of first.'

'Oh, look at that, Cole. Already you're a "we". Isn't love the best of all drugs? I'm so happy for you,' and I knew she was. 'Now see, aren't you glad we had our little talk on the beach?'

My thoughts drifted back to that night, Grey on her knees before me, the warmth of her breath, the soft, experienced rhythm of her hands.

'Yeah,' I said. 'I am. I'm glad I came down to visit you. You were a bright spot in an otherwise dark stretch of my life, Grey. I owe you.'

'Nonsense, darling. You don't owe me anything. I wouldn't have been at all upset had you let me finish what I almost started beneath the stars that night with you, but that's more my own personal selfishness than anything else. What matters is you told her, the two of you are in love, and the rest will take care of itself.'

'We're working on it,' I said. 'There might be a way you could help us.'

'Anything,' she said.

'Well,' – taking another pull from the Beck's, glancing around the room looking for my cigarettes, then remembering Savannah had tossed them out the window of my car. She'd leaned over at a red light to kiss me and had come away with the taste of Chesterfield, and apparently hadn't found it pleasing – 'Remember you were telling me about Philip, about how he had all that money and that it wasn't really money, just little lights blinking in some computer somewhere?'

'Ah, yes. Poor Philip, whose prick is too small to span the cleft of time. He really is terribly perturbed with me right now. I suppose I'll have to make it up to him later today.'

'I've all confidence in your ability to do so, Grey.'

'Anyone with warm hands and a heartbeat could manage just fine, I think. He stole the money, of course. You knew that.'

'I figured as much. I kind of thought most of the people at your party had.'

'I don't know about most. Certainly some. I've never really asked those types of questions, and it rarely comes up on its own, as you can imagine.'

I could hear someone speaking in the background, then Grey's voice, away from the telephone: 'In a minute, dear. I'm on the phone with Cole.'

'That Philip?'

'Yes, the poor tortured soul. He's just informed me he's taking the jet-ski out for a few hours' wandering. We're fifty miles off the nearest coast, it's nighttime and he's going riding on the jet-ski. You men really should get over this whole penis-size thing. You'd be so much happier for it.'

'I've never given it a lot of thought, tell you the truth about it.'

'Nor do you need to, Cole. You're quite the handful. Philip's fine, too, but he's past the point of listening to me. I've offended his masculinity. He needs to do dangerous things and kill small animals now. But you were speaking of his money and the fact that it's stolen. It isn't the life it seems, Cole.'

'It appears pleasant enough.'

'Oh, sure, the money's pleasant, and I do think it suits him well, but he's relegated to spending his life sailing from port to port because of it. He's on the move constantly.'

'With beautiful women who play international dateline games with him.'

I could hear her smile.

'You've found a pot of honey, then?'

'A what?'

'A pot of honey. A honey pot. It's what they – the people who do this sort of thing – call large sums of money just sitting around, waiting to be grabbed. I imagine they fancy themselves masculine marauding bears with immense genitalia, no doubt. '

'Oh. Yes. I think so. I think I've found a honey pot. It's – '

'Careful, Cole. Honey pots aren't the sorts of things one should discuss over the tele. Would you like me to have Philip call you?'

'You think he would?'

'Oh, I would think so. I've bruised his ego a bit, but he is still very much who he was before. If you've really found one, he'll likely be too interested not to at least ring you up and ask you a thousand questions.'

'He couldn't call me here.'

'No, you're right. You can't be too careful with this sort of thing, Cole. I really do wish you'd reconsider even seeing this through another day. Money often costs too much. I've had gobs of the stuff for most of my life, and aside from the things it buys it does very little.'

'I don't need it to buy anything. I need it for her.'

'Does she know about this?'

'She knows some.'

'And is she pushing you?'

The question irritated me. 'No. This is my thing. I'm looking for a way out without hurting anyone.'

'A way out. Of the race.'

'For starters.'

'Will you write your books?'

'Yes. Eventually. After she and I make love on every beach we can find.'

'Are you absolutely set upon this? This taste of illicit honey?'

'I think so.'

'Then you will need to speak with Philip. He's the best there is at it. One of them, anyway. If he doesn't drown himself tonight at sea I'll have him contact you. Do you have email?'

'Of course.' I gave it to her.

'He'll email you later.'

'How later?'

'Oh, I don't know. A few days. Within the week, I should think.'

THIRTY-TWO

Intermezzo; emails and phone-calls

I take it this Philip character emailed you,' the girl said – Tezra was the name she was using, and it was about as authentic as a skinny Santa Claus – 'since you're here.'

'Yeah,' I said. 'I'm here.'

Another month had passed in Roatan, another series of days which varied from one another in no appreciable way. I spent my mornings on the balcony of my second story hotel room, over-looking the incredible blue of the water, tossing muffin crumbs to the little songbirds and dropping mousers to Brasco. Brasco liked the balcony, and though he pretended it was for the breeze and the smell of the coastal air, we both knew it was for the songbirds. One day he may catch one, though I doubt it. Domesticity had hampered his agility.

Around noon, when the sun was directly overhead and the heat began to weigh upon me, I would shower. Occasionally I'd shave. Sometimes I'd order room service afterwards and eat in front of the television. They had HBO and MTV here and sometimes CNN. Sometimes I walked the quarter-mile to the beach and read American novels that I found in the hotel lobby; other times I slept atop the sand until evening, the sounds of the surf and of children laughing dancing like images through my dreams.

For supper it was always the same, and it likely always would be. I would come here, to the little café down the street from my hotel, and find my table and order my food from one of the three same waiters each night. It was a small café. I had the menu memorized. The three waiters were the sons of the couple who owned it. They smiled a lot, spoke broken English, made passable meals, and never asked questions.

It was here, at this little café, that I met Tezra and her husband, who called himself Jack, which meant that whatever his name had been in America, it wasn't Jonathan or Jackson or John.

She was a pleasant-enough woman, nearing thirty if not there just yet, with long blonde hair and steady eyes she usually kept covered with sunglasses. Lately she had taken to joining me for meals, occasionally with Jack, usually without. They'd been living here for years now, and Jack had found a love for scuba diving. According to Tezra he explored the reefs beyond the breakers every evening. Sometimes he brought her shells.

'It gets easier,' she said, stirring a packet of Equal into her tea. 'Leaving. It gets easier with time.'

'Everything gets easier with time,' I agreed. 'It's the time that's so hard, though.'

'Does it help you to talk about her?' she asked.

'Sometimes. Usually.' I forced a smile. 'It's against the rules, though.'

She laughed. 'The rules. Part of all this is to stay away from their rules.'

'Whose?'

She shrugged. 'Whoever's rules it was you left behind.'

I sipped my beer. Budweiser is imported here, so it's no cheaper than Beck's. I'm a wealthy man now, multiple times over, but I still can't help glancing at the prices first when I open a menu. Time will change that, too, I'm sure.

'What did you and Jack leave behind?'

She touched her chin with her napkin. 'Everything. When you leave for good you leave it all behind.'

'But you have each other.'

'Yes. We do. I would die without him.'

I nodded.

'I'm sorry,' she said. 'I'm an idiot.'

'No, no,' I said, shaking my head. 'I understand. What the two of you have is what I wanted with her. I would have killed for it.' The English teacher I had once been pointed out that I was speaking in the wrong tense. 'I did kill for it,' I corrected myself.

Philip's email read: *Spoke with G about sweet things. Sugar and spice and the taste of fresh honey. Email safe number. We'll talk.*

It was late February now. I was in the library at the College of

Charleston, downtown. Outside the sky was a slate gray with dark, rain-filled clouds hanging motionless throughout. It was noon Saturday morning, and what company I had here on the basement level of the library looked about as interested in me as they were in whatever they were supposed to be studying. The subtle smell of alcohol and morning-breath permeated the air down here.

I had wedged myself into the computer carrel farthest from the staircase leading upstairs to the main floor. My back was in a windowless wall, and the carrels on either side of me were empty. I was wearing gloves, which I felt silly about even then, but I didn't want to be tied to any of this if things got ugly before I disappeared. All I knew about Philip was that he was a wealthy thief with an apparently little prick, and this was not enough to warrant my trusting him.

But I needed him. I needed his knowledge. So I slipped on my gloves and glanced around to make sure I was in relative solitude, then clicked 'reply.' I typed out a phone number, followed by the message: *will be there from ten pm to ten-thirty eastern time for next five nights. thanx.*

I paused for a moment, reread it, then went back and deleted the *thanx.* Somehow it sounded too juvenile for our purposes.

I glanced around once more, clicked send, then went into my email account and deleted Philip's message from the in-box, and my message to him from the sent-box. It was still there, I knew, still able to be retrieved if the right equipment was used, but hopefully before anyone knew to look I'd be long gone.

That was the plan, at any rate.

When I was confident I'd deleted everything, I turned the computer off and left the library. Savannah and I had a date; she was meeting me at the East Bay pier at one and I didn't want to be late.

The payphone in the West Ashley bowling alley rang at a quarter after ten that night. I was standing there, nibbling on nachos and jalapeños, watching folks bowl and thinking about my date that afternoon with Savannah. We'd gone from the pier to the old movie house on King Street, a place called American Cinema Grille where you sit in big easy chairs and a waiter comes around and takes your order while you watch the movie. When the movie ended at five she'd had to go home to make dinner for her mother and brothers, so I'd come here, to the Brunswick Bowl, where I'd bowled a few games and drank a few beers and waited for ten o'clock to roll around.

I answered on the second ring.

'Who is this, please?' the voice on the other end asked. Right away I knew it was Philip. He sounded someplace far away where the nights are warm and everything smells of suntan lotion.

'We have a mutual friend,' I said. 'I'm looking for a good recipe for honey.'

'What you do with it once you get it is entirely up to you, young man,' he said. 'I'm more interested in acquisition than utilization. Tell me what you know. And use no names. None. The moment you utter any name at all this conversation ends. Is that clear?'

'Yes.'

'Good. Go ahead, then.'

'I know of a large amount of honey that's shipped to this particular storehouse annually in June.'

'How large is large?'

'I'm not exactly sure on that, but I've done a bit of looking and some figuring and my best guess is roughly sixty million gallons of the stuff.'

'That is a lot of honey,' he said. 'How much of it do you have plans for?'

'All of it.'

'Whatever could you possibly need with sixty million gallons of honey?'

'Maybe nothing. But getting some of it is just as hard as getting all of it. I don't see any reason to leave any of it behind.'

He laughed. 'Dear boy, you are every bit as precocious as our mutual friend says you are. Bravo! I like your style. What else can you tell me about it?'

'I know the keymaster.'

'Keymaster. Be more specific.'

'There is a person who for a limited time has access to the storehouse where they hold the honey until they divide it up and send it off. Some honey for this group, some honey for that, some for this group over there. This person is the individual responsible for determining each group's annual need and then facilitating the transfers.'

'You know who this person is?'

'Yes.'

There was a pause. I could hear him breathing.

'It's time to end this conversation. I'm going to give you a number. Call it tomorrow night, ten o'clock your time. There'll be a recording on the other end, asking you to punch in your code. Use the date of the morning you met our mutual friend. Day, month, year, two digits each.'

He gave me the number. I scribbled it across a napkin between nacho cheese smudges.

'Don't be late. At ten after ten the recording comes down, this conversation never happened, and you and I shall never speak again. Good?'

'Got it.'

'Not yet, you don't. But if you're as clever as our mutual friend thinks you are, and if you want this more than you've ever imagined you could want anything in your entire life, you might stand a chance of at least seeing it.'

'Oohh, that really is exciting,' Tezra said. 'Jack and I had nothing like that. Everything we took was already stolen.'

'You stole it from the thief?'

'Not exactly. Someone we knew stole it from the thief, then killed the thief. I exchanged something I had for a portion of it.'

'What was that?'

'My dignity,' she said, and her tone said there'd been scars there once, scars which, while faded now, had never fully healed.

I nodded, flagged the waiter for another beer, asked Tezra if she wanted anything. She shook her head.

'I'll need to be getting back before too long,' she said. 'Jack'll be wandering in shortly.'

I nodded again. 'Thanks for listening.'

She smiled a wan smile. 'We've been doing this for nearly eight years now, he and I. We criss-crossed the globe by train, plane, boat, even horseback. A week into it Jack bought an American paper and I read that my father had been implicated in a scheme to embezzle millions from a political party. He committed suicide rather than stand trial for it. To this day I haven't been able to speak to my mother, to see how she's doing, to tell her I'm all right. We left our entire families behind, forever.'

She stood.

'There's an enormous world out there to lose yourself in, and if you've got the means to do it you can stay hidden forever, no matter who's looking for you. The hard thing is to not look back. That's where they get you.'

'I know.'

'But you want to look, don't you?'

'I do,' I said. *'God yes I do. More than I ever wanted to leave.'*

At one minute after ten the following night I dialed the number given to me by Philip. I was at a different phone booth this time; I'd driven all the way to North Charleston to the Trident Tech campus. There were half a dozen pay phones in the main lobby, and at this hour I was the only one on any of them.

After a few rings a mechanical voice came on, just as Philip had said it would. It asked me to punch in my pin. I did. The date I'd stumbled onto Grey in her big, stupid hat on the Isle of Palms beach, a chance encounter which had, I suspected even then, the potential to change my life forever.

There was a click, then another ringing, then another mechanical voice. This one gave me another number, which I scribbled across the palm of my left hand. Then it hung up, and left me alone with a dial tone in the Trident Technical Campus main lobby.

I considered driving across town to find another payphone, but I wasn't sure how much time I had to call the new number. Philip had been pretty specific last night. Ten minutes after ten the voicemail would be taken down and I'd have no way of contacting him again. I could always get in touch with Grey – she'd given me the number to her cell, which she was never far from – but I knew better than to think Philip would give a stranger a second chance at something as risky as this.

So I opted instead to simply switch phones, bouncing two phones down in the row of six, knowing it made absolutely no difference but feeling nonetheless that it'd be better to switch something than nothing at all.

I dialed the number – all 14 digits of it – and Philip answered on the fifth ring.

'Remember,' he said first off, 'no names. Not one. We're on a secured line, but even the most secure lines aren't secure more than a few minutes.'

'I understand.'

'Good. Here's what we'll do, then. If you're interested, tell me and we'll set about beginning. If not, tell me that and we'll hang up and go our separate ways. Either way, this is our final conversation and you and I have never spoken.'

'Okay.'

'What I'm about to say is non-negotiable, irrevocable, and once it's set in motion is unable to be recalled. You can't get soft or sentimental or find religion halfway through it.'

'I understand that.'

'Good. You will sometime in the next twenty four hours set yourself up an email account, the address of which will be your cat's name backwards, followed by your favorite city's name – minus the vowels – forwards, followed by your age, in numbers. Register it with Yahoo. Henceforth this will be our sole method of communication.'

'Got it.'

'Not yet you don't. You'll receive a message from a contact of mine, asking you for specific information. Amounts, transit routes, sources and destinations. Anything you have. You'll also likely be asked the keymaster's name, address, family, schedule, habits and haunts if you know them. You'll be contacted in person, probably at night, probably while you're alone. Then you'll fade away until I contact you again. Go about your usual day. Under no circumstances are you to try to contact me. Under no circumstances are you to initiate contact with our mutual friend. Do you have any questions?'

'A couple. What's your end?'

'Fifty percent. That, too, is non-negotiable.'

'That's a lot of honey.'

'It had better be, which brings me to my next point. This is not a game. If at any point you find yourself forgetting that, remember that you're not in this alone. Some very serious people with serious things to hide are going to become involved, and they don't take well to being toyed with.'

'How do I know I can trust you?'

I heard him chuckle. 'Dear boy, the first thing you'd better learn in this is that you can't trust anyone.'

And then he hung up.

THIRTY-THREE

B

March passes as March does, slowly and wet and gray. I spent my days in class pushing The Kids through the literature, the grammar, the vocabulary. I spent my weeknights at home on the phone with Savannah or, when she couldn't talk for one reason or another, out at a bar with Julian.

Several times I'd almost broken down and let Julian in on my plan. He'd been a solid friend these past ten years, and it seemed the right thing to do. He'd walked side by side with me through my despair after Autumn had called things off. I couldn't count the number of times he'd listened to me tell and retell the same stories about her over and over, all the while pretending it was the first time he'd ever heard it. Julian was gold, and I owed him more than simply disappearing on him, leaving a whirlwind in my wake. That sort of thing only plays well in poems and bad movies. In real life it's bullshit.

But I had no choice. I'd conscripted myself into a situation where I was gradually losing my options. Others were involved now. Serious people with serious things to hide.

B, as he had instructed me to call him, approached me ten days after my final call with Philip. And Philip had been right; it'd been at night, and I'd been alone, walking across George's parking lot after a night of beer and wings with Julian, Julian having just driven off, me trying to fumble my keys into the door.

'Cole,' I heard behind me. It was a voice I'd never heard before.

I turned around, still holding my keys.

'I'm B,' he said, stepping forward. He was an older man, a full head taller than I, mid-fifties probably, dark hair going white around the temples. 'I'm told you have some information for me.'

I looked at his hands. They were empty. I wondered if he was carrying a gun.

'I might,' I said, trying to sound confident. 'I'm going to need more than just a fucking letter, though. You understand.'

He smiled a little, as if to himself. 'You contacted a mutual acquaintance regarding a shipment of honey.'

I nodded. 'You want to talk here?'

'No,' he said. 'In the car.'

So I drove downtown and caught the James Island connector, B riding shotgun, and told him what I knew.

'Under your seat there you'll find a folder. I've been carting it around waiting for someone to ask me for it.' I said. 'It's not much. Just copies of district finance reports, personnel numbers and salaries, appropriations for various departments. Food services, transportation, alternative-educational setting, athletics, vocational programs, salaries, textbooks and supplies, all that shit. It's all last year's info, but this year can't be too far off.'

'Where'd you get this?' he asked, thumbing through the copies.

'City library. Made the copies there too. It's all public knowledge.'

'I know it's public knowledge. I want to know if anyone else knows you're interested in it.'

I shrugged. 'I don't see how they could.'

He fanned through the pages.

'Tell me what you know.'

'Her name is Emily Cosgrove,' I said. 'She's in her late thirties, married, couple-three kids. I teach one of them. Her oldest graduated a few years ago, just had a baby.'

'What's her official position?' B asked.

'She's the district's finance officer. She handles all the comings and goings of the money. She disburses paychecks, makes sure each department has their funds for the year, that sort of thing. When the state sends its annual allotment to the district, she's the one who receives it.'

'So she knows the codes.'

The James Island Connector ended and I made a U-turn and crossed it going the other way. The city glimmered before us low on the horizon like jewels under glass.

'She either has them or has access to them. All the money that Winter's Cove receives from the state each year in June goes through her hands. She's the one who actually sends it to the appropriate departments. Exactly how that's done I don't know. That's why I need you guys.'

'It doesn't matter how it's done,' B said. 'It only matters that she's able to do it.'

'How do you mean?'

'It's just a matter of access codes, account numbers, routing numbers, that sort of thing. All of which, according to you, this Emily Cosgrove has. The most sophisticated password system in the world is only as strong as the person controlling it. If she can distribute it for the district, she can distribute it for us.'

'What makes you think she'll do that?'

B kept his face forward, off toward the city's skyline, except I could tell he wasn't looking at it. He wasn't looking at anything anyone else could see.

'Experience,' he said. 'People will do anything if their motivation is right.'

I nodded. I was pretty sure I didn't want to know much of B's experience in motivating people to do things.

'Tell me again,' he said, 'about her family.'

I let Savannah in on things a little at a time. I let her know when we'd be leaving, when to be ready. I told her to pack lightly. But the details stopped there for her. She didn't need to know everything. She wouldn't have wanted to know it all. Parts of my plan were ugly and wrong, and the only way I could go through with it was to focus on the whole, which I still believed was just and right and on most levels worth the means necessary to see it through.

I did tell her what I saw after leaving the Southern Belle that night. I'd told B as well, although it was with a sickening sense of something breaking that I realized that night in the car with him as we drove back and forth on the James Island Connector that he was much more interested in Emily Cosgrove's family. Her 'motivational avenues,' he called them.

When he'd asked me about her daughter's newborn I thought I was going to throw up.

So that part I kept to myself, preferring instead to shelter Savannah from the darker details of it all. That was part of my job, after all. To shelter and protect her. It's what I wanted to do more than anything else in the world.

But I told her how I'd followed Collins, how I'd crossed the Cooper River Bridge with him and sliced through the night up the center of Mount Pleasant, all the while keeping a healthy ten or twelve car lengths between us.

I watched him pull up in front of an apartment complex near the Isle of Palms Connector that I knew good and well he didn't live in. It was pushing four in the morning now, and there he was, my principal, Mr. Ricke Collins, climbing out of his SUV and walking up the sidewalk towards one of the units, smoothing out his shirt and squirting breath freshener in his mouth. From where I was parked I couldn't hear, but I was fairly confident the man was sniffing away like a bastard, too. I wondered if he did that when he fucked.

Part of me admired his stamina. He'd just spent an hour with Chessie – whose youth and flexibility we all bore witness to every Friday afternoon at the pep rallies as she danced, flipped, and tumbled across the gymnasium with the rest of the dance team – in a little dark room surrounded by music and strobe and all the pleasure money could buy. Yet here he was, ready for round two.

I wasn't overly interested in the whole deal, and I was by this time sufficiently tired to the point where I thought I could go home and sleep without missing Savannah too much. I was getting ready to leave when the door he'd knocked on opened, and the women he'd come to see answered.

I recognized her, of course. Even from this distance I knew who she was. I'd seen her face in the *Winter's Cove Journal-Scene* numerous times, whenever the District Office had a comment to make about the budget, teacher pay, any of it. During our orientation, she'd given a talk about the importance of Federal Cards, and how vital it was that we as teachers handed them out and picked them back up. Federal Cards determined how much money the district received from Uncle Sam. And Emily – Winter's Cove's Finance Director, divorced mother of three, grandmother of one, and Ricke Collins' hostess tonight – handled the money.

Or, as Grey's crowd might have said, guarded the honey.

THIRTY-FOUR

Cole grades on a curve; intermezzo

At a quarter after six in the evening, everyone but the maintenance crew having gone home for the day, the computer screen in my classroom read:

ORION
<
Enter Password

My classroom door was shut and locked, the blinds closed over the windows. The lights were off. Aside from the milky white glow emanating from the computer screen before me, the entire room was dark.

Enter Password
Enter Password
Enter Password

It flashed every few seconds, the steady, staccato tempo serving as a reminder that this was it. I was standing at the proverbial edge looking over, looking to the other side, wondering if I had what it took to cross without falling. On the other side was a sandy beach and a girl with copper hair and cotton hands dancing on air and laughing at the moon. Beneath me, waiting for me should I fall, there was more than likely a life of regret and pain and second-guessing, for myself and for Savannah.

Enter Password

I typed: Brasco.

Select Screen

I typed: Student Records.

Select Student

Savannah Bellington.

Select Year

Current.

Savannah's grades materialized on the screen before me. It was mid-April now; third quarter had ended last week. The deadline for teachers to turn in grades was yesterday. And there, before me, were the marks of a young woman who had been a near straight-A student until this year. Until she met me.

Government 72%
Calculus   77%
Chemistry 78%
French 2   67%
English 3 97%

Savannah had been right. So long as our plan worked, it didn't matter what her grades were. You go to school to get good grades to get into a good college to get a good job to make a good living to have a good life. That had been Savannah's plan before I'd come along. But not now. Now we'd found a way to skip the grades, the college, the job, the good living, and go directly to the good life. The Good Life. It'd become my mantra of late. I – we – were risking everything, including any hope of ever living a normal life, all in exchange for the good life.

And to that end I couldn't afford suspicion. A previously good student struggling with C's and D's and an F sparked a certain level of concern, even curiosity. But that same student struggling with C's and D's in every class but one prompted something more. Anyone who cared to look – a generous assumption in any bureaucracy, but a possibility nonetheless – would see that the teacher in that A class was a young, single male with a fairly high failure ratio. It wasn't exactly holding her hand in the hallway, but it was more than I could afford at this point.

So I played with the numbers a bit. The grade file was closed yesterday, so everything was in by now. Report cards went out four days from now; for the next four days Guidance would actually have to work. They'd be verifying credits and printing reports and licking and sticking and mailing for nearly two thousand students. Then, ORION would be closed to everyone – teachers included – except guidance and the administration. Unless someone was specifically searching out Savannah's records, no one – especially her teachers – would notice her grades had been changed. I would simply have to go back in and re-enter the correct grades as soon as the grade file was opened next quarter.

So Government became a 95. Calculus a 93. Chemistry a 99. French a *très bon* 100. And English. I punched a few more keys, flashed through a few more screens, and ran her new numbers against those of the entire junior class. She was ranked number eleven out of 488. Top 3%. Not bad by any measure. Good enough for virtually any college, in any distant corner of the country she desired.

I sat back in my chair, closed my eyes and rubbed my temples with the heels of my hands. There were fourteen days left in April. Thirty-one in May. By mid-June we'd be somewhere else, leaving in our wake enough ripples to keep them guessing and wondering for years.

Another month in Roatan. Another series of days and nights filled with nothing memorable at all. I slept a lot. Drank more than I should have. And I wrote long, wistful letters to Savannah that would never be mailed.

After six months in the massive, tourist-filled hotel I finally decided it was time to move on. I didn't know where, not exactly, but I hadn't been running far enough for long enough yet to grow roots.

'Roots aren't what get you,' Tezra told me the afternoon I mentioned my plan to relocate. We were on the beach, stretched out beneath the sun in adjacent lounge chairs. She was wearing a white two-piece that fit her well. Her husband, Jack, she said,

was off yachting with their child, an eight-year-old boy named Quentin.

'I know. But I don't feel safe here.'

'You're probably as safe here as you are anywhere else. Staying isn't how they find you. It's trying to go back that does people in.'

'I'm not going back.'

'That's a good thing,' she said, sipping her drink. 'Because they'll be waiting if you do.'

I nodded silently. My skin was so dark I could pass for Hispanic. Darker than Julian back home had ever been.

No, I corrected myself. Not back home. I'm darker than Julian back in Charleston had ever been. Charleston wasn't home. Roatan wasn't home. Home was some place I hadn't found yet.

'Where will you go?' she asked.

I shrugged into the sunlight. A young couple strolled in front of me, hand-in-hand. Her hair reminded me of Savannah's.

'I don't know. Any suggestions?'

'Jack and I wandered everywhere at first,' she said. 'Mexico, then Paris, then Barbados. We lived in the Caymans for almost three years before we moved on again.'

'Caymans no good?'

'Too many tourists.'

'This place is crawling with them.'

'In the Caymans they seemed to all be American. Besides, everyone in the world has a Cayman bank account. They make movies about it.'

'I need somewhere warm. With beaches.'

'And young girls in bikinis?' she smiled. 'There's nothing wrong with it, you know.' I was facing the sun, my eyes closed behind my sunglasses, but I could feel her looking at me.

'It's healthy,' she continued. 'Necessary even. You can't pine for her forever.'

'I know.'

There was a lengthy silence then, during which I might have fallen asleep.

'There's this place I know,' she said abruptly, in such a way that I wondered if she'd ever actually stopped talking, unaware that I'd dozed off.

'Jack and I lived there a few months. We wouldn't have left except it's an island and Jack was beginning to feel water-locked.'

I heard her sit up. I opened my eyes behind the dark lenses and watched clouds work their way across my field of vision.

'Where is it?'

She told me. I nodded.

'Have you been?'

'No. Seen pictures, though. Someone I knew went once.'

'It really is spectacularly beautiful,' she continued. 'Wonderful restaurants, excellent banking system. Everyone there speaks English and they love Americans. Being wealthy doesn't stand out at all.'

'No, I don't imagine it would.'

'Well,' she said, then stood and gathered her things. 'I've got some errands to run before Jack comes home. If you have the chance, say goodbye before you go. Jack would be upset if you left without coming over for dinner at least once.'

'Sounds nice,' I said.

'How's next week? Say, Monday?'

'What day is it today?'

'Thursday, I think. Yes, I'm sure it's Thursday.'

'Monday sounds fine,' I said, knowing full well I wouldn't be eating dinner there Monday or any other day.

I don't remember speaking much with her after that. I wiped a fresh sheen of sweat from my forehead, then closed my eyes and allowed myself to drift. When I woke up it was nearly dark, Tezra was gone, and the ocean breeze had turned cold.

Brasco and I were in the cab when the ominous thunderclouds began forming overhead. Thunderbolts clapped through the night every few minutes, causing his ears to drop and his hair to rise.

As I settled into my seat on the little twin-engine puddle-jumper, Brasco in his carrier on the seat next to me, the rain began to fall. By the time we'd taken off, heading south, I was sleeping.

THIRTY-FIVE

Getting ink done

I took my eighth sick day on the second to last Friday of April. Savannah cut as well, which was stupid, but I was getting to the point where I didn't care. We were almost gone. Each day began to seem shorter for me, each week moving more rapidly toward the next. There were times I felt that if I closed my eyes I could hear the rest of the world whirring past my ears, all the little ants marching forward with their insignificant little lives filled with quiet desperation.

I worked amongst men and women who'd given themselves over entirely to the myth of the teacher, that it's somehow noble to be underpaid, under-appreciated, and over-worked, that the doctors and lawyers and other professionals out there had sold out, traded purpose for money, settling for big houses and expensive vacations when they could have had the intrinsic reward of driving old cars owned by credit unions. I felt badly for them, because most of them had come into this gig with the best of intentions, and, despite the prevailing wisdom, a goodly number of them were in fact quite intelligent. But like Geist, they'd gotten caught early, sucked in by cost-of-living increases and summers off. It was criminal – an unjust edict, handed down by the district. I viewed disobedience as a moral imperative.

Savannah was at my apartment by seven that morning, having driven there directly from her trailer. She curled up beside me and slept, her head on my chest, an arm draped over my stomach. I lay there and ran my fingers through her hair, listening to her breathe. I watched a rhombus of sunlight the color of old bone gradually climb the bed, our bodies, then the opposite wall. I closed my eyes and focused on her scent, the smell of soap and conditioner and surrender.

At noon I kissed her slightly parted mouth and woke her up. She smiled and stretched.

'What time is it?'

'Twelve,' I said. 'You're beautiful when you sleep.'

She blushed, then rolled onto her stomach and turned so she was facing me, her head still on my chest.

'Are you hungry?' she asked.

'I could eat.'

'Let's go downtown,' she said. 'We can eat at a café.'

'In broad daylight, no less,' I said.

She smiled. 'And then I want to show you something.'

I nodded.

We ate at Doriano's, splitting a large veggie-lover's. It occurred to me halfway through the meal that I hadn't been glancing over my shoulder every few bites to make sure I didn't see anyone I knew. It didn't matter at this point.

When we finished we walked down King, her hand enfolded softly in mine. The mid-April sun was warm and welcoming, giving the entire city that fresh, washed-over look and making all the buildings, trees, and cars shimmer, like they'd been painted on the skyline by some skilled artist's hand. The air was still free of the oppressive humidity that would begin in another six weeks or so and last until mid-autumn. There was a pleasant breeze coming in from the harbor half a mile in front of us, smelling subtly of salt and fish. The sounds of gulls cawing at one another rode the breeze into the city like a wave.

We'd gone only a few blocks when Savannah stopped us.

'Let's go in there,' she said.

I looked. We were standing beneath a large, purple awning with the words 'Grannie's Goodies' written across it in script. The shop front was entirely glass, with tie-dyed shirts and hemp sandals and dancing bears situated hodge-podge behind it. It didn't look like the kind of place I would ever intentionally go in.

'Really?' I asked, half-waiting for the punch-line.

She nodded. 'There's something we should do.'

The inside of Grannie's Goodies was the deadhead's dream. It was cool and dark to the point you had to stop and let your eyes adjust. The walls were lined with tie-dyed everything, Birkenstocks, beads, posters, rearview mirror ornaments, raggedy jeans peppered with holes, wigs, hats, belts, socks, suspenders, and backpacks. There were racks of clothes all around, with huge signs proclaiming '40% off thru April' and 'Buy 2 get 1 free.' It didn't seem to be working. Near as I could tell, we were the only shoppers in the place.

There was a collection of water-bongs for sale near the back of the store, along with numerous displays of incense, aroma candles, mood rings, karma crystals, and instrumental CD's. In one of the back corners was the piercing station, where you could do everything from switch out your earrings to run a three-quarter inch stud through your cock. They had nipple rings, lip rings (for lips both south and north of the equator) navel-loops and studs, nose-rings, and eyebrow rings. There was an entire section of multi-sized silver, gold, and jade studs reserved exclusively for the tongue. And there was a series of tiny little bells no bigger than a dime that hung down from a thin, half-inch chain.

'It's for your clit,' the man behind the counter said. His forearms were covered in vivid blue and red tattoos. His hair was a shiny black that was almost blue in the lack of light, and both ears were run through with various sized pieces of shrapnel, like a grenade had gone off near his head. The word 'PAIN' was inked across his neck in large black letters. The backs of his hands had been tattooed almost entirely blue.

'Come again?'

He slid the glass back behind the counter and retrieved one of the little bells, holding it out for me to see.

'You run this pin here through the clit, and as long as you don't wear underwear it jingles when you walk.' He looked at me. 'Not you, of course. Women.'

'Yeah,' I said. 'I know what a clit is. You sell many of these?'

He shrugged. 'Some.'

Savannah had joined me now. The human bruise behind the counter looked like he might offer the little bell to her.

'We can fit any of this right here on the premises,' he said.

'What about tattoos?' Savannah asked.

'Those're illegal here,' I said. 'To get, anyway.'

Both of them looked like they were trying not to laugh.

'We have a guy comes by sometimes,' bruise-man said.

'What times?' Savannah asked.

He looked at her. 'You thinking about getting ink done, love?'

'We,' she said.

'We?' I repeated.

'Lots of folks do it,' the bruise piped up. 'You two getting married? You see some couples get their other's name tattooed beneath the wedding band. That way, you ever take the ring off...'

'I was thinking something a little bigger,' she said. 'And somewhere else. Is your guy here now?'

Bruise shrugged. For the first time I was aware of a stale haze of acrid smoke emanating off of him, from the dope he smoked on his last break, no doubt.

'He could be. What are we talking about?'

Savannah shrugged. 'Just names. His on my ass.'

Bruise nodded, then glanced at me. 'And you?'

'I ...' – pause, stammer, the idea of getting ink done not one I'd ever considered for even the shortest second – 'Hers, of course. Not my ass, though. The arm, I guess.'

'Run you about two hundred total,' Bruise nodded. 'More if you want color.'

Savannah slipped her hand into a front pocket and pulled out a series of hundred-dollar bills. She peeled two of them off and set them on the smudgy glass countertop.

'It sure would be convenient if your guy was here now,' she said.

The Bruise palmed the two bills and came out from behind the counter without a word, walking towards the front of the store and locking the double glass doors. He flipped the open sign around to 'closed.'

'Follow me,' he said, motioning to the back of the near-dark store with a nod of the head.

Half an hour later I had my first tattoo: Savannah, in black cursive script across my left shoulder, weeping blood beneath the bandage.

'It's hard to believe,' Savannah was saying, trying to get comfortable on my bed without rolling onto her right cheek.

'What's that?' I was lying on my right side, touching her face. My arm was itching beneath the ointment and the bandage, and I had to consciously keep myself from scratching it.

'I have my teacher's name tattooed on my rear,' she said, then giggled. 'Kind of sexy when you think of it. Your name on me. Like a little poem.'

'You may want to keep it hush-hush for now,' I suggested.

'I don't regularly run around showing off my derriere, Mr. Archer. Not anymore, at any rate.'

'This is a good thing.'

'I still don't feel right about it.'

'About not showing your ass?'

'About taking money from you.'

'Don't even think about it. All you have to do is keep doing what you've been doing. We're almost there.'

'Where's it coming from? You couldn't possibly have had that much in savings.'

'Don't end your sentences in a preposition.'

'From where is it coming? That sounds stupid.'

'It's right, though.' I winked at her. 'From the wonders of our modern credit system. It's not even mine.'

'Won't you have to pay it back? They don't just give it away.'

I shrugged. 'They're predatory lenders, all of them. Visa, MasterCard, American Express, Discover, the lot of them. It won't hurt them to take a little hit here and again. Besides, they've got losses like the one I'm going to hand them built into their system. It won't be so much as a blip on their daily balance sheet. No one will even blink.'

After an extended silence that was as comfortable as a warm bath, Savannah's eyes met mine and she said, 'You think it'll work out?' Her tone was sadder than I'd heard it in a long time. 'I mean really?'

'I think it has a good chance.'

'People are going to come after us, aren't they?'

I nodded.

'For a long time?'

'Maybe forever.'

'But you're smarter than they are, aren't you?'

'I think so.'

'We won't know, though. If they ever stop looking.'

'No.'

'Forever's a long time to run,' she said.

'Yes.' I paused. 'We could wait, Savannah. We could wait until you graduate and then just go then. I can quit teaching and find another job wherever it is you go to school.'

'My grades have fallen,' she offered. 'I've let them slip.'

'That doesn't matter. I can probably fix them well enough. And even if I can't, you could go to a tech school somewhere long enough to drive your GPA back up. Transfer to a four-year and the med. schools won't know any different.'

'Do you ever worry about your plan not working?'

All the time, I thought. 'No,' I said. 'It will work if …well, if a lot of things. If it doesn't work, I'm in deep. They'll know I tried. I'll have to run regardless. Without the money. I'll be a Mexican without pesos.'

'And you're sure it's worth it?'

'Yes,' I said. 'Yes, I am. If it works, we'll have the rest of our lives to spend with each other. We'll be able to fill our time with anything and everything we want, and nothing we don't. We'll have the kind of life people spend their whole lives dreaming about.'

'I want to have your baby,' she said, and it was like getting hit in the face with a sack of thousand dollar bills. Hard and unforgiving and without warning and wonderful. 'I know we can't do that now, Cole, but I want it badly; my insides ache for it. Every time you hold me I can feel how badly I want it. We've got some things we have to do first, I know, but I wanted to tell you that. I wanted you to know that it's something I think about. Your baby growing inside of me.'

Sometime later, the sweat on her neck glowing a warm gold, she asked me, 'Why can't you tell me where the money's coming from?'

'It's coming from a great-aunt. I already told you.'

She smiled. 'I don't believe you.'

'You don't have to. Just trust me.'

'I do. And even if it doesn't come, I will. I'll come with you anyway.'

'I wouldn't let you.'

'You couldn't stop me.'

I marveled at her, not at what she said but at the fact that she'd had the stuff to say it at all. Her loyalty pulled tears to my eyes.

'Don't worry,' I whispered, pulling her head to my lips. 'We're going to be all right.' I kissed her forehead. 'We deserve it.'

THIRTY-SIX

B pays Cole a visit;
visions of a van

The following Monday I walked into my apartment a little after four, my briefcase in one hand, a six pack of Beck's in the other. The light was off, the shades pulled down, just as it was every day. I instinctively scanned the living room for Brasco, who always met me with an approving chirp.

'Brasco,' I said. 'Hey little man. Where are you?'

I set the briefcase on the floor, having resolved to let it spend the night where it fell, resting undisturbed, for I was not grading a thing for the next couple days. I'd spent most of Saturday and a good chunk of Sunday poring over student essays, grammar quizzes, and unit tests. Tonight I was drinking beer and watching TV. Tomorrow I was drinking more beer, TV optional. And Wednesday after work would probably find me hunched over the bar at George's with Jules, which meant Thursday would be another sick day for recovery. I might even take Friday too; make it a four-day weekend.

'Brasco,' I called. 'Here little man. Kitty-kitty-kitty. Here boy.'

No sign of him. I figured he was probably in the bathroom, squeezing one off in the litter box, a nice little surprise for me now that I was home from work.

But still. He never missed greeting me at the door. Never.

I was replaying my morning – mentally retracing my steps, seeing myself grab my briefcase, squat down at the door, rub his ears and under his chin, then step outside backwards so as to make sure he didn't shoot out between my legs, watching him watching me, then closing the door and locking it, leaving him safely inside, the same routine every time I left the apartment – when it occurred to me that it was possible a maintenance man or bug-guy might have come in and left the door open.

Of course, if he was taking a shit or preoccupied elsewhere – maybe he'd found a mouse or particularly entertaining cockroach – it wouldn't take but a couple seconds to find him. A quick search of the apartment and –

And then I saw him, sitting atop the card table in the kitchenette. I saw B then, too, sitting at the table, his big, heavy hands atop Brasco, rubbing him almost absently. B was looking at me, petting my cat, sitting in my apartment. Aside from his hands, he was completely motionless. He was a statue, a solid, graying statue made of marble and covered in weathered skin, all of it blended into the pool of shadows in the corner.

'What the fuck are you doing in my house?'

'Waiting for you.'

'How'd you get in?'

B shook his head.

I took two steps to my left and opened the shades, letting sunlight pour in. B squinted, which pleased me inexplicably.

'Shut those,' he said without moving.

'Take your hands off my cat.'

His meaty hands lifted half an inch and Brasco bolted across the room towards me, rolling on my feet. I stooped and picked him up.

'Shut the blinds, Cole.'

I looked at him sitting there, thought that if I got close enough to his face I could probably find dust in the wrinkles and weather-lines.

I closed the blinds. The room fell to shadows.

'Why are you in my house?'

'We need to talk.'

'Then you can call me on the phone like a regular fucking person and set up a time and a place to meet.'

His hands were folded over one another. He was very still, but in his legs and trunk there was a sense of an enormous amount of potential energy, as if he could at any second spring like a panther from that chair and be upon me.

'I'm not a regular person, Cole,' he said. 'That's fact number one. Neither are the people I'm working for. That's fact number two. Fact number three is one you shouldn't forget: once this is done, you'll never be a regular person again, either.'

'That's the plan,' I said.

He nodded. 'The girl.'

'What girl?'

'The one you were locking lips with downtown last week. The student.'

'What about her?'

'What does she know?'

'Listen to me, B,' I said, slowly. 'You stay away from her. She's got nothing to do with any of this.'

'What does she know?'

'She doesn't know anything.'

'Doubtful.'

'She knows we're planning a trip.'

'To where?'

'She doesn't know yet. Neither do I. And if I did I wouldn't tell you. No offense, but I don't need any pen-pals once I'm gone.'

'She could talk.'

'She can't talk because she doesn't know anything. I'm serious. You leave her alone. Don't go anywhere near her.'

'The people I work for – '

'We can cancel the I-Spy shit too. I know who you work for. I called them, remember?'

'The people I work for are averse to risk.'

'Bully for them. If any of your people go anywhere near her I swear to God you'll have to move to Mars to get away from me.'

'To get away from you,' he repeated.

I stood my ground. 'That's right.'

'Cole,' he asked, his hands still now, his entire mass as motionless as stone, 'have you ever been butt-fucked?'

My intestines turned to icy jelly.

B stood, a moveable wall of muscle and purpose. 'You heard me correctly. I asked if you've ever been butt-fucked.'

'No.'

'It's not too much fun,' he said, taking two steps in my direction. I felt Brasco tighten into me. 'Not even if you do swing that way. First time a fag takes it in the ass he bleeds for a week. Can't hold his shits in, can't even fart without crying. Now I want you to picture something for me. Picture a field somewhere, big and open and spacious. Nothing anywhere near it except the surrounding forest, and nothing in the forest except for trees and squirrels. And in the middle of that field is a van without windows. Maybe it's a black van, maybe it's blue. Doesn't matter because you've never seen the outside of it. You wake up in the inside, gagged, hands tied behind your back, ankles roped together. You're naked. You're being butt-fucked, and you're tearing on the inside. You feel your blood dripping down your thighs, pooling around your knees in warm puddles, and you're trying to scream, trying to get away, but the fucking just keeps on and on and on, until you feel something give in there, something that'd been firm and resistant now torn and giving way, and it feels like you're on fire inside, and then you vomit, and you choke on it because of the gag, and still the fucking keeps coming. The fucking always keeps coming. The fucking never stops. Can you see that, Cole? Can you see that picture?'

I didn't say anything.

'If this thing we're doing here – this money thing – doesn't happen the way my employers want it to happen, that other thing – the field, the van – will. With a few variations, such as you watching it happen to her. Your quim. She'll get to look you in the eye while her insides turn to pulp, and then she'll feel her throat slice open, and there'll be about a minute, minute and half as she realizes that she's bleeding to death, and the fucking will keep coming. The fucking never stops, Cole. And you'll get to watch it. You'll get to watch her watch you watch it.'

B glanced at his watch.

'Now did you want to tell me anything else about Mars, or did you want to make sure that little piece of bang-tail you're so fond of keeps her mouth shut?'

'She doesn't know anything to tell,' I said, struggling against the image of the van, the field, the pools of warm blood.

B nodded, then turned and sat at the card table again.

'We've got to go over some specifics, then, if you've got a few minutes.'

I realized I'd been holding my breath. I set Brasco down.

'That Beck's?' B asked, nodding at the six-pack sitting at my feet.

'Yeah.'

He nodded. 'You're just like me, Cole,' he said. 'I like my beer dark, too.'

B left my apartment three hours later, having gone over – and over and over and over – the plan to get the account numbers and the routing codes. It isn't something I'm proud of, and it isn't something I want to think about. I don't think I'll ever be able to think about the things B was willing to do to get Emily Cosgrove to share her information, because I know he would have never been able to do it were it not for me.

My part in it was simple. There were three payphones situated side by side outside the Publix in Mount Pleasant, just over the bridge from the city. Between midnight and two the night after the district received the money in its account, the phone would ring. B would be on the other end. He'd give me a phone number, then hold while I dialed it on one of the other payphones. That number would connect to a phone in another part of the world, answered by a man I'd never met and hoped I never would. B would then feed me the account and routing numbers, which I would then feed to him. Presumably he'd access the district's account, move the money, take fifty percent, and redirect the other half to my account, which I would have set up by then.

'How do I know your guy will send me my half?'

'You'll have to trust us.'

'Would you trust me if the situation was reversed?'

'The situation isn't reversed. The situation is what it is. You can either accept it or not.'

'I take all the heat on this. When I'm gone they come looking for me. You people have no risk.'

He shrugged. 'If you could do it without us you would.'

That was true.

'Why can't you just call your guy yourself? You don't need me playing middle-man at some grocery store somewhere.'

'This is the way it's done,' B had said. 'It's the only way it's done. None of this is negotiable.'

I knew good and well why, though. When the district realized the following morning they'd been robbed, there'd be shit hitting fans all over the place. Publix had cameras everywhere; inside the store, in the parking lot, at all the ins and outs. It would only be a matter of time before the phone records led them from Cosgrove's house to the phones at Publix. A quick check of the security tapes and there'd I'd be, a phone to each ear. They'd know I was working with someone, but they'd never know who. They never would know, either. These people had no permanent address, had no permanent friends, no permanent citizenship, no permanent anything, save wealth. They were wealthy and crafty and had an entire world in which to hide. I, on the other hand, was known, had a history, a face, and no experience at all in this most serious of games. The investigation would start with me. They'd set themselves to finding me, then squeezing me until I told them what I knew about the people I'd been working with. Which, aside from the fact that one of them had a little prick and was rather sensitive about it, was very little.

'What if she won't talk?'

'She'll talk,' B assured me.

'What if she won't?'

'She will.' He looked at me, and I thought I saw the slightest hint of a smile. 'Eventually they all talk.'

THIRTY-SEVEN

Collins' office; intermezzo

That'd been Monday. The next morning I was in Collins' office, sitting in one of the two vinyl chairs opposite his big mahogany desk, the whole room smelling of his after-shave – Brut, by Fabergé – and self-importance while he clipped his nails, leaned back in his chair, and regarded me like I was something he'd found in his soup.

'Archer,' he started, in that tone that told you nothing that came next would be anything you wanted to hear; it was all a bad business.

'Yes, sir?'

'We've got a problem here, Archer.'

'Sir?'

'Now I'm not gonna bullshit you, Archer, so don't you bullshit me.' He was working on a particularly stubborn hangnail on his left thumb. 'Can we agree on that?'

'Not to bullshit one another?'

'That's right. We're in here. Door's closed. No one's listening but you and me." Sniff. "Can we be men in here, Archer? Real men, I'm talking about. Not women or sissies with all the excuses and doubletalk and faggoty tears. Can we agree to do this thing we gotta do here that way, leave the puppy dogs and ice cream for the little girls?'

I nodded.

'Good. Seems ORION has you logged in middle of last month, after hours. Same time there were a few anomalous grade entries.' He said this, then set his fingernail clipper down, leveled his eyes on mine. 'Re-entries, actually. This mean anything to you, Archer?'

I chose my words very closely. It was the end of April; there were still five weeks before we disappeared.

'I think I need clarification as to what you're speaking of specifically, sir,' I said.

He grimaced. 'Okay,' he said, sliding open a drawer to his right, retrieving a manila folder and setting it on the desk before him.

'In this folder is all the clarification you'll ever need, Archer. We open this folder, and it's like opening a world of wonders. Every how-full-of-shit-am-I question you might be considering right now is going to be answered." Sniff. "Right now there's one copy of the stuff in this folder. Things don't go well with you in here this morning, by lunchtime there'll be ten. Betty'll fax copies to the district, from Waters down to personnel. The contents of this file will become agenda item number one on every DO desk until it's taken care of. Am I making myself clear here, Archer?'

'Yes, sir.'

'Good. Do you have a lawyer, Archer?'

'No, sir. Do I need one?'

He shrugged, a heavy lifting and lowering of his shoulders beneath his expensive suit. Ricke Collins, GQ educator, lover extraordinaire.

'A lot of that depends on you,' he said, resting his hands atop the closed folder. 'Maybe there's a way we can not worry about what's in this folder.'

There was a full half-minute of thick, uncomfortable silence in the room, time I spent picturing Savannah and myself lying side by side on a beach the color of bone, our skin an Inca gold, our troubles far away in some world that didn't exist for us anymore.

'Say—" sniff— "say you knew a teacher here had this unhealthy affection for one of his students. Now, maybe you do, maybe you don't. But let's just say for the moment that you did know this teacher. We're just speaking hypothetically here. And say you knew he'd accessed ORION and changed her grades. Maybe she paid him money, maybe she's showing him what teenage tongue on his balls feels like. Hell, he might even think he loves her and he's helping her out. The point is you know this about him. And you know your principal knows, knows enough to warrant initiating an investigation, legal proceedings, all the rest of it. Now let's assume this teacher you knew hadn't made himself many friends at the board, or the district office for that matter. Would you assume he was pretty much fucked?'

'I would assume he's in for some rough swimming, yes sir.'

He nodded softly. 'Sports analogies,' he said. Sniff. 'Always apropos, aren't they?'

I didn't say anything.

'Now say this principal was twenty-nine years into a thirty-year stint, and had recently accepted a superintendent's spot at a little piss-ant district couple-three hours up the road. Say this principal squeezed into that job against the wishes of some misguided members of the Board in that backward district, and that something like the situation we're speaking of here – and mind you, we're speaking only hypothetically, of course – would cause him a headache on the way out just as he was trying to ease into his next job.' He looked at me. 'No one likes a headache, Archer.'

'No sir,' I agreed. 'No one likes a headache.'

More silence.

'Say I pulled you in here,' sniff 'told you about this suspicion I had, about how this teacher changed grades for a little filly with a cute smile and a French vanilla ass. Would you warn him? Would you tell him we spoke?'

'Would you want me to?' I asked.

'Say I would.' Sniff. 'Do you think you could convince him to go in there, fix the grades back, then ease off? To lay low and coast the rest of the year through. Just do his job and keep his hands and dick to himself, leave the ittie-bittie-tittie alone until summertime, then get busy finding alternate employment.'

'I think I could convince him, yes sir.'

Mr. Collins nodded, the hypocrisy radiating off of him like cologne.

'I know it's tempting,' he said. 'Teachers,' sniff, 'have the toughest job in the world. Half these kids are raised in a home with no dad but plenty of cable TV, and they send their child to you and expect you to fill in the gaps where they've failed. The liberals and the bureaucrats have eviscerated the discipline code, and everyone's scared shitless they're going to be sued if they put their foot down too hard. So the foot never comes down, and the problems rise because of it. Hell, we can't even make the little shits stand for the pledge of allegiance anymore. What does that say about this system?' Sniff.

He sighed. 'Toss into all that a few hundred seventeen-year-olds swishing their little tails around the halls in those butt-twitcher skirts they're so fond of, and you've got a recipe for disaster. I understand that. I'm sympathetic to it. It's a tough gig, Archer, with shit pay, and I don't want you to think I don't appreciate the job you're tying to do.'

His words hung there, as though he were considering saying what came next, but then he simply tapped the desk and slid backwards in his roller-recliner-chair.

'Thanks for stopping by,' he said, sniffed. 'I think it's good we had this talk.'

'So do I, sir,' I said, standing.

I turned to go, then hesitated. Collins saw this.

'Was there something else?'

'Yes, sir. I was wondering if I might speak freely for a moment, off the record.'

He nodded. 'What's on your mind?'

'Well, assuming you had caught one of your teachers doing … doing what we just spoke of – hypothetically, of course – wouldn't you run the risk of an even bigger headache if it got out that you buried it instead of pushing it through the proper channels?'

'Good question, Archer.' Sniff. 'Couple ways you can answer it, too. One, I'm out of here in a matter of days. I think you might be, too. I'm betting you can keep yourself in line until May, when we both move on to greener pastures.'

Greener pastures, I thought. He had no idea.

'And the other?' I pressed.

He shrugged. 'You've got balls, Archer. I knew it way back at the beginning of the year, when you nailed that Watherstein kid for being a little shit in class. Called him a dirty Jew, remember that?'

'I didn't actually call him that,' I said. 'It was more of a –'

'Whatever,' he said, waving my words away. 'It was like that in the old days, when I was in the classroom.' Sniff. 'A kid gets out of line and you did what you had to do to get him back in. That was back before everyone got so sensitive.'

I tried to picture Collins in the classroom. He'd be one of those men you'd be afraid to challenge, because you knew if you did he'd take you out in the hall and smash you into a couple lockers on your way to the principal's office for a paddling.

'It takes balls to get through most anything in this life, Archer. But it's also balls that gets us in trouble. Your little thing with what's-her-name, perfect example.'

'I don't have a thing with anyone, sir.'

I considered asking him if Chessie had showed him what teenage tongue on the balls felt like, but I didn't. There was no need. We both knew the answer.

'No,' he said. 'No, of course not. That'd be against the law. If I thought you were sleeping with one of our students I'd have to call the police, have you taken off in handcuffs.'

He paused, searched my face for signs that the image bothered me. But the image I had was one of Chessie the Bad Student giving Collins the GQ principal head in the back of the Southern Belle. 'Have a nice day, Mr. Archer.'

'You do the same, sir,' I said, and I left his office.

'You can't be sure,' Savannah was saying. 'He's probably just bluffing you.'

'No,' I said, shaking my head, a useless gesture given that I was on my bed alone, talking to her through the phone. 'No, he knows. You could see it in his eyes.'

'Well, he knows then,' she said. 'So what? You said yourself he said he didn't want any headaches. He isn't going to do anything. He's just biding his time until the end of the year, waiting for his new job to start. I wouldn't worry.'

'I'm going to anyway.'

'Of course you are. How many days are there left?'

'Thirty, give or take a couple.'

'Are you going to be stressed like this until we leave?'

'Probably. There are a zillion things that could go wrong, Savannah.'

'I bet I can think of at least that many ways to help you relax.'

I smiled to the empty room. It was late, nearly eleven. The Kids had a test tomorrow. I still hadn't typed the first word.

'If I was there now I might try a few.'

'Like what?' I asked.

'Oh, I don't know. I've got a few tricks you respond to pretty well.'

'You've got more than a few, Savannah.' I closed my eyes. 'Tell me what you'd do if you were here.'

'Tell you?'

'Walk me through it.'

'Cole,' she giggled. 'My brothers – '

'You can whisper,' I said. 'Shut your door and whisper me through it. It'll help me sleep.'

'My door's already shut.'

'Are your lights on?'

'Yes.'

'Turn them off,' I said. 'Climb up in bed and get under the covers. Come on, sweetie.'

'It's too hot for covers.'

'Then you'll sweat,' I said. 'Even better. You're gorgeous when you sweat.'

'You're disgusting, Mr. Archer.'

'Oooh, teacher-student games. I'm going to have to keep you after class, Miss Bellington.'

There was a pause. 'My light's off,' she said.

'Are you in bed?'

'Uh-huh. Under the covers.'

'What are you wearing?'

'Nothing.'

'You're fibbing, but that's okay. I appreciate the effort. Keep going.'

And she did.

The plane – no puddle-jumper for this one, but a big 737 I'd caught in Rio two nights after leaving Roatan – touched down to my final destination at ten AM local time. Tezra had been right; it was very beautiful, very green, very wet, and very much an island. On the descent I could see every last inch of it, glistening like a string of emeralds floating in a sparkling blue pool.

I stepped off the plane – a carry-on in one hand and Brasco's carrier in the other – and climbed the metal flight of steps down to the tarmac. The plane was full of tourists, many of them American, most of them old, wearing wide-rimmed hats and colorful clothes and carrying cameras and guides and lots and lots of cash. A four-some of light-skinned black men started up with the reggae as we made our approach towards the main building, which was the only building, as far as I could tell.

I checked through customs, listed my purpose for visiting as 'pleasure', and slid the man a thousand US dollars when he handed me a quarantine form and advised me of his country's mandatory six-month quarantine for all domestic animals. The man palmed the ten hundreds and slipped them into his front pocket as he crumpled the form and tossed it into a trashcan behind him. He hadn't missed a beat.

That's another thing Tezra had mentioned. Nearly everyone who lives here is wealthy, except the people who were born and raised here. They survive off tips, kickbacks, and bribes. Someone with ready money should have no trouble quietly blending into the landscape and purchasing privacy.

An hour later and a friendly cabbie named George drove me to my hotel, which was the largest on the island. Two hundred seventy-five rooms, the brochure had proudly declared in bright blue letters. I'd reserved a month over the phone from Brazil, not long after leaving Roatan, and planned on using the time familiarizing myself with the island, learning the customs, and finding permanent residence. Maybe I'd buy some land, if any of it was for sale, and build a place. Maybe I'd rent a villa near the beach. Maybe I'd get tired of this place and leave in a few months, the way I'd left Roatan, and Mexico, and America, the way it seemed I was always leaving.

But even as I considered it I knew that I never would. I was tired of running. I was tired of not having a home. I needed a place of permanence, a port of call to cling to as my own. Here was as good as any, and better than most.

I spent that night alone – all my nights were spent alone now, even the ones spent with others – save Brasco, on the bed in the four-star hotel that jutted out of the ocean like Neptune's trident, writing letters to a Savannah that was gone forever.

THIRTY-EIGHT

The end begins;
Cole turns in his Long-Range Plan

When it went it went fast. I'd planned it for months, waited raptly for it for what seemed like years, but once it arrived it did so with a speed and weight I was ill-equipped to handle. For the large majority of that day – in retrospect it's difficult to conceive that it all went down over the course of just one day – I felt as though I were some observer, a benign interloper standing on the sidelines, watching it all unfold before me. Until the end, the very end, I was impotent.

June 1st – the district's big payday from the state – was a Thursday, which meant the day after the 1st – the 2nd, for those of you keeping score – was Friday, which meant we'd be leaving that morning. Savannah's desk would be empty and there'd be a substitute in my place, and no one would put two and two together – except possibly Collins, who wouldn't care at that point, his own greener pasture days within grasp, and Chessie's adolescent assets available for hire that night at the Belle – until we were below the border.

That was the plan, and it was laid as best I could manage. That I failed so miserably is no indication of how much I wanted it.

On the morning of June 1st, Savannah had worn one of my shirts to school, a long-sleeve, navy-blue button-down, Chaps logo over the left breast. She had it tucked into her jeans, which were old and tight and faded. I was sitting at my desk when she'd walked in. I felt myself go hard and remained seated, grading papers, trying to look busy. There were already five or six other students there, with a steady stream of them filing in behind her, and though I was past worry – had been for weeks now – I didn't want them to see me with a blue-veiner. That's the sort of thing high school kids don't miss. You can lecture them for hours on the Renaissance, give them notes on the overhead, hand out study-guides, outlines, timelines, all of it, and you'll still have students who don't know that Shakespeare wrote sonnets. But sprout a stiffie in front of them and they all see it, remember it, and take the opportunity to share it with everyone they meet for the rest of their educational careers.

She'd spent the night with me last night, and when I rose this morning to shave and shower I paused momentarily to look at her. She was on her stomach, still sleeping, her auburn hair fanned out behind her the color of secrets and fire, the cream-colored, translucent bedsheet pulled up to the small of her back, just covering my name. The room was dark but growing less so by the second as the June morning broke the blood meridian beyond my window and slipped between the blinds, giving the room the velvety, smoky hue of night's final moments. I could barely discern the outline of her small, pale breasts, hidden by her body. At the base of her spine danced a pool of shadow, breaking and fragmenting as the light dripped into the room. I closed my eyes and inhaled slowly through my nose, finding her scent beneath ours, holding it in the hopes of tasting it.

She was everything, my world, all I'd ever need, and we were almost there.

I dressed quietly, setting the clock on her side of the bed, the alarm set early enough to give her time to dress and make it to school. Or she could turn it off and sleep all day, wait for me to return. It didn't matter to me. None of it mattered to me. Tomorrow we were leaving before the sun came up, beginning the rest of our lives on our terms, at our pace, our way.

I got through the rest of that day the way I'd gotten through virtually all the others, watching the clock, waiting for bells, enduring each minute because it was a bridge to the next.

We were wrapping up Salinger's *The Catcher in the Rye*, closing out the final scene, the big surprise-ending where the students learn that Holden is writing everything from a mental institution, that he isn't really cool just because he can buy beer and order prostitutes and swear every five words. I remember when I was a sophomore in high school back in Georgia, and some grandstanding school Board member made a big stink about the book, said it taught immorality, said Holden was a negative role-model, had no respect for adult authority, etc, etc, blah blah blah. I can't remember the guy's name, but I remember all the teachers got a bit of a kick out of it, because this Board member's son was a sexual predator, listed on the city and state-wide registries. Apparently he'd been a coach at a prep school somewhere and had shoved his hand down some little boy's gym shorts. I can't remember how it all turned out, but I know we all enjoyed the book that much more because of it.

By five that evening the butterflies in my stomach were flailing away like mad. I felt on the verge of vomiting every few seconds. My stomach was lurching foul-smelling hiccup-burps up my throat with all the gentleness of a rabbit punch. There'd been a note on my door when I'd gotten home, a single word written across it. No name, and no matter. I'd gotten the point, and I knew the author.

Tonight, it'd said, and it was right. If everything had proceeded as it should have – which is to say, if the cumbersome, slow-turning wheels of big government had managed to stay on schedule – then sometime today while I was toiling away at The Creek, Columbia had wired countless millions to Winter's Cove, via one Emily Cosgrove.

I broke another rule and called Savannah, checking my watch. It was a quarter after five. I had Ramen noodles on the stove. Brasco was sleeping in the window, enjoying the early-summer sun. I reminded her to pack lightly, not to worry about leaving too much behind. We'd be able to buy whatever she needed once we got there. She said she would.

'Two bags' worth is all,' she'd said.

I told her she needed to leave her home as soon as possible and be at our meeting place by eleven. She asked why she couldn't just wait at home for me to call. I told her it wasn't safe. She asked me why. I told her I'd explain it to her later, not wanting to go into my fear of vans with no windows in wide open spaces.

'I can be gone in twenty minutes,' she assured me.

'Good. Stay away from places you normally go. Take alternate routes, if you can. If you think you're being followed –'

'Is something wrong?' she asked.

'No. I'm just being cautious.'

'Well, I'm leaving right after we get off the phone, and I'll stay gone. I'll meet you at eleven.'

'Perfect,' I said.

'And my brothers? How long do you think before we can send for them?'

'They'll be watching for that. We'll have to wait a while. A few months. Six, nine. Maybe a year.'

I'd bought her a cell phone two days ago exclusively for tonight. Before we left I'd toss it in a trashcan somewhere, or give to a stranger on the street, let them make all the calls they wanted with it. But for now I had to be able to get in touch with her, should something go wrong. I reminded her to keep it with her, to keep it on.

I'd asked her if she was nervous. She said no. I asked what she was doing tonight.

She said she had to go tell someone goodbye. I asked whom. She said an old friend, and I hadn't pressed the point. I should have, but I didn't. Instead I told her I loved her. She told me she knew, she could feel it, and that she believed in me and trusted me and loved me, no matter what happened.

No matter what happened, she said.

No matter what happened.

By four I'd eaten the noodles, and was resting for the last time of my life on that old garage-sale couch, waiting for B to call.

At 8:45 PM, Thursday, June 1st, my telephone rang, pulling me from a semi-sleep in which I'd been trying to focus on not throwing up. I knew who it was before I answered it.

'Hello.'

'It's time. Assume your station.'

'You said between ten and eleven.'

'We're moving things up a bit.'

'Why?'

'Why's not important right now. Have you set up your account?'

'Yes. Where are you?'

'I'm on my way. You need to be there in half an hour.'

The line went dead with a click.

I went to the toilet and leaned over it for several minutes, my mouth pouring saliva like a faucet. I squeezed my eyes shut until the nausea subsided. Then I gathered my keys and wallet and headed for the Publix in Mount Pleasant, fifteen minutes away.

By 9:08 PM I was there, standing before the phone, waiting for it to ring. People passed behind me pushing carts filled with food; the electric doors slid open in a whisper and rushed cool, conditioned-air past me, chilling the sweat that had begun to gather along my neck, back, and forearms. The security camera, angled downward at the phones and me standing at them, taped it all for later viewing pleasure.

Eleven minutes later the phone rang.

'I'm here.'

'Good. Stand by.'

I could hear crying in the background; of pain, not sadness.

'What's going on there?'

'Business. I'll be calling within the hour. Stay there.'

More crying. Higher-pitched. A long, squalling sound. A baby.

'What the fuck are you doing over there?'

'Don't concern yourself with it. You worry about answering that phone when it rings. If someone else tries to use it, you tell them no. Be as insistent as you need.'

The baby's cries kept on, but they sounded muffled now.

'Listen, we talked about this. I told you not the baby. If you want to scare Cosgrove a bit, fine, but not the baby.'

But he'd already hung up.

I called Savannah's cell phone, but there was no answer. I waited five minutes, then tried again. Nothing. Five minutes later the same thing. And five minutes later. Then two minutes later. And all the while the sound of that baby screaming echoing throughout my head, growing louder and more desperate, and the image of B's massive hands atop Brasco, just resting there on his spine like that, pressing him down into the table, not hurting him – not yet – but not letting him move, either. I'd thought then that those hands could crush Brasco's back into powder, that B could do something like that and get up and wash his hands as though he'd just squashed a spider.

Tell me again, he'd said, about her family.

What if she won't talk, I'd asked.

She will. Eventually they all talk.

But they don't. They don't all talk eventually. Emily Cosgrove's little granddaughter couldn't talk. All she could do was cry.

I was at her front door by a quarter to ten that night, the same front door I'd watched Ricke Collins stroll into after the Southern

Belle. I knocked, every nerve-ending on fire. A little girl of maybe eight answered. Her face was wet and sticky with tears. Her nose was running.

I didn't say anything. I stepped past her, shutting and locking the door behind me. The television was turned up loud, loud enough to drown out all but the most piercing scream, but not so loud the neighbors come over to ask you to turn it down.

I glanced back at the little girl and she pointed past me, down the hall. I nodded, walked down the hall, and there was B, Emily Cosgrove, and Emily's little granddaughter, wearing nothing but a diaper. B was sitting in the rocking chair. He was holding her. He was feeding her a bottle.

Emily Cosgrove was on the floor, her face a glistening wash of tears. She was resting back on her haunches, her hands over her mouth, ready to catch a scream. Eye-shadow and lipstick were smeared over her face in a sort of upward, diagonal arrow, like a bizarre war-paint. Her hands were shaking.

'What's going on here, B?'

'Where's the little girl?' B asked.

'She's in the hallway.'

'Annabelle,' B called out. 'Oh, Annabelle. Come on back in here, sweetheart.'

She came walking in the room, her hands folded in front of her, her chin down. She was trying not to cry.

'Sit over there next to your mama, Annabelle,' B said from the rocking chair, which he was rocking in. 'That's a girl.'

'What are you doing with the baby?' I asked.

'You aren't supposed to be here, Cole. What did I tell you about sticking to the plan?'

'I heard the baby. There wasn't supposed to be anything with the baby. We discussed this.'

He ignored me. The baby sucked hungrily at the bottle, her little hands resting along the side of it, guiding it into her mouth.

'*You are my sunshine, my only sunshine,*' B was singing softly. His hands – his hands far too enormous for just one man – were holding her the same way they'd been resting atop Brasco. They looked like steel traps, waiting to snap shut.

'Please,' Emily was saying. I realized then she'd been saying it since I'd walked in. In her terror, she'd considered me someone who could help.

'You make me happy, when skies are gray.' B was looking down lovingly at the baby, as though it were his first granddaughter, and there he was at the hospital, holding her and feeling all the wonderful things grown people feel when they hold a baby that's related to them.

'Did you know,' B was saying, still looking down at the little girl, 'that all babies are girls at first?'

I didn't say anything. I was thinking about a van in a field somewhere, and fighting to stave off the accompanying images.

The sound of the television blared in the background. A familiar commercial was on at the moment, but I couldn't place it just then.

'I asked you a question, Emily,' B said. She jolted as though a wave of electricity had been pumped through her. 'You know that all babies are girls at first? In the womb. Did you know that, Emily?'

Emily shook her head. 'N – no.'

B just nodded. 'It's true. Boys are the weaker sex. We're all XX's for the first few hours of our lives. For some – for the weaker ones – a little piece of that second X breaks off, leaving a Y behind in its place.' He lifted his head and looked directly at Emily.

'Isn't that shit fascinating, Emily?'

'B,' I said, but he cut me off with a look that told me absolutely everything I'd never wanted to hear.

'How strong do you think little Sterling is here?'

At that Emily let out a long, wailing yelp, burying her face in her hands to muffle it.

'Please please please pleasepleaseplease don't hurt her don't hurt her please oh God don't hurt her I'll do whatever you want whatever you want I swear to God just please don't hurt her ...'

'Nobody here wants to hurt anyone, do they Cole?'

'No,' I said.

'But I need something from you. It's something you can give me to make me go away forever. You'd like that, wouldn't you Emily?' He asked this last in the tone of someone talking to their five-year-old about ice-cream on the way home from little league practice. If you're good we'll stop by the Baskin-Robbins and get ice-cream. You'd like that, wouldn't you?

'Yes,' her trembling mouth tried to say, but nothing came out.

B stood. 'Good.' He squatted down, set the baby – Sterling, her name, and I'll never forget it – in the rocking chair, and stood. Little Sterling kicked and pumped her fists a bit.

B then looked at Emily, a shivering, leaking mass of muffled yelps and moans. She couldn't take her eyes off the baby. He looked at me, his face stone, but I could tell he wasn't pleased and considered me something he'd have to deal with later. How I wasn't sure, and wasn't willing to think about.

He removed from a side-harness a revolver the size of a pot roast. Emily's entire mass tightened and shook even more frenetically. Her whimpers became screams, only partially stifled.

He then turned a little, keeping the rest of the room in his peripheral vision, and slid the muzzle about half an inch into the baby's mouth. You could see her rooting on it, sucking the mouth of the gun the way she would a bottle or pacifier.

'Oh God no please no please –'

'Stop crying, Emily.'

Emily buried her face in her hands and shook her head from side to side.

'I can't! Don't you see I can't you can't do that please don't do that I'll do anything! Anything at all! Just don't hurt her. Don't hurt her please!'

'I've already told you I don't want to hurt anyone. But I need to know you appreciate how serious a situation this is. I'm not here for fun. You have something I want, and you're going to give it to me, Emily. You're going to give it to me before I leave. Let that be the point from which all your thoughts and actions begin tonight. You are going to give me what I want. The only question is how much suffering you and your family endure before I get it. And Emily,' B said, as didactically as ever, 'the only person who can answer that question is you.'

He pulled the trigger back. Little Sterling kept sucking, oblivious to it all.

'B,' I said. 'That's enough. For the love of God it isn't worth this.'

'You've got three seconds to walk out of here and get back to your station.' With his free hand he removed a small cell phone. 'In five minutes that payphone is going to ring. If you answer it, we'll proceed as planned. If not, consider the arrangement off. You can live your life with the knowledge that you killed an entire family.' He glanced down at the baby. 'Little angel and everything.'

I squatted down next to Emily Cosgrove. 'Don't worry, Mrs. Cosgrove,' I said, touching her shoulder. The little girl who'd let me in was curled up next to her, hiding her face from it all. She had her hands pressed over her ears.

I leaned forward and pressed my mouth next to Emily's ear. 'Give him what he wants and he'll go away. Just tell him. Whatever he asks, tell him. Please, Mrs. Cosgrove,' I pleaded, and I wasn't surprised to find that I meant it. I didn't doubt B's resolve at all. I didn't think Emily Cosgrove did, either.

What I still had to learn that night, though, what I would have to find a way to live with for the rest of my life, was my own resolve.

B had nothing on me.

Within seconds of my reaching the phone outside the Publix it began ringing.

'I'm here.'

'Good. Coming here was stupid. You're an amateur, Cole.'

'Is the baby all right?'

'Don't concern yourself with it. You knew the possibility for collateral damage when you set this in motion.'

'I did not sign on for baby-killing, goddammit.'

'It's not something for nothing in this world. Do your penance on your own time. Dial this number.'

'Not until I know the baby's all right.'

I heard him breathing through his nose.

'You don't want to draw lines in the sand with me, Cole. There are things in the world that'll make you shrivel up and want to die just from seeing them.'

'I will not be a party to killing innocent children, you fucking sick fuck!'

There was a moment of agonizing silence in which I was sure I'd hear a gunshot, and everything around me started to close in. My head began to swim; the world whirled.

Emily was on the line.

'Please do what he says,' she whispered between sobs. 'Please. Please don't let him hurt my babies.'

My hands were shaking, and B was back on the phone.

'Here's the number.'

I could hear the baby crying again in the background as B gave me the number. I wedged the phone into the crook of my neck and punched the number into the other phone with fingers I had trouble steadying.

'It's ringing,' I said, a phone in each hand now.

B said nothing. I could still hear him breathing. In the background I could hear little Sterling cooing. I tried to focus on that sound but I couldn't. I tried to picture Savannah's face but couldn't hold that either.

The phone stopped ringing with a click, followed by the voice of another man. I couldn't tell if it was Philip or not. Philip with his sub-par cock.

'This line is clean for sixty seconds,' the man said. 'You have the account numbers?'

I spoke into the other phone. 'They're waiting, B.'

'Good. Read these numbers exactly as I give them to you. 0-595-09399-X.'

I repeated the numbers and dashes into the phone in my left hand.

B continued. '09-2919-79 –'

Again I repeated.

'0-1301-984.'

Once more into the phone in my left hand.

'Very good, Cole,' B said. 'The first number is the District's holding account. The second one is the passcode. The third is the routing number.'

I repeated this information as well.

'Excellent,' said the man on the other end. 'Now listen closely, because we're down to a few seconds. I'm going to give you a phone number in Singapore. It'll be active in precisely five minutes and will stay that way for precisely two. This is your only window, and there will not be another. Call the number and wait for the recorded message. Then leave your holding institution and relevant account numbers. Provided everything has been handled properly on your end, your share of the money will be deposited within twenty-four hours of it clearing our account.'

He gave me the number; I dropped B's phone and hurriedly scribbled it across my left forearm, then hung up the phone.

Across the parking lot, on the other side of Johnnie Dodds Blvd, was the BankAmerica, its big, rotating clock shining through the night like a beacon. It was 10:22 and 88 degrees.

'B,' I said into the other phone. 'B.'

But the line was dead.

Five minutes, the man had said.

Enough time for B to leave Cosgrove's and get here. Show me how unhappy he is with my interrupting his work like that.

10:23, the clock said. Still 88 degrees.

I walked into Publix and bought a pack of gum, a small keychain-size can of mace, and an eight-inch carving knife. The mace wouldn't do anything more than piss B off, if I was even able to hit him in the eyes with it. But maybe it would buy me a few seconds. Enough to get away, in any case. Or maybe enough to stick the knife in his throat, if I could bring myself to do something like that.

And it occurred to me then for perhaps the millionth time since I'd called Grey and first contacted Philip that there existed the very real possibility – probability, even, depending on how deep your paranoia ran – that he and whoever he was working with would simply take all the money and continue playing musical yachts and time-zone games, leaving me to spend the rest of my life a fugitive, on the lam, without so much as a dime. Savannah had said she'd come anyway. But if that was what she'd be coming with, I had no right to let her.

By the time I got back to the phones the BankAmerica clock read 10:27. It had cooled down to 87.

I scanned the parking lot and saw no sign of B. I held the tiny single-serving can of mace in my right palm, lifted the receiver, and dialed the number scrawled across my arm. The knife was still in the plastic grocery bag.

When the machine answered, I followed my instructions, reading off from memory the account numbers to my bank – the National Bank of Antigua – and wishing that what I was doing wasn't so undeniably wrong so that I could at least pray to God to help me.

By eleven I was back at my apartment – the mace clutched tightly in one hand, grocery-store carving knife in the other – half-expecting B to be waiting for me again.

I shut and locked the door behind me, leaving the lights off. Brasco was at my feet, purring and chirping as he rubbed against my shins. I squatted down, set the knife on the carpet, and scratched his ears and chin for a few seconds. The apartment around me was deafeningly quiet.

First I called Savannah again. Still there was no answer. I put an inordinate amount of energy into keeping out thoughts of B and her together, B doing what it was he so clearly enjoyed doing, Savannah not understanding any of it, only that it all had something to do with me.

My single duffel bag – packed with two pairs of underwear, two t-shirts, a pair of jeans, pair of shorts, a gray nylon sweat-suit, sneakers, and sandals – sat in the center of my bed.

I grabbed from the top shelf in my closet the old, worn shoebox I'd spent the previous two months filling with hair dye (two shades of blonde, a jet black, and a reddish-brown), colored contacts (two different greens and three different browns), scissors, putty, (for that Kennedy-esque cheek-pad look), and sunless tanning cream. I stuffed the box into the duffel bag. It bulged the bag to the point where I couldn't zip it closed, so I removed one of the t-shirts, one of the pairs of underwear, and the sandals, tossing them to the floor. It zipped this time, though barely.

I called Savannah again. It rang forty-three times. Forty-three times her cell phone rang without her answering it, without a mechanical voice coming on to tell me that the person I was calling was either out of area or had their phone off. Which meant she wasn't out of area, and she didn't have the phone off. It was on. She just wasn't answering it. Which meant she wasn't able to answer it.

I took the duffel bag and tossed it by the front door. The Honda had a full tank of gas. I'd gotten it tuned up and had the oil changed two days ago. From beneath my mattress I'd retrieved $2,700 in cash, courtesy of those great American leeches, MasterCard and Visa. I'd just assisted a professional extortionist and probable murderer in stealing God knew how many millions of dollars from the State of South Carolina. This was done and couldn't be undone. I had to leave, and I had to leave tonight.

I dialed her phone again. This time I let it ring forty-seven times before I hung up.

At 11:20 I called Jules. We'd met at Tommy Condon's downtown a few evenings back, laughing and smoking cigars and telling old war stories over salmon and dark beer. We'd sat out on the veranda and watched the sun sink beneath the horizon and breathed in that Charleston harbor air and worked our way through the history of our friendship, the cities in which we'd gotten plowed, the girls we'd hooked up with, the ones we hadn't but lied about anyway.

It was a bittersweet experience for me; I knew this would be our last time doing this. I was trading my friendship in – along with everything else – for a stolen fortune and foreign soil.

Jules felt it too, I think.

'You wanna talk about it?'

I'd sipped my beer, managed a smile, and shook my head. 'Maybe one day,' I'd said.

Jules had nodded. He never pushed. It was a good quality in a friend, and a rare one.

He'd taken a long, slow sip of his Guinness, then held the beer up in the waning sunlight and looked at it almost reverently. 'They're plenty of days left, pal,' he'd said, sipping again. 'Plenty of days.'

I'd nodded, and we'd both known it was a lie.

Jules answered on the fourth ring.

'Juliet,' I said, trying to sound okay, it's cool, everything's everything.

'Colon cancer,' he said. 'How goes it?'

My guts were burning but I focused on my breathing and tried to push through it. 'I catch you at a bad time?'

'I'm taking a shit.'

'I'm surprised you're there. You staying in tonight?'

'I'm waiting on Skylar, that fucking mollycoddle. He's supposed to have been here half an hour ago. Jenna's working the bar over at Liquid Lounge so we're gonna hit that for a few.'

'Liquid Lounge, huh? Classy place.'

'Yeah, but Skylar's banging Jenna so the drinks are free. He said she's got a clit the size of a fucking thumb. Rubs the roof of his mouth when he's dining downtown. Makes my stomach turn just to think about it. Hey, you wanna come, man? We're not staying there any longer than it takes to knock back a few shots. We'll probably hit Jack the Ripper's or Blind Tiger. Maybe even end up at Wet Willie's, check out the tourist pouch. You should come. Do you good to get that little girl off your mind.'

'I'd like to, Jules, but tonight's not good. I've got some things I need to take care of.'

'They'll be there tomorrow, teacher. Fuck it. Come out tonight and we'll turn it loose like we used to. I got a case of Icehouse tall-boys sitting in my fridge. We'll get all fucked up and go hang out at the dorms. We can even give ol' Max a call, see if that Jew fuck can pry himself away from his wife long enough to hang with men.'

'I wish I could, man,' I said, and I did. Right then I wished I could have my old life back, that life I spent so much time trying to change or escape, where I had a job and a couple solid friends and I lived in the most beautiful city in the world. In that life a big night was getting drunk with Jules in one bar or another, smoking cigars and telling lies and looking for girls who looked like they might be looking for us. I puked from alcohol then; now I was puking from anxiety, my asshole stayed puckered with fear, and I would spend the rest of my life wondering what a normal life might have held for me.

I saw a bumper-sticker once that said: Hate your job? Join the club. It's called Everybody and it meets at the bar. I laughed, because I did hate my job, and I'd met many people at many bars in my day. That sticker's point was clear. Life's tough. Bills have to be paid. Working isn't always about self-fulfillment or finding your purpose. Sometimes it's about keeping the lights turned on, or putting a carton of orange juice in the fridge. Work is that thing you do to stay alive, so you can spend the rest of your time doing those things you do that make you happy. Work is survival.

The sticker hadn't read: Hate your job? Collude with criminals who feed guns to babies. Steal millions and run the rest of your fucking life.

No. The sticker hadn't said that, but that's what I'd read. I'd looked at what my life had become and wanted something different. I'd fallen in love with a seventeen-year-old girl and discovered a need to protect and provide for her. I heard the call of worlds away and wanted to answer them with her, and had put everything I was and would ever be on the line in the hopes of making it happen.

Now, talking to Jules on the phone was as close as I could afford to get to the life I had used to lead. His offer to go out drinking might as well have been an offer to put on diapers and sit around sipping bottled formula while we shit ourselves; both were phases of my life I'd necessarily outgrown.

'Listen,' I said – thinking that this was survival too, this here, this thing that I was doing with Savannah and B and Cosgrove and her little ones, this was about surviving too – 'I gotta tell you something.'

'Talk, motherfucker. I'm listening. You don't mind if I wipe my ass do you?'

'You have to let me get through it without interrupting me, though. I don't know if I can say it right in spurts and jerks.'

'Cole, if you tell me you're a fag I swear to God I don't know what I'll do.'

'Shut the fuck up for a minute here. This is serious.'

'I'll shut the fuck up when you tell me you're still a cunt-hunter.'

'Jules, just listen. I got this thing I have to do, and after I do it there's going to be a lot of things said. A lot of people are going to ask questions, and a lot more are going to have answers that aren't always right. I wanted to let you know at the outset, for lots of reasons, really, but mostly because I think I'd be hurt if the situation was reversed and I found out the same time everyone else did. Particularly after all you and I have been through.'

'What's going on, Cole? You in some sort of trouble?'

'Yeah, I am, but that's not what I'm talking about. I'm talking about all of it, and you'll see soon enough. But I wanted to tell you something else, too, so just shut up and listen because this sort of shit is hard for me to say, even though I know it needs to be said.'

I paused. Jules didn't speak.

'You've been a good friend, Jules. The best. I know I can lean on you no matter what happens in life, and I'd lean on you now through this if I thought I could do it without hurting you too much. But I can't, so I'm not going to try. This thing I'm doing I'm doing for me, because if I don't do it I won't survive. I'm not cut out for things the way you are. I'm not made of whatever stuff it is that lets people get up and go to work everyday and come home and live their little lives of silent envy and constant want. I thought that was a good thing at first but I'm not so sure now. About all I am sure about is that if I keep doing what I've been doing I'll die. Not physically, but there are plenty of dead people walking around out there, and I don't want to walk with them. I could talk about this all night but what I'm trying to say is pretty much just thank you, bro. Thank you for being the pal you are, for being that rock I could count on for these past however many years. I wish it wasn't so hard for me to say but I love you and I hope I've been half the friend to you that you've been to me. I don't think I have, but I tried. I want you to know I tried.'

'I'm coming over.'

'You don't have to, man. But I know you would. I know you always would.'

'No, no, no. Fuck that. I'm coming over right now. Something's wrong, bro. Something's obviously wrong when you're talking like that. I'll be there in ten minutes.'

'Don't. I won't be here. I've got to go take care of something. But I'll stop by Liquid Lounge tonight.'

'No you won't.'

'I will. I promise.'

'When?'

'In an hour. Wait for me at the bar.'

'An hour from now,' Jules said. 'One hour from right now you'll be at Liquid?'

'Sixty minutes,' I said. 'Clock's ticking.'

He paused. 'I'll see you then, then.'

'Yeah,' I said. 'See you then.'

And again we both knew it was a lie. But that's one of the hallmarks of a truly good friend. You can lie to them and they know you're doing it, and you know they know, which means you aren't really lying at all. You're just being pals.

'Yellow.'

'Last I checked, yellow was a color, not a greeting.'

'Well Mr. Archer,' Capers said. 'Fancy this. Is it 11:30 at your house? Because it's 11:30 here at mine.'

'Yeah, I know. I've got to leave town for a couple days. I wanted to call and say bye before I did.'

'Is everything all right?'

'Yeah, everything's fine. My mother's broken her leg and needs someone around for a while. Her sister's flying in from Oklahoma Monday night but I don't want her alone until then. I went ahead and scheduled a sub for tomorrow and Monday. Hate to burn the days up this close to the end but I don't have any choice, really. Mom's always been so damned independent; she was trying to fix a gutter by herself and she fell off the ladder.'

'Ouch. Just a leg?'

'Yeah. Lucky she isn't hurt worse. She'll be fine. It'll be an inconvenience more than anything else.'

'Well, you're doing the right thing. Don't worry about the kids. Unless you're testing tomorrow you probably didn't even need to call for a sub. We don't get much out of them this late into the year. Aside from one last vocab quiz I'm showing movies from here out. But I'll poke my head in here and again, make sure things are going smoothly. You just worry about looking after your mom. Moms are special, you know.'

'Yeah,' I said. 'I know.'

'You driving tonight?'

'Early tomorrow. Listen, I appreciate all you did for me this year. Helping me out, guiding me, all that stuff.'

'Part of my job, Mr. Archer.'

'Yeah, I know. But...what the hell. Thanks. In case I get hit by a meteorite on the way back from Augusta, I wouldn't want to croak without telling you I appreciate your looking out for me this past year.'

'It wasn't hard, Cole. I can tell you're worried about not getting offered a contract for next year, but don't be. There are plenty of other districts out there who'd love to have a young, male, and good English teacher. We'll find you a job. If it doesn't work out in Winter's Cove, I'll put in a few calls. See what I can do.'

'I appreciate it.'

'Drive safely. And take care of that mama of yours.'

'I will. One more thing, then I'll let you sleep.'

'Shoot.'

'If you ever did get that sailboat, would you really name it Winter's Cove?'

He laughed. 'Who knows? Good sailboats can run into the six figures. It'll take a hell of a raise for me to go shopping for one anytime soon.'

'Yeah, well, you never know.'

'This is true,' Capers said. 'You damn well never do.'

When I hung up, it was 11:40.

Almost Friday.

Time to run.

Savannah's cell rang from 11:47 to 11:51 without an answer. My stomach tightened into a small, burning fist. My hands were shaking again.

I stood there for a moment, considering my options. They were rapidly dwindling. If I assumed B was out of the picture – a generous assumption and quite possibly wrong, but one I had to make for logistics' sake at this point – then I was left with the aftermath of his visit to Emily Cosgrove's. If she was still alive she would have called the cops by now. They'd be at her house at this point, perhaps had been for hours. I don't know if she recognized me – we'd never spoken in person before, though she had taught one of the induction classes I'd attended back in February – and I couldn't remember if B had used my name. I thought he had, but so much of those few minutes was hazy now. The sight of B sliding the barrel of his gun into that baby's rooting mouth was all I could remember with any real clarity.

They'd trace the calls, though. B had called me at Publix from Cosgrove's phone. They might even know that already. It was an intentional move on his part meant to keep my feet to the fire. If I was on tape there'd be no backing out, no changing my mind, no deathbed discovery of God. I'd be more malleable then, B would have assumed. And, of course, he'd been right.

The Publix security tapes would have me standing there like a thespian on stage, lead role in one serious sequence of criminal events. I never looked directly at the camera, but there'd be a good minute, minute and a half of my profile on tape. And when I'd walked in to buy the mace and knife? I'd lowered my head and looked at my feet, but I doubt it mattered. The FBI has people trained in that sort of thing.

I had to go. Soon.

But there was one more small piece of business to attend to first.

Superintendent Charles Waters lived in an old, historic section of Winter's Cove called Tea Tree Plantation. In the days of Southern slavery Tea Tree Plantation had stretched across most of the area that was now Winter's Cove proper, producing more tea for colonials and, later, the Confederates, than any other single plantation in the South. Now it was mostly pavement – roads and strip malls, Wal-Marts and self-storage centers, apartments and corner gas stations. Tea Tree Plantation existed only in name these days – like many of Winter's Cove's older families – and had been reduced to a mid-sized neighborhood filled with massive houses for people who made a lot of money and needed others to know it.

I'd never been to Waters' house before. I'd looked it up in the phone book a few weeks ago, when I'd decided to make this last stop before leaving town. There was a certain touch of the poetic there for me; Waters was the man who would ultimately decide to fire me at year's end, thanks to my challenging him at the Board meeting. And it was Waters who'd have to deal with the maelstrom of bad publicity and even worse reality once I was gone.

I pulled up in front of his big, spacious three-story at 12:35 AM. All the lights were off save the one on the porch, which glowed against the red brick and made the house look even bigger because of it. There were several large, sweeping oaks in his front lawn. As I walked across it, carrying my Long-Range Plan in my hands, I wondered if Superintendent Waters even owned a lawn-mower.

I stepped up the three brick steps to his large wrap-around porch, and leaned my Long-Range Plan against the shiny brass kick-plate running along the base of his oak wood door. Forty-seven pages, three-hole punched and bound at Kinkos for a $1.99. Forty-seven pages representing some twenty-plus hours of my life, the only writing by this writer old Waters was ever likely to read. My fucking Long-Range Plan.

It was supposed to be the definitive document of your first-year teaching, a summary of everything you planned on doing in the classroom, right down to the number of staples you used. How you graded, samples of your lesson plans, your tests, the textbook you used. How you communicated with parents, how you maintained discipline, what your goals were for your students' learning.

I started to walk away, then stopped. I'd spent a long time on my Long-Range Plan – LRP, as it was referred to in teacher-talk. I'd spent many a night typing away as I waited for Savannah to call.

I squatted over on my haunches and retrieved it. The front light was just bright enough for me to read by. It occurred to me that a concerned neighbor might glance out their window and decide to call Waters or, worse, the police, informing them that someone strange was loitering on their front porch at nearly one in the morning, but I didn't care anymore.

I flipped the document open to page 1.

Table of Contents

Description of Students
Learning/Developmental Goals
Units of Instruction
Instructional Materials and Resources
Major Assessments
Rules for Student Behavior
Student Records

Daily Classroom Procedures
Communication with Parents

I fanned through various sections. My Description of Students was legit, but from there I'd deviated enough to ensure that the bureaucrats cloistered away in their little carrels at the Winter's Cove District Office would never offer me another contract. Contract. That's k in law-lingo, the brass ring in teacher-town, and none of it mattered to me anymore.

I read in a book one time that once you let go and realize that the rules are someone else's problem, all you've got left is freedom. I wasn't sure if that was true or not, but I had decided some time ago that the rules didn't apply to me anymore. The freedom part I was still working on.

Confession's good for the soul, they say, and I think they're right. For the most part. My Long-Range Plan was my confession; in it I'd documented my first – and last – year as a teacher, confessing all of it, my affection for Savannah, my decision to rob the school district, my plans for the two of us disappearing. And it was good for me. The writing was, as it always is, an exercise in catharsis. I didn't think Waters would find it the best he'd read, but he'd read it all, every word, of that I was certain. My guess is he'd be sure to pass it on once he was done, too. And that's all any author can really ask for, after all.

But I changed a few things, of course. Any writer knows the value of reality in his writing. The backbone of all the best fiction is fact. How well it comes off is a matter of how well those facts are twisted and obscured. So I added in a number of details that would throw them off-track for a long, long while, and probably for good. I suggested some things that weren't true, and went to great pains to lead them in directions I was sure I'd never go. How well it would work I guess Savannah and I would see down the line.

I set the LRP back against the kick-plate. Then, for reasons I didn't bother trying to determine, I unzipped my pants and fumbled my prick free. I pissed all over it, over the nice Kinkos flexi-folder they'd given me, over the forty-seven pages, over the shiny brass kick-plate and the expensive oak-wood door. When I was done, I zipped up, turned, and left.

When I walked into my apartment, Brasco was waiting, it was 1:21AM, and the telephone was ringing.

THIRTY-NINE

Cole considers legal counsel;
just drive

C'ole?'
    'Savannah. Where the hell are you? I've been calling all
night. We needed to be on the road hours ago.'

'I – I'm in trouble, Cole. I'm in big trouble.'

'Are you hurt? Where are you? What's going on?'

'I think he's dead, Cole. I think I killed him. I didn't mean to do
it – I was just trying to get him off me. I promise I didn't mean to
hurt – oh Cole, I think he's dead and I've killed him.'

'Killed who? What the fuck is going on, Savannah? Where are
you?'

'I didn't want you to know. It's the last thing I had to do before I
left. I had to tell him goodbye. I had to let him know I was going to
be all right. But he wouldn't let me leave. He'd been drinking and
he wouldn't –'

'Savannah, listen to me. We need to get out of here immediately.
We need to go now. Tell me where you are.'

'Embassy Suites downtown.'

'What room?'

'I don't know.'

'All right. Wait outside. I'll be there in ten minutes.'

'I can't.'

'You can't what?'

'I can't wait outside, Cole. I'm – oh, Cole, I'm so sorry. I'm so
sorry about all of this. I only wanted to tell him goodbye. I –'

'Savannah, why can't you wait outside? Are you hurt? Did
someone hurt you?'

'Sort of. Most of the blood isn't mine. But it's all over me. I have
– I need to shower. I'm covered all over in blood. I think he's dead,

Cole. I think he's dead and I think I killed him.'

'Savannah, listen to me. I can't get to you if I don't know what room you're in. It's a big hotel. Can you check the door, tell me the room?'

'Wait a second,' she said, her voice cracking, wavering, breaking across the surface like ice atop a lake. There was ten seconds of silence, followed by her voice again.

'Room 408. Fourth floor. I'm scared, Cole.'

'It's going to be okay,' I said, not bothering to tell her that I was scared too. 'I'll be there in ten minutes. Don't open the door for anyone except me. Make sure it's locked.'

'I love you,' she said.

'I love you, too,' I replied.

I drove as fast as I could without drawing attention to myself. The idea of getting pulled by the boys in blue at this stage of the whole ordeal was more irony than I could stomach.

At 1:40 AM I pulled my little Honda into the Embassy Suites parking lot. Two minutes later I was knocking on the door of room 408, Savannah was opening it, and the hell that was within entered my consciousness forever.

'Oh my God,' – stepping quickly into the room, the air smelling of old sweat and warm meat, shutting the door behind me – 'Oh my God, Savannah, what the fuck happened?'

She was wrapped in a towel, her hair dripping wet, her skin moist with steam. From between her legs a drip-drip-drip of blood fell steady as a leaky faucet, thumping softly into the plush carpet.

I saw her eye, then, too. The left one, raw and swollen, the beginnings of a bruise forming, a hint of blue and black and yellowish-green rising beneath the surface.

There were large welts on her neck – three, no, four – that were clearly bite marks. Her lower lip was split down the center, secreting a shiny mixture of blood and saliva.

But none of this prepared me for him.

He was naked, his white, puffy body lying prone on the floor beside the bed. I stepped gingerly around Savannah and made my way towards him. His head was twisted nearly all the way around, his neck craned at an angle necks were never meant to know.

'His neck's broken,' I said.

She didn't say anything.

'What happened, Savannah?' I asked, keeping my voice calm and steady, for her sake as well as mine.

'What happened up here?'

She'd sat down on the edge of the bed and pulled her knees up to her chest. A thin river of blood had inched its way down her inner thigh and calf and was pooling around her heel.

'I don't know,' she said, her eyes glazed. 'I...I only came here to tell him goodbye. I knew we were leaving and I felt like he should know I'd be okay.'

I looked down at the pudgy corpse at my feet. I could smell him now; a thick, meaty smell of poorly gelded sausage. A trickle of blood escaped his nose and mouth.

A million thoughts swarmed throughout my head, none of them cohesive or lucid enough to grab hold of.

'Who the hell is he?' I finally managed.

Savannah didn't say anything.

I tapped his side with my foot. His skin felt rubbery and tight. His hair was matted through with blood. He looked to be in his mid-forties or so, but it was difficult to tell. Death, head trauma, and nudity can all be convincing obscurers of age.

'Who is he, Savannah?'

I looked at Savannah. She was sitting motionless on the side of the bed, looking at me. Droplets of water collected and pooled in the hollow of her neck like dew.

'This doesn't change anything, does it, Cole? We can still leave, can't we?'

'Savannah you're hurt.' I nodded towards her lower body. I didn't know where to start. Why was she here? Why hadn't she told me where'd she'd been going tonight? What the fuck had happened to her?

I crossed the room to her, took her face in my hands.

'Savannah ...what happened here tonight? Why are you bleeding?'

But they were rhetorical questions. She'd come here voluntarily, in secret. She was bleeding from between the legs. He was dead. Whatever had happened there that night, I didn't want to hear it. But of course I knew I had to hear it.

She glanced down at herself, saw the blood running down her leg and ankle, and stood.

'I thought it'd stopped,' she said, stepping over the body into the bathroom and grabbing a handful of toilet paper. She turned her back to me, and tucked the paper beneath the towel into her crotch.

There were bright red welts on her rear, contrasting sharply with the black whispery text of my name, and I knew, even as I fought the knowledge, that they'd come from the dead man's hands.

'Oh Savannah. Dear God, Savannah, what have you done?'

She turned and regarded me, her eyes filled with tears.

'I'm sorry,' she said. 'I'm so sorry Cole. I …I'd changed my mind. About all of it. I wanted to leave with you. I wanted to be with you. I just – I just wanted to tell him goodbye. I felt like I owed him that much.'

Balled up in the corner were his pants, a shiny black belt made of some sort of reptile's skin snaked through the loops. I picked them up, found his wallet in the back right pocket, and retrieved it.

'He was just so angry, and he'd been drinking. He was never angry unless he was drinking. He was …he was on top of me when I got him with the pen and he fell off the bed.'

Inside his wallet he'd had eight, nine, ten one hundred-dollar bills, all crisp and feeling freshly ironed. I disregarded the money and found his license. It said his name was Steve Kinerly, age 48, living in Charleston. Height was six-two. Weight 220. Two hundred and twenty and lessening by the minute now.

'Steve Kinerly,' I said aloud. 'Why do I know that name?'

'He's a lawyer,' she said. 'He looks … he used to look after me some.' She closed her eyes against the tears, but they fell anyway. I wanted to tell her that they always would, that tears fall whether you fight them or not, but I didn't.

'He's the one who did this to you?' I asked, glancing downwards at her legs, at the area between them.

She nodded. 'He was upset I was leaving. I told him I loved you, Cole. That I'd fallen in love with you and I wanted to be with you, to go away with you. I knew I wasn't supposed to do that, to fall in love with you or anything like that. It wasn't part of the plan, but –' she stood then, letting the towel fall, crossed the room and pressed herself against me, wrapping her arms tightly around my back, – 'but I couldn't help it. I couldn't help it. I love you. I just want to leave. Let us leave now, Cole. I don't even care if you got the district's money or not. I just want to go far away from here with you. Please. Please just let's go now.'

I held her close. She buried her face in my chest, and I could feel her body shudder as she fought the tears. I pressed the open palm of my hands against her back and closed my eyes. Her skin was warm beneath my hands. Warm and pink and alive. I ran my hands downward over her naked skin to the small of her back. I kissed the top of her head, touching her wet hair with my tongue. I could feel her hips against mine, the place between her legs pressed into my thigh, naked and warm and wet with blood. I wanted to pick her up and make love to her even then, make love to her through the blood, through the hurt, through the pain that would be my world if I was still in Charleston five hours from now. We could make love in the bed there, make love as the sun broke through the watery horizon and stained the morning a broken rust and gold, then pull the sheets over our heads and hold each other and maybe, maybe if I tried hard enough I could lose myself in the smell of her breath and the feel of her skin and the history we'd formed and the future we'd almost had, and it wouldn't matter when the knocking came at the door.

None of it would matter because I would always have this, this moment here with her now, regardless of what might happen to me.

She'd always had a certain smell to her, a light, subtle hint of jasmine and cotton and something else I'd never been able to place. But it was always there, and it was there right now, and I breathed it in and held it and tasted and swallowed it and breathed it in again, because I knew it was the last time. I'd been led for nearly nine months. Now it was time to go.

(I don't even care if you got the district's money or not.)

It had already clicked for me then – her being here, the dead lawyer, Grey, The Keys, all of it. I understood it all then. There was a momentary feeling of the floor opening up beneath me, of the hotel, the city, the stratosphere above crashing down atop me, smashing me into tiny pieces, then smashing the pieces into atoms, pieces of atoms, into quarks and pieces of quarks, and I could hear the blood rushing in my ears and my mouth turned coppery, but it only lasted a second. The vertigo passed and the taste of pennies passed and then I was just standing there, holding a naked, hurt little girl in the middle of a hotel room in downtown Charleston, a dead man on the floor beside us, and every cop in the city mere hours shy of me being their first priority.

'Savannah,' I said, my eyes still closed, a single strand of her hair in my mouth, 'how did you know the money was coming from the district? I never told you that.'

She stopped crying. Her body went rigid in my hands.

'It's okay,' I whispered, stroking her hair. 'I love you. It's okay. It's okay because I love you.'

'Cole –' but she lost it in the tears.

There was a clock on the nightstand beside the bed. It read 2:08.

'We have to get you to a hospital,' I said.

'I'm fine. I want to come with you. Please, Cole. Please don't leave me now. We can just walk out of here and get in the car and go. There's still time.'

'You're hurt, Savannah,' I said. 'He hurt you inside. If you don't get help you might never be okay down there again.'

'It's not serious,' she said. 'I have my period. That's all. I just need to –'

'No.' I shook my head. 'That's not all, little angel. We have to get you looked at.'

She was crying again, and I understood the tears. The worst part before the bad is the moment when you realize that the bad is coming, and there's nothing you can do to stop it. That's the part that takes its toll. That's the part that makes the tears fall.

We were in the car when I asked, 'Did he leave semen behind?'

'No,' she said.

'How do you know?'

'Because I stabbed him in the eye with a pen before he could finish.'

I carried her in my arms into the emergency room. I made the lady behind the counter get off her ass and find the doctor. When the doctor came I carried her into the examination room behind him, laid her on the paper-wrapped bed, and told him what happened.

'Was it rape?' he asked, as Savannah pulled down her pants.

I looked at Savannah, then looked away. 'I don't know,' I said.

The doctor rested a hand on Savannah's stomach for comfort, I suppose, and asked me to leave. I left.

Half an hour later – 2:45 in the morning – I was sitting in the waiting room. A woman dressed in a baby-blue hospital uniform and wearing too much lipstick for this hour touched my shoulder from behind and told me I could see her.

She was sitting up on the side of the examination bed, the protective paper wrap beneath her wrinkled and speckled like a robin's egg with blood. I closed the door behind me and leaned against it. Her head was bent over, like she was studying the floor.

'Savannah,' I said.

She wouldn't look at me.

'Did he say you'd be all right?'

She nodded, still looking at the floor.

'There's some tearing, that's all. It'll heal.'

I nodded to myself.

'He's writing a prescription to prevent infection. He said I should abstain from sex for the next two weeks.'

She raised her head then, looked at me through eyes red and swollen from crying.

'I guess we won't have to worry about that now though, will we?'

There wasn't anything to say to that, or rather, nothing I could bring myself to say aloud.

I came to her then, pulled her into me, hugged her tightly, then took one step back. I held her face in my hands and kissed her mouth. Her lips were salty with tears.

'Listen,' I said. 'Listen to me. I can fix this. Not all the way, but mostly. I can fix it for you, Savannah.'

I tried to go on but the words got stuck in my throat; I felt that deep, overwhelming shudder, the one that starts in the belly and climbs up through the chest, throat, and face before escaping in a burst of sound and tears. I fought it with all I had. I was running out of time.

'There's so much I wanted for us, Savannah. So much I wanted to give. But I can't. I can't give you what I had to give –'

'Please Cole, please let me come with you. Please let's just go now. The money doesn't matter to me. I don't care –'

I was shaking my head. The tears had come; it was the rushing tide of emotion I was fighting to stave off.

'I can do the next best thing,' I heard myself say. 'I can give you back your future, the one you nearly lost because of me. I can give you a new start right now, but,' – an involuntary pause, my entire torso wracked with waves of nausea and pain – 'but you have to ask me to.'

'No Cole,' – her face red and shiny with tears – 'no no no no no no no. I won't. I can't. Not like this. Not us. We weren't meant to finish like this. We can just go. It's not too late yet.'

'It's been too late for us for a while. But not you. It's not too late for you. It's all there in front of you, all waiting for you to grab it. And I think I can help you get it, Savannah, help you have a chance at it at least, if you ask me to, and if you tell me you'll forgive me for the way I have to do it.'

The police were on their way. I still didn't know if it was rape or not (I do, of course; I do know, but I want to be unsure on that. I need to be unsure) but when young girls come in bruised and bitten and bleeding from their privates the cops get called. I needed to be elsewhere when they arrived.

I kissed her forehead, then each of her eyes, then her mouth, bringing the saltiness away on my lips, running my tongue over them.

'I love you, Savannah. Know that above all the rest of it.'

'Will you … can you forgive me, Cole?'

'Oh, Savannah,' I managed before kissing her, longer this time, longer because it was the last time. My night had been filled with experiences I was having for the last time, but the taste of Savannah Bellington's kiss was the most painful of the lot.

'How long have you known him? The lawyer. Kinerly.'

She just shook her head.

'It doesn't matter,' I said, because it didn't. None of it did now.

'Tell them it was me that did this to you,' I said. 'Tell them I did it out of jealousy and anger. Tell them we'd had an affair and you wanted to end it and I went insane.'

'No, Cole,' she said. 'I can't do that. I can't –'

'Tell them nothing about Kinerly or the hotel room. Nothing. You were never there. You never knew him. You and I were out, you broke things off, and I forced myself on you. I wanted you to run away with me and you wouldn't go so I got violent. That's what you have to say.'

'I won't do it –'

I touched her lip with my thumb. 'You will, little angel, because you have to. It's the only choice to make.'

I smiled for her sake.

'Think of a sunset on a beach somewhere far away, and do it. Do it if you ever cared for me at all.'

Her eyes were bluer than I'd ever seen them. She wrapped her arms around my neck and pressed her lips to my cheek. 'Remember everything up until tonight,' she whispered. 'Just forget tonight and remember the rest of it; that's the part that's true, Cole. That's the part that's real.'

I took a deep breath then, shut down everything inside myself except the will to survive, and turned and left.

I didn't say anything on the way out, and even though Savannah did, I didn't let myself hear it.

It was nearly 3:30 when I reached the room again. I'd taken the passkey from Kinerly's wallet when I'd checked his ID. I slipped it into the door, waited for the little red lights to yield to the little green ones, and pushed the door open.

Once inside, I made sure the door was locked and the curtains closed, then set about doing what had to be done. None of it makes me proud. But it was about survival, and sometimes the things we do in order to survive aren't things we should be proud about. Sometimes it's enough that we could just do them.

I grabbed the towels from the bathroom and rubbed down every surface in the room. The headboard, the countertops, the nightstand, the light switches, the window sill, the television remote, the clock, the television, the pictures on the wall, the walls themselves, the toilet, the sink, shower handles, shower doors, everything. When I was finished I balled the towels and tossed them at the door.

From the plush sandstone carpet I pulled several thin fibers free and stuffed them into my front pocket.

The clock on the nightstand read 3:52. Somewhere in the city the police were looking for the people who'd broken into Emily Cosgrove's home and pushed her family to the edge. Somewhere else they might be looking at Publix videotape by now. And closer still, less than two miles away, the police would be taking the statement of a scared little girl who might or might not have been raped, brought in by person unknown, currently missing. Sooner or later everyone's description would match, and they'd show up at my door.

It was probably too late for me now. The possibility of them waiting outside my apartment for me when I arrived home was rapidly becoming more and more feasible. The sun would be coming up in a couple of hours. I could walk them in and pet Brasco while they searched my place, found my get-away bag, all my cash, and a shoebox full of appearance-altering paraphernalia.

3:53.

I retrieved Steve Kinerly's wallet from his pants again. I opened it and found one of his cards. It had come to me in the waiting room. The name. Kinerly. A lawyer. I realized where I'd heard – and seen – it before. Kinerly, Walker, Smith, and Herndon, attorneys-at-law. I didn't need confirmation. But I did need the card for something else.

I slipped the card into my other front pocket. Kinerly, Walker, Smith, and Herndon, attorneys-at-law. When I'd picked Savannah up downtown all those months ago – after she'd called me – her hair dotted with mist and her eyes wide with relief upon seeing me, she'd been wearing a sweatshirt with the same logo. Same names, same confident, sturdy lettering.

And again at her trailer, a different-colored sweatshirt – maroon, I remember; the details surrounding my time with Savannah will always be remembered – but the same logo. The same law firm. Same lawyers.

('…he used to look after me some…')

And Key West, too, with Grey, who'd wanted to look after me some.

I could be your patron, she'd said. Every good artist needs a patron.

It'd been on Grey's mug that morning, the morning before I left. Kinerly, Walker, Smith, and Herndon, attorneys-at-law. The steam had twisted up out of that mug in whispery ribbons and she'd blown it away as she smiled and told me to make Savannah mine.

And from somewhere out of the fragments that were my memories of my time in the Keys came Grey's soft, careless voice and the warmth of her hands as she led me by my wrist throughout the rooms of her winter home and introduced me to her wealthy friends. Bartholemeu, with his barren, leathery scalp and silken voice. The Kleinfeld twins. Madeline the human insect. Darcy of the Honduras, formerly of Detroit. Ned/Ted, who appreciated a good bibliography. M.J., the Caribbean island-hopper. And someone else. Tall. Dirty-blonde hair going white around the temples. I never got his name but I remember he'd had his arm around Grey when I'd stumbled in after my conversation with Bartholemeu on the porch. I'd been swimming in Crown by then, looking for a phone, having resolved in my drunken state to give Autumn a call for reasons decidedly less sensible when considered sober.

3:54.

I didn't have time to think about it then. If I made it, if I got away, I'd work through it then. If I didn't, well, I'd have plenty of time to think about things in that case, too.

I steeled myself, took a couple of deep breaths, and bent over and grabbed Steve Kinerly – wealthy lawyer in life, something less in death – and with a heave I got most of him on the bed, his head flopping loosely at the end of his neck like a doll's. Savannah hadn't been kidding; she'd buried a pen deep into his eye. And not just any pen, either. A Mont Blanc. The trademark white tip stuck out of his bloody sclera like some sort of three-dimensional cataract. A stream of frothy blood had flown out of the cavity there and dried down his cheek and chin. I pressed my thumb and forefinger onto the pen and held it for a count of three.

I held his face in my hands and stared at him, tried to picture him without the pen in his eye and the blood all over his forehead, face, and neck. His hair was soaked through with blood, drying and beginning to flake now, but it looked like it might have been dirty-blonde under better conditions. And around the temples it was beginning to whiten, though this too was obscured some by the blood.

3:56.

I climbed atop the bed and hooked my arms beneath his armpits, pulling the rest of him on the bed. I took care to touch his chest, his face, his ears, his legs.

I then removed several hairs from my head, dropping one above his beat-less heart, where it mingled with his graying chest hair. Two I let fall to the carpet. One I placed on the windowsill. The last I set on the bathroom counter.

3:57.

I took Steve Kinerly's hand in mine. It was heavy, lifeless, like a leather-covered paperweight.

Whatever he'd done when he wasn't lawyering hadn't been labor. His palms were smooth, like polished glass; his nails were manicured, short little perfect crescent moons. I held his left hand in my right, his gold wedding band catching the overhead light and glistening, and dragged the nails down my neck. Then again. And once more, hard enough this time to make me wince.

I let his hand fall and picked up the other one, and repeated the process over my left forearm. A second time, my skin peeling off beneath those expensively-done nails.

3:58.

In the bathroom I washed my hands and dried them on my shirt. I then removed the toilet paper roll and set it on the counter. I took the little spring-loaded dumbbell off the fitting and walked back into the bedroom with it. I stood there for a moment, wishing there were another way, knowing there wasn't, knowing it was pointless to even think about it now.

I held the aluminum tube in my mouth and turned Kinerly over. His belly and buttocks rippled and jiggled. I spit a mouthful of saliva on the end of the tube and inserted it into his flaccid anus, the sphincter loose and open, holding my breath, looking away, thinking of the Atlanta Braves, mortgage rates, the works of Chaucer, whatever it took to keep my mind off what I was doing.

I moved it back and forth several times, fast, slower, deeper, shallower, deeper again. Then I took it out and set it on the bed without looking at it. I could smell it though, and it smelled of shit and death.

4:01.

I left Kinerly on his side, then took the aluminum tube, washed it, slid the toilet paper roll back over it, and put it back together in the wall opposite the toilet.

4:02.

I wanted to do this next part – this most difficult, and most important, part – in the bathroom, but I knew I couldn't. For it to look real it had to be real, which meant I had to be in there, in the bedroom, where he was.

I positioned myself on the floor, on my knees, my back to Kinerly's corpse. For the second time that night I fumbled myself free with intentions of leaving behind a part of myself to be discovered. Making water on Waters' front porch had been easier, though.

I closed my eyes and began. It was hard at first, which is to say I wasn't hard at all, but I continued. Young, single men are blessed with an ability to ejaculate at a moment's notice; there's virtually nothing in the concrete that we can't shut out in the abstract long enough to push past the critical point. Years of practice refines this to the level of near-art.

I thought of her, of course, of my Savannah, my little angel who'd pulled me in with a smile and held me with a whisper. There on my knees in that downtown hotel room with a lawyer stiffening on the bed beside me I granted her last wish and remembered everything up until tonight, all that was real and true, all that we'd ever had together. I kept the part we'd never have at bay and focused on the part we'd have forever, and when it was time I stood and aimed at Kinerly's open, torn, leaking anus, then quickly upwards, to his hand, his neck, his half-opened mouth.

It sent my stomach roiling and I bit my fist to keep from puking.

4:13.

I left the hotel. I arrived at my tiny West Ashley apartment at 4:32. No one was there but Brasco, who stood and stretched dutifully upon my entrance. I stepped over him, reached into my pocket and retrieved the carpet fibers, scattering them in the air like dust. I then stepped into my closet and slipped Kinerly's card into the breast pocket of one of my dress shirts hanging on the hanger. It wouldn't take them long to find it, and with luck they'd think they'd found a clue.

I grabbed Brasco, my duffel bag, and left. By 4:50 my little Honda was pushing its way up I-26. At a quarter after six I-26 yielded to I-20 in Columbia, and we began heading southwest. I was still reasonably sure we'd be caught before we made Brownsville, but there wasn't anything to do about it except keep driving, so that's what we did. When you're out of options and out of time that's about all you can do.

Just drive.

EPILOGUE

I spend most days on the beach, and a lot of the nights as well. A few months ago I met someone, a young woman named Anna. She lives on the other side of the island. She was born here. Her father's a water-purification worker for the government. Anna's twenty-four. She says she'd like to go to America one day to become a teacher. The first time she told me that I choked on my beer. Now I just smile and nod.

We've been seeing each other for a while, now. Nothing serious. She's into her work at one of the preschools here on the island. I'm into nothing at all. So far it works for both of us.

It's been two years since I left America for Mexico, crossing over the border in Brownsville, Texas, like so many who came before me. Two years since I saw Savannah; maybe a few days since I last thought of her. But the pain doesn't come with the memories now; the pain doesn't come at all anymore. Now when I think of her, when I think of those days and nights we shared, it's like thinking of a movie I saw once, or a dream I had when I was younger. The images still come, but their colors are duller and their lines not as sharp. Even the smells are weaker now, memories of a memory.

At the end of my fourth month here I bought a little four-room bungalow on the beach. It has a front porch and a back porch and a pier that stretches all the way out to the water. I paid cash to a British man who'd had the place built for his daughter a month before she died in childbirth. He said his therapist told him part of healing was letting go, so he sold the house she'd never seen and boarded a plane for London with his wife.

Brasco likes it here. He spends most of his time on the pier, sleeping. In the early morning he likes to go down to the sand and chase the crabs as they scatter towards their tunnels to beat the sun. So far as I know he's never caught one.

Six months after disappearing I wired a million dollars to my mother's account in Augusta, Georgia, from an account I'd set up in Luxembourg for that purpose. I wanted to send a card, tell her I was all right, but I didn't. That sort of thing is against the rules. Tezra knew it, and I knew it too. Tezra also knew the difficulties that come with that kind of commitment. I'm still learning those.

Grey's people had been legit; all told B's gun in Sterling's mouth had netted just under sixty million dollars, half of which Philip – or someone like him – had transferred to the account in Antigua, just as we'd planned. I'd moved it into Mexico City the next day from a payphone in Western Alabama.

I read the Charleston papers for a while after leaving; Emily Cosgrove's family – baby Sterling included – was fine. According to the article, Mrs. Cosgrove was still the finance director in Winter's Cove. The state stepped in and propped up the district the following school year, covering the loss through a series of loans. The district would have to float bond referendums in order to pay it back, a move likely to raise taxes on Winter's Cove homeowners, but other than that there wasn't much in the way of tangible effects from my sudden departure. The bells throughout the Winter's Cove schools heralded the first day of school the following August as they had every other August, and teachers and students alike filed in to begin another year.

I sent Jules a chunk of the money, too, enough to ensure he never buys Bud Light instead of Guinness again. Geist, too. He was always a good egg.

Some time later I contacted a company in Australia that makes sailboats. I had them build a big one for Capers. I did it all through a mailing service in Amsterdam, and wired the money to their account from the one in Luxembourg. Luxembourg understands the first two rules of running. Cash makes no enemies, and it tells no tales.

I didn't name the boat for him. I don't even know if he'll keep it – Capers was funny about that kind of thing. But I like to think he did, and I like to think he named it WINTER'S COVE.

I was telling the truth that night in the emergency room. I did forgive Savannah, and not just because I loved her. I forgave her because I wanted to be happy wherever I ended up, and to be happy

I knew I'd need to forgive myself. We weren't that different, she and I. We both saw something better and thought the other one could help us get there.

How she came to pick me or know that I was vulnerable at that time in my life I'll probably never know. But it wasn't random. It was no more random than Grey happening upon me that day on a deserted Isle of Palms, wearing that silly hat and talking about her most recent divorce.

I'm pretty sure their connection was the lawyer – Steve Kinerly, who paid the highest price of all. Steve Kinerly, who I may or may not have seen at Grey's place down at The Keys. Steve Kinerly, who bled to death with his five-hundred-dollar pen sticking out of his eye, his body going rigid on the floor next to the bed he'd shared with a teenager. The news said he was a tax attorney, so he would have known plenty about the collection of property assessments and the state's distribution of the funds. He would have known – because Grey would have told him – that Grey knew people who could get to it, provided they had someone who was willing to take the risks and, if necessary, take the fall. Someone like a teacher, young and unattached and disenchanted with his world. Someone susceptible to the songs of innocence and opportunity.

Grey's role is less clear to me. Maybe she sensed my hopelessness and shared it with Kinerly. Maybe she really did think she was helping me, guiding me towards a life free of need and filled with all the time in the world to write my novels. It doesn't matter, anyway. None of it was an accident, of that I'm certain. When I'd been trying to push myself away from Savannah, Grey had been there to nudge me back toward her. Always, always, she'd softly encouraged me to make her mine. Tell me you love her, she'd said that night on the Key West sand, her mouth wet and waiting, tell me you love her and that's why you have to keep your stress and pain and angst. That you're keeping it so you can remember what it's like without her, that you're remembering so you'll know why you have to have her.

She knew all sorts of interesting people, Grey did. People who moved throughout all sorts of interesting circles. The third-floor apartment, the one on Stoll's Alley downtown she'd wanted me to rent, belonged to Kinerly; Kinerly, the non-boyfriend Grey occasionally slept with – Jules himself had covered that aspect of the story, standing in the center of that enchanted, secret garden, surrounded by the flowing green vines of jasmine and ivy and the vibrant flowering trees. CNN was borrowing him, apparently feeling his close association with me gave him extra insight to it all. A wealthy tax attorney lived in this picturesque little hideaway and died just up the road there, Jules had said, in an Embassy Suites hotel room. What was his connection to a teacher gone bad? Was he involved in the theft of millions of dollars in state money, earmarked for public education? Was it a deal that went sour? And how did he fit into a bizarre, ultimately fatal lover's tryst involving fugitive teacher Cole Archer? That story at 11:00.

I was proud of him. He looked like a million bucks standing there holding the microphone, his suit new and looking it, his face and hands tanned from golfing, his eyes a mysterious black. Brasco and I had watched it from our hotel room in Mexico City.

He hadn't mentioned Savannah, which meant my gambit in the Embassy Suites room worked. She'd come out of it unscathed. She had her life back.

How Kinerly had come upon Savannah I could imagine. He'd probably seen her at the club where she'd danced, and he'd probably smelled the hunger and the need on her like perfume. Men like that have an eye for people's weaknesses, and men like that have a talent for preying upon them.

Or maybe, maybe he saw the same things I saw. Maybe he saw a little girl lost in a big world, with so much to offer and no one to help her. Maybe he felt that same need I'd felt, that need to touch and protect her, and maybe she'd let him because she hadn't seen another way.

I used to try to play it out in my mind. Their plan. I used to run through the various possibilities and try to figure out just what had been going on around me while I was busy falling in love with my student. My best guess is that Kinerly was the catalyst. I think he used Savannah to get to me, betting I'd see the bait – the millions of dollars in district funds – and, if properly motivated, make a play for it. Grey's crowd in Key West had been a carefully calculated move, as well. Wealth and plenty are intoxicating aromas. Kinerly knew that, and he knew that if anyone could show me and make me want to taste it, it was Grey, with her wild abandon and casual trot through life. All it took then was my falling in love with Savannah, my craving for eternity her kiss and touch, the lure of which Kinerly probably knew all too well.

I used to try to figure it out. Now I don't think about it much. Savannah had fallen in love with me. Whatever their plan had been, whatever her role in it was, she'd fallen in love with me. She'd told me that in the hotel room that night, and again in the emergency room before I left. It doesn't matter why she'd first approached me, why she'd taken the time to stay after class to thank me for teaching her, why she'd called me that night downtown, alone and afraid. It didn't matter why she'd hugged me in the living room of her trailer and told me she needed a friend, or why she'd kissed me that afternoon in Savannah and told me I was her savior. She'd fallen in love with me. Even though it wasn't part of their plan, she'd fallen in love with me. In the end, she hadn't cared about the money. She was going to leave him, the money, all of it. In the end, she'd only wanted to run away with me. And for me, knowing that is almost as good as what we nearly had.

I don't blame Savannah for any of it. You can't blame someone you love for letting you love them.

So I spend most days on the beach, and a lot of the nights as well. I take long walks around the island. Sometimes I find an interesting seashell or shark's tooth and pick it up. Usually I just leave it in the sand. Everything, even a seashell, needs a place to call home.

The evenings are warm here, and I plan to one day stay the night, to see it through to morning. I think I'm ready for that now. I really do.

And in the morning, when the new day's light begins to slip through the clouds, I might let myself think of her, of the time we shared, and I might even look in her direction, into the warm breeze that sweeps in across the water like a gift or an invitation to some distant land, and wonder if she found her sunsets. My first few months here I'd let the tide wash in around my feet and ankles and wonder if that same water had ever touched her. I don't think like that anymore. Not much at all.

She said something to me once, not long before that last, fateful night when it all came unraveled so quickly and permanently. We were lying in my bed in that little one-bedroom apartment I called home that year, and she'd rested her head atop my chest and listened to my heart as she slid her hand beneath the covers and down my stomach, and she told me that a burning bridge was the best light to read a book by. I hadn't known what she meant then, but I think I do now. I think it means we do our best when we have to, and that in the end that's all we can hope for. That's all we have a right to expect of ourselves. A lot of life is luck and chance, and a lot of who we are is what we do with it when it happens to us.

I think about that occasionally, usually when I'm out here, on the beach, as the sun is lowering itself into the ocean and the air is growing cooler and the daylight starts to dim, and sometimes when I do I feel better. Because I did what I did for the right reasons, for what I believed to be the right reasons at the time. I didn't ask to fall in love with her. I didn't ask to need her. These things happened and I dealt with them the best way I knew how. I know that now. Here, on the beach, on the island I call home, I know that.

And here it is enough.

CODA

In August, 2000, I flew from Raleigh, North Carolina, to Las Vegas, Nevada, for a dear friend's bachelor party. He's that type of friend you grow up hoping you'll find some day, a one-of-a-kind article, and this was to be a one-of-a-kind bachelor party, the type you grow up hoping you can be involved with some day. It was to be a four-day, non-stop affair, attended by eleven of his closest pals (and three goofy tag-alongs he'd not so much invited as not explicitly disinvited, and who, lacking proper upbringing, had thus shown up) – the sort of thing one writes books, and not home, about.

The trip was indeed an event, but now, sitting here as I read over the last sentence of the last page of the final draft of this book which has taken nearly two years to complete, it occurs to me that what stands out the most from that trip isn't the round-the-clock gambling or the late night limos, and it isn't the free booze or the cheap food or the 110 degree heat at two a.m. It's not the mid-day hangovers by the pool or the midnight turn of the roulette wheel where my buddy Pat – in utter fealty to that most alluring of cocktails, the one that's equal parts adrenaline, ego, and alcohol – put his last thousand dollars on red to the near-deafening chant of 'come on, red! come on, red! come on, red!' only to watch the wheel and the world go black at once. All of that was fun, and the stuff of stories that guys retell guys for years to come, but it isn't what stands out the most for me.

What has retained its salience more than all the rest of it is the story of M—, about whom I still – in the quiet, reflective parts of my days – find myself occasionally thinking. For reasons those of you just finishing the novel can understand, her real name, out of courtesy to her and hers, cannot be shared.

I sat next to M— on the plane that early August morning. She was a seventeen-year-old high-school student, glowing in that happy, smiles-and-secrets way girls of that age glow. She was striking to look at; her hair did something with the mile-high sun that now and then still visits me when I close my eyes at night, and her scent was that of hope and possibility and lilac.

I'm not a particularly good flyer. I've never vomited on any plane yet, and I don't quite qualify for a bona-fide white-knuckler, but I do spend a goodly portion of my time in the air in silent communion with God, reviewing my life insurance holdings, hoping those I've left behind on the ground will think of me as a good son, brother, husband, father, and friend should the unthinkable happen. I'm never entirely certain that it won't, and I spend each flight vowing that it will be my last, and praying that it won't be.

This flight was no different. We'd been in the air around ten minutes when she switched seats from several rows back behind me, wanting a seat by the window, the window seat to my left being available. The flight attendant made the comment that she'd been in the business for over twenty years and hadn't seen more than a dozen flights bound for Vegas with vacant seats – particularly vacant window seats – in her entire career.

Ever, Fate has her way.

I'm not haunted by Fate, however. Fate I accept. As Cole might have said, it is what it is. What does haunt me, what has haunted me nearly every day now since that morning, came in pairs.

First, her smile, and then, the story behind it.

She was scheduled to begin her senior year of high-school three days later, but was giving it all up for this trip to Las Vegas, she explained breathlessly. Her Biology teacher had taken a job out there at the end of the year.

'Big gambler, is he?' I asked, not making the connection.

She shook her head. 'He did it to get away from me.'

That one caused me pause, but nothing like what came next.

'We fell in love,' she said. 'It just happened. He left to keep from hurting me. I told him if he left I'd follow. He didn't believe me, and neither did I, and the night he left I cried so hard I threw up blood. Two days later he sent me a one-way ticket and,' she rummaged through her bookbag, the same bookbag, I mused, which must have carried her biology book to Mr. Pedophile's class, 'this letter.'

She produced a folded piece of plain white paper with a single, whispery line of script across it.

'I love you and miss you and will die if I don't walk through this world with you.'

I didn't know what to say. I was disgusted by him, but on another, not entirely separate level, I was excited for her as well.

'How'd it happen?' I asked, handing the note back to her. She read it again and giggled the way a small child might giggle on Santa's lap. In that moment she was as happy as anyone I'd ever seen.

'It's a long story,' she said, and she was right. It lasted from somewhere over North Carolina all the way to the edge of Nevada. She told me most of what you've just read as we flew through the clouds that morning on our way to that quintessential city of big dreams and bigger risks, I to bid farewell to my friend's single life, and she to begin the rest of hers. The only part that would ever matter, she said.

Somewhere in all that I'd asked her how old he was. She told me thirty-four. I asked her if she was worried about being hurt by him. She said she could never hurt the way she did the day he left. I wasn't sure of that, but I kept it to myself. She asked me what I did for a living. I told her I was a teacher in Charleston, South Carolina, and we both got an ironic little laugh out of that one. Had I ever fallen in love with any of my students, she asked, as though it was the sort of thing teachers do any given week, after homeroom and just before lunch. No, I'd said, but I'd met my wife when she was seventeen and I twenty-six, and I'd waited until the night of her eighteenth birthday to call her and see where it went.

'Where did it go?'

'All the way to the altar,' I said.

'It will for us, too.' And there wasn't the first seed of doubt in her, which I think is a lot of what made her so memorable to me.

'I hope so,' I said.

'Do you?'

'Do I what?'

'Do you really hope it works out for us? Because if you do, then that means that other than him and me, you'll be the only person out there pulling for us.'

I thought about that. It seemed neat to me that I could have that role: that I could stop off in Vegas for four days of carefully-controlled decadence before returning to my life of husband, writer, teacher, and sole supporter of her unorthodox introduction into the austere world of love and pain.

'He's good to you?'

Her whole face lit up. 'He's wonderful. He's the kindest, most loving, thoughtful man in the world.'

If a high school teacher can tell you anything it would probably be that hyperbole is the law of the land in the world of late-adolescent girls. But bliss can be a contagious elixir, and I found myself wanting it to work for her. Doubting it strongly, but wanting it just the same.

'Then yes,' I said. 'I do. Count me your first official fan.'

Shortly after we touched down in Vegas, the captain coming on over the intercom to tell us the local time, the weather, and all the rest of it, I asked her if she ever had kids, a daughter specifically, did she have any idea what she might name her?

'Savannah,' she said, so quickly you might have thought she'd been asked it before.

'Why Savannah?'

'Because I've always loved that name. If we have a little girl I'm going to name her Savannah. I used to wish it was my name, but giving it to my baby will be just as good.'

So M—, wherever you are out there, here's your book. I named her Savannah, but her smile was always yours. I suspect it always will be.

Goodbye, and thanks for the story.

Wade Tabor
Charleston, South Carolina
December 2003